THE MINOR YEARS

A Narvan Novel

Jean Davis

The Minor Years: A Narvan Novel

www.jeandavisauthor.com

ISBN-13:   979-8-9850814-0-4 (print)
                  979-8-9850814-1-1 (ebook)

First Edition: October 2021

Printed in the United States of America
Published by StreamlineDesign LLC

Also by Jean Davis

The Last God
Sahmara
A Broken Race
Destiny Pills and Space Wizards
Dreams of Stars and Lies
Everyone Dies
Not Another Bard's Tale
Spindelkin
Frayed
19

The Narvan

One Shot at the Sphinx
Trust
The Minor Years
Chain of Gray
Bound in Blue
Seeker
Tears of the Tyrant

ONE

Rhaine

He sat with his elbows planted on the table, head in his hands, as I often caught him in the mornings before he realized I was up. Within a breath, he saw me coming into the kitchen and jumped to his feet. The fluid motion of his large form unfolding to its full impressive size had drawn my attention for years, but now it only reminded me of how he moved when we'd worked together. Back when he'd worked for me. Back when I had the life I'd worked so hard for.

The life that he'd taken from me.

The High Council had demanded that he kill me. And he had. Just not the way they'd wanted.

Not that I wasn't grateful to still be breathing, but hiding here on Veria Minor under an assumed identity wasn't living. I was supposed to be advising the Narvan, guiding the lives on the worlds in my charge, protecting them, shaping the system to what I knew it could be if given the chance. But the High Council had ripped that from my hands, the position I'd clawed my way into and killed for.

They'd handed my position to him.

"What do you want for breakfast?" he asked.

"Nothing."

I shouldered my way past him, which is to say I bounced off his chest as I tried to get by. He moved aside like a wave retreating from a rocky shore.

"You need to eat," he said.

I turned to glare at him. Damned bossy man, always trying to tell me what I needed to do. I needed to do what the Council told me. And only then, the parts I agreed with or couldn't avoid doing. I needed to do what was best for the people of the Narvan. I needed to—

"Stass...Rhaine. Please. I'm sorry."

He apologized at least once a day. Today was earlier than most. And he'd slipped with the alias, the one he'd given me, the names he'd demanded we use even when we were alone in this life he'd chosen for us. That he'd chosen without one iota of input from me.

He could have given me the chance to recover from surgery for at least an hour or two. Maybe get more than half the sedation out of my system so I could coherently make a plan with him if he was so intent on keeping me among the living. But, that had been asking too much. He'd taken it upon himself to set up my future.

Even though he'd just offered his daily apology, I wanted to kick him. Not that it would do any good. We were stuck here now. Both of us.

His hair stuck up in clumps. I hated it. He'd had the most glorious mane of black hair, but he'd cut it off when we'd come here to better fit in with the Verian culture. Not that a dark-skinned, seven-foot-tall giant of an Artorian had any chance of fitting in with the petite, flat-faced, pale-skinned Verians we now lived amidst. Even as a human, I wasn't much better at blending in, but I'd grown up around the Verian people and Vayen had known that. As far as places to hide, it was a smart choice and I couldn't fault him in that regard, but this wasn't where I wanted to be.

I probably shouldn't blame him for half of what I did, but he was my available outlet. If we did happen across any of those who truly deserved to be the target of my frustrations, the two of us would either be hauled in front of the High Council and killed, or simply killed on sight for a payout later.

He'd always been an easy target for my frustration, loyal to a fault, ever-present, taking everything I slung at him and rarely firing back.

He'd been a target on another front too. I'd avoided his charm for years, pushed him aside, distracted myself, but he'd eventually worked his way past my defenses. Or maybe I'd given in to temptation. Probably a bit of both. We'd had something enjoyable yet tenuous back in the Narvan, undefined in its newness. He'd made it clear, despite bonding to me without my consent, that the kind of life we had here wasn't what he wanted either. Yet, here we both were.

In the month and a half since we'd arrived on Minor, he'd inserted himself neatly in the colony, this house, as a father to my son. His seemingly easy acceptance of the situation he'd crammed us into pissed me off most.

"Come on, eat something," he said.

My stomach cramped, protesting my protest of eating. I knew it hurt him when I refused his meals. I could feel it through the cursed bond he'd inflicted on both of us. Fasting was one of the few weapons I had left.

Upstairs, a wail sounded. Daniel was awake. Again.

"Fucking hells," Vayen muttered. "He barely slept last night."

Neither had he. He was still wearing the same green tunic as yesterday. It was deeply wrinkled and sported two sour-smelling dark spots, one on his chest and the other on his shoulder. He'd never been a particularly fastidious man, but the baby had brought him to a new low.

"You were the one who chose to take him out of stasis."

The deep brown pools of his eyes narrowed. His jaw tightened to a point that I almost indulged the sudden twinge of regret for snapping at him. But this *was* his fault.

He could have picked anywhere to hide us, maybe on a space station or with a crew headed anywhere outside the Narvan. We could have found work more in keeping with our skills, working security, or anything else for fuck's sake. Instead, he'd picked this slice of utter vanilla normalcy that I had zero experience with. And now here we were, living together under the guise of a joined couple, with my son, in a little house in a small colony, far away from everything that mattered.

His brother, Daniel's father, had to be laughing his fucking head off in whichever level of hell that man had ended up in. I hoped it was at least one of the mid-levels for getting me pregnant and then getting killed. Not to mention putting me through the misery of carrying a hybrid child, but even more so, for introducing his younger brother into my life. This man I now couldn't pry my attention from no matter how angry I was with him.

"Starve yourself then, if that's what you really want." He spun around and stalked toward the stairs.

It wasn't, but I had nothing left. Nothing but terrorizing him, and now that I'd managed to piss him off, that didn't have the gratification I'd hoped for.

"Vayen."

"Isnar," he corrected on his way up the stairs, near yelling over the shrieking of the angry baby in the cradle that was fast becoming too small for him.

He disappeared into Daniel's room. The baby stopped crying a moment later.

I watched the doorway, but he didn't reemerge. Alone in the kitchen, I sank into the seat he'd left, half-wishing he was still in it with me and yet glad that he was gone.

Isnar was my friend's name. Isnar Fa'yet. Granted, it was a very common Artorian name. Vayen claimed he hadn't been on a first-name basis with Fa'yet, that he hadn't considered it a problem when he'd rushed to pick his new name. It was a good alias as far as Artorian names went, but didn't belong to him and I had a hard time thinking of him as anything other than Vayen, especially in my own head where using the wrong name didn't have major consequences.

I wished he'd slip up a little more often. I didn't mind at all when he called me Stassia. It made me smile inside every time, not that I'd let him see that, at least not now. The first time he'd used it, I'd thought he'd only slurred my name. He'd been dead drunk after I'd forced three ultra-strong shots on him and took him back to one of my houses, away from my other bodyguards, to sample what I'd been trying to keep myself away from. But he'd privately called me that ever since.

Now he called me Rhaine.

Except when he was exhausted. Which he was now. I checked the time. He had to be at work in two hours. He'd said something about a big delivery coming in at dinner last night. I hadn't been listening all that closely. I'd been busy glaring at the plate of noodles that he'd made that smelled so damned tempting that I'd almost caved on my hunger strike and shoved them into my mouth with my bare hands.

I sighed. If he had to work, it was my turn with the baby.

My son. My mind refused to wrap itself around that word, this situation. Around everything that had befallen me over the past couple of years since I'd gone on a High Council killing spree to repay them for going after those I held dear in an attempt to control me.

They'd imprisoned me, tortured me, and screwed up my link beyond repair. Every day since I'd stormed down the hall of my ship with Vayen hot on my heels had been a swarming buzz of headaches I didn't want to remember. I'd locked myself in the armory as he screamed for me to not leave on the other side of the door. Maybe I should have listened. We might both still be in the Narvan if I had.

But now he was here, also without everything he'd worked so

hard to achieve, that I'd trained him for. Here, in hiding with me. The man I'd seen spattered in blood too many times to count, who had taken at least as many, if not more lives than I had, was now upstairs, rocking my son back to sleep. As he had every time Daniel cried since we'd arrived.

Whereas he was good at this parenting thing, I had no idea what I was doing. Wasn't I supposed to have innate maternal urges? Shouldn't I feel attached to my son? I seemed to be missing the whole nurturing end of the spectrum. My childhood memories hadn't left any lingering inkling of what that was supposed to be like. Each day, I waited for something to kick in, something Vayen had with Daniel that I didn't.

I got to my feet and crept up the stairs. Peeking into the doorway, I saw them in the chair beside the cradle. They were both sound asleep. Daniel looked normal-sized in Vayen's arms, a father correctly proportioned to a child of his race. My son bore little resemblance to me.

I'd never, not in dreams or even nightmares, envisioned this man in a fatherly role. He excelled at drinking, swearing, and making people quake in their shoes. But that was before, I reminded myself. Since we'd arrived, he'd been different. Entirely. If he drank, I didn't see it. He'd made every effort to be polite to our Verian neighbors and, from what he told me, the staff at Dugans, the shipping and trading business he'd bought into the week before. That whole endeavor had to have been a challenge, considering that without our links to translate, he'd had to rely solely on speaking Trade since he knew no Verian. Thankfully, most of the people here did speak some Trade because they had to deal with outsiders from time to time. Veria Minor was slightly more inclusive than Veria Prime.

He did still swear. Mostly it was at me, under his breath.

I crept in closer. Neither of them stirred, not the baby whose round cheek was pressed against a broad chest, nor the man whose head had lolled back over the top of the chair. That was going to leave a crick in his neck for sure, but I wasn't going to chance waking either of them. Instead, I reached into the cabinet, pulled out the clean blanket I'd folded the day before, and covered them both. Backing away, I headed downstairs. For what, I didn't know.

Most of my time on Veria Minor had been spent in bed recovering from the surgery where they'd removed my link implant and attempted to fix the damage the Council's torture had caused. They hadn't fixed enough. I'd lost my telepathy as well as my link, leaving me isolated from everything I was used to having in my head. There were moments where it was too quiet and others where my tornados of thought were near deafening. Through it all, I was alone in my mind. I missed Vayen's voice there. Merkief's, Jey's, everyone else we'd left behind.

My eyes began to water.

Stupid damned eyes. I sniffed and went to sit on the couch to stare out the window. The evergreens didn't care if I held myself together or not. They didn't judge. We'd become quite close, spending a good amount of time the past few weeks watching one another.

What the hell was I supposed to do here? As soon as Vayen had been sure I was all right, that it was safe to leave me alone for a few hours at a time, he'd gone out to see what opportunities the colony offered. It had only taken him two days to find his place, to invest his way in, to make connections.

I didn't want to talk to these people, to have to embrace my alias, to make it real.

But Anastassia Kazan was dead.

Pulling a pillow from the corner of the couch up to my face, I screamed into it. It made a good silencer. In the first days I'd left the bedroom, I'd tested a couple of them before settling on this one.

There was nowhere to be alone. If Vayen was gone, Daniel was with me. If I wanted a few minutes to myself outside of the bathroom, I'd have to leave the house, and I wasn't willing to do that yet. Inside, I could close my eyes and pretend we were on Frique in the first house I'd owned, the one I'd designed and had built there in the woods. I could pretend there weren't neighbors just beyond those evergreens out the window. That we had links and could Jump to Artor or Jal or anywhere else in the blink of an eye.

But we couldn't.

Vayen had given up his link even though his had still been fully functional. He'd handed it over to Kess, my ex-partner, to sell the story of our deaths to the Council. I hoped it had worked.

Every creak of the house made me start, freezing to listen for the sound of a gun being drawn, just waiting for the day someone from Kryon found us and took us out for real. I yelled into the pillow again.

The pillow smelled like Vayen, I realized as I clutched it tightly. He'd been sleeping on the couch more often than not. For the number of nights he had, I was surprised he hadn't bought a bed of his own and moved into the third bedroom upstairs. Or for that matter, bought his own house, somewhere else.

It had to be his idiotic bond that kept him around. No sane person would put up with all the sleepless nights between taking care of Daniel and bearing what punishment I was up for doling out on any given day.

He absorbed it all, every ounce of anger I wanted to let loose on Merkief and Jey for going along with Vayen's plan, Kess for fulfilling it, and Fa'yet and Gemmen for not talking sense into him. What the fuck had they all been thinking? I threw the pillow across the room.

It knocked into the one bowl I'd set on the table in a singular attempt at decorating with the eclectic collection of furnishings Vayen had bought and had delivered here upon our arrival.

The blue bowl was made of glass rather than plaz, as I belatedly discovered when it slid across the table, flew off the edge, and shattered on the floor.

The commotion brought a thunder of giant feet down the stairs. Arms empty and with eyes wild and still swimming with sleep he'd desperately needed, Vayen shot to my side like one magnet drawn to another.

"Are you all right?"

I nodded. "I'll clean it up. Go to bed."

Daniel was still quiet upstairs, amazingly the noise hadn't awoken him. Maybe he was finally worn out for a few hours.

Vayen followed my gaze, taking in the pillow in the kitchen and the scattered field of blue glass. "I doubt I could get back to sleep after that. Besides," he checked the time on the wall, "I have to get ready for work soon anyway. Bring the reclamation container over here. I'll help."

He was down on his knees, picking up glass in his big hands before I could even take a step.

"You don't have to do that. Go take a shower. I'm sure you're well aware of how you smell."

"There's plenty of time for a shower. The container?" He held out one hand already filled with jagged, glittering blue shards.

I went to the closet and then carried the container to the table. While I considered dropping it on the floor next to him, I wasn't willing to wake Daniel. Periods of silence were too precious and far between.

He set the glass in the shallow container already half full of other detritus of our time here. A plate I'd thrown at him last week that had shattered the floor when he'd knocked it away. A mug he'd dropped on our fourth morning after three nights and days with nearly no sleep and too many stims. And one irreparably bent spoon that had suffered my wrath upon hearing his explanation of why Merkief and Jey wouldn't be coming to visit or sending us news about the Narvan. He'd drugged them and now they thought we were dead.

After picking up the last shard without any assistance from me, he got up and put the container back in the closet. Then he went into the common room and came back with the cleaning bot under his arm. With a few quick touches to the control panel, the bot quietly hummed to life. Once on the floor, it began vacuuming around the table. Without another word, he went back upstairs and into the bathroom. The shower started a minute later.

Why did he have to be so damned nice?

Oh yes, because he was sorry. As he should be.

I picked up my pillow, brushed off any lingering glass dust, and went back to the couch. That's where he found me half an hour later. He was much better smelling, hair combed, and wearing fresh clothes. I only gave him a glance before turning back to the trees.

He stood behind me, hands on the back of the couch, not quite touching my shoulders. We might not be able to talk to one another like before and the bond wasn't the same either, it had lost something when my mind speech went out the window, but I could still feel him in my head enough to sense his mood. Today he did his best to stifle what little connection remained to us, but concern drifted from his mind to mine.

"Make sure you eat something. I'll be back before dinner, but call if you need anything. I mean it, if you feel anything weird coming on, let me know. I can be back here in fifteen minutes or less."

By weird, he meant a seizure. He wouldn't use that word. As if he did say it, one would hit me.

"I have the doctor on standby and she left an injector here. I know how it works, thank you very much."

"I know you do."

He leaned over to kiss my forehead and then he left, closing the manual door softly behind him. The automated locks he'd installed clicked into place. A bird chirped loudly and flitted from the tree, probably annoyed by the invasion of its outdoor space.

Only after I heard our little transport fire up and then fade as it traveled away, did I realize Vayen hadn't eaten either. He hadn't even brought anything with him for later. The man loved to eat. He needed to with a body that size.

I wondered how he was getting through days at the office on so little sleep. He'd run out of stims shortly after our arrival and the colony doctor didn't know what we were talking about when we'd asked for more. Maybe with his new shipping connection, he could import some. He was going to need something to keep him going unless Daniel decided to start sleeping more than two or three hours in a row very soon. Mister Bossy had decreed I wasn't going to take them, even though he'd been willing enough to shove one in my face right after waking from brain surgery.

He'd also repeatedly told me to go back to sleep when I'd tried to get up and give the damned martyr a break from wailing baby duty. He claimed the doctor had told him I needed to rest as much as possible, but the doctor hadn't said as much to me. At least, not that I remembered. The stern-faced Verian woman and I had spent a good deal of time together those first few weeks, but most of that was a medicated blur.

I hadn't had a seizure in over two weeks and I didn't plan on it again. They scared the hell out of Vayen. He didn't bother trying to stifle that. The loss of consciousness and body-wracking convulsions weren't high on my list either.

I sat on the couch with my pillow, watching the trees and birds, ignoring the occasional hum of a transport traveling on the road just beyond them. What could I do here for the rest of my life? With this man now named Isnar. With my son. In a house that wasn't mine, here on a world far away from everything that mattered.

TWO

Rhaine

The door closed with a muffled click, signaling Vayen's arrival. I held onto the counter, willing the headache that had started an hour before to hold off on hitting full intensity for a little while longer. My plan had been to meet him at the door, to say hello in a civil tone, maybe even attempt a smile, to make an effort to try making our cover work at home before I had to sell it outside to strangers. Instead, I stood clutching the edge of the counter, second-guessing my efforts.

I'd spent every baby-free moment of my day darting around the house, putting the furnishings in tolerable order and using the antiquated vid terminal to research how to make a meal he might enjoy. For all my efforts, the house still didn't feel like home and I'd never cooked anything in my life so the results were sure to disappoint. Now he was already inside, my smile couldn't have been more forced, and I couldn't think of a single civil thing to say that wouldn't quickly devolve into a tirade. I rubbed my temples and took a deep breath.

His footsteps came closer. They weren't the heavy-booted ones I knew by heart. Verians favored a soft-soled shoe or clogs made from recycled plas. Neither of which came in anything close to his size, but he'd convinced someone to make a set of both for him. From what he'd told me, he hadn't even used a gun. They were all locked away in a trunk in the back of our closet. His armored coat sat folded on top of it. His boots beside it. All of the man I'd known sat hidden behind a hanging row of Verian clothes he'd also had custom-made for his size.

Vayen was gone too. Isnar was here. I repeated his alias over and over until it began to lose meaning. To make this cover work, I needed to drive it into my aching brain. Using his new name was a small step, but a start.

If Daniel hadn't been quiet, I had no doubt Isnar would have been calling for me by now, making sure I wasn't passed out on the floor somewhere. I could feel his concern rising with every second.

"I'm in here," I said now that he was close enough that I didn't have to yell and chance waking Daniel.

He came to a dead stop in the archway, looking like he was waiting for me to drop him with a shot between the eyes. I could only imagine that the utter awkwardness of my efforts to be civil and mundane were as clear on my face as the mess was on the counter, the sink, and the cooktop.

"I...made dinner," I managed to say.

His lips opened and closed a couple of times, then he glanced back at the stairway.

"No, I didn't drug him and he'll likely be awake again soon, so we should eat while we have the chance."

I'd already put the food on the table, knowing he'd been like clockwork in returning home from his first week at work. He walked over to the table and sat down but didn't reach for anything.

"I'm not trying to poison you. Though, it may be an unintentional byproduct of my first ever attempt at cooking."

I convinced my fingers to let go of the counter and walked over to the table to sit down across from him. Was this what normal people did every night? Did they actually pick a specific time in the evening that they prepared food and sat down together to talk and eat?

My family had worked at all hours. They each ate when they were hungry, usually something pre-packaged. Work always came first. I was the same, food was an interruption, something my body needed that I didn't have time for. When I'd worked with Vayen, Jey, and Merkief, we'd eaten when we were between meetings or contracts, and more often than not, one or two of them were sleeping and caught the leftovers when they woke up. Was this one of those normal things the work we'd done had allowed the majority of the population to enjoy? Why wasn't I enjoying it?

Isnar had lost his utter startlement, but now he seemed to be waiting for me to explode either with a vocal tirade, or from the level of confusion flowing from his mind to mine, possibly literally.

In an effort to put him more at ease, words dribbled off my tongue. "I watched the cooking vid three times before I even started. How the hell do you know how to do all that stuff? What everything is for? It's like an alien chemistry lab in there, I swear."

"Stassia?"

Oh damn, I really did have him befuddled. "Yeah?"

"You cooked."

"I think, more accurately, I made a giant mess."

He grinned, something I hadn't seen since before our arrival on Minor. The sight of it warmed me, causing my earlier awkwardness to dissipate.

But now that I was in close proximity with all the smells of what I'd made, the headache convinced my stomach that it would be wise to continue my several-day hunger strike. I took a small scoop of the beans and the buttered grains so that he would maybe leave off the chastising for once. I left the fish for him. It was burnt on one side anyway.

He proceeded to fill his plate, then took note of mine. "Headache?"

I nodded. "Eat. You skipped breakfast and didn't pack lunch."

"One of the women in the office went home and made me lunch when she saw I wasn't eating." He pointed his fork at me. "You better eat even that little bit or I'm sending her over here to feed you too." He shook his head. "Don't Verians have any appreciation for spices? In anything? Ever?"

"They appreciate the natural flavors of their food."

From his pained look mid-chew, I gathered the flavor of my beans was off. I took a bite. No, not the flavor, they'd only half-cooked. I tried the grains. Those weren't half bad, or more so, not half good. They'd turned to tasteless mush. He'd made the same thing before and I'd liked it. Why did everything in the kitchen have to be a damned challenge?

Despite the lack of flavor and bad texture, I ate the four bites I'd put on my plate just in case he was serious about sending that woman over. I wasn't ready to talk to anyone one on one without him around to help sell our new identities. He'd already established our story here. I didn't want to get any details wrong that I may have missed while medicated.

Isnar picked at the fish, mostly on the less blackened side, eating every speck of meat off the bones. "You could maybe help me with dinner a few times, you know, to learn what all that stuff is for...if you wanted," he said while keeping his gaze on his plate.

"Maybe."

He was a good cook, though how he'd managed to become one in the short time we'd been on Minor, I didn't know. Sure, he'd made food for me a time or two before when we'd worked together, but he certainly hadn't been cooking on a daily basis. If he could do it, I'd figure it out too.

I stood up to start clearing the plates, to end this disaster of an effort I should never have attempted.

"Go lie down. I'll get this," he said.

"I can do it."

He was suddenly right there, on his feet in front of me, taking the plate out of my hands. "I know you can, but you're not feeling well, and neither of us wants this to get worse. Get some sleep. You said that helps."

I massaged my temples, which was a futile effort but habit made me try. "What would help is a visit with Peter. He worked wonders on my headaches when I carried Daniel. I'm sure he could help with this."

"Doctor Weeda isn't the best out there, but she's competent and you're getting better. She's using the best medicine this colony, or any other nearby has to offer. It would take days to reach the station over Prime to see your doctor." He gave me a pointed look. "The doctor that thinks you're dead. For your safety."

That was the problem, the thing that made my insides twist into a knot all day and every night. The people I cared about thought I was dead. And he'd had a hand in that. The headache made my irritation hard to mask despite my intention to try to be civil for one night. I took a moment to double down on my efforts to be calm.

"Can't we at least let Merkief know we're all right?" I asked. "You still have a natural connection with him, don't you?"

"I severed it," he said firmly. "They have to believe we're gone. Entirely. If there's any doubt, the Council will question Kess's story. If they suspect he's lying, they'll issue new contracts for us and Kess will undoubtedly take action if we become a problem for him. Violating our agreement would mean he'll also cause trouble for Merkief and Jey. We need both of them to be as focused as possible since they're now holding the Narvan."

That all sounded logical, but the situation flooded me with frustration all over again. Yet, I managed to keep my mouth shut.

He'd finished clearing the table in the time it took for me to get rid of the remains of the fish. The pulsing in my head made me regret the few bites I'd eaten. The flaring light in one eye caused the perspective of the room to stretch and contract. I reached backward, searching for a chair while trying to focus on a singular point on the counter with the malfunctioning eye squeezed shut.

His hand was on me a moment later, guiding me to the chair. "Sit."

"I was going to." I waved him off. "I'll be fine."

Not that I felt at all fine, but I was so sick of him hovering, watching me what seemed like every moment. He had to be because every time I might possibly need even the slightest amount of help, he was right there. Like I was the fucking delicate glass bowl in danger of being flung off the table, about to shatter into a thousand tiny pieces.

Then his hand was on my forehead, the other on my shoulder. His warm, fish-scented breath buffeted my face. I turned my head away, needing fresh air. Needing space.

"Do you need the injection?" he asked.

I did. The headache wasn't going to go away and the distant feeling I'd come to associate with an oncoming seizure permeated my awareness. Despite my efforts, my precarious hold on calm and civil cracked. I pushed him away. "I said, I can do this myself. Back off."

Putting one foot in front of the other, with one eye on the stairs, I started across the room. Again, he was right there, concern near drowning me in my shrieking mind, one hand out, not quite touching, but waiting to catch me if I faltered.

Who the hell had I been trying to fool all day? This cover story was impossible. I didn't cook or greet my supposed spouse at the door with a smile. I didn't want to raise a kid and certainly didn't want to fucking be here.

I gave up trying to get away and turned to face him. "Why didn't you just stay?"

"Stay where?" His hand dropped to his side.

"With Jey and Merkief. At least I'd know the Narvan was being taken care of. Why the hell did you toss it all aside to pretend we're living this happily-ever-after shit story, because, trust me, we're not."

"I've noticed." His smile was gone, along with any hint of warmth. "Since you brought it up, I hadn't planned on being here. I'd intended to stay, to take the drug with them."

For all my annoyance at his constant hovering, the thought of not having him around at all, of having him think I was dead, that he would do that to himself even with the bond, made my throat tighten.

My voice came out strangled and broken. "But your idiotic bond convinced you otherwise? Did you really think we could make this cover a reality?"

Upstairs, Daniel started to cry. Why the hell couldn't he sleep for six hours in a row like any normal person? Why was this all so fucking hard?

I wanted to be upstairs, medicated, dead to the world until tomorrow. If Isnar wanted this life so badly, he could have it by himself.

He had backed away a few steps, giving me the breathing room I needed.

Or maybe it was the room *he* needed.

The man I'd worked with made an unexpected reappearance, the muscles in his face tight, eyes narrowed. It was an unsettling sight out of context, here in this bland house, the baby crying, and him in the long, unclasped, flared grey overcoat with a dusky orange tunic underneath that hung down to his knees. No boots, no armor, no weapons, but his stance was all work.

The never-ending, stifling stream of concern I'd grown so used to vanished. Our bonded connection had suddenly gone flat and dry, a minute trickle, as through he'd stopped making the effort to hold the door open. I was more alone in my head than I'd ever been.

The quiet and solace I'd hoped to find wasn't there.

"While we're being honest for once, the idiotic bond, as you enjoy calling it, wasn't my idea. Blame the fucking Council for that."

That couldn't be. He had to be lying out of spite now but he looked dead serious, almost relieved, as if this was a confession he'd been longing to make.

My heart stuttered as my mind tried to balance what he was saying with his month-and-a-half of actions. "You said you had to want it. You explicitly said so."

"Their drug, you—" he broke off into a fuming stream of Artorian that rolled way too fast for me to follow while my head was spinning with both the headache and his revelation.

He punctuated the end of his rant with a snarl, almost as if it pissed him off even further that I hadn't understood what he'd said. He switched back to Trade. "The bond was just another way to control me. Or try to, anyway."

If that was true, was anything between us real? Had he only been making a far more convincing show of our cover than I'd bothered with? Was his presence here only a lingering obligation from his role as my bodyguard? A hastily made choice he'd quietly been regretting the entire time? When the Council had attempted to control me by killing Res, my Seeker mentor, I'd gone on a Council killing spree. Perhaps my deadly partner had learned from my mistake and found leaving the playing field a more appropriate response.

Looking at him now, hearing the menace in his voice and seeing the anger in his eyes, my gut told me he was baring the ugly truth behind the supportive and tolerant act that was Isnar.

The floor seemed like it could give way at any moment. I reached for the wall to steady myself. For once, he made no effort to assist me.

The quiet in my head, the lack of anything sensory beyond the pain the Council had tethered me with, was far more stifling than he'd ever been. There was nothing to distract me, nothing to focus on, no anchor. My thoughts swirled, echoing in what now seemed like a vast space filled with too many shadows.

"The bond is manageable." The kind and patient tone I'd grown used to lately was replaced by the hard-edged one that matched the fists clenched at his sides. "Obviously, it's easier when I'm around you, but I can deal with it. I did before. I can again."

If it wasn't the bond, if it was manageable, if he hadn't wanted to be here... Did I want the answer, the real answer, while he was in brutally honest mode? I pushed myself off the wall. "So why *are* you here?"

I started for the stairs again, toward the promise of relief offered by the injector in the bathroom cabinet. Maybe in the oblivion of sleep I could make sense of all this, somehow rationalize my actions and his. I worked my way upward but he didn't move. He stood at the bottom, strangling the railing.

"Because you couldn't get to the transport alone. Because the Council's last attempt on you made the damage even worse. Because the LEs told me you'd be plagued by intense headaches and possibly seizures and that they might never go away. You needed time to recover, and you couldn't protect yourself or Daniel while you were doing that."

Obligation. That's all this was? Memories raced through my mind, moments between us that I was sure had been real, both here and back in the Narvan. He'd never been good at lying to me, and he sure as hell didn't seem to be lying now.

Everything between us couldn't have been strictly duty. He'd been in charge since I'd come back from my imprisonment, even I couldn't deny that. He could have ordered either Merkief or Jey to go into hiding with me.

"But why are *you* here? You could have—"

"Sent someone else? Would you have preferred that?" He took to the stairs, stalking upward. "I didn't kill Fa'yet either, though the Council ordered me to. He's in hiding somewhere, likely not any more grateful for it than you are."

He'd been ordered to kill the real Isnar? My stomach went cold. How well did I really know the man I'd been living with? I thought I had, that I knew all his buttons and how to push them, but maybe that had been the man I'd known before I'd taken on the Council and lost. Holding the Narvan and dealing directly with the Council had changed him.

Before I could reach the top of the stairs, he took three in one long stride, planting himself right next to me. I'd worked beside him for years, watched him do his intimidation routine on countless others, but I'd only ever been afraid of him twice before, when his bond had made him lose his shit in a jealous rage. This time was different. He was cold, a finely-honed blade at my throat without touching me, without being armed. He seemed to tower over me even more than usual, filling the stairway with his presence.

I tried to tone his fury down in my mind so that I could pretend I wasn't afraid of him now. The last three steps were difficult, my gaze locked forward, each breath forced to a pseudo calm. When I finally found myself at the top, I left the safety of the railing behind.

He was right there, imposing, looming. My feet betrayed me by backing away. Daniel's cries for attention grew louder. My one eye cast a halo around the man who shadowed my every backward halting step toward the bathroom.

"You want to do this alone?" he asked "Maybe you want to hunt down the real Isnar and see if he makes a more agreeable cover story with you?"

I realized he'd stopped following me and was standing at Daniel's door.

He shook his head. "Have at it. I've done my part, you're settled in and mostly on your feet. You don't need me, and Geva knows I don't need another second of your shit." He opened the door and went inside.

The injector with its promise of relief was only a few steps away, yet I couldn't move. "What are you doing?"

I didn't like the shrillness of my voice or the uneasiness in my stomach. It felt too much like a thing I didn't do: panic. He wasn't threatening me, not dragging me toward the bedroom with the injector in hand, not yelling at me. There wasn't a whisper of him in my head beyond the knowledge that he was alive, and only then because the place where the bonded connection existed was still there.

The last time I'd felt this unpleasant emotion was when Chesser had died, leaving me pregnant and alone on a world where I barely half-understood the language.

The man now known as Isnar emerged with a quiet baby in one arm and two bags in another. "I'm leaving. You'll be out for a good twelve hours. I'm taking Daniel with me."

He drove me back with a flat stare that was as empty as the place where he'd been in my mind. My conscience urged me to protest him taking my son, but I couldn't find the voice to do it. In the same logical way I'd forced that voice into silence when working Kryon contracts, I told myself he was doing me a favor. I did need my medication and I would be out. It was best if my son went with him. Left with him.

He was leaving.

The finality in his tone refused to be ignored no matter how hard I tried to tell myself we were just having another argument, that he'd get over it and be back in the morning.

He'd never left me of his own accord before, certainly not without extending some offer of reconciliation. But I'd never seen him as angry as he was now.

I waited one heartbeat. Two. Three.

No offers to talk about it in the morning passed his lips. Not a hint of concern shown on his face, no regret.

After all the shit I'd thrown at him since our arrival on Minor, it was this one night when I'd tried my best to be civil that pushed him over the edge. He'd wanted out of this bond, this thing the Council had dragged him into, this cover of a bonded Artorian that might have had feelings for me that he'd tried to make work. Had I done him a favor by pressing him to confess the truth of it all? Was letting him go the best thing for both of us?

The sick feeling churning in my stomach made the best course of action on any front hard to discern. Was it from dread over him leaving or the result of the headache? My breath came in short gasps as the finality of his tone amplified my panic.

He was really leaving.

"Where are you going?" I found the voice to ask.

"My office. I'm used to sleeping on a couch. That will suffice until

I can get my own place." He set the bags down and filled the hallway as he brushed past me to go into our bedroom.

My hands shook as I opened the cabinet in the bathroom. Everything seemed to be in the way as I searched for the injector, items spilling onto the counter and floor. My fucking eyes were too full of liquid to even attempt to focus. I finally recognized the feel of the small hard case the doctor had left for me. With my relief in hand, I felt my way to the bedroom as I wiped at my eyes to clear my vision.

Daniel lay in the middle of the bed, legs kicking in the air, a finger in his mouth. Isnar had wrapped his pile of clothes with one of the long overcoats like what he wore now, tying the long sleeves around it all. He stood in front of the mostly empty closet, staring at the chest that held his weapons and the coat that sat on top of it.

From the way he stiffened, I gathered he'd heard me enter. He glanced at Daniel and shut the closet door. My wondering how he planned on carrying his clothes along with Daniel and the other bags was answered when he grabbed the wrapped bundle and pitched it out the door. The bump and tumble that followed informed me the bundle was on the way down the stairs.

"Recall the transport in the morning. I'll have everything out of it by then." He scooped up Daniel off the bed.

I sat hard on the edge of it, unable to stand. The pounding in my head blossomed and the tightness associated with an oncoming seizure started to take hold. I was almost out of time. I fumbled with the latch on the case.

He just stood there, watching me. No offers to help, no setting Daniel down to tuck me into bed, no comforting hand on mine.

I took a deep breath. I didn't need any of that. I could do this by myself. Being on my own was what I wanted. It's what he wanted too, I firmly said to myself to silence the urge to plead for him to stay.

The injector finally freed and loaded, I sent the medicine into my vein. Knowing I only had a minute or two before my eyes shut whether I wanted them to or not, I scrambled fully onto the bed. Belatedly, I realized I'd chosen the side he used when he wasn't banished to the couch. It was too late to try to move now. The welcoming calm slithered through my body, soothing my muscles and quieting my head.

He didn't tell me to call him if I needed anything. He didn't come closer to pull the blankets over me that I'd not given thought to a moment before when I could still move. He didn't say anything at all as he turned and walked out of the bedroom, not even closing the door behind him.

The door downstairs closed without a slam, without any last burst of insults. He was just gone, leaving me alone like I'd all but been begging him to do since we arrived here.

I closed my eyes and sank into the pillow that I was glad was his instead of mine.

THREE

Jey

Standing in the foyer of the Artor house with Merkief looking utterly distraught, I couldn't shake the feeling that something devastating had just happened. But what that might be, I couldn't put my finger on. The more I tried to figure it out, the more confused I became.

"Why are we here?" I asked him.

Merkief shook his head, opening and closing his mouth a couple of times before leaning against the wall as if he expected the floor to open up and swallow him. "What just happened?"

"I don't know."

The weight of my coat felt normal, nothing missing. I wasn't sore, hadn't been in a fight. Wasn't tired, hadn't just eaten. My armor was clean. No helpful diagnostic information came to the forefront.

Had the Council been screwing with our heads? Vayen had said they'd done that to him when Kazan was imprisoned. I opened my link to him to find out what he knew.

There was nothing there. Not the quiet open connection of him sleeping or even unconscious somewhere, just nothing. Kazan's had been malfunctioning, but I tried it anyway. Again with the nothing.

My stomach plummeted to my feet and the devastation looming over me grew heavier. Good Geva, if something had happened to them, to both of them, we were so screwed.

"Can you reach either of them?"

"No," Merkief whispered.

"What about your other connection with Vayen?"

"Severed. Gone." His eyes took on a wild cast. "What happened just before we got here? Where are they?"

Before I could drive myself crazy with speculation, a High Council summons hit me. I hadn't been singled out for that before, but

Vayen had warned me about those too. If something had gone horribly wrong, this was a logical step. The Council would notify me. I'd been working with Vayen for the two years Kazan had been gone and even somewhat after she'd returned. I prayed that this summons was anything but logical.

"Sere," I told him.

He nodded and Jumped. I gave him a few seconds. If something bad was going down there, I hoped he'd give me a warning. All I got was aggravation from having to wait for me.

Aggravation was better than both of us walking into a trap. Not that I explained that to him.

Merkief had been off his game since Kazan had gone on an assassination frenzy with the Council and gotten herself imprisoned. Vayen hadn't fully trusted him, not like before, and I had a hard time not trusting Vayen's instincts even if Merkief and I still got along fine. Then again, I wasn't the one that had awoken to Merkief standing over him more than once.

Sere was much the same as always, creepy, quiet, and full of people I didn't trust. A set of grey-suited guards detached themselves from the rest and ushered us to a large meeting room.

People filled the room, but one in particular didn't belong. Kess.

My insides executed an unpleasant shimmy and bile threatened to do a follow-up. I took a deep breath and tried to find a sliver of reason and control. Sere wasn't the place to show weakness of any kind.

Fellow Kryon stood in clumps along the walls, many of them murmuring to one another and eyeing us up along with Kess. A host of cloaked Council members stood apart at one end of the room. Kess, looking like someone had beat the shit out of him, stood alone in the middle.

Screw courtesy and protocol. That vicious bastard hadn't been Kryon for years. "What's he doing here?"

A trio of cloaked Council members approached Merkief and I. One of them spoke. "You will want to sit down." A shuffling behind me signaled the likely arrival of chairs.

"I'm fine on my feet." It was easier to Jump or to fight while standing, and if Kess was here, one of those two things was going to happen.

Merkief glanced over his shoulder at the chairs. He also remained standing.

There were too many bodies near me. A crowd of grey-suited

guards had gathered. They circled the two of us. Why the hells were they leaving Kess out of the loop? If anyone should be under guard, it was him.

Not that he looked up to causing much trouble at the moment. In fact, he looked like he was hoping someone would offer him a chair too. No one did.

Two more cloaked Council members entered, skirting the ring of guards to consult with the trio. "We have confirmed that the links belonged to Vayen Ta'set and Anastassia Kazan."

The chinking of two metal objects traveled from one cloaked member to another. Something niggled at the back of my brain, something about Vayen and Kazan's links. Now they were in the hands of the Council.

Belonged. Past tense.

Merkief was already seated. I dropped into the other chair. I forgot how to swallow, how to breathe. Blackness edged my vision.

"Mr. Atta, tell us one more time how you came to be in possession of these links?" asked one of the cloaked figures.

I'd wanted to kill Kess before, but could I do more than kill him? Maybe tear him to pieces slowly with my bare hands? Cut him into thousand thin strips with a sharp knife? I could beat him within a breath of life and then toss him in the regen tank and do it all over again. Endlessly. Maybe some of all of that. Yes, that's what I'd do. I got up and started towards him.

A wall of weapons stood between us, unmoving and unimpressed by my intent approach. One of them fired into my coat. A second one fired. That knocked the breath from me. Someone dragged me backward. I realized it was Merkief.

"Sit, dammit," he growled in my ear.

I also realized that all of the cloaked figures were facing me because the ring of guards had backed away to allow the view. Kess was right there with them.

Kazan had once killed four of the Council before they'd apprehended her. How many could I get?

"Look around us. Don't be stupid," said Merkief in my head.

Kazan was gone. Dead. I couldn't think of any better time to be stupid. I shook Merkief off and went for Kess. He was going to look a whole lot worse when I got ahold of him.

Kess backed into the crowd of Council members. He was limping. He wouldn't even be on his feet once—

Two stunner blasts hit me, one from either side. I gritted my teeth and fought to stay vertical while my armor absorbed most of the charge. Again, Merkief was there, dragging me back to the chair. Half-numb and tingling all over, I let him. For now.

"Mr. Atta?" prodded one of the cloaked figures.

"Could we do this elsewhere?" Kess asked, watching me warily.

"The employees of Ta'set and Kazan will hear your story now."

Whatever game the Council was playing with all of us, I wanted no part of it. I'd not been a fan of dealing with them before, but I'd always had Vayen to take that on for me. Now he was gone. Fuck. How the hells had Kess taken that raging maniac down? Kess must have pulled the hit off quick because I'd seen Vayen go into bonded asshole mode and no one was getting out alive from that.

That he'd taken Kazan out wasn't as much of a stretch. She hadn't been herself, not since these same cloaked bastards had screwed her up hard. She'd tried, and we'd all been working with her, but they'd broken her link and that was a distraction none of us could get over, especially her.

If one of us had been with them, they would still be alive and bickering back at the house.

I couldn't wrap my head around the fact that they were gone. They'd both been alive just hours ago. Though, I still couldn't pinpoint the last time I'd seen either of them. The last time I would ever see them.

Merkief finally found his tongue. "Where are they? I demand their bodies be returned to us."

"They've been disposed of. Links are all you'll get," Kess said from the safety of his Council entourage.

"Mr. Atta," prodded one of the cloaked figures.

"Yes, all right, but you better keep them away from me like you promised."

Several hoods bobbed in agreement. One of them came closer to us. "Mr. Ta'set's wishes were for the Narvan advisory position to fall to the two of you should he die. Do you accept this obligation?"

He'd planned for this. Of course he had, the conniving bastard. We'd all suffered the chaos of Kazan's safety net when she'd been imprisoned. The change of hands on the Narvan had caused far more delays and deaths than necessary. He wouldn't want us to go through that again.

Could I step into Vayen's role and deal with the Council's demands face to hood? My skin crawled at the thought of it.

"Yes, we will," Merkief declared.

He appeared calm and rational enough, but when I touched his link, it was all gnashing of teeth and seething. At least he hid it well.

As much as I liked Merkief, I wished he'd been the one to die beside Kazan. Vayen had the Narvan down and the Council in hand. As unlikely of a pairing as we'd been, it had worked. I knew him and what he needed from me. He would have been a mess, losing Kazan, but he'd go on because she'd want him to take care of the Narvan. Dammit, now I had to do exactly that. For both of them.

"We will," I said.

"Then you will honor the arrangement we have with Mr. Atta. We are well aware of the ongoing feud. Anastassia Kazan is dead."

Anastassia Kazan is dead. The words lodged in my heart. The woman who had trained me, raised me to positions I'd never dreamed of holding, who had become my focus, was dead.

"All hostile actions between you ends with her. Kess Atta has been reinstated into Kryon. He has proven his skills worthy."

By killing them.

Thank Geva, Kazan wasn't alive to see this. She'd be spitting teeth and spewing curses.

I already missed her curses. It was bad enough having my access to her limited by Vayen's possessive bonding shit, now she was entirely gone.

They weren't even going to give us bodies.

"We should have tried harder to kill him before he was Kryon again," muttered Merkief.

"We *did* try."

Merkief glared at me. I focused on the cloaks in front of us rather than let him feed the anger that was already close to boiling over.

Kess said, "One of my contacts spotted Kazan at the Artorian University. Rumor was, her link was malfunctioning and she only had one guard with her. She thought she was safe there."

She wrongly thought she had the University in her pocket. I wouldn't make the same mistake. I would find Kess's contact and end them.

"Vayen was distracted by the discussion of her treatment," Kess continued. "Couldn't have asked for a better opportunity. My contact slipped me into the surgical team."

I could easily see Vayen getting caught up in Kazan's wellbeing.

He'd been worried about her since her return to us. We all had. I was glad he'd convinced her to go to the University, to let the Link Experts examine her, but dammit, he should have taken one or both of us along for backup, knowing he'd be distracted. Then again, they both had thought they were safe in the heart of the University.

"The LEs took them into an operating room. Separated them— her on the table and him in an observation room above."

Being separated while she was defenseless had to have driven Vayen mad. Memories supplied the sound of his boots pacing and him cursing under his breath.

"They put her under. Then it was as simple as offing the treatment team and putting a bullet in her head. By the time Vayen pulsed the plaz and leapt down, the deed was done. He didn't go down easy, her death hit him as hard as I did. Probably wouldn't have succeeded otherwise." Kess rubbed his bruised face gingerly.

"The surgical tools were right there and links are easier to carry than bodies. Vaporized the rest. I didn't want to chance anyone else trying to cash in on my kills."

His kills. My boss. My partner.

The cloaked Council conferred quietly. One of them pointed to us.

"They have been probed. No subterfuge was detected. Mr. Atta's accounting has been confirmed," he said. "You are free to go, Mr. Atta."

"What are they talking about?" I silently asked Merkief through our linked connection.

"They probed us. It was very light, you probably didn't notice."

I hadn't. Being Artorian, he was more sensitive to invasions of the mind than I was.

Leaving brought Kess closer to us. He paused near the door. "If you want something of hers, Vayen dropped her armor when he leapt down from the observation room. It may still be there."

I watched him leave, momentarily stunned by his revelation of a conscience. Merkief was already on his feet. Other Kryon followed Kess out the door.

"Before you leave, there are some terms to this arrangement that you need to be aware of," said the cloak closest to us.

"Terms?" Merkief asked.

"You have been offered the advisory position for the Narvan. This includes Narvan worlds only. Kess Atta will advise the free worlds of the Rakon Nebula territory, including Merchess."

"Merchess is our largest source of income," I said.

"Merchess was not included in Mr. Ta'set's wishes. Nor ours. It now falls to Kess Atta. You will respect this ruling," the cloak said firmly. "You have one week to conclude business there. Any further business arrangements will need to be cleared through Mr. Atta."

The ninth hell would freeze over before that ever happened. We were so very screwed.

Why would Vayen leave Merchess off? Had he been in a hurry and simply overlooked it or was there a valid reason? I prayed he had the whole world rigged to blow in a week and a half and that Kess would go down with it.

"Your position will be probationary with weekly evaluations. Mr. Ta'set split the Narvan worlds between you. His assignments will be relayed to your links shortly. We expect the same level of service as your predecessors provided. Any open hostility between the Narvan and the Nebula will not be tolerated. Do we have an understanding?"

"Kess kills our people and now we have to work *with* him?" Merkief asked with the same level of incredulity that I felt.

"You don't have to work with him any more than any other system advisor. You will do your jobs and stay out of each other's way. That is all."

I nodded an acceptance I didn't feel. Merkief followed my lead.

"Good. In lieu of remains, you may have these. Mr. Atta took little care with preserving any information stored on either of them, but they may offer you some consolation." A gloved hand held out two link implants.

Merkief took them, cradling them in his hand. For a split second, that seemed like a familiar image. Then the notion was gone.

"You're free to go," said the cloak.

The room emptied around us. I couldn't stop staring at the two blackened implants. Hours ago they had been in the heads of people I cared about. I swallowed hard and forced my voice to remain steady. "Think we can get anything helpful off them?"

"The LEs might be able to," he said quietly.

"The University then."

He nodded and we Jumped.

FOUR

Rhaine

When I woke from my drugged slumber, I stayed there in bed, listening, waiting to hear some hint that he'd come back. There wasn't any. There were sounds in the house for sure, but none I could attribute to the man I knew so well or the baby he'd left with. It was only the mundane creaking of the hurried construction of a typical colony home.

I got up and went downstairs. No one was on the couch or in the kitchen. My stomach cramped and growled with the demand for sustenance. Unfortunately, the one who could cook was gone. I went through the cupboards one by one, assessing what I dared attempt. Protein spread on crackers ended up on my plate. What I was really hungry for were the noodles he'd made before, but the crackers filled the void well enough.

Once my stomach was satiated, I sat down at the terminal and checked to see if he'd left any messages. He hadn't. Staring at the blank screen, I worked up the nerve to use the identity he'd created for me. With a hesitant few commands, I delved into my current financial situation. I hadn't needed to do here. He'd taken care of everything.

Like he'd taken care of me.

I sighed. Too much care. Too close, too often. I didn't need him. I'd been on my own before.

I peered past the vid to the window by the kitchen table. The sky had a blue-green cast, heralding the impending arrival of a storm. Heavy rains and high winds seemed to hit hard every two standard weeks. The days were longer here than on Prime, rather like Moriek and Syless, far out of standard, making the reliance on universal time a definite necessity rather than using day and night cycles.

The financial report came up on the vid, pulling together all the resources he'd set out for me into one neat place. He'd invested in several local businesses within our colony, as well as a few of the larger companies elsewhere on Minor. Beyond the house and the transport, which were both on the higher end compared to our neighbors, he'd set me up with a substantial fortune. It had to all be directly from him. He'd never had access to my funds.

If he'd taken a portion of his wealth with him, I didn't see any record of it. The last of his spending was the business he'd bought into. The date caught my attention: Mere days after our arrival. Not weeks like I'd thought. Maybe he was better at lying to me than I'd realized.

I watched the report for a while as if I could see what he was thinking. As if a large portion of credits would disappear any moment when he purchased his own house or a transport, or whatever else he'd need if he actually meant to leave me.

Two hours ticked by and nothing had changed other than my back growing sore from the chair. Maybe he'd grabbed a few of his own credit chips when he'd had his last-minute change of plans back at the University—when he'd decided to toss everything away to make sure I was safe here.

Fucking martyr.

I got up and paced around the common room. Had that really been his plan, leaving at the last minute? Running up the stairs to check what was left in his closet, it appeared he was telling the truth. He'd only had the clothes he'd been wearing, but he'd packed for Daniel and I. The single pair of pants and a shirt of Artorian make were the only things still hanging in the closet. He'd left the belongings of Vayen Ta'set behind, here with me. Isnar Ka'turoc had walked out the door last night with a bundle of clothes and a baby.

The trip to my son's room was much slower than my assent of the stairs and dash down the hall. With both trepidation and anticipation, I opened the door. The cabinets hung open, shelves empty. Daniel had arrived here with one bag and left with two. Other than the furniture, Isnar had taken everything.

He'd taken my son.

I sat down in the chair the two of them had napped in the day before. Yes, I'd given birth to Daniel, but he'd been in stasis for twelve years. Most of the time we'd been here, I'd been medicated and in bed. I tried to find it in me to be distraught or that I was missing a giant part of myself, but none of it felt genuine.

Peter had kept watch over Daniel all those years in stasis. Isnar had spent nearly every waking moment with him here. I'd only started to take full shifts with him when Isnar had gone to work. It was quiet in the house for once, and I couldn't find it in me to be upset about that. If that made me a terrible mother, I wasn't surprised. That was a fact I'd long known and the reason Daniel had been in stasis to begin with.

When I'd told Vayen about Daniel, I knew he'd wake him. Maybe not right away, but he would. He would do the right thing, the thing I couldn't bring myself to do. And he had. Dammit. He always seemed to do the right thing. More often than not, anyway.

Maybe he didn't know I was awake yet, maybe that's why he hadn't tried to contact me. I went back downstairs and used the terminal to recall the transport.

Fifteen minutes later, it arrived. I went out to the covered charging station to see if he'd left anything inside for me.

It was empty.

I walked back inside before any of the neighbors were inclined to come over and introduce themselves upon seeing me out in the open. Isnar had met them all and told me about them. Thanks to my medicated state at the time, I didn't remember much of what he'd said. The only Verian I'd talked to since our arrival had been the doctor. I didn't want to talk to anyone, certainly not until I knew my true situation here and what angle I'd need to take with this new identity if I was going to live on my own.

Safely inside, I reset the door alarm and walked to the kitchen to check the terminal. Still no messages. Maybe he was busy with work and Daniel. Midday mealtime had passed. I'd have to wait until he was done with his workday.

When he did get angry with me, it was intense for a short while, but he calmed quickly. If he hadn't already leapt on buying a place, he just needed a little cool down time. This wasn't permanent. I just needed to do something to make the hours pass until he was ready to talk.

I didn't need him here exactly, but he was the only person on all of Minor who knew who I was, what I was. He knew *me*. The one person I felt safe talking to. And he did have my son. Cutting contact altogether wasn't an option.

Isnar would need to be around me somewhat thanks to the bond, or he'd be in no mental state I'd want around Daniel, unsuitable mother or not. He claimed he could deal with it, but Merkief and Jey had both cautioned me about how work-centric and intense he'd been while I'd been incarcerated.

Back in the Narvan, he'd been adamant about not wanting a relationship like he'd set up for us here. He'd been brutally firm about not wanting to bond with me. I'd suspected he'd only formed the bond to prove his loyalty in the wake of my accusations that he'd been working with the Council to get rid of me. The real Isnar had dropped hints along the same lines, though he'd been sure I'd demanded it. Like I'd want to entangle myself in a mess like this intentionally?

If what Vayen said was true, if the Council had lulled him into the bond or demanded it of him, it hadn't been by his choice, and he was stuck with it for life. My life.

What would it do to him if I died? I'd done enough research upon initially learning I'd been involuntarily roped into a bonded relationship to know that dealing with a broken one was rough. Rough on a normal Artorian. What would it do to a volatile and deadly one?

Maybe that's why he hadn't trusted anyone else with keeping me safe and alive. Maybe being here wasn't for me, but to maintain his sanity.

We were both stuck. Bonded, fugitives, here on a world where neither of us belonged.

Watching the bland public vid feed only made time crawl. Instead, I delved deeper into colony news and eventually ventured into job listings. Like hell was I going to be a stay-at-home parent if I did decide to go after joint custody.

Like we were getting a divorce. I laughed out loud.

We weren't joined, married, whatever cultural word we wanted to call it. We were only partners in this bland beige shit situation— assuming he was still speaking to me.

In keeping with the normalcy level of this colony, the current job listings ranged from childcare, field work, and one opening for a medical assistant, all the way to general physical labor in the small port that serviced Dugans and the other businesses nearby. Working there wasn't going to be an option for me. Isnar had the corner on knowing what was going on in the greater universe. If I wanted to know, I'd have to hang out in the port and find a contact or two of my own.

The market was also at the port. I'd need to find food options that I could prepare. I'd lived on Veria Prime long enough to know what might be available and what it was called. Maybe I could make this work. Hell, maybe someone would save me a load of trouble and have a case or two of meal bars. Though, that was unlikely out here. Isnar had already remarked about the lack of food imports. That, I did remember.

I was halfway up the stairs to change into something socially acceptable for my first foray into possible interaction when the proximity alarm on the door went off. Had he come back? My heart started to race. I ran back down the stairs and peered through the view hole on the door—such primitive security, but ordinary. We were supposed to be ordinary.

It was Doctor Weeda. I opened the door just enough to talk to her. "Did he send you?"

"He? Your Ishlan? Your...mate? Did I get that right?"

I nodded, waiting to hear her tell me that my doting and concerned mate had contacted her to check on me. Needing to hear her say so because if that was true, my conscience would feel a hell of a lot better.

"I've been trying to brush up on Artorian culture. There hasn't been much need for it here, but your Isnar is such a nice man." She stood there, holding her brown case, waiting.

"Nice, yes." If she only knew that man half as well as I did. "Did he send you?"

Weeda shook her head of fading yellow hair. "We have an appointment. Did you not remember?"

Disappointment tore through me. I'd really pissed him off, pushed him too hard. Pushed him right out the door.

"It must have slipped my mind." I opened the door the rest of the way and let her in.

"Why would your mate have sent me?" She gave me a thorough once over from head to foot. "Did you have another episode? I'd hoped we had those under control."

"Almost, but I caught it in time with the medicine you left."

"Good. Good. Would you mind having a seat? We'll get this over with. You've made it quite clear how little you enjoy being poked at."

We settled into the common room. She spent the next half an hour scanning my head, neck, and spine and then drilling me with questions, most of which pertained to my health, but then she ventured off into territory I was already feeling damned guilty about. "How are you doing with Isnar going off to work? Do you feel able to care for yourself throughout the day?"

"I'm fine. He needed to get out of the house. We both needed some space." That sounded like a socially acceptable answer.

She nodded. "And your son? Having a newborn is stressful and stress will only magnify your symptoms. Let that man take care of you. He does such a good job of it."

He did, but he also did a good job of rubbing my nerves raw. "He took Daniel to work with him. It's plenty quiet here."

"That was thoughtful of him." She smiled warmly. "Make sure you hang on to that one, not many like him around."

No, thank all that was good in the universe, there were not. Isnar might have been a kind man, but I'd seen the real Vayen that lurked just below that considerate exterior last night. Minor, or all of the Verian Cluster, for that matter, didn't need more than one of those. He'd have it all under his thumb in no time. I'd seen how he'd held the Narvan, and I had to admit that he'd done a far more intricately productive and efficient job of it than I ever had.

Weeda cleared her throat, watching me with a calculating gaze. "Is something bothering you?"

The woman had seen me at some pretty low and loopy moments in my first weeks here. I'd followed Isnar's suggestion to keep my mouth shut when at all possible so I wouldn't blow our cover while under the influence of the medication. Weeda was used to my short answers or not answering at all, so why was she digging now?

"No. I was just on my way out to the market. Are we done here?"

"I don't know as that's a good idea, Rhaine. You haven't been on your feet that long. Is Isnar going with you? I'd feel better about it if he were."

"I'm fully capable of leaving the house on my own."

She wore a tight smile. "But if you have an episode while in the transport or at the market, who will know how to help you?"

No one would. I swore what I thought was under my breath, but Weeda had good hearing. She took a step backward and busied herself with returning her equipment to her case.

"I'll take the injector with me, all right?"

"It will knock you out in minutes," she said quietly.

That was true, but come on, did I need her permission to leave the damned house on my own? "I guess I'll have to wait until Isnar gets home then."

Relief rolled off the slightly hunched woman. She handed me a fresh vial for the injector. "I'll be back next week unless I hear from you or Isnar before that. Call me if you need a refill."

"I will. Thank you." I herded her toward the door.

Once the sound of her transport had faded, I went back up the stairs to change. I didn't need Isnar or Weeda or anyone else for that matter. I could make a life here for myself. What I needed was to get out of the house and start solidifying my alias.

I walked out to the charging station and activated the transport. The sleek little tube's engine hummed to life. I opened the door and settled into one of the two narrow seats. It might have sat four Verians comfortably, two per seat facing each other, or Isnar and I if I didn't mind his long legs entangled with my feet.

Hoping to avoid any headaches or stressful situations, I set the destination using the interface on the door. The transport trundled off for the center of our colony, where the market, the port, and Isnar's business all sat within minutes of one another.

FIVE

Merkief

Jey and I arrived at the University and made our way through the security checkpoints without exchanging a single word between us. That was just as well because I was torn between being relieved that Vayen was gone and terrified that we were on our own. Spilling any hint of my relief to Vayen's right-hand man might cost me everything.

When Kazan had given me the order to off Vayen if he tried to take her position, I'd been appalled. Vayen and I had been friends, peers. But then she *had* been taken out, in one manner or another, and he *had* taken her position. However, he'd never crossed the line to the point where I'd been inclined to kill him without hesitation, and he had kept his word to return the Narvan to her.

I shouldn't have hesitated.

Had I followed her orders two years ago, I could have prevented this vacuum now surrounding us. Jey and I could have protected Kazan after she'd been released, when she needed time to recover. She wouldn't have felt like she needed to reclaim her position from Vayen. Maybe if she'd eased back into everything, her link would have recovered too.

Hells, even if she'd never reclaimed the advisory position for herself, she'd have been able to mentor us as she always had, she would still be alive, still an asset.

Kazan knew the Council and the intricacies of the Narvan. She had a host of contacts, a seemingly endless list of people who owed her favors, and a freighter-load of credits. As difficult to get along with as she could be on a personal level, she got the job done, held the Narvan together, and kept the peace my people deserved.

She might have even thanked me for following her orders, might have welcomed me into the position Vayen had held beside her. I'd never know because I'd fucking hesitated. Multiple times. And now she was gone forever.

We paused at a security point to offer a palm scan and were waved through. Jey's expression remained tight and closed, as though he were wrapped up in his head too. He took off at a brisk pace. I followed, body on autopilot as my spinning thoughts again took over.

There had always been competitiveness between Kazan and Vayen, some driving force that kept them at each other's throats like they knew the Narvan wasn't big enough for both of them. But then the asshole had to go and bond with her.

I'd thought a bond might have calmed Vayen down to a degree, reined him in a little, that maybe he'd let her have her way for the sake of making her happy. After all, that's what bonded males typically did. But no. He pushed her too damned hard, and knowing everything she was missing out on, she'd let him.

She'd seen what he'd done with the Narvan in her absence, how it had flourished, how much he'd accomplished. She'd heard the abundant admiration of the Primes, Premiers, and the High Council themselves. She'd confided how much it hurt, how it drove her crazy. And when he'd leave the two of us behind to go work with Jey, she became sullen and resentful. I understood completely. I'd been feeling that way for years.

How could anyone bonded to another not feel the pain they were causing? A bond was supposed to solidify a relationship, to tie a couple together in understanding and openness, but theirs seemed to do the opposite. I'd never seen a bonded couple fight like they did. Only Geva knows what his true motivations were.

He sure hadn't talked to me about them. Instead, he'd latched onto Jey during Kazan's absence. Jey. The man he'd hated for years. Not me, the one he drank with and could talk to. I, for some Geva fucked reason, wasn't the man he wanted to work beside. Granted, I'd been ordered to off him. But I hadn't. Neither of them quite trusted me after that, though Jey had made a good show of it.

Trust wasn't an issue now. Kazan and Vayen's death necessitated that Jey and I work together.

Kazan had molded me into someone fit to take on the advisory position. All that shit I'd done for her and the Council had to be for a purpose greater than landing me a prime seat in the ninth hell.

Geva had handed me what I'd been waiting for, not the way that I'd wanted, but I would make the best of it for the sake of my people and Kazan's memory.

Feeling a little more at peace, I took a deep breath and let it out as we arrived in the belly of the University, the domain of the LEs. An assistant assured us an LE would be with us in a few moments.

Jey appeared ready to tear into something or someone at any second. His calculating blue-eyed gaze judged the threat level of everything around him and what weapon might be needed to eliminate it.

He'd lost his partner and his idol. Their murder had hit him hard, blinding him to the opportunity Geva had handed us. We could do this.

I was going to have to watch out for Jey, keep him from getting himself killed until the grief wore off. After working closely with Vayen, Jey knew the advisory position a whole lot better than I did. Which meant I'd need to be on top of everything or he'd try to roll right over me and take the lead straight out of the gate. If I couldn't pull lead, we were at least going to be equal partners. I wasn't going to accept any fucking less, dammit. I'd done my time in the shadows.

An LE approached with a hesitant step that told me she'd been warned of the deadly situation she was walking into. "You have a pair of extracted links you'd like examined?"

I nodded, holding them out to her.

After she'd taken them from me, Jey finally spoke.

"You will transfer any salvageable data to us. No copies are to be made. No backups. Nothing. Is that clear?"

"Yes, of course, sir." She bobbed her head and backed away.

Jey had been here beside Vayen so it figured that the staff was all *sir* and *of course* with him. They were going to learn to be that way with me too.

"You can wait in there if you'd like." She pointed to one of the empty recovery rooms.

There were chairs inside and Geva knew how long the retrieval process might take. "We have plenty of work to do while we wait. Let's go," I said, walking in.

"I'm not in the mood to work right now," Jey snarled as he paced the hallway.

His rhythmic stomping reminded me of Kazan. The entire orderly list of tasks I'd pictured for myself shattered. Tears blurred my vision.

Fuck. They were gone. Really gone.

We'd never know if the two of them would have made the bonded relationship work, or which one of them would eventually bend and let the other lead. Equal was a word neither of them understood.

If I ever allowed myself the level of attachment Vayen had, I was going outside Kryon. It would have to be someone able to protect herself, but damn, I couldn't be in the middle of the screaming wars those two had. I might have entertained the thought of being in a relationship with Kazan early on in my employment, but she had too many secrets. And she'd been seeing the leader of the Assassin's Guild for fuck's sake. That hadn't stopped Vayen though.

On reflex, I sought Vayen out through our Artorian connection, to assure myself that the insane asshole was still breathing. As long as he was, the Narvan was under control. Those two things went hand in hand.

A second later, my brain slapped me with the reason I was here. The dead silence of nothingness hit me a heartbeat later. The Narvan was no longer safe in his hands.

After years of being overshadowed, the Narvan was finally in mine.

I could do this. Do it differently. Less crazy, less iron-fisted, more orderly. Better.

The Council's message relaying Vayen's assignments pinged my link. Eager for what information he might provide, I cleared my mind and read it. The brief note included the names of three worlds, two Artorian-ruled and one Jalvian, meaning Jey had received the opposite. Vayen had left no farewell, no instructions beyond the planetary leader's names, and a few lines on how to best deal with them. Overall, not very helpful.

Jey's footsteps halted. And then there was a second set, coming closer. The LE had returned. I stood and went out into the hall to meet her.

"Well?" I asked.

She looked to Jey rather than me. I gritted my teeth. This was *not* how this was going to be. I stepped forward and held out my hand. She had to look at me then. The links dropped onto my palm.

"I'm sorry for your loss. We all are," she said to both of us. Then she stepped back, hands clasped together. "I'm very sorry to report that beyond identity, we were unable to recover any viable information from either link. They both encountered irreparable damage."

"I'd hoped there would be something, fragments even, but we were told they were destroyed by a reputable source," Jey said.

She shifted her stance, gaze dipping to the floor. "The Board of

Directors was informed of your arrival. They wish to meet with you if you have a few moments?"

Jey didn't even spare me a glance before answering. "Yes, we might as well get that out of the way while we're here." Before she could make her getaway, he added, "I was told Kazan's armor was here, in the roomwhere...it happened. Could you bring that and anything else either of them may have left to the boardroom?"

"Yes, of course, sir." She bobbed her head again and scurried off.

I hadn't been to any board meetings at the University, having been busy supervising research teams when I'd had cause to be here. But apparently Jey had, either with Kazan or Vayen. He headed off as though he knew right where he was going, leaving me to follow along.

"I hoped there would be something," Jey said as we walked. "Names, maybe some leads on either of their credit stashes. Geva, the man had a million contacts and investments in just as many companies. No way in all hells I can track even half of what just fell apart when Kess took him out."

"You make it sound like Vayen was some sort of master cog holding the entire system together."

"He was."

Jey walked the rest of the way in silence. When we arrived at a wide set of heavy-looking black doors, he nodded to the young man at the station beside them.

"They're assembled, sir," the man said. "I'll have the items you requested waiting here when you're finished."

"Thank you." Jey opened one of the doors and went in.

I followed a step behind. Nine men and women, ranging from elderly to near the same age as the aide outside, sat around a long table. Some wore suits, others lab coats. All of them were looking straight at us.

"Our condolences," said the white-haired man at the head of the table. "We regret that this heinous attack took place at our facility. As you are aware, we pride ourselves on our security, but it failed miserably in this instance." He cleared his throat. "Please tell us how we might make amends."

"They're worried we're going to cut their funding," Jey said.

"Vayen would." He'd always been heavy on punishment. We didn't need these people terrified of us. We needed them to cooperate—fully and without hesitation.

"Kazan would have too, had any of us been killed here," he said.

"We're not them."

Jey cast me a sideways glance. For once, I couldn't tell what was on his mind. Grief made great camouflage.

As I was considering how to answer the board, Jey spoke up, "You will provide us with direct access to the LE department. A jump point, safe and guarded. If there is ever a need for us to be there again, no one outside that department will know about it. Is that clear?"

"Yes. Set your point. I'll accompany you myself and make sure your instructions are followed." While he seemed agreeable enough, he also seemed to be waiting for bullets to start flying.

"Everything else shall continue as before," I said. "I will be directly advising Artor. All reports and funding requests will be addressed to me."

The bastard looked to Jey first and only after he nodded did the man address me. "It will be as you say."

Not even a sir at the end of that? I started to consider slamming a fist into the table so they might better understand the new situation. A little voice pointed out that action was something Vayen would do, what the Board expected me to do.

"Good. If we need anything else, you'll be the first to know." I initiated a direct connection with him. He accepted without hesitation.

That was one contact off of Vayen's supposed million. As long as they were all this eager to stay in good standing with us, I wouldn't need to resort to his methods.

Today, the Narvan had new advisors.

SIX

Rhaine

I'd only been at the port for an hour, still feeling my way around the whole being out in public as someone other than Anastassia Kazan, when a harried-looking woman flocked by four small children approached me. As a human towering above everyone else in the market, I immediately felt conspicuous. I braced myself for whatever outsider slur she might be going to throw at me.

"Ishla Ka'turoc" were the only words I picked out of the flurry of formal Verian. Lady Ka'turoc. I laughed to myself. I'd never entertained the thought of that word being applied to me.

When I'd studied with Seeker Res, we'd had a few higher-class supplicants, but Res always served them. I hadn't ever learned anything beyond the hybrid of informal Verian and Trade that the majority of the populace could understand, even if they didn't prefer it. The common Verians on Prime hadn't liked me but would put up with being served by an outsider if no one else was available.

"I'm sorry, what did you say?" I asked.

Her pale, near-translucent skin flushed. She glanced around the busy market as if hoping no one would see her talking to me. She switched to Trade. "It is said that you are a Seeker?"

So that was Isnar's angle and why we were accepted so easily among them. Seekers were rare among the Verians, the mind speech ability being as uncommon among their kind as it was in mine. They were highly revered.

"An acolyte Seeker, yes." Though, no doubt, what had been done to me had severely hampered my abilities on that front as well.

"You will have to do. My Ishlan is ill. You will attend to him?"

"There is no other Seeker here?"

Two boys ran around her legs, chasing one another. Two girls, one the oldest, by her height, held the shoulders of the youngest of the four. The lady barked out a command in formal Verian that brought them all to a stiff-backed standstill. She smiled tightly at me.

"The Seeker that served these colonies when they were formed has long since passed from this world," she said.

"These colonies? How many are without guidance?"

"Most of them, Ishla Ka'turoc. Will you help us?"

I had no supplies, no place to work, no idea what abilities were left to me, but to be needed brought me peace, a purpose that I'd not felt since before I'd been imprisoned by the Council. Vayen certainly hadn't needed me upon my return, not for the purpose I wanted, anyway. He'd had the Narvan well in hand by then. It was only the bond and perhaps a touch of nostalgia that had tied him to me.

To be a Seeker here, in whatever capacity, would bring news to me and favors owed. It was a job that wouldn't require me to be tied to anyone else, on my own terms, on my own time. I could make this work, no matter what arrangement Isnar and I came to over Daniel.

"Yes, I will see your Ishlan."

She reached into the bag hanging from her shoulder and drew out a card to hand to me. I took it, reading her address and their names. I stifled a gasp.

Well, this was one way to get my foot wedged in the door. My first client was the prefect of our colony. I wondered if Isnar had managed to work his way close to the man yet or if I'd beaten him to it.

"What troubles him?"

"He cannot sleep and it is making him ill."

I was already busy compiling a list of supplies I'd need to purchase. "When is he available?"

"He is at home now," she said

"I will need a few things. I'm not set up here yet. I'll contact you as soon as I am able."

"Thank you, Ishla." She bowed her head slightly and left with the children in her care.

I spent the next hour hunting down the supplies I needed for the prefect as well as a basket full of fruit that didn't need anything other than a knife for preparation—at least I knew how to use one of those. During that time, no one else approached me. I had little doubt that Isnar would be tracking our transport if only out of curiosity. He probably knew exactly where I was in the market, but I didn't get the feeling of being observed.

Maybe he really had written me off.

It had been years since I'd been out in the open without anyone at my back, without the ability to contact anyone in an instant through my link or the few contacts I trusted enough to form natural telepathic connections with. Kryon could be anywhere, looking for me, for us.

The stalls in the market suddenly seemed too shadowed, offering too many places to hide. Distant conversations that had been nothing but harmless background noise became whispers. Were the stares of strangers indications I'd been recognized or were they just because I wasn't Verian?

With my heart in my throat and not a single weapon on me, I hurried out of the market as fast as I dared. The transport sat waiting, parked between a host of others. All of which offered plentiful cover for anyone watching me, or worse, taking aim. My hands shook as I opened the door and shoved my purchases onto the empty seat beside me. The door wouldn't close fast enough. Hitting the return to charging port button served as the quickest way to bring me home since my brain seemed to be too fixated on evaluating everything I had with me for use as a weapon rather than typing coherent commands.

Though I arrived home without incident, paranoia refused to abate. I ran to the door and then dropped the basket of fruit while fighting with the damned manual lock. With the door finally open, I darted inside and sank to the floor, my back pressed against the wall. I very much missed my formidable, towering Artorian shadow just then.

I drew a deep shaking breath and then another slightly more controlled one. My shadow was gone and I didn't need him. This was Veria Minor for fuck's sake. No one in their right mind would think to look for us here, not unless they'd gotten a solid lead. Vayen may have thrown our vanishing act together in a matter of hours, but he'd planned for me to be safe here with or without him. He wouldn't have allowed anything that might even have been misconstrued as a lead, solid or otherwise. And if Kess wanted to keep his reputation intact, he'd be doing everything in his means to quell any rumor of our existence no matter where we might be.

If anyone found me here, it would be an unfortunate coincidence, maybe an offhand comment passed along and overheard third-hand by some contact of a Kryon member desperate enough for Council favor that they'd look into it. That kind of crap, I couldn't prevent. All I could do was to be more prepared when I left the house. And when

I was in it. Alone.

With my wits again around me, I went upstairs to the bedroom and opened Isnar's near-empty closet. Thankfully, he'd used one of our regular codes for the chest. I sifted through the weapons he'd brought with him the day we'd left the Narvan. Everything was clean, charged, and loaded. Whether it had been that way since our arrival or he'd been taking care of his horde without my knowledge, I didn't know. I also didn't know if he'd removed anything before I'd found him packing. My gut told me that man wouldn't have walked out with my son if he'd been unarmed. Besides, he had a bigger price on his head than I had on mine. He had to be just as paranoid.

Most of his usual arsenal was sized to be masked by his bulk and his armor. While the weight of armor would have made me feel more confident in public, neither of us could get away with wearing it here. Not to mention, his coat was twice my size. I ran my hand over the rough surface, considering shaking the folded armor out. It would be better to store it hanging up so that if he needed it, it would be ready to go, not plagued with deep creases. Not that hanging the coat up would make it easier to envision him standing there wearing it. That had nothing to do with my urge. Nothing at all.

I shook my head and set the folded coat down. Selecting the most compact gun and a short, thin-bladed knife, I put the rest back as I'd found it and returned the coat to the top of the closed and locked chest.

With a couple of weapons secreted upon my person, I took a deep breath and headed downstairs. A knock at the door brought me to a halt halfway down.

Was it Isnar? I wanted to slap myself for how damned reliant I'd become on having him around. I'd been on my own before. I could do this. Bolstering my resolve to handle whatever waited for me, I strode over and peered through the peephole.

A Verian man I didn't know stood outside, peering back at me. "Ishla Ka'turoc? Hello?"

From his casual clothes and blatant nosiness, I concluded he was likely one of our neighbors. I opened the door enough to get my head through while wedging my foot against it in case he attempted to push his way inside.

"Yes?"

"You dropped this." He held up the basket, now again filled with the fruit that had been scattered over the ground outside.

I took the proffered basket and set it on the table behind me by feel so I could keep my eyes on him. "Thank you."

"Are you well?" he asked.

"Well enough."

The mild breeze ruffled his thinning hair as he stood there on my step, hands clasped together before him. "I see your transport is here. Is your Ishlan home?"

Was he going to try something if I was alone? Was he looking for Isnar? I fought the urge to reach for the gun, to point it in this little man's face and tell him to get the hell off my property. Logic informed me that might be a bit hasty, but my hand hovered at my side anyway.

"He's at work. Thank you for retrieving the fruit for me." I started to close the door before this got out of hand.

"I was wondering..."

A hundred ends to that sentence flashed through my mind in the time it took me to pause reaching for the gun again. Making sure my foot was still firmly wedged into place, I tried to keep my tone pleasant. If Isnar could do this socializing thing, so could I. "Yes?"

"Your Ishlan, he mentioned you had some training as a Seeker."

"Yes." Best to keep my answers short until I knew where this was going.

"Would you see to my daughter? She has a rash and a cough that won't go away. The doctor is very busy. We were hoping you might be available?"

A rash and a cough didn't require any telepathy to fix. Neither did the prefect's sleep issues. I might be up all night narrowing down what the problems were and possible treatments, but hell, I wasn't doing anything else.

"I have to see the prefect shortly, but I can take a look at your daughter before I go."

The man offered a grateful smile and beckoned me to follow him across the street. After assuring myself that my weapons were in place, I locked the door and stepped into my new life as Seeker Rhaine Ka'turoc.

SEVEN

Jey

Merkief seemed to be wanting to take lead on things I had no idea he was interested in. Vayen had willed half the system to him, but I figured it was to keep the Council happy. We'd had the arrangement of one Artorian and one Jalvian before. It made sense that Vayen would try to maintain that balance to make this easy for us in the event of his death.

Death. Every time I even considered that word and Vayen in the same sentence, my brain went blank for a second.

He'd recovered from so much in the five years we'd worked together, endured hundreds of injuries, lived through gunfights beyond counting, pulse blasts, a fucking all out Kryon attack. Then Kess had killed him.

It bothered me immensely that we didn't have his body, that we couldn't see what had taken him down. Maybe that's what made it all seem so unreal.

Kazan was also to blame. And she wasn't.

Sure, he'd been distracted with watching over her and taking care of her. I would have done no less were I in his place. But if he hadn't been bonded to her, or if he'd buried the bond like he had when she'd been imprisoned, he might still be here. I could be in my room, happily grabbing six solid hours of sleep while he took three and worked through his link until I got up. I would know that tomorrow, he would have a list of things we'd need to accomplish and he'd hand me my quarter while he did the rest. For the most part, I just had to stand beside him and let the man do what he did best while keeping an eye out for anyone who disagreed with his plans with possible deadly intent.

Now my morning looked like a fucking endless list of shit to do while leaning on Merkief. And that was another whole unsettling proposition right there.

He was intent on work, dour, like he'd skipped right over any grief and had taken on a persona of Vayen-lite. Like he felt entitled to his half of the Narvan because he'd put in the time working with all of us. I couldn't fathom why he was so eager for the endless stress of constantly proving yourself until one day when Kess or someone like him erased you from the universe.

At least it wouldn't be Kess taking me out. The odds against it were pretty high anyway, with the Council's rules in place. Us working with him was a definite no-go but avoiding each other, if it meant not having to ever see him again, that I could work with. Because if I *did* see him, I would be inclined to ignore the Council entirely and do my best to kill him.

Vayen would thank me for sending Kess straight to the ninth hell. No doubt, he was waiting there for just such an arrival. People like us didn't bother entertaining the hope of landing at Geva's feet for some form of eternal bliss. No matter which hell Vayen had ended up in, at least Kazan was probably there beside him.

I'd have to find some way to rein Merkief in, but not piss him off. We needed to stick together, especially in these first months. We had to present a united front—like we'd done when Kazan had been gone. I knew how to do this, and thankfully, it wasn't going to be near as hard as before, but I'd prayed this day would never come.

The University staff had provided us with the belongings of Vayen and Kazan: her armored coat, a pulse pistol and a gun he'd dropped, the clothes Kazan had changed from for her surgery and her boots. I'd hung her clothes from my closet door, the boots stood below. It was like she was there but invisible.

We'd examined the operating room where they'd died, but it had been cleaned. All evidence of any attack had been removed except for the missing plaz panel in the room above and some deep laser burns on the floor and one wall. Standing there, I'd tried to envision how it had all gone down as Kess had described it. I could almost hear Vayen's voice, see Kazan on the table. I drew a ragged breath. Then Merkief had nudged me and suggested we get some sleep while we could.

Sleep was hard. The Artorian house was too quiet. No one sat at the security station. Merkief and I both needed to rest, and I knew the system was set on high alert. So much as a bug crossing one of the sensor grids would set it off, but there were only two of us left.

There was no screaming couple in the kitchen and there never would be again.

What I wouldn't give to walk in on the two of them yelling at one another just one more time. Or to catch a glimpse of them getting all soft and personal when they thought we weren't looking. They both worked so hard to keep appearances up that it was almost impossible to imagine them relaxing enough to be in a somewhat normal version of a relationship. Maybe they didn't.

Maybe they hadn't, I corrected myself.

When Merkief nudged my link to see if I was awake, I realized I must have dozed off at least lightly for a little while. Kazan's shadow in the coat told me to get to work. I got up and changed.

Merkief and I didn't speak as we ate whatever he'd pulled from the cold storage and heated. I was busy touching base with my contacts and the leaders of the planets Vayen had entrusted to me. What Merkief was doing, I didn't ask, but I assumed it was much the same.

"We should see Gemmen and pick up a Kryon contract to show the Council that we can handle this," he said at last.

"Both of those should be safe enough, neutral territory. I'll take Gemmen if you want to pick the contract."

"Sure." He smiled as he put his dishes on the counter for the bots to take care of.

If picking contracts made him happy, I would gladly let him have that responsibility. I'd never had an issue with jobs he'd picked before and Sere wasn't my favorite place. After he'd left, I Jumped to Cragtek on Rok.

Being there without Vayen felt wrong. While Cragtek had been Kazan's project before we'd come to work for her, Vayen had taken it over early on and he'd run with it. His fingerprints were everywhere. He'd talked about the place with well-deserved pride.

Cragtek staff went about their business with extreme efficiency. The stock was well organized. The equipment was in good repair. I'd lost track of how large the Cragtek fleet had grown, but I supposed it was now my business to find out.

A guard met me before I'd gotten too far into the warehouse from the jump point.

"Here to see Gemmen?" he asked.

"He in?"

"Always." The guard chuckled and nodded me back toward the offices. He followed along in my wake, hand not exactly on his sidearm but not relaxed either.

I kept some of my attention on the armed guard as I contemplated what to say to Gemmen. The old man had some sort of relationship with Vayen that had never been fully defined in my presence, and Vayen wasn't the sort to spill his personal shit to anyone. I didn't quite know what I was in for.

"That one," the guard behind me said.

I'd guessed which office from how many steps it was from Vayen's. He'd called Gemmen in enough when I'd been there to assume it had to be within twenty to forty steps and there weren't many doors in that hall. Gemmen's was the one at the end, before the hall turned and headed back to the warehouse. The corner office. My wondering about the view was cut short by the door release clicking after one half knock. The automated door slid open without a sound.

There was no view. Solid walls. Secure walls. No wonder he and Vayen had gotten along.

Gemmen sat there, his eyes red, one empty hand on the desk, the other around a half-empty glass of brown liquor that I could smell the moment I walked in.

"You've heard, I take it?" I dropped into the chair across from his desk, wondering how many times Vayen had sat there.

Gemmen nodded. "Go on." He waved the guard away and pressed a button on his desktop. The door closed. He held up his glass. "Want one?"

First thing in the morning? Well, my morning, meaning I'd recently slept. The actual time of day was irrelevant. Did Vayen normally drink with him? He did...*had* drunk quite a lot.

"Sure."

"Is that wise?" he asked.

Was this a trick question? "Just one? Yes. Four, definitely not."

"Fair enough." He offered a half-hearted smile and reached down to pull a clean glass from somewhere. When he'd filled it from a bottle that he'd also pulled from what may have been a drawer in his desk, he pushed it toward me.

Just how close had they been? Did the old man have his own orders or agenda? "Not poisoning me, are you?"

He took a sip off the top and pushed it farther my way. I grabbed it and drank. It was the strong shit indeed. It burned pleasantly all the way down.

"So what are you going to do about this?" he asked.

"My hands are tied in the retaliation department, but I can tell you what I'd like to do." I took another swig.

"Tied by who?"

"By people I can't afford to cross. Vayen couldn't either, if you follow me."

"Not exactly, but you might want to see if you can find a way around those people. Kess needs to be exterminated. He was a thorn in Kazan's side for too damn long, and now this. Taking Vayen out. Taking them both." He rubbed at his eyes and then stared into his glass.

"I'll see what I can do." I wasn't the only Jalvian missing the irritable, insane Artorian.

"You let me know if you need any help." He emptied his glass and poured another.

While he'd no doubt been a formidable force in his prime, the old man looked hollow now and mostly drunk. I doubted that was a daily thing or he wouldn't be able to keep Cragtek running to Vayen's standards. And as much as Vayen liked to drink, he wouldn't have tolerated it on the job from anyone he worked closely with.

"I'll keep that in mind." Cragtek did have stealthy forces, ones that weren't tied to any particular military branch or planet. Much of our untraceable weaponry also came from Cragtek storerooms.

"I can almost see the wheels turning," he said, hoisting his glass.

Perceptive, even while drunk. Maybe I was underestimating him. "Do you think I could see his office? Just for a few minutes?"

Gemmen thrust himself up from his chair and grabbed the bottle. "Lead the way."

We walked the thirty-two steps to Vayen's door. Gemmen fumbled with the multi-layered code pad for a moment before it opened.

The lights came on as we walked in. Everything was just as it had been the last time I'd been there.

Gemmen lifted the bottle to the empty desk and took a long pull. He handed it to me. I took an honorary sip and handed it back.

"Will there be a service?" Gemmen asked.

"We don't have their bodies." Proper Jalvian services required a body to cremate.

"Wasn't Jalvian. Don't need one."

From the short answers, I gathered the liquor was adding up. Best to make this quick before he forgot what we'd talked about. "Maybe we could do a private memorial on Artor. For both of them."

"I'd like that. Tell me when. I'll be there."

"Look, Merkief and I are taking over. Vayen's wishes. If you need anything, you let us know, all right? And about your offer? I'll get back to you."

He pointed the bottle at me. "You do that."

Gemmen didn't appear to be in any condition to cause us trouble at the moment so I considered that another successful meeting. Maybe assuming control wasn't going to be so bad.

EIGHT

Rhaine

The house had been too quiet for seventeen days. Too many days. Isnar had been silent for all of them. Not even a written message, though I still checked several times a day. Seventeen days without my son. While I had set up a shop within walking distance of the house and clients had been contacting me for treatment since word of my successful efforts with the prefect had spread, something was missing. Something that goaded me to get into the transport and drive to the port rather than send a message of my own.

I tried to convince myself it was curiosity. What had he gotten so wrapped up in that he hadn't even checked in to see if I was all right? Surely his bond demanded that he spend at least an hour or two at my side by now. Was Daniel sleeping through the night yet? If I could plan on a semi-regular schedule, I might be able to balance having Daniel at home with me to give Isnar a break. He had to be wanting a break by now.

The houses near ours fell behind as the transport sped toward the port. In the distance, freight ships traveled in a carefully planned upward and downward pattern. What were they carrying? Had Isnar managed to convince anyone to import a case of frozen prantha yet? He'd been craving meat from home. The stock animals here did have a distinct taste from the native grasses that he didn't like. There were a selection of birds at the market as well, but they also fed on Minor's flora and had the same issue. Only the fish agreed with his stomach.

Minor's trees were short, the majority not much taller than Isnar. Their wide, sprawling canopies covered the landscape in varying shades of greens and yellows. A flock of birds, tiny things with bright orange bellies shot from the woodland as I sped past.

What was Isnar doing? Where was he staying? Not a single credit had left my account that I hadn't spent. A wave of heat blasted over me. If that helpful little Verian woman who had cooked for him that day he'd forgotten his midday meal had taken him in, she wouldn't survive the day.

Not that I could see him putting up with a Verian woman, tiny as they were compared to him. He'd likely step on her by accident or roll over and crush her. The heat came again. If he was in one of their beds...

The transport came to a stop quicker than seemed possible for the fifteen-minute trip, but when I glanced out the window, I had arrived at the port. The lot was nearly full of transports. Most of the colony's workforce was employed here, either in importing, exporting, or supporting those who did with food, entertainment, and supplies.

I hadn't been able to find anything similar to a Seeker's robes in the stores, and I certainly wasn't going to ask Isnar to import one from Prime. Besides, I didn't want the real thing. I wasn't a full Seeker or even half of one in my current state. However, the rusty red overcoat I'd bought the week before had a suitable swirl to it when I walked and it went all the way to my feet, which was a surprise in itself. The merchant had seemed happy to be rid of it, probably because it hadn't fit anyone else. Sunlight caught on the golden embroidery that ran along the hem, up the front edges, and all the way to the neckline. I checked my reflection in the window of the transport. The coat was undoubtedly the showiest piece of clothing I'd ever owned, but it did an appropriate job of advertising my services as a knock-off Seeker.

I tucked my hair behind my ears so I could see clearly. It still felt odd to be out in public with my hair down, but most Verian women didn't bind their hair back and the majority grew it out to their waist or beyond. If I was going to sell this Rhaine Ka'turoc act, I was going all in.

The more I talked to people and visited the port market, the more obvious it became that word of our separation was making the rounds, along with wild speculation as to the cause. Being different among the Verians was one thing, but if word of us got out too widely, someone might put real names to our faces, and then it would all be over. Daniel deserved a longer life than that.

For both of our sakes, and as much as it might drive me mad, I needed my estranged Ishlan to come home.

I made my way into the port complex, pausing only to scan my ID chip at the entrance. He had to know I'd been here frequently over the past two weeks, purchasing herbs, candles, and furnishings for my shop, but he'd kept to himself. Entirely.

My shop was almost ready and I was looking forward to a time when clients could come to me rather than me traveling around the colony and beyond on my own. Even here in the bland safety of rudimentarily-settled Veria Minor, with my knife and gun when I dared carry them, it made me nervous to be too far from Isnar.

Our bonded connection remained so muffled, it might as well have not existed. Maybe he was getting settled in somewhere on his own just as I was. I wasn't quite sure how I felt about that other than it brought me no ease or satisfaction.

Uncertain of what reception I might get, I spent a good hour in the market. Half the time, I was exploring possible meal options I could put together myself. The rest, I was touching ingredients that were already in my kitchen that I had no clue what to do with. Maybe Isnar would agree to at least come home long enough to cook the kind of meal I was hungry for.

If he was happy to work himself to the bone here, and it wouldn't surprise me if he was since he was avoiding the bond, he could at least keep up appearances by coming home at night. We could figure out some sort of arrangement we could both tolerate.

Acknowledging that I was only delaying the inevitable, I gathered my nerve and left the market empty-handed. The building that housed his shipping operation was only a short walk away. Every step seemed to bring another pair of eyes on me, judging, evaluating, taking notice. Who knew what rumors I was spawning just by being here. Was my next step a move toward fixing this or only making it worse? What if we ended up in a screaming match in his office and his staff overheard everything? It wasn't as though we could keep it silent while we raged at one another like we had before. It was out loud or nothing these days. I'd just have to do my best to keep calm. This was only a negotiation, like thousands of others I'd brokered before. I could do this.

Seekers didn't get angry, and they didn't raise their voices. I had an identity to solidify.

A guard waited at the door. One set by Isnar, no doubt. The typical Verian wouldn't have considered the need for such a thing.

"Welcome," the smiling Verian man said. "Your business here?"

"I'm here to see my Ishlan, your boss."

"Of course, Ishla Ka'turoc, but he is not taking visitors today."

I kept the pleasant smile on my face despite my inclination to ram past him. "I'm not a visitor."

His demeanor slipped faster than I expected from a Verian, turning hard and decidedly unfriendly. I wondered how many hundreds of men Isnar had interviewed to find this one. "I said, he's busy."

"Then he can tell me that himself." I glared at everything that might have been a camera.

The door behind him clicked open. The guard scowled at the traitorous door. I imagined he didn't get much of a chance to dip into his darker side around here.

"Don't worry, you're doing a fine job. Keep it up, just not with me," I said as I strode past him.

Inside the building, bright lights illuminated rows upon towering rows of boxes, crates, and loose goods on heavy-duty shelving. Dugans was a far cry from the size of Cragtek on Rok, but also much cleaner, more organized. I could see what had drawn him here, something familiar, a place to utilize his less deadly skill-set.

Mover units traveled between the rows, beeping and humming along as they followed their programming—shelving stock, or retrieving orders. A woman wearing a long blue tunic and loose pale green pants dodged between a set of them to hurry toward me. Her plump face was flushed.

"Ishla Ka'turoc?" she asked breathlessly.

"Yes?"

"Oh thank goodness," she leaned over, one hand on her side as she huffed to catch her breath.

"I'm here to see my Ishlan, he let me in."

"That was me. Come. Quickly." She gestured for me to follow as she hurried back into the depths of the warehouse. The building was narrow but much longer than it seemed on the outside, not that I'd examined it too closely. This was his place. Like his private office at Cragtek, he needed a little breathing room of his own even when we were getting along.

"Where are we going?" Thanks to my longer legs, it was easy to keep up with her. My overcoat flared out behind me. I pulled it close to keep it from catching on the movers or stock as we passed by.

She remained intent on her path until we reached a door at the back of the building. Another guard stood there. This one didn't bother with a smile or greeting.

"You're sure about this Atalina? If he gets mad, I'm not covering for you."

"He can fire me for all I care. She's a Seeker. She can help."

The guard shrugged and shook his head, but he opened the door.

"What can I help with?" I asked, wishing Isnar would just get off his ass and yell at me in person so we could get on to negotiations, preferably somewhere more private than the open office space I found myself standing in.

A host of Verian women, varying greatly in age, popped up from their workspaces. Their gazes locked on to me. Some curious, most full of accusation. They all made my neck muscles tighten and my heart beat faster. What the hell was going on with the entire staff of women? And why was I the bad guy? Isnar had left *me* and taken my son to boot.

I was about to have a serious departure from my Seeker persona when Atalina took control of the situation. "Back to work, all of you. We've got a business to run. Just because the boss is down, doesn't mean we are."

That caught my attention. "Down? What do you mean, down?"

"Come." She gestured for me to step closer as we turned our backs on the judgmental staff to face a single door in the middle of a wall of windows. Window covers had been drawn down over every one. The plaz was clean and gawking faceprint-free. I couldn't help but wonder what waited inside. Did he want me kept away or brought in despite what his guard thought? What was Atalina up to?

I let go of my coat, the loose fabric falling around me in a comforting wave. I pretended it was my armor, wherever that had ended up. Isnar hadn't packed it, but I would have liked to have been wearing it right then.

She palmed the panel beside the door and swallowed audibly as the door slid open. The office was silent. The wide space wasn't very deep, but it comfortably allowed for a table, a couch, a large desk, and a tall chair filled with a glassy-eyed Artorian who was staring vacantly at a vid screen with a sleeping infant in a sling across his chest.

"Take care of him, would you?" Atalina whispered. "He's done good things here, but he can't keep this pace up." She started for the door.

"Stay, I may need you." I didn't like his coloring, it had a grey-green cast, and he'd yet to acknowledge that we'd entered the room.

"Isnar?" I said, not going any closer.

He blinked slowly and raised his head to look around, his gaze unfocused. This wasn't the intense single-mindedness I'd expected. I wasn't sure he even recognized me.

Taking the chance that I'd get a head full of fury, I expended what little force the Council had left to me and pried our bonded connection open a few degrees further. All I got from him was a trickle of exhaustion.

I approached slowly. Atalina lingered by the door. He made no move to stand.

Empty feeding tubes from Daniel, three cups with sludgy liquids at the bottom, and plates of partially finished meals littered the desk. He hadn't changed in that regard.

"Sorry about the mess," Atalina said. "He's wanted to be alone for most of the last week. I make sure he's fed, and the baby, but that's all he'll allow."

So this was the woman who was taking care of him. I found a small measure of gratification in the fact that she wasn't doing a very good job of it.

"You're here?" His voice was quiet. His lips were dry and cracked.

"I think you're sick."

"Maybe." He nodded slowly.

"I'm going to give Daniel to Atalina for a little while, all right? Then we're going to get you onto the couch."

For the next few minutes, he ceased to be the man I missed and was also still annoyed with. He became a client, someone in need of healing.

Daniel woke as I removed him from the sling. He launched into a bout of red-faced crying and was in sore need of changing. Isnar's shirt was wet and a revolting stench rolled off the two of them. At least the baby was alert and his coloring was normal.

"Take Daniel and get him cleaned up and fed. Please. And send that guard in to help me move Isnar," I added before Atalina got out the door.

"I can walk," Isnar said as he shivered and hunched in upon himself now that Daniel's warmth was gone.

"I doubt it." The heat coming off of him concerned me greatly. I'd never known him to be feverish before. Then again, our frequent use of the tank had kept common trivial illnesses at bay.

We no longer had access to the tank.

Acting as a confidant, therapy sessions, massages, stitches and bandages, and using the minuscule trickle of telepathy I had left to soothe troubled minds, I could do, but whatever was strong enough to knock Isnar down was very likely beyond my skills. Seeing him this way shredded my nerves. I didn't trust myself to take the time to figure it out. He needed help now. I pushed his chair back far enough that I could use his terminal to send for Doctor Weeda.

"How long have you been sick?"

"A few days, maybe?" He looked truly miserable and like he wanted nothing more than to go to sleep right there. "You were in the market. Again."

The guard from outside the office popped his head in the doorway. "You needed me?"

"Help me get him up and onto the couch."

It was a troubling sign that Isnar didn't utter a single word of protest as the two of us got him to his feet. The bundle of clothing he'd taken with him sat in a folded stack on the squat table in front of the couch. A folded blanket lay over one end along with a pillow. Given the state of his desk, I was sure I had Atalina to thank for all of the neatness.

It wasn't until we were getting him situated that I nearly tripped over the cradle tucked between the table and the couch.

"You've been staying here? All this time? The two of you?"

He didn't answer, his eyes already closed, hand limp on my arm. I found it very disconcerting that he was so unresponsive. Why hadn't he let me know he needed help?

"I've sent for a doctor," I told the guard. "Please see that she gets in as expediently as possible."

"Yes, of course." He bobbed his head and backed out of the office.

Not knowing how long Weeda was going to be, I got the pillow situated under Isnar's head. His legs from the calf down hung over the low arm of the couch on the other end. It wasn't made for a man his size. The couch was barely wide enough for him to lay on. I draped his arms over his chest to keep his weight centralized. If he tried to roll over, he might well end up on the floor.

Hours later, Doctor Weeda found me there, sitting on the table beside him, attempting to bring some order to the sweat-tousled short hair that I hated.

"Ishla Ka'turoc." She nodded curtly.

"Let's go with Rhaine, Weeda. I have a feeling we'll be seeing a lot of one another now that I'm practicing here."

"As you wish. What seems to be the problem?" She set her bag on the table beside me and opened it. Weeda pulled out a tube, squeezing out the knot of clear gel that began her hand cleansing ritual.

"He has a high fever and appears quite dehydrated. He said it came on a few days ago. It may have been longer according to his staff. I would guess it wasn't this bad at first or he would have contacted me to take Daniel."

"So you're still separated then?" She gave me a disapproving scowl.

"Not for much longer." Not if I had anything to say about it. If he'd listen to me after how badly things had gone the last time we'd spoken. I kept my sigh to myself.

Continuing with her usual routine, she started with running a scanner over his body, pausing to rescan his chest three times before continuing. She checked his eyes, his mouth, and felt around on his neck and behind his ears.

Weeda turned to me with a scowl. "You did get the required immunizations before taking up residency here, correct?"

"I lived on Prime years ago. I should be set, shouldn't I?"

"Possibly, but all of this should have been covered with your residency application."

"He took care of all that." I looked down at the miserable man shivering even in his sleep. Clearly, he hadn't thought to check that little detail when he'd made the spur-of-the-moment decision to live here with me.

"Minor is not Prime," Weeda chided. "The initial round of planetary engineering only finished eighty years ago. We're still discovering new issues and will be for a very long time. Minor is still a very wild place outside of the colonized zones. We'll need to go over all of your records carefully to see how this lapse occurred so we can prevent it in the future." She shook her head and set the scanner down. "This is very serious."

"Do you know what it is?"

She nodded but didn't look any happier about it. "I take it he didn't live on Prime with you?"

"That was long before we met."

"With all the cargo coming and going here from all over Minor, it's not surprising that he picked up this virus."

"What about our son?" I bit my lip before I could make a correction or further explanation. According to our cover, he was *our* son.

Hell, according to the amount of time and effort he'd put in, Isnar had far more claim to Daniel than I did.

"He may have acquired some immunity from you, but again, this isn't Prime. There are new diseases here, allergens, and who knows what else and how it might affect an Artorian or yourself. The residency board should have researched this and given all of you—"

"How can we help him?" I blurted, hoping to distract her from concerns about the details Isnar had foraged or bribed his way past.

"Get him home and cleaned up. We'll need to try to get his fever down. Artorian systems aren't known for their tolerance of high temperatures, one of the downfalls of all their genetic manipulation." She searched around in her bag and came out with a black fabric-covered case that she unzipped. A host of small, narrow vials were tucked into padded slots on either side. She ran her finger over several of them, reading the tiny print on the labels.

Weeda removed an injector from the bag, a more compact model than the one she'd given me. She fit one of the vials into it, pressed the needle tip into his arm, and hit the button on the top. "That may help."

"May?"

She rested her hand on my arm in an utterly practiced consoling way that I instantly recognized. "He's Artorian, Rhaine. Our medicine is intended for Verian chemistry. I'll do what I can, but honestly, there is no simple cure even for us. It's something he'll live through, or he won't. You want to help him? Pray."

NINE

Merkief

Jey floated in the tank. Our second Kryon contract hadn't gone well. Jey's head had been elsewhere since that fated meeting on Sere. Admittedly, we were both not paying as much attention to the job at hand as we should have been.

Running the Narvan was a distraction from the ninth hell. Even in the middle of tracking down and wiping out an underground drug distribution ring that was competing with Council-approved channels, requests for funding, complaints, updates from contacts, reports from planetary heads, all of it funneled in, bombarding my link. Every fucking moment of the day. And this was just from my three worlds and the few active contacts I had on Jey's. We didn't even have Merchess to contend with, which was likely an even bigger distraction. How the hells had Kazan and then Vayen managed it all themselves?

Maybe it just took a lot of practice and delegating. However, most of these decisions had to go through me or I'd lose my hold on what was going on and why. If I fumbled with my worlds, Jey would think I wasn't fit for this. He'd make a play for the whole system.

Neither of us had come this far in Kazan's service without a healthy dose of ambition.

I needed to prove myself, buy some time to gain experience. I needed a majority hold on the Narvan so both Jey and the Council would see that I was in control.

There was one world within the Narvan that hadn't been in Vayen's will. Frique. Small and mostly useless except as a source of food exports, the small world posed no threat or strategic benefit. It had no military force beyond a civil militia in times of crisis. And in my memory, there hadn't ever been a crisis there. They wouldn't put up a resistance as long as I maintained Vayen's deals. I could gain the majority with a single meeting.

I double-checked my weapons and the couple thin spots in my armor where the weave was repairing itself from our last contract. Nothing appeared to be an obvious weakness. Jey had another hour in the tank and two to sleep before we could get back to work.

By the time he woke, I'd be running lead on the Narvan and he wouldn't be able to do a thing about it. With a grin I didn't bother to hide, I Jumped to the house on Frique.

The small structure looked as it always did, a few leaves on the roof, quiet, and empty. A house like that needed a family, a couple of kids playing outside, maybe a few animals in a barn nearby. Clearing a few trees would make room for a garden. Everything grew twice as large on Frique, especially here on this zone of the continent. But like all of Kazan's houses, it was only a series of walls to sleep and eat within. The woman had been sharp and deadly, and she'd done good things for Artor and the Narvan as a whole, but she had no idea how to live beyond her job. Her entire being was wrapped up in work. No wonder she and Vayen had hit it off. The two of them were identical in that regard. Then again, maybe it wasn't so much hitting it off as defaulting. It wasn't like either of them had a social life.

I wasn't going to be like that. I would not let this job swallow me whole. The Narvan needed the hand of a living being who felt emotions beyond anger and satisfaction. There was more to life than that. There had to be.

This house would be a silent monument to those who had slept inside but never lived there. A reminder for me to do better.

I turned away and set off toward town.

As it turned out, the city council wasn't in session when I got there, and unlike any civilized world, their governing system wasn't operated out of any central complex. All of their councilmembers worked from their own public offices, usually above their homes. Only a few of them lived within this town.

Vayen had always seemed to arrive when there was a meeting in session or at least scheduled. I made a note to watch the official Friquen newsfeed more carefully. If he could keep up on events here along with every other damned thing, so could I.

The secretary working inside the council building informed me the next meeting was in four days. When I calmly suggested she contact the city council and have them convene today, she gave me a tired smile and said, "I'm sorry, sir, you'll have to come back in four days. We have a schedule."

"Right. I'll be back then. Thank you."

While I could have thrown my weight around and demanded to see someone, that wasn't the image I wanted to portray. Four days wasn't too long to wait, I repeated to myself while surveying the town proper to set up a jump point closer to the council building. I had no urge to see Kazan's empty house ever again.

I returned to the ship to wait for Jey to wake up. While I waited, I touched base with the Premier of Artor through the vid terminal in what had been Kazan's office. The entire time I was on the call, my skin crawled, my conscience telling me I shouldn't be sitting there. Vayen had taken over her office for two years. It hadn't seemed out of place to see him sitting here, so why did I feel so out of sorts? I deserved to sit here. He'd decreed I should, for Geva's sake.

I made myself stay in the chair, and rather than work through my link like Vayen or Kazan or even Jey would, I made the effort to meet face to face—even if it was by vid rather than in person. The memories of all the ways those in-person meetings had gone wrong when Kazan's safety net had unfurled were too fresh, even years later. Any in-person meetings beyond harmless Frique were going to be as a pair until we were sure things were working in our favor.

When I heard Jey get out of the shower, I finished up my last meeting and went to see him.

"Did you file the completion?" he called from his room. The shuffling and shifting told me he was getting dressed.

"Yeah. We pulled that off, barely. You've got to get your focus back. I know this whole thing has hit you hard."

"*Whole thing?*" Jey emerged as he settled his armor onto his shoulders. "They're fucking dead. Our people. Our friends. Kess is out there, free as can be on the other side of the Nebula, enjoying his cloak of protection from the Council. That seem right to you?"

"As long as he stays out of our way. I'm not prepared to lose our advisory position in the name of revenge. Neither Kazan nor Vayen would thank us for that."

Jey stared at me for a moment. "Then I'll take care of it myself."

"Didn't you hear me? You need to focus, dammit. The Narvan needs both of us. Let this go."

"I can't. And I can't believe that you can."

Ah fuck. He had the same implacable set to his face that Vayen had worn ninety-eight percent of the time.

"Give it a week. If you still feel that way, we'll revisit the how-do-we-kill-Kess planning."

"A week?" he sneered. "Sure, a week for Kess to further embed himself within his new territory. Why not? He's never been much of a challenge before, so sure, let's wait."

Jey hadn't used that snide tone with me since our first few days working together. I hadn't appreciated it then and I didn't need it now. Time for redirection. "You wanted to do a memorial service? Work on that. At least a service won't get you killed."

"So you're afraid of him." Jey managed to look down at me even though he was only slightly taller. The look of Jalvian superiority, Vayen had called it.

"Yes, I am. And you should be too. In case you missed the memo, he managed to kill Vayen." I gave him a hard jab in the shoulder in case he wasn't paying attention. "Even distracted, Vayen would have been difficult to take down. And yet, Kess managed to do it."

Jey's narrow-eyed glare didn't ease in the slightest. Dammit, time to change tactics. "Taking Kazan out while she was sedated shows you how low he is. She deserved so much more than that."

That seemed to sap some of the resolute ire from him. He shifted backward, relaxing his stance a few degrees. "She did."

"So...the service," I said.

His gaze drifted to Kazan's closed door. "She had no family, no friends other than Gemmen that I'm aware of. Same for Vayen. What am I supposed to do, invite the planetary heads and some Kryon? Maybe a couple of High and Mighties for fun?"

I hadn't considered the lack of attendees when he'd first brought up the idea of a memorial. Jalvians prided themselves on a lengthy death service. Their family read a list of lifetime accomplishments with medals and commendations on full display. Artorians did that to some degree but it was more about sharing memories and comforting one another in the time of loss. There was usually drinking involved. That sounded more like Kazan and Vayen to me.

Jey needed some form of closure, an emotional reset. If I gave him that, I hoped he would snap back into his usual self. He knew this advising routine better than I did, and dammit, I couldn't shadow his actions if he wasn't taking any.

"Then invite Gemmen. We'll go to Vayen's beach, and we'll have a drink for both of them," I said.

"Doubt the old man needs another drink, but sure. What's this beach?"

I flashed him the jump point. "Vayen told me he used to fish there with his father when he was a kid. I mostly know it as one of the places to look when he would vanish."

"When I pissed him off," Jey chuckled softly. "Kazan ever go there?"

"He didn't mention it. He didn't mention much to me, not like he used to when we were first hired."

Jey nodded. "He kept it in tight."

He said that like it was some motto to live by. Like a new goal for himself. It wasn't mine.

"He did. And look how happy he was," I said with heavy sarcasm.

"Didn't know the meaning of the word," Jey cracked a grin.

"Let me know when this is happening. We both have a lot of work to do. Speaking of which, I got a lot done while you were out. Do you need me for anything?"

I hoped he did, and that he didn't realize how much I was gleaning off of every interaction.

"Actually yes, I could use your friendly face for a visit to Karin. The Premier isn't on board with following my orders. He was Vayen's man and the change isn't setting well."

"But you were there with Vayen. He knows you're legit, right?"

"He's Artorian. He's used to working for one of you. Specifically, the one who handpicked him for the job."

That made it sound easy enough to step in and take Karin from Jey. But that would mean he'd want to trade for the Jalvian holding of Syless. While the Sylessian government wasn't entirely in my pocket either, they had been mostly cooperative so far. Holding a portion of the Jalvian forces made me feel more secure than relying solely on the Artorian military if a revolt broke out. Or if, for some reason, Jey might decide running the Narvan would be neater with one advisor.

Vayen had been wise in dividing the Narvan's worlds as he had. I just wished he'd mentioned this contingency plan. Despite the unease between us, I would have shadowed him more rather than focusing on my own jobs and projects.

"Sure, I can help with Karin. What do you want me to do?" I asked.

"Show him we're united. That the Narvan is unified, for Geva's sake. That we're not going to devolve into a war next week that might pit the Artorian worlds against one another."

"So smile and nod and let you talk."

His tenuous better mood wavered back to the callous one. "Too much to ask for?"

I held up a hand and reminded myself to keep my tone neutral. "No problem."

"Good."

We Jumped to the office Vayen had set up in the Karinian capital building. He'd been smart to do so, eliminating travel time between outside jump points to the building itself and removing the possibility of attacks during those times. I supposed Kazan's imprisonment had brought about a few positive changes for us.

The aide in attendance inside Vayen's office was on her feet and had a weapon on us in the matter of a breath. Vayen had probably handpicked her too.

Jey spoke calmly, "Hello, Marit."

"Oh, hello." She sighed and slid her gun home.

"Are you familiar with Advisor Ma'Tep?" he asked.

I wasn't aware we were going with outright titles. Vayen and Kazan never had. But I liked the ring of it. I offered Marit a polite nod.

While she did return the gesture, there didn't appear to be much heart in it. She sat back down at her desk, which inhabited a corner of the spacious room opposite Vayen's desk. She stared at the vid in front of her.

"I don't think you're the Artorian she was hoping for." Jey chuckled in my head.

"I'm far more available than the other one was." Not that Marit appeared interested.

"We're here to see the Premier," I said.

"I'll let him know you're waiting. Let me check his schedule a moment." Marit's fingers tapped over the terminal. "He should be finished with his current appointment in a few minutes. Would you prefer to meet with him here or in his office?"

"Here," said Jey.

Jey settled in behind Vayen's desk. The black high-backed chair fit Jey well. I went around to stand beside him, leaving the only other chair open for the Premier. Marit noticed me standing, and for a split second, showed apprehension before returning to her pleasant expression.

"Would you like my seat, Advisor Ma'tep? I didn't mean for you to stand. Or I could bring another chair in?"

"We won't be long. This is fine. Thank you."

"As you wish. Please let me know if you change your mind. Do you need anything while you wait? Something to eat or drink?"

"Damn, I could barely get a word out of her on my last visit, and she wasn't nearly this accommodating," Jey said.

"Maybe you're not as charming as you think you are."

Jey shook his head. *"I assure you, I get no complaints on my charm from Jalvian women."*

I shrugged. *"There's your problem. She's not Jalvian."*

"That's why you're here. This is our problem."

"Right." The solution was going to take more than the smiling and nodding Jey had assigned me.

"Marit, could I talk to you outside for a moment?" I asked.

Her apprehension made another appearance, this one more marked and it didn't vanish. Her gaze darted to Jey and then to me.

"The Premier will be here shortly. Would you prefer to wait?" she asked.

"I think Advisor Te can handle the Premier by himself, seeing that he is the advisor to Karin. I'm just visiting. We could perhaps offer them some privacy?"

"Of course." She stood, and after one last look at Jey, walked stiffly to the door. She palmed the panel and waited out in the hall for me.

"What are you doing? You're supposed to be helping me with the Premier, not hitting on his aide." Jey said.

"I know how Vayen worked. I am helping you. Trust me on this one."

Once out in the hall, I closed the door behind us. "Is there somewhere we can talk?"

She nodded. Marit led me down a hallway past two closed doors and into the last room, which was open. She turned on the lights and closed us inside. Hands at her sides, she stood there, trigger finger twitching slightly.

"Has anyone explained what happened to Advisor Ta'set to you?" I asked.

"Advisor Te told me he'd been killed. Assassinated."

"Yes. It was unexpected for all of us, and we're doing our best to keep everything running smoothly. We would appreciate your help."

"My help?"

Marit stood next to a square table surrounded by four low-backed chairs. A single ivory and orange weaving hung on the wall facing the door. The square meeting room was otherwise devoid of any personality. Kazan would have liked it.

"I'm not sure what you think I could do. I'm just a guard that was drafted as an aide to Advisor Ta'set on his infrequent visits."

"I rather doubt any of that is true." I stood there watching her, making no effort to hide my appraisal.

A pretty woman, but not overly done up, alert and quick with a gun, she seemed just the type Vayen would pick to guard his office.

She watched right back. All hint of apprehension had vanished, though her one finger still twitched.

Steady under pressure too. I considered the orderly piles I'd seen on her desk and the single datapad that sat on Vayen's. She'd been working when we'd arrived. None of the other planetary leaders' aides shared an office with the advisor of the Narvan. If I hadn't known better I would have assumed Vayen had given her a job here for personal reasons but bonded Artorians didn't screw around. Yet, it sure seemed like Marit had some sort of close relationship with him, something that belied the short periods of distracted time he would have spent in that office with her.

The job we'd taken in this same building long ago where we'd taken out Karin's then Premier rushed to the forefront of my mind. She'd had bodyguards, good ones even, and we'd still completed the contract, albeit not in an ideal manner. As I recalled, the fallout from that job had nearly cost Vayen his. Kazan had been pissed at him for months afterward. Would that have been enough to spur him to better protecting the Karinian Premier when he took control of the Narvan?

Planetary heads were vital to keeping the Narvan running smoothly. We worked closely with them on a daily basis. Having one assassinated would cause huge problems we didn't have time for. Vayen was one to find unconventional solutions.

I released Marit from my unwavering gaze and threw my cards on the table.

"Advisor Ta'set is gone. I'm guessing from your demeanor that you were one of the few that might actually be mourning him. I'm also guessing that you're the actual Premier and the man Jey is meeting with is only the public face."

"That would be quite a convoluted way to manage a world. Why would you think such a thing?"

"Because I knew your boss quite well and he was a big fan of convoluted."

I had to give her credit, she didn't reveal a thing.

"Hiding you from the public eye protected you from exactly what happened to him."

At that, her gaze did finally waver. "Will there be a service?"

While Jey would probably be overjoyed to have another person present at the memorial, it was going to be hard enough to censor everything we might say about Kazan and Vayen around Gemmen, who was not privy to Kryon or the High Council. Bringing a civilian into the mix was only going to make things more difficult.

"We're keeping it small, private."

She nodded. "But you will have people there?"

"Yes. Why?"

"That's good. I'd hate to think there would only be a couple of you at a service for a man like that. He was important to this world, the system, even if near no one knew he existed. He always seemed very alone, apart from everyone."

That summed Vayen up well. In the early days of our time in Kazan's service, we'd spent most of our off time together, drinking, venting, me trying to smooth things over between him and Jey, but once he'd taken on Cragtek and fully became Kazan's partner, he forgot what off time was. We'd still talked, but not as often as before, and then that had dried up altogether. I gathered that he'd talked to Jey more later on, but if any of it had been of a personal nature, I'd have been surprised.

If Marit had grown that close with Vayen, maybe she wouldn't be opposed to trying out a different advisor, one who wasn't in a bonded relationship. "Maybe you and I could talk sometime, outside of this office?"

"Maybe."

I allowed myself a smile, hoping to set her more at ease. "Are you going to confirm my speculation?"

"Believe what you want."

Vayen's people didn't crack easily. They were used to him, for Geva's sake. Maybe nice wasn't going to work with her. Knowing I was likely killing any chance of a possible talk, I tried a different route, likely one she was more familiar with.

"How about we go back into that office, and I put a gun to the Premier's head. We'll see what happens when I pull the trigger."

"I'd prefer you didn't. It would ruin his pretty face." She scowled.

"It is hard to find good help, isn't it?"

Marit exhaled loudly. "The public loves him. Me not so much. He's not near as attractive as he thinks he is."

"So, shall we go back into the office, kick out the face, and get some real work done, or would you rather keep wasting Advisor Te's time?"

"I wasn't wasting his time. I was right there for the meetings."

"Taking notes, but not taking part in the conversation. How is that productive?"

Her level gaze was impressive. "It worked under Vayen. He told me what to do. I did it. Everyone was happy. Not much conversation needed."

"Wouldn't you rather have some input? This is your world after all."

She gave me a look that made me wonder if I'd missed something. "You people do read my reports, right? That *is* my input."

"Well, yes, I mean, I'm sure Jey does. I do read those from the leaders of the worlds I advise. But wouldn't you rather have more say in what happens here? Some back and forth conversation?"

"You have the bigger picture, the financing, the connections. I'm just doing my part here, funneling every damned report that comes to me, that came from hundreds of others below me, into one relatively concise list of what we need and why. That's worked for years. I don't see any reason to change the system now."

"So you're happy with how things are."

She shrugged. "I don't have any complaints."

"Then why are you giving Jey a hard time?"

Marit glanced away, her shoulders dropping. "I don't like him. He's not the one I want here."

I wondered if Vayen had ever realized what he had in Marit. With his head buried in work and brain set in blind-to-other-women bonded mode, very likely not.

"I get that, but Vayen is no longer with us. He asked Jey to take Karin. This wasn't Jey's choice, but he's trying to do right by you for Vayen's sake. I suggest you cooperate while Jey is still in that mindset. Once you get on his bad side, it's hard to come back."

"Vayen put a Jalvian here? Why would he do that to us?"

"To maintain balance. I'm advising Syless."

"I see. I'd like to have a word with him about this."

"I'd like to have words with him on a lot of topics, but unfortunately, that option was taken from both of us."

Her hands finally relaxed at her sides. "All right then. Thank you for taking the time to explain."

"You're welcome. Can we go save Jey now?"

She grimaced. "He's going to be pissed."

"Better he be pissed now while I'm here to calm him down than the next time he shows up and you have to explain your system yourself."

"Right." She palmed the door panel. "After you then."

As we walked back down the hall I wondered how many other twisted surprises Vayen had left for us.

TEN

Rhaine

In order to get Isnar home, Atalina suggested we transfer him onto a mover. The guard I'd met helped Weeda and I get him out of the office. From there it seemed the entire staff had assembled to gawk as we hoisted his unconscious body onto the flat platform.

Atalina handed me the sling. I slipped it around my chest and then she held out my son to me. 'You carry him', was on the tip of my tongue. I should want him near me, to know he was safe. Rhaine was a mother, maybe even a good one, and I was supposed to be Rhaine.

I took my son and settled him into the sling. He was heavy. I didn't blame Atalina for wanting to give him to me, no matter how sturdy her little Verian frame might be.

We escaped the offices and moved back into the warehouse. "My transport is in the market lot," I said.

The guard gave me a sideways glance and shook his head. "West bay doors. Clear the path," he called out.

Two women ran ahead. One of them stopped a mover ahead of us with a vocal command, and after a quick few taps on the programming pad, sent it off into an aisle on standby.

"I'm Roshonomen." He offered a quick polite nod that we'd skipped earlier. "You'll never be able to get him in or out of a personal transport on your own and there's not enough room for anyone else to help you. We'll take him in the delivery unit."

I did appreciate that Isnar had found capable staff here, especially just then. My brain had stopped functioning properly from the moment Weeda had said either he'd live or he wouldn't.

Atalina walked beside me. A host of shuffling footsteps told me that most, if not all of the office staff were following. The solemn procession through the warehouse was interrupted only by the distant beeps of movers rows away and the squeak of a single out-of-whack tread every twenty-seven seconds on the unit carrying Isnar.

It was one thing to be stuck here on Minor with my son and a job I could tolerate, but quite another to be stuck here alone. Walking beside Isnar as the mover traveled the warehouse, I felt exposed. Not just that our cover story was under scrutiny from Weeda and the rumors racing through the colony, but now this host of women were watching me with him, like my every breath was being judged.

Squeak. The distant beeps of the other movers began to form a rhythm of their own that my steps refused to conform to. Even my breathing was uneven. I stroked Daniel's arm in an attempt to assure my squirming son that his father would be fine.

How many times had I rolled his unconscious body onto the gurney on the ship to get him into the regen tank? He'd always lived. This was the same, I repeated.

Except we had no tank. We didn't even have Artorian doctors.

He'd risked everything to be here. For me and the baby in the stinking sling I now wore around my chest.

What an idiotic thing for him to do.

"I'm sure you and the doctor will take good care of him," Atalina said as she walked beside me. "He'll be all right. Strong man like that."

I realized I was on the verge of outright sobbing and that's why she was talking to me.

Seekers didn't cry when their clients were in dire need of treatment. But an Ishla would...if she were very worried and maybe even scared at the prospect of being on her own. Sinking into the Ishla role for a little while would be in our favor. No one here knew who I really was, they wouldn't judge me for being weak just this once.

"Don't you dare fucking die on me," I said in my head, wishing to all of his hells that I could convey those words directly into his mind like I used to be able to do.

The mover slowed and then stopped beside Roshonomen. The rest of us gathered around him.

"Kray, bring the delivery unit around. The rest of you, convey your well-wishes and get back to work," he said.

I had the sneaking suspicion that he was more than just a guard, but I'd have to delve into that later when my wits were less scattered. And really, Dugans wasn't my business, it was Isnar's.

Anastassia would have kept her eye on it anyway. I had to keep reminding myself that I wasn't her anymore. I had my shop to take care of, my son to figure out how to raise, and an Ishlan who wasn't speaking to me. What happened in these walls, other than Isnar's wellbeing, was none of my concern. Except, as I listened to the hushed voices of the crowd of women pausing one at a time to lay a hand on my unconscious Ishlan, I couldn't push *that* one thing down. That was a valid concern an Ishla would have, a meeting of both of my identities. We were definitely going to have a talk about his office full of adoring women once he was back on his feet.

The bay door rolled upward and a large, boxy transport backed into the opening. The majority of the warehouse employees took that as their cue to get back to work. Roshonomen worked a couple of latches on the back of the transport and released a ramp door. It hit the floor with a loud clank that made me jump. Isnar didn't stir.

Daniel squirmed in the sling, one of his hands grabbing onto my overcoat. His weight made me feel front-heavy, like I might topple over.

"Come now, we're almost there." Atalina held on to my arm, not in a way that made me want to shake her off, but comforting, support-ing even. "If I'd have known he was so sick, I would have called the doctor myself. He hid it well."

I nodded. "He's good at that."

"Don't fret. He'll be back on those giant feet of his in no time."

If it was a common illness, the kind everyone got from time to time, a passing inconvenience, I would have believed her, but this wasn't. It was a virus he never should have contracted if he'd only had the forethought to get the proper immunizations—for the trip he hadn't planned on taking to the life he hadn't planned on living.

"He better be." I'd meant it as a threat, to him, to the Council who drove him to be here, to everyone who hadn't stood in his way and kept him in the Narvan, but it came out brittle and rather choked. My heart was really getting into this Ishla role.

The coat grew too warm, too confining. I tried to undo the latches, but Daniel and the sling made it impossible with my shaking hands.

"Rosh, how are we doing?" she asked loudly.

"It will just be a minute or two." He took a good look at me. "Why don't you get Ishla Ka'turoc settled up front?"

"That's a good idea," she said more to him than me, as if I wasn't standing right there, listening.

I did shake her off then. "I'll ride with him."

Roshonomen drove the mover up the ramp and into the dark back end.

"We can't have you bouncing about in back with the baby. I'll stay with him," said Atalina.

Like hell she would. "Then you take the baby and go sit up front." I'd slipped Daniel out of the sling and held him out to her.

"But you haven't seen your son in weeks. He needs you."

Strangled laughter poured out of my mouth. "He needs his father far more than me."

Atalina gave me a skeptical glance but took Daniel. "As you say, Ishla."

I waited until they got the mover strapped in and then walked up to stand beside it. They closed the back door, leaving us in darkness. It was much better that way. I could hold onto his hand and mumble the calming chants I'd memorized long ago without anyone noticing when I got the words wrong or my voice broke.

Whether the chants did anything more than provide a calm environment for an actual doctor or a conscious patient, I didn't really know. Res had always said my skills didn't favor the healing arts as much as administration and evaluating people, seeing the truth in them. But healing was what it seemed these people needed most, what Isnar needed, so I was going to have to learn to be good at it.

The box swayed as the unit got underway. The floor vibrated under my feet, the jittering traveling up my legs. Isnar's fingers moved in mine, gripping with faint pressure.

"Where are we?" he asked.

"I'm taking you home."

"I don't live—"

"You do." I held onto him tightly. "We'll talk about it later. Rest."

"Daniel?"

"Up front with Atalina."

He fell silent, his hand relaxing again as he drifted off. The ride wasn't smooth like our little transport. Atalina's warning had been valid, and I was glad she'd had taken Daniel. Even holding on, I almost lost my footing twice as we turned corners. The straps twanged as opposing sets snapped tight, eating up the slack.

The unit came to a stop. The back door opened a couple of minutes later. I blinked in the bright light. Roshonomen stood there with Atalina and another Verian man.

"Let's get him inside," Atalina said with Daniel on her hip. "Can you get the door for us, Ishla?"

Having her take control of the situation irked me greatly, but I wasn't up to the task. Someone had to do it. I let her.

I walked down the ramp, my feet tingling from the constant vibrations of the ride. The two men got the mover unstrapped and guided it down the ramp and toward the door. I opened the locks and let Atalina in.

"Daniel's room is upstairs. The middle one, by the bathroom. Can you put him down in there while we get Isnar settled?"

Atalina nodded and went into the house. It was unnerving to let her in unsupervised, but there was nothing to be done about it for now. The men got the mover as close to the door as possible. A few of the neighbors came out to watch. An audience was just what we needed. I sighed. We...I was going to have to do a lot of social wrangling to get all of this out of everyone's conversations.

Being taller than the Verians, I nominated myself to take one side of Isnar as we half-stood, half-dragged him into the house. The stairs were a trial in and of themselves, but we got him up them and onto the bed.

"I can get him from here. Thank you." I'd wrestled him around enough in the past to have a good handle on that.

The men nodded and headed for the stairs.

Atalina emerged from Daniel's room. "Will you be needing anything else? You'll want to keep him in bed for a few days, I'd guess. He's not getting much sleep between that couch and the baby."

"No, I bet not. Yes, I'll keep him here."

She nodded. "I'll have Rosh submit his reports in writing as he's been doing. Your Ishlan can read them when he's up to it. I'm sure he wouldn't want the progress we've made over the past month and a half to slow now. He's got so many deals open. Don't worry, we'll do our best to stay on top of it while he recovers."

"Thank you." A month and a half? So he'd not only bought into Dugans far earlier than I'd thought, he'd been actively working there too. Had he been sneaking out or solely working through the terminal? Anastassia would have delved into an investigation to confront him with, but I needed a few peaceful conversations with him before I'd consider broaching that topic.

"Don't worry about a thing," said Atalina. "I'll send some of Daniel's belongings back here for you. It looks like he could use some clean clothes and his room is empty. I'll check in on you later." She smiled and left the bedroom. Her footsteps traveled down the stairs. The front door closed. The deep rumble of the delivery unit sounded a minute later then faded.

Daniel was quiet for the moment, so I concentrated my efforts on getting Isnar out of the disgusting tunic. It occurred to me then that all of his Verian clothes were back in his office and Atalina hadn't offered to send anything back for him.

With a doctor visit in his near future, I decided to leave him undressed rather than put him in the clothes he'd left here. There was no need to further advertise his true self.

No clothes also made it easier to wash him. His office might have been getting him by for a place to crash, but clearly, it did not have a shower. The fever sweat only served to further accentuate the stench rolling off him.

It worried me greatly that the cool cloth all over his body didn't cause him to stir in the slightest. With both of my men quiet and cared for, I went down to the kitchen and sat at the terminal to consult with Weeda.

I'd been doing small healing tasks here so far and I'd assisted in the care of sick Verians during my time with Res. Verians often came to a Seeker first, hoping for healing by more natural or spiritual means, before resorting to medicinal. And we, the Seekers, were the ones to call the doctors in, working with them, under their guidance. I had no idea if Weeda and I could settle into that sort of partnership for the good of the people here. But for the good of the one very sick man upstairs, I was going to try.

She answered my call with her usual dour demeanor. I quickly explained what had transpired since she'd left Dugans.

"What more should I do for him?" I asked.

"You are quite attached to your Ishlan then? To wish to heal him?" Weeda was one not to mince words. In that regard, she reminded me of Arita Palaz, the second in command on the Verian Station, my long-suffering nemesis there. Maybe that's why Weeda rubbed me the wrong way most of the time.

"Of course I am. Why would you ask such a thing?"

"Your household is less than harmonious. Perhaps letting him go would solve this? Would it create a more stable environment in which to raise your son?"

"It would not," I said tightly. "As you well know, he's the one doing the raising."

"So you wish him healed that he can again take on that duty and leave you once more?"

Just who was the Seeker here? For this colony lacking one, Weeda sure seemed to have the leading questions routine down. Though, I supposed she'd had to play both roles for most of her practice.

"We're working on resolving our issues, but we can't continue to do so if he's dead."

"As you say." Weeda turned her attention to a datapad in her hand. "I've been consulting with another doctor here on Minor that has had an Artorian male in his care for many years."

"Did he also fall ill like this?"

"No, he had the proper immunizations for his kind. If your Ishlan recovers, I now know what to give him. I've also begun an inquiry into the matter of the sloppy residency processing your family encountered. Don't worry, I'll make sure this doesn't happen again."

I forced a smile. How fucking helpful of her. If she starting digging, she might uncover our false documents. Without my link, I couldn't access the files or systems needed to head off her inquiry. This terminal was too old and clumsy for delicate work like that. I pondered the datapad in her hand. Unless I could make one of those work. It would take much longer, but it was possible.

"So this other doctor, does he have a hospital, a clinic, anywhere we might take Isnar for proper treatment?"

She visibly bristled. "I can offer him *proper* treatment right here."

If we were elsewhere in the civilized universe, a doctor would have him hooked up to monitoring equipment. He'd be pumped full of fluids. He'd have medication meant for Artorians.

"Rhaine," Weeda's voice interrupted my seething. "It doesn't matter what building he's in. His body will decide if it will survive or not. There's nothing we can do." She shook her head and returned to her business-like tone. "Wake him if you can, get him up to use the bathroom, though he'll probably sweat everything out as long as the fever persists. Get him to drink if he wakes. I'll be by tomorrow afternoon to check on him."

"Thank you, Weeda."

"Call if he gets worse. I can give him something to ease his passing."

So worse was dying. I wanted to throw the terminal at her, but instead, I said, "I will."

She offered her usual curt, professional nod and ended the call.

I went back up to our bedroom. Daniel was awake, rustling around in his crib but not crying yet. I let him be and focused on the man I wished was rustling around. He lay still and his skin was still that same awful sickly color. How many times had I sat beside him after a dip in the tank, waiting for him to wake? But this was altogether different. There was no drying sheen of gel on his body, no assurance that he'd wake whole and healthy, ready to get back to work after a quick shower. The thought of him not waking, of Weeda coming tomorrow with her promise to ease his passing, made my stomach turn cold and hollow.

Had he felt this helpless when I'd been recovering from my surgery? I picked up the cloth and rewet it, washing him again, doing my best to cool his burning skin.

Daniel's shrill cry signaled a peak in his seemingly constant hunger. Maybe if I ignored him for a while he'd stop growing so quickly. It was freakish really. I was no expert on babies by any means, but he seemed to be outgrowing everything almost by the week. Isnar assured me it was normal, but I had a feeling it was only normal for his kind. Daniel was going to be towering over everyone here just like his father, and at this rate, by the time he was five.

Cursing Chesser for the hundredth time since we'd arrived here with a squalling infant, I went downstairs and warmed a feeding tube. With the pillows propped behind me, I settled onto the bed beside Isnar with Daniel in my arms, contentedly sucking at his meal. By the time Daniel had finished and was quietly contemplating his toes, I started to get hungry myself. We went back downstairs where I warmed a meat and vegetable-filled pastry, one of the two flavors of pre-made meals I'd found at the market. It was tolerable... the first few times I'd eaten it. I'd lost track of how many times it had been now, but the joy was gone. It was food and it was warm and I didn't have to waste time cooking it. I ate quickly, changed Daniel, and felt compelled to go back and sit beside Isnar in case he got worse or woke up. I picked up the one datapad we had in the house and decided I might as well see if I could do something useful while I was sitting in bed in the middle of the day.

Two hours later, a raspy voice asked, "What are you doing?"

I about threw the datapad aside, only remembering Daniel was right next to me at the last second. "Oh thank goodness, you're awake! Do you need water? To go to the bathroom? To eat?"

"Yes." His head dropped back onto the pillow and his eyes closed.

"Oh no you don't. Give me ten minutes before you resume your nearly dead routine."

"I'm tired."

I shoved his shoulder. "You're sick, idiot. You skipped some very important immunizations, and now Weeda says you could die. And I'll have you know that you're not allowed. If anyone gets to kill you, it's me, not some stupid Verian virus."

He started to say something but a fit of coughing took over.

"Hold on, I'll get you some water. Don't crush Daniel." I pushed the baby further toward the middle of the bed so he wouldn't fall off.

After a quick dash to the bathroom and back, I handed Isnar a cup, which he drained in a single swallow.

"More."

"That, I can do." I'd never been good at the hovering caregiver shit Seeker training required. Triage I could handle, give me a specific task and I'd be all over it, but just sitting there waiting was torture.

Two more glasses later, he looked like he might explode. "Need to get on your feet? Weeda said it would be good if you could."

By the time he got his legs to the edge of the bed, he was already coated in a new sheen of sweat. He sat there shivering. "Why is it so cold in here?"

"You have a fever. A very high one. And yes, you're naked. Your clothes were disgusting, and they're not clean yet so deal with it."

Isnar sat there on the edge, blankets pulled around him, shivering so badly that I swore his teeth were clacking together. I went over and pulled him to his feet. He stood there swaying. His color instantly deteriorated back to the sickly green-grey.

"Come on. I'll help you."

He nodded, leaning on me. I tried not to grunt as a large portion of his weight shifted to my shoulder. I was going to be sore tomorrow. That arm had never healed quite right after the Council guards had taken me down. Their medical staff had set it, but the tank would have healed it like it had never happened. It was a relief when we reached the bathroom and I could shift his weight off of me and onto the doorframe.

The bathroom was narrow enough for him to hold onto the counter to get to the toilet. I let him have his privacy and stayed in the hallway. He was silent for too long.

I was about to go in after him when I heard him making his way out, the counter creaking under his weight. To make him look even more miserable, he was now scowling while shivering.

"What?"

"There was blood," he mumbled.

"That can't be good."

"You kind of suck at this."

I got us heading back to the bedroom. "I never made it to full Seeker, or even close, if we're being honest. My training seems like a lifetime ago."

He managed an acknowledging grunt and shuffled along beside me, his strength flagging before we'd made it even the few steps back to the door of the bedroom. If he fell out here, I'd have a hell of a time getting him back on his feet.

"We're almost there." On my better side this time, I took even more of his weight, which made talking all but impossible as I wrestled and dragged him back into the bed.

"Tired," he whispered as his eyes drifted closed.

I covered him with every blanket we had, grabbed Daniel, and ran down to the terminal to call Weeda.

After I'd conveyed what had just transpired, she nodded and said, "I expected as much. Do what you can to try and lower his temperature." Then her tone softened, reminding me more of Atalina than the Weeda I knew. "This virus is putting a lot of strain on his organs. His weren't designed for that. If we had the luxury of time and he wasn't contagious to any other Artorian, I'd say to take him to his homeworld and let them treat him, but no one would let him onboard in his condition. Stay with him tonight. I'll be by tomorrow." Then she ended the call.

I swore then instantly felt guilty when I realized I had Daniel in my arms. I needed to be more mindful of that now that there were little ears in the house.

That thought sent me into another round of swearing. *Little ears? Really? What the hell was I doing here?* I shook my head.

By the time the clock told me it was time for bed, Isnar still hadn't awoken again. I walked Daniel to sleep, put him down, and crawled into my bed, now nearly filled with a large sweating, naked man. If he'd been well, I'd have been thinking of one last barb to fling at him for the day. But if he'd been well, he wouldn't be there. He'd have been on the couch in his office, uncomfortable, unshowered, and probably with several barbs of his own.

We hadn't been sharing a bed much before we'd come to Minor.

That had seemed awkward while living with Merkief and Jey. Most of the time, if we did sleep together, we'd done so quietly, covertly. More often than not, he'd been off working with Jey while I was left behind, trying to catch up on everything with Merkief playing watchdog. However, here in this house, where we were alone, I didn't exactly dislike having him in the bed. When we'd first arrived here, in my lucid moments, he was an evil I knew. But now I realized he was also someone who knew me in a world of strangers. The only one I could really talk to, who understood how frustrating this was, to be apart from everything we'd worked for. And I had to admit, when he'd been gone, I'd missed him.

As I followed our bonded connection, trying to offer what calm I could, more of my long-disused training came back. Tomorrow, I'd bring a candle and some of the herbs from my shop to do a proper healing chant. For now, I'd done all I could. He seemed less restless, at least.

His labored breathing and the creaking of the house kept me company in the dark. My thoughts wandered to the Narvan. Were Merkief and Jey thriving thanks to the friendly handover? Were they standing up to the High Council's demands? What did my contacts think of my supposed death and what did that death mean for Merchess and the constantly feuding families there? And Gemmen, that poor man, to lose us both. There had to be some way to let him know we were all right.

There had to be, but as the hours passed, a safe way didn't come to light. Isnar was right, the only way we got to stay alive was if the Council didn't hit upon a single whisper of doubt. The only way to guarantee that was to stay quiet. I fell asleep while silently begging for everyone to forgive us.

ELEVEN

Jey

The three of us standing on a rocky shore hadn't been what I'd had in mind when Gemmen had suggested a memorial service. I didn't know the side of Vayen that had come from a family. To me, he'd always been a fully formed pain in my ass. It was hard to imagine him as a kid. Could someone that focused ever have had a regular childhood?

When we'd first met, I'd hated him on sight. Mostly because he was the enemy. Faces like his had been on the government propaganda since the war had begun. Sure, I knew it for what it truly was now, but at the time, Artorians being the enemy was my only truth. They'd taken advantage of us, thought they deserved more of the Narvan. They viewed us as mindless brutes fit only to fire weapons at Fragians or whatever invaders their explorations brought down upon us all.

He was also several years older than me, and I'd assumed that meant more experience and a higher rank. He was a threat to my one-day lead on gaining Kazan's favor. To make matters worse, he'd hated me too, and he hadn't had any qualms about showing it.

Kazan had done her best to keep the peace between us, dividing her time equally. I had no idea how she stayed on her feet those first few weeks, training and mediating between the three of us. I'd never met a woman more driven than her. Or stubborn. We all admired her devotion to the Narvan, even though she could take things too far, take one job too many, push herself to the ends of her nerves and ours. The Narvan was better for it. My people thrived because of her, of everything she'd done and pushed us to do.

She was the reason I was standing on a beach with two other men, each of us with a bottle in hand. I would never have set foot on Artor had she not hired me. Would never have gotten to know the Artorian that had aggravated me to my wit's end until one day he didn't. Until I saw how he was taking better care of Kazan than she was. Someone had to do it before she put herself in an early grave, and she certainly hadn't welcomed my advice.

Maybe I cared too much about pissing her off to really put my foot down or openly disagree. I'd lost count of how many times she'd fired Vayen. She may have threatened to fire me a time or two, but thank Geva she had never actually said those words. It would have crushed me. Maybe she knew that. I hoped she had.

There were words I would have liked to have said to her. To thank her for all she'd done for me, everything that had been offered to me due to her training, but the right time had never presented itself. Besides, even though Vayen and I had reached an amicable middle ground, when it came to anyone else getting personal with Kazan, he had no tolerance for it. One didn't mess with a bonded Artorian, especially not that one.

Gemmen raised his bottle. "If they had to go, I'm glad they went together."

They didn't *have* to go. Fucking Kess took them. But the old man knew that and arguing about semantics wasn't on the agenda for the evening. I drank. So did Merkief.

"May they find peace wherever they are," said Merkief.

"They wouldn't know what to do with it," I muttered.

"Probably not." Gemmen took another drink.

We followed suit.

Merkief looked to me. Fuck. My turn. "You could have left some fucking notes," I yelled at the lapping waves. "Hiding the Karinian Premier in plain sight? Just love to make me look stupid, don't you?" I considered throwing my bottle, but in the end, I drank from it instead.

"For what it's worth, I don't think he planned on getting killed," said Gemmen.

"He'd planned enough to leave assignments on the Narvan." I shook my bottle at him. "He might not have planned on it that day, but he'd given it some thought. And yes, he could have hidden some damned notes, encrypted them, something."

"That would have been helpful." Merkief took a tame swig.

I pointed at his bottle. "You got somewhere to be tonight?"

"Maybe. Don't worry, I'm not rushing off. We'll do this right."

"If we're doing this right, you won't be on your feet later. What are you drinking anyway?"

I grabbed the bottle out of his hand. My heart faltered as I turned it to see the label of Kazan's favorite red wine from Frique. "Oh." I handed it back with far more care.

Why hadn't I thought of that? The fact that I hadn't only pissed me off more. Then again, it would have taken several bottles before the wine had half the effect as the potent piss I'd taken from the cabinet on Artor. This was what had filled Vayen's sturdy silver flask that he'd kept in his coat right beside his tin of stims. I knew because he'd shared it with me on several occasions during the couple of years we'd worked closely together.

But I should have been the one remembering her more. She'd been my center for years, the one to give me all that I was now. The one that I'd loved even though she'd never reciprocated or encouraged the emotions I'd never openly shared with her.

When I'd first learned of Kess, that Kazan had had a Jalvian partner, I thought I had a chance of stepping into his position. If I tried hard enough, proved myself enough, maybe she'd see it. Despite my efforts, she'd picked Vayen instead. I'd hated him for that too.

"I don't suppose you two composed their accomplishment lists?" Gemmen asked.

"Doubt any one person could compile either of those lists." Merkief settled onto a dry windswept area of rock. He picked up a pebble and threw it into the water.

"It would take days to read them." I sat down nearby.

"And most of them would no doubt be classified," Gemmen added as he gingerly worked himself down onto the rock between us.

I raised my bottle and we drank. The waves rushed the shore and retreated for a long while before Gemmen broke the silence.

"Do you think they would have ever joined, those two?"

Merkief snorted. "Can you imagine Kazan's face if he'd been stupid enough to ask?"

A bark of laughter burbled up my throat and exploded from my mouth.

Merkief cast me a sideways glance and grinned. "How about a couple of little Vayen's running around?"

"Like she'd ever permit that to happen," I said.

"Like the universe could handle a couple more Vayens." Gemmen raised his bottle and we drank.

Was that what we were trying to do? Be a couple of Vayens? A pair of Kazans? As much as we admired both of them, we weren't them and would never be. But maybe the Narvan didn't need them anymore. It needed us.

❧

When I woke the next morning, I vaguely remembered Jumping Gemmen back to Rok. I'd handed the wavering old man off to his annoyed-looking eldest son before returning to the house on Artor to collapse in my bed.

Three empty bottles sat on the counter in the kitchen, trophies of the night before. I grabbed a stim from the bulk supply we kept in the cupboard and swallowed it down. When I reached out to Merkief through my link, I found him asleep. He'd left a message that he was elsewhere and when he planned to return. I had several hours to kill.

The Artorian house didn't belong to me. It was Merkief's world, his territory. If we were going to do this right, the two of us, and not step on each other's feet, we'd need some space.

We would need to work together. I certainly didn't trust anyone else at my back at the moment, but maybe living together wasn't necessary. The sudden itch to get out, to find a space of my own, was near uncontrollable. Part of that may have been the stim taking effect.

I got dressed and suited up before making a lap through the house, the first house that I'd slept in with Kazan and Vayen, where Merkief had first joined us. There were so many memories here. I needed a few less of them so I could focus. Merkief hadn't been wrong.

My nerves peaked as I opened the door to Kazan's room. It felt wrong to even consider walking inside her space. Everything was neat, put away. Nothing personal adorned her walls or any of the surfaces in the room. She wasn't there.

I went to Vayen's room. As usual, it was a mess. A few empty bottles perched as he'd left them, two on their sides, one precariously close to the edge of the bedside table. Food wrappers, clothes, and what looked like a sheet lay scattered on the floor. A tangle of blankets and pillows lay heaped on one side of the bed. The jumbled stack of datapads on the floor beside the bed beckoned to me. Sitting on the edge of his bed, I activated the first one and prayed to Geva it would offer me some guidance.

Rhaine

I'd figured out how to successfully toast bread without charring it, and was enjoying a slice covered with semi-melted cheese when Weeda knocked on the door. I scooped Daniel up off the blanket on the floor and let her in.

"He's still breathing, I take it?" she asked.

"I would hope so."

And Isnar thought my bedside manner sucked? Maybe she was this way with me because I was a Seeker, or not Verian, or perhaps it was because I'd snapped at her twelve too many times when I'd been under her constant care.

I led her up the stairs with Daniel on my hip like Atalina had done. She was on to something there. It was a much more comfortable place for his chunky weight.

Weeda walked into our bedroom like she lived there. I supposed she'd been treating me in the same room during our first weeks on Minor so maybe it wasn't as brazen as it seemed.

She set her bag down, pulled back the blankets, and gasped.

"What?" I ran to her side, expecting that he'd turned purple or stopped breathing or was covered in some horrible rash. But he appeared normal. Sickly, but normal.

"He's quite...large."

Since she only had the blanket down to his waist, I didn't know what to make of her comment. "He *is* Artorian."

"I mean," she poked a finger into his shoulder. "Muscles. Everywhere. A man doesn't look like that from sitting behind a desk. Don't tell me he got that way from working in a warehouse either. I've treated most of the staff down at Dugans at one time or another and none of them look anything like that."

I had to admit, even as aggravating as he could be, he was not at all hard to look at. The more I looked, the fact that Weeda was also looking grated on my nerves. If anyone was going to drool over my naked Artorian, it was me. Only me.

"He does take good care of himself." That body was a weapon, honed as sharp as any blade. It was a good thing he wore a lot of loose clothing here or he'd have a lot more people gawking. "Did you bring anything to help him?" I managed to ask without snarling.

"Help him?" She blinked and shook her head. "Oh yes, let's see how he's doing, shall we?"

Weeda sanitized her hands and then pulled out her scanner and went over him, head to waist, several times. "The good news is that his organs don't seem to be liquefying."

"That *is* good news." I glared at her. "Do you talk to all your patients this way?"

"I'm here to deliver the truth. You, Seeker, are the one to offer comfort and kind words."

Daniel started to squirm and whine. I realized I was squeezing him and loosened my hold. "You might consider not being quite so blunt. It would make my job easier."

Isnar began to toss and groan. I realized he was saying something. Rather than the common trade language we normally spoke here, this was all in Artorian, a soft pleasing cadence to listen to even if I didn't know most of it. Unfortunately, "Stassia" came out in the flow quite clearly.

I grabbed his hand and would have liked to shove a loud 'shut the hell up' into his head if I could have. "She's gone. I'm here," I said instead.

Weeda's brows rose.

"He was joined before me. She died," I said as calmly as I could manage. That was somewhat true. I was Rhaine now and I had died. Sort of.

She put the scanner back in her bag and pulled out the black case of tiny vials she'd used the day before. After selecting one from the case and loading the injector, she sent another dose of medicine into his veins.

"You know what would make my job easier?" she said. "The two of you not taking me away from my own people who appreciate my time." She shoved the case and the injector into her bag.

"You're fortunate that he," Weeda nodded toward Isnar, "has

been good for this colony. I'm swimming in medical supplies thanks to his taking over Dugans. Otherwise, I'd be inclined to report the two of you, because Seeker or not, I don't smell a whole lot of truth in this house."

Why did the damned woman have to be smart? Caught in a debate between putting Daniel down so I could cause Weeda to have a fatal accident on the stairs or thanking her for her services, I let her leave in silence. The colony needed their doctor, and we didn't need any further suspicion cast in our direction, even if she was the only one entertaining it at the moment.

Weeda certainly would have scented the lack of truth in my thanks. Silence was my best option. Neutral, as it were. I'd have to figure out some way of playing this out in my favor because Weeda and I were surely going to need each other again.

I stayed with Isnar, hoping that he'd quiet down and go back to sleep so he could get better. I didn't want to have to call Weeda back if I could help it.

It took a good long while before his breathing started to settle into a slow and steady rhythm. It was hours later that his eyes finally opened.

"Hold on, I'll get you some water."

"You're here," he rasped, repeating the same thing he'd said in his office.

I nodded, wondering what exactly he was implying by that, but plowing onward anyway. "Weeda stopped by earlier. She gave you something different today. Hopefully, it helps."

With Daniel settled on the floor, I ran to the bathroom to fill the cup with fresh cold water. When I returned, Isnar was trying to sit up, but his arms were shaking and his head was bobbing to and fro like his neck was a spring.

"Bathroom?"

He nodded more frantically.

I set the cup down and dashed over to get him on his feet. He wasn't much help on our walk to the bathroom, but he did manage to stay vertical. He was in and out and back in bed five minutes later. I made him drink the water, but he only took one cup this time.

"Have you ever been sick like this before?" I asked, hoping to keep him awake for a few minutes while I washed his face with a cool cloth.

"No. My insides are clawing their way out."

I put the cloth down and sat back. "Let's keep them inside, all right? Do you know where you are?"

He blinked several times and finally seemed to focus. "House?"

"Yes. I need you to remember to call me Rhaine. Weeda is already suspicious. She launched an investigation. I've done what I can to cover our tracks, but you set this up. I need you to see if more can be done."

"Datapad."

I grabbed it from the table beside the bed where I'd left it. "Do you feel up to this or do you want to talk me through it?"

"No."

Well, wasn't he just a cheery patient? As he didn't clarify, and given his exodus from our house, I handed him the datapad and gave him some room to work.

Watching his shaking fingers made me cringe. What if he didn't recover from this? What if Weeda's investigation exposed us? I did my best to keep my concerns to myself now that he was awake and semi-alert, but his grasp of our bond was a hell of a lot more sensitive than mine. He was watching me. I could feel it even as I picked Daniel up and busied myself with checking him. It figured that when I wanted an excuse to leave the room and change him, he didn't need it.

"Damned Verians and their home health care," Isnar muttered.

The system here was far different than the Artorian way. 'Fucking primitive', he'd called it when I'd been stuck in the same bed. But it did make sense within their social structure. Family served as caregivers. A doctor was shared by all, their living expenses and supplies paid for by the community. Trading companies like Dugans, purchased medicines when and where they could to care for themselves and the community as part of doing business. It was all quite symbiotic. Seekers filled the gaps. Except with this particular patient, where it seemed I wasn't welcome in either capacity.

At least when he was delirious he'd asked for me. Or maybe cursed me. My actual grasp of the Artorian language was fairly rudimentary. I missed my link and its nearly seamless translation function.

Since Daniel wasn't cooperating, I went down to the kitchen to get my irritable charge more water and a piece of toast with protein spread—the closest thing to cooking for him that I was qualified for. He had to be hungry by now, no matter what his insides felt like.

When I got back upstairs, Daniel had managed to scoot his way off his blanket and was busy sucking on the corner of the sheet that dangled near the floor. That didn't seem to be anything dangerous, so

I left him to it. A man's voice came from the datapad. Roshonomen. Atalina had said he'd be submitting reports.

I set the cup and toast on the table beside him. "Everything going as planned?"

An icy glare told me the answer was a definite no.

"Anything I can do?"

Though he didn't say it, the prickly sensation through our bonded connection suggested me leaving the room was a good start. I grabbed Daniel and retreated downstairs. Forcing Isnar to talk to me wouldn't help anything.

I spent the next hour resuming my brushing up on Seeker practices while feeding Daniel and balancing him on my lap to keep him quiet. When I heard stumbling footsteps upstairs and the shower come on moments later, I debated the best course of action. We had to find some measure of peace between us so we could pull this joined couple thing off for the rest of our lives.

Starting small seemed a wise choice. I eyed the stack of his clean clothes on the counter. The sling was there too. I put it on, situated Daniel into it, grabbed the stack, and went upstairs.

Hair still dripping, he sat on the end of the bed wearing only a damp towel. Both hands were on his temples, massaging.

I set the clothes down beside him. "Thought you might want these."

He didn't bother to look at me or the clothes.

I hazarded a few steps closer, smoothing his wet hair back so I could feel his forehead. He stilled but didn't look up.

"I think your fever has finally broken." I didn't hide my utter relief.

"Bad for business if I died in your care."

A full sentence. We were making progress.

It wasn't easy, but I let his jab go. Progress for me too, I supposed.

"Are you still hungry?" I asked.

"Maybe."

I nodded and left him to get dressed. He'd probably fall on his face rather than accept help from me now that he was more alert. I began to wonder if when he'd said 'you're here' before in that empty tone, it was supposed to have been more of an accusation or distasteful observation than any measure of relief.

While one of the pastry pockets I'd been living off of was heating up, I put Daniel down for a nap. Rustling came from the bedroom along with more heated muttering in Artorian. There was enough 'she' in there to understand whatever he was bitching about wasn't in my favor. He also repeatedly used a couple of words I'd only ever heard in the context of Chesser yelling at me when we were fighting.

The fights between Chesser and I had always been loud. Both brothers had fierce tempers, but the older one hadn't enjoyed the physical outlet I'd offered the younger. Enforcement and assassination with limited rules did have venting benefits.

I'd never thought much of whatever derogatory Artorian slang or obscenities Chesser had thrown at me. They were just words I didn't know, and I'd wielded an equal arsenal that he didn't understand. What had been between us had burned fast, consuming, and often confusing. Vayen was more of a slow burn, worming his way closer even when I'd tried to push him away for his own good. He was familiar and safe. He'd stuck by me when I was utterly certain he wouldn't, even when I'd thrown my doubt right in his face. He could be so damned earnest and, since we'd come here, outright kind.

He'd had hard words for me before, but never like this. To hear them come out of his mouth even if they weren't to my face, stung. Beyond stung, I admitted to myself. They hurt deeply.

I hadn't been easy on him then or now. Especially not here, after he'd given up so much, after the Council had screwed him over as badly as they had me. He had been trying like hell to make this work, and I'd shoved it all in his face and pushed him out the door.

Dammit, I'd missed him, despite trying not to. Having him here again, being near him, felt right.

I stared at the blurry floor. Every relationship with my past partners, Chesser, Zsmed, Kess, had gone wrong, deadly wrong for them or me, or both. Even Marin, who I'd kept at a distance, had ultimately betrayed me. They all had in their own ways.

Except for Vayen. I wiped my moist eyes on my sleeve.

We weren't partners anymore. We weren't in the Narvan. We didn't have to work together in anything other than keeping our cover secure and raising Daniel. I took a deep, shuddering breath and let it out slowly. It wouldn't be easy to unwire my defensive habits after all this time, but I owed it to him to try.

If he would let me.

I gave him a few more minutes to vent while I grabbed the plated pastry and more water from the kitchen. His head came up like a starving animal scenting a meal as I walked into the room. He was still perched on the end of the bed, though drier and wearing pants now. I handed him the plate and cup and backed away to the chair in the corner of his side of the room. It was normally covered in his discarded clothes, but those were all currently at his office where Atalina was dealing with his messy tendencies.

I wondered if she was enjoying her break or pining for his return. Either way, she'd better be keeping her oh-so-helpful hands to herself. And he'd better be keeping those shades drawn when he was sitting there eating without a shirt on. In fact, he'd better keep a shirt on at all times when he was there, dammit.

He paused mid-bite and gave me an odd look but said nothing. The pastry was eaten with a single-minded focus. The glass was drained. Then he was back to rubbing his head.

"I could help with—"

"Fine."

I chose my side of the bed, the one a sick, sweating man hadn't been occupying for two days straight, and sat at the head. We'd done this a couple of times before, so he knew what I was up to. He settled his head into my lap and closed his eyes. Though, I suspected that was more to avoid looking at me than anything else.

It was hard to not talk to him. There were so many questions, so much that needed to be said, but none of it would help his headache. I supposed this was a good test of my conviction to embrace my Seeker training.

Clearing my mind took longer than it should have, but I managed to shove everything else aside and create a calm place to draw him into. I set my fingers to work on the hard corded muscles of his neck and shoulders while pushing quiet and peace into his mind. Eventually, he relaxed, his shoulders becoming heavier on my legs as I worked my way over his scalp and alongside his face. It was a very nice face, and though my fingers missed slipping through all the silky hair, he was here in our bed, where he belonged.

If I could just keep him perpetually sleeping, I could pretend everything was great between us, that he was actually my doting Ishlan and I, his adoring Ishla. The absurdity of the daydream bubbled up into a bark of laughter that I barely caught.

Nothing had ever been great between us, not for more than a few minutes at a time here and there. Maybe it could be now. I'd even settle for a few hours rather than minutes if we could manage it, but that would require him to be awake and speaking to me.

For now, I enjoyed the weight of him against me, the soft sound of his unlabored breathing, his skin at a normal temperature and color, and was thankful.

THIRTEEN

Merkief

Jey had moved out of the Artorian house two weeks ago, but I still kept thinking I heard someone there as I lay in bed questioning every decision I'd made since we'd taken on the Narvan. I understood why he'd left and part of me appreciated it. Neither of us had been on our own in five years. It was time. We had our own worlds to advise and as long as our people weren't trying to kill us, we could save our partnered time for when it was necessary, like briefings and Kryon work.

Besides, it made seeing Marit easier. She worked for Jey. Karin wasn't mine, but the Premier was. At least for now.

Jey and I had cleaned out the house on Merchess the day after the memorial service, two days from our deadline of vacating Kess's new holding. I'd suggested leaving it empty and in Kazan's name, but Jey had been adamant about selling it before Kess had a chance to get his hands on it. The thought of Kess walking the halls where we'd lived and worked had made me ill so I'd agreed. Atashi Ka'Opul had purchased the house at top price for one of his sons.

The big question had been what to do with the belongings of two people who were no longer with us. Jey arranged for a few pieces of furniture to be transported to the house on Jal, along with his belongings and some of Vayen's and Kazan's—items he said he wasn't ready to part with. The rest he said he'd donate to a social services organization Vayen had had a stake in on Artor.

I didn't need anything other than my clothes and the few trinkets I'd picked up during my employment. That was all easy enough to Jump by myself.

Kazan's room on Merchess had been like every other one I'd entered, clean, generally bare and everything put neatly in its place.

If I had the urge to get nostalgic, I had three of her rooms to raid. The same went for Vayen's pits of chaos. When I got back to the Artor house, I changed the bot settings to perform the same level of services to his room as Kazan's. Once his room was cleaned, I'd figure out what I wanted to do with their stuff.

There were two useful things we discovered in our room explorations. One being that Vayen was a serious packrat with weapons. He had at least one, if not two, in the case of Merchess, chests full of assorted weaponry and stockpiles of ammo in each of his rooms. No wonder I'd rarely seen him anywhere near the armory on the ship where the rest of us regularly restocked or traded weapons out. The second was the assortment of datapads we found scattered around their rooms.

After Jey had mentioned finding a few in Vayen's room on Jal, I'd gone on a hunt in what were now my houses. While I didn't discover anything life-altering, it did give me a place to start on some of the threads both of them had dropped. We'd drained all the Merchessian accounts that we had access to and split them between us. Jey had suggested a joint credit pool, but I wanted control over my half. Having to justify our spending to one another would be a waste of time that neither of us had to spare.

As I went over the morning's credit requests from the leaders of Syless, Artor, and Moriek, I yet again cursed Vayen and Kazan for dying with their multitude of overflowing accounts kept to themselves. Kazan had years of Kryon-earned credits stashed somewhere that she'd drawn from as needed. Only Geva knew how widely Vayen had invested his credit horde from his time employed with Kazan and then his two years of high-intensity Kryon contract fulfillment. Jey had his half of the payout from many of those same contracts since they'd been working closely together. I'd shared in a little of that, but not to a degree that was showing my account any appreciation now. Jey and I were going to have to hit Kryon contracts hard if we wanted to maintain the level of funding Vayen and Kazan had provided.

"Are you available?" Marit's voice sidled along the natural path we'd established.

"I can be. What do you have in mind?"

The image she sent convinced me that funding requests could wait.

"Give me half an hour." I finished the two most urgent matters and then Jumped to the office Jey shared with Marit on Karin.

Marit inclined her head toward the steaming meal on Jey's desk. "You should eat first. You're not doing that enough."

"Been kind of busy." The food on the plate smelled delicious. My mouth watered. "Maybe just a few bites."

"I'll wait." She settled onto the desk beside me, her hip barely leaving room for me to grab the fork. "One would think you're not eating except for when I remind you."

The fish was too perfectly flaky and dripping with a buttery sauce to take a break from chewing to answer. The plethora of wrappers from the bars Vayen must have regularly shoved in his face were starting to make sense. Going out to get food alone meant putting myself at risk. Cooking wasn't something I had the time for. Warming up leftovers from the cold storage worked when I thought of it, but those would run out soon. Vayen's stash of bars in the kitchen were much better than the ones Kazan had lived off of before hiring us. They were produced for proper Artorian nutrition and contained additives to maintain muscle mass. Leave it to him to find the perfect answer to eating when one rarely had time. Maybe not quite perfect, they didn't taste near as good as this did.

"Delicious, isn't it?" Marit asked. "I had my chef make up a second plate for you."

"You didn't tell him I was here, did you?"

"I have a guest. That's all he knows. Don't worry."

I ate in record time and pushed the plate away. "So then, here or did you have somewhere else in mind?"

She shook her head and tsked. "Right down to business aren't you?"

"I'm on a tight schedule."

"You always are. A woman might think you're just using her for a few pleasurable minutes."

She thought correctly, but every time we got together it seemed to me that we had a mutual using. Premiers had to be just as careful when it came to allowing people access to their minds and bodies. Neither of us were joined. As long as no one knew we were together, we were both safe to enjoy what pleasure we had time for.

"You're the one who invited me here," I said, reminding her who was doing the using today.

"I did," she conceded. "Here is fine." She dropped down off the desk and sat on my lap. Her lips met mine. She was in my head a moment later.

We spent a good half hour wrapped up in each other, not that I was watching the time. Exactly. When we'd both been satisfied, I rested my forehead on hers.

"Do you ever do more than answer a lonely woman's call?" she asked.

"For what it's worth, yours are the only calls I'm answering."

She smiled. "I mean like stick around after, maybe do a little more chatting before, anything that might constitute a relationship."

"Those aren't wise in my line of business. Tricky in yours too."

Marit nodded, but she pulled away and stood. She straightened her shirt and ran a hand through her hair to smooth it back into place. "So this is all you get then? All you need?"

My needs weren't getting much priority since the Narvan fell into my lap. While I was inclined to establish an actual relationship at some point, I couldn't see a way of peacefully making that happen with Marit, not while she remained the Premier of Karin and under Jey's control.

Vayen had chosen wisely. Marit was good at her job, at taking care of our people. Asking her to step down was out of the question. So was going public.

"I thought we agreed to keep this casual," I said.

"We did." But her forced smile said she was having second thoughts. "I'm the Premier of an Artorian world. Isn't that good enough for you?"

"Rank is not the problem." At least not in the way she thought it was.

"Then perhaps you could explain what the problem is." She stood with her arms crossed, glaring down at me. She'd missed one of the buttons on her shirt but it didn't seem like the time to point that out.

"I'm the problem. Like I said that first night, this is what it has to be. This or nothing."

Someone knocked on the door.

Marit scowled at it. "I'm busy. Go away."

"Ma'am, there's been an explosion at one of the Haralex facilities. It took out several surrounding blocks. Casualties are estimated in the thousands. Should we wake the Premier?"

"I'll do it. Transfer all the data to my terminal immediately."

"Yes, ma'am." Footsteps retreated from the doorway.

When Marit turned back to me, all evidence of the talk of relationships had vanished. The Premier of Karin asked, "Is there anything you can do about this?"

I held up my hands. "Not my world. Contact your Advisor. Speaking of which, I should vacate the office before he arrives. He may have seen the news feed himself."

"Merkief, I think we should tell him. I don't like—"

"Why are you here?" Jey's voice cut off whatever Marit had been going to say. "Sitting at my desk, no less?"

Doing my best to get up casually, I attempted to straighten my clothing. I wasn't even wearing my armor. It was on the back of the chair in my home office on Artor.

"You heard about the explosion?" Marit asked, stepping between Jey and I.

"Yes, I happened to be monitoring the feeds on all my worlds. As I often do." His gaze drilled into me as if Marit didn't exist. "So, one more time, what are you doing here?"

"It was a personal visit. I was just leaving."

He seemed to take in my lack of armor and Marit's disheveled shirt. "In my office? Seriously?"

"It's my office too," Marit said.

"You're not helping," I muttered.

Jey slammed a fist against the wall. Marit jumped.

"Find a new office or I'll find a new Premier."

Marit scrambled out of Jey's path as he lunged for me. In the interest of not making the situation worse than it was, I let him grab my shirt and shove me against the wall. My lack of fighting back seemed to suck a bit of the ire from him.

"Keep your personal shit off my worlds." He shook me once, hard enough to knock my head against the wall again and then let go. "Get out of here so I can concentrate."

Marit spun to face me. *"Don't leave me here alone with him."*

"Don't hurt her," I said to Jey.

"Hadn't planned on it, but you and I are discussing this later. Leave."

"He's pissed at me, not you. I have to go." I blocked out Marit's protest, severed my natural connection with her, and Jumped back to Artor.

Dammit. I had one bright spot in my day and now that was over. I didn't have to wait for the discussion with Jey to know what he was going to say. The voice in the back of my head had been telling me the same thing since the night of the memorial when I'd left Jey and

Gemmen to find a little comfort of my own.

Kazan had preached her decree loud: you did not have sexual relations with anyone directly under you. That included anyone you worked directly with and for good measure, anyone they worked with. If we had an inch in need of scratching, we were to find a one-nighter, or if we wanted a repeat, someone so far down the chain of command that they wouldn't be an issue.

One had only to look at Kazan's past to see why she'd laid out those rules. Marin was dead thanks to Vayen, and Kess had killed Kazan. At least Vayen had waited to be stupid until he was working on an equal level, even if he'd technically still been employed by her. The end result was the same though. He was dead.

I'd had a real relationship once, before Kazan had hired me. The job had ended that quite unpleasantly.

If I wanted more bright spots in my future, I was going to have to start looking on my own worlds for someone unknown. But right now, I had a pile of funding requests to go over, reports to read, and a meeting with Jey to dread.

❧

Jey arrived in our Kryon quarters, limping and in a shitty mood. I'd suggested this as our meeting spot to maintain neutral territory. While we'd gotten past my indiscretions with his Premier, at least to the point where he'd stopped shoving it in my face, the explosions on Karin hadn't been an isolated problem. They'd hit Artor too. Whoever *they* were. We'd been trying to figure that out for the past eight days.

"It's Kess, I'm telling you," he said.

"And I still don't see why Kess would venture outside his territory when the Council expressly told him not to. He'd be risking his advisory position."

Jey growled something unintelligible.

"We both have teams on this. Let's let the investigation run its course for a few more days. If nothing else turns up, we'll look closer at Kess," I said.

"Always backing down."

He did that Jalvian stare down his nose thing again. I began to see why it aggravated Vayen as much as it had.

"I'm going after him, with or without you," Jey decreed.

"Hold the fuck on. We don't have any evidence it was him."

"He's always been after us. Why would he stop now that Vayen and Kazan are out of the way? He's got the Nebula, but you know as well as I do that he wants the Narvan. Jal is his homeworld too."

"Have you talked to anyone on Sere? Asked around?"

He shook his head. "Have you?"

"No. Been kind of busy."

"Same here. Speaking of which, Artor's prices for the upgrades to the Jalvian fleet are out of line," he said.

"They are the same prices they've always been."

His eyes narrowed. "They're not. You haven't even looked at the cost negotiation I sent you?"

I was pretty sure I had. But the way his unnerving stare was drilling into me, I had a feeling I'd overlooked a recent communication. There were just so damned many, between Jey, and the three worlds, and my contacts.

"I'll review it tomorrow. I swear. Can we go do this contract so we can maybe finance something next week? I don't know about you, but I'm running low."

"Then stop granting every damned request."

"I'm not."

Jey scoffed. "You're granting twice as much as Vayen would have and he had the credits to support that. You don't."

That couldn't be true. "If I don't offer the funding, people are going to be angry. Shit won't get done."

"That's how the universe works. Grant less. They're taking advantage of you."

"How would you know?"

"I have contacts too. I know you're using yours so why would you doubt I'm using mine?"

If he knew I was keeping tabs on him, one or more of my contacts weren't solely mine. I wanted to hunt down whomever it was and make an example of them. But that would be showing weakness, that he'd gotten to me. I wouldn't do that. Maybe I just needed to trust the sole allegiance of my contacts a bit less.

"I hear Frique didn't accept your offer either," I said, not able to let his comment go without some form of retaliation.

The prominent vein in his forehead began to visibly pulse. Dammit, I should have just nodded and let him think he had the upper hand. I needed the credits from this contract far more than he did.

"I think I'm busy," he said snidely. "You can do this one alone."

We'd agreed from the start of this joint effort that we wouldn't do solo Kryon work. Calling off the job would piss off the Council, but that was preferable to one of us out there alone with the possibility of not making it to the tank. Unless he wanted me out of the way so he could have the system for himself. That wasn't going to happen.

"I can wait. I have plenty to do. How much time do you need?" I asked. Better to act like I'd missed his true intention than to end up dead on my own.

His upper lip twitched into what could have easily become a snarl if he let it go. "I'll let you know when I'm ready."

He Jumped before I could nod.

In the hopes of making a bit of peace between us, I delved into the nightmare of manufacturing contract reviews and interplanetary price negotiations. Jey and I might be at odds, but if Artor and Jal devolved to the same status, we were all screwed.

FOURTEEN

Rhaine

Daniel's tossing around in the crib down the hall woke me. I realized I'd fallen asleep with Isnar's comforting weight and warmth still in my lap. Slipping out from under him, I gladly noted that his fever hadn't returned. Hoping to enjoy the silent peace of having him home for a little while longer, I grabbed Daniel and went downstairs.

Two hours later, footsteps sounded up in our bedroom. Isnar was awake.

Daniel rested on my lap where I sat on the couch. Instead of watching the birds in the morning sunlight, I watched my son toothlessly laugh as I tickled the bottom of his feet. His laughter was a vast improvement over the crying he'd been so fond of up until now.

The sheer joy of the sound distracted me from the negotiations I'd been playing out in my head with the irate man upstairs. None of the approaches I'd tried had worked. He knew me. I knew him. We were both stubborn, and I supposed I was every bit as prickly as he was. That was one of the things I needed to rewire.

It seemed like I'd done this adapting routine too many times in my life, barreling forward until I hit a wall. There was always a wall: My family dying had led me down the path of trying to be a Seeker. The Jalvian occupation turned me into a soldier. Chesser's death left me with a baby I hadn't known what to do with and spurred me to join Kryon to gain enough clout to put an end to the war in the Narvan. Zsmed, my first Kryon partner, betrayed me to the Fragians, a deep wound that sent me into a drugged oblivion that nearly caused to me lose everything. Just when I'd regained favor with the Council and thought I had a good Kryon and personal partnership figured out with Kess, he turned against me, leading me to hire bodyguards, and bringing Vayen into my life. And then the Council ultimately turned against me, wanting me dead, landing me here, on Minor.

What would it be next time? How long would I have to put myself together and explore this incarnation before it all fell apart?

Daniel kicked his feet into my hand. I toyed with his toes. Isnar and I had to figure something out, to make our time here at least tolerable, if not enjoyable, for Daniel's sake.

I'd always wanted my son to have a childhood far different from my own. One where he could where he could play, laugh, and have the benefit of two parents. Initially, I'd thought the answer was adoption, but I'd never settled on a family. I'd wanted him to fit in, which he wouldn't have done on Veria Prime any better than Isnar was doing here. Hybrid children were frowned upon on Artor. Due to my uncertainty, he'd sat in stasis for twelve years while I'd gone on living my life. I'd never anticipated being in a position where I would be the one he grew up with or that I might have an Artorian available to step in as his father...if I could learn to swallow my frustration at the universe.

I stroked my son's soft cheek. He grinned toothlessly. I found myself smiling back.

This was my new normal. Only a trickle of telepathy, not able to host a link, never able to go back to what I was before. I was a Seeker now, or as close to one as I'd ever be. And Seekers always chose peace. How far backward was I willing to bend to fix things with Isnar?

For all his bonding with me against his will, he could have easily set himself up elsewhere in this colony or anywhere else on Minor. He could have kept an eye on me from afar if his sanity had been his only reason to be here. Instead, he'd chosen to live here with me, with my son, to attempt to be a family.

I could almost hear Res, my Seeker mentor, the man who'd been my second father, leading me on an introspection. I'd always hated those, too much sitting and thinking and no doing, but I gave into the half-daydream now, fondly remembering the sound of his voice. As with the many other times he'd gently chided me for my actions, he urged me to look inward to examine what I'd done, the whole situation, as if I were someone else, to give it distance so that I might find truth.

The truth was right there, glaring at me, a mirror into the cause of my current problem. Me. I swallowed hard.

Time seemed to stretch out in the quiet until Daniel gurgled as he suddenly kicked enthusiastically and flailed his arms. And then he stilled, looking upward with his round dark eyes.

Isnar stood over my shoulder, barbs loaded. I could feel them over our connection.

"Playing mother for a few minutes?" he asked in a dry snarl. "You going to keep him here for the day or should I just take him back with me?"

"I need you both to stay here," I said, keeping my attention on Daniel. It made it easier to avoid matching Isnar's tone. "There are enough rumors about us floating around already."

"That might be, but I can deal with them. I have people who actually like me."

I'd seen that at the warehouse. They'd been genuinely worried about him. The few clients I'd helped needed me, or at least, my services. They were polite, appreciative, but would they stand up for me against the wagging tongues of their neighbors? I wouldn't bet on it.

He'd simply had a head start with entrenching himself, that's all. I could do the same.

Maybe.

I watched Daniel suck on his fingers. Did my son like me? He barely knew me, his own mother. What did I have to offer a stranger? I had no idea how to make friends anymore. I prodded or threatened people to do what I wanted. They did it because it was in their best interest or I would withhold funding and make life hell for them if they resisted.

I groaned inwardly. I'd lost every bit of leverage I'd had. I was nothing here. It would take months to build up a social standing I could begin to rely on.

"They do like you. All those women," I snapped, unable to stop myself.

He smiled, the kind he used to use when we were working together, the kind that was a promise of something bad about to happen.

"I want you to stay here," I said quickly. "I would *like* you to stay here," I amended, my brain informing my willful tongue that it was doing a shitty job of sounding contrite.

"I won't."

"Please." I didn't use that word often and he knew it.

He walked around the couch to stand at the end of it, arms crossed and glare in full force. "I came to Minor to make sure you were all right, that you got back on your feet, that you were protected.

I did that. You made it abundantly clear you didn't want me here. You know where to find me if someone is causing trouble you can't deal with." He pointed at Daniel. "Now, are you taking a turn being a parent or am I taking him with me?"

My heart sank. I'd known repairing the damage I'd caused wasn't going to be easy, but knowing was nothing compared to facing the impossible-looking challenge in front of me. Before I could screw things up further, I returned to my state of distance, silently thanking Res for drilling that rudimentary Seeker lesson into my brain. Anastassia would have screamed at him for being difficult. But he wasn't difficult. He was angry with me for a good reason.

An outright apology wasn't going to fix this and old me would never have apologized. He wasn't going to believe a few useless words. If I wanted him back, I was going to have to find a way to show him that I was sorry and prove that I meant it.

"I'll keep him here for the day," I said calmly. "Come home for dinner, and we can trade off. That way you can work in peace. I'm sure you have plenty to catch up on."

His arms dropped to his sides, but the glower remained in full force. "I'm not sleeping here."

"Take the other bedroom. Send over a bed for it. The couch in your office can't be comfortable for you."

"We'll see," he said with slightly less venom.

He leaned over the end of the couch to rub his big hand over the dark fuzz on Daniel's head. His hair was starting to curl. I wondered if it would stay that way or if it would straighten as he grew. My brother had had curly hair. So far, it was the one thing about my son that might have come from me. Maybe he would spout facial hair after puberty. I laughed to myself, imagining a beard on an Artorian face. It seemed like Artorian genes trumped human on every other front.

"Call Weeda and have her set up whatever immunizations you need. Neither of us wants you to go through that again," I said.

He nodded. "What about both of you?"

"I'll take care of it."

He started for the door.

I wanted to say that he should stay here and rest, take it easy, recover for a day or two before going back, but he was determined to get away from me. Guilting him into staying wouldn't win him over. Instead, I sat there, shaking inside my calm exterior as he got in the transport and left.

Res was right. I'd never been a very good Seeker. Calm wasn't my default emotion, not unless it had to do with assessing the situation during a fight. But if I wanted Isnar back, fighting was one of the things I was going to have to put aside.

I wasn't happy with how this conversation had gone, but it was a step. A small step. I took a moment to do a few breathing exercises, letting the tension I'd kept inside flow out in a series of long, slow exhales.

Rhaine the Seeker was going to be doing a lot of breathing exercises.

Resolved to my course, I considered what I needed to do for the rest of the day while Isnar was at work. I had a job of my own, one that needed to become my lifestyle if I truly wanted a future here.

Without the luxury of a second transport, I put Daniel into the sling, donned my coat, and walked to my shop. The weather was pleasant enough and traffic near non-existent in the middle of the day. If Isnar could run Dugans with Daniel strapped to his chest, I supposed I could do my appointments. No more 'playing mother', as he put it. I was going to have to sell being a family not only to Isnar, but the entire colony if we wanted to put an end to any rumors that might get us unduly noticed.

And truly, while I'd not missed my son in the same way as Isnar, now that I had him in my arms, I was intrigued by the idea of giving motherhood an honest try. The only memories I had of my own mother were from still frames that I'd lost in my drug haze when I'd been on the Blue thanks to Zsmed. I might not end up being very good at it, but at least Daniel would have more than I ever did.

Pushing the door to my shop open, the scent of herbs and incense washed over me like a sea of memories. I congratulated myself on finally getting the smell just right. It was like standing in a Res's house on Veria Prime. I could breathe here.

Memories of the most carefree days of my life washed over me, the laughter of the other acolytes in the long dorm house where we lived, sharing simple meals over an easy conversation, and Tomias's half-hearted flirting as we worked through lessons together. There had been dark moments there, but they were few comparatively, and I tried not to think of them now, not in this space where I needed every possible hint of positivity and security.

The deep red walls welcomed me. I closed the manual door. They were all that way here, but it was still something I found myself having to get used to, like at any moment I expected to wake up back in the Narvan where so much was automated.

The tiny bells attached to the handle tinkled as the door closed behind me. Two chairs sat across from one another on a large woven-grass mat. Several long shelves of dark wood along the wall behind the chairs housed thick white candles, oils, and jars of herbs. Others hung in bunches from hooks beneath the shelves. Potted plants I'd collected from the nearby wildlands filled the floor-to-ceiling front window and the one at the rear where the massage table sat behind a curtain wall. There were no terminals or datapads here, no hint of the more civilized parts of the universe.

My shop occupied a fairly small space at the end of the building, but it was all that a Seeker workspace required. I shared a bathroom in the back hallway with the weaver and a bakery, which was my source for the bread I'd figured out how to toast. They were only open until early afternoon but offered a few food options beyond the fruit and pastries I'd found at the market. I supposed I shouldn't rely too heavily on the breads and baked treats or I'd be buying larger clothes in short order. After the time we'd already been here, I could see my body suffering from the lack of my usual level of activity. The couple weeks of going through the Seeker forms on the soft mat I'd now kept here had helped, but it was a vast departure from weights or actual fighting. Even if Isnar and I had been on speaking terms, there wasn't room for a devoted exercise space in our house for the two of us to do hand-to-hand work together like we'd done long ago.

Daniel was sound asleep by the time my first client arrived. I put him down in the back room on the mat and got to work on being Rhaine.

My second client had just left and I was stripping the cloth from the massage table when I heard a transport pull up. I gathered the towel I'd used to wipe the oil from my hands and the table covering and glanced out the back window to see that the sky had darkened.

The bakery was closed as was the weaver, and all her assistants had already left for the day. Like me, she lived within walking distance. I checked on Daniel where he sat on the floor gnawing on a cloth toy. With the laundry under one arm, I pulled the curtain aside and blinked in the brighter light of the main space. The transport's headlights made the raindrops on the windows sparkle. Good thing I'd worn my coat and it had a hood.

The bells tinkled. A large form filled my doorway. Isnar.

I checked the time on the wall. He wasn't due home for another couple of hours. Not wanting to infect my peaceful place with an argument if I could help it, I waited for him to lead.

He seemed to be waiting for me to start. When I didn't, he went over to sit in one of my chairs. It was far too small for him and couldn't have been at all comfortable, but he shifted around until he'd managed to wedge himself in.

"I called Weeda to set up the immunizations. She was appalled I was at work and pitched a fit, quite loudly, until I agreed to leave."

"I'm not surprised."

"Everyone's gone?" he asked, as though he were annoyed at the thought that anyone else had been here.

I glanced at the laundry in my arms. "Just cleaning up."

"Figured you might want a ride home."

'I can walk' almost made it through my lips, but I kept them firmly closed and nodded.

"Daniel?" he asked.

I went into the back room and opened up the closet where the cleaning unit was hidden. After getting the laundry going, I retrieved Daniel and handed him to Isnar. I could have been done right then if I thought he needed to get home and into bed, but his color was holding, and as soon as I backed away, he started talking softly to Daniel.

I'd not had much occasion or inclination to pay attention to the two of them together beyond being grateful that someone else was dealing with the squalling infant, but now, as I puttered around the shop, putting everything in order, I enjoyed the heart-warming sight. They belonged together.

Both of his parents had been in the military, but maybe he'd had a normal childhood, as much as one could with a war going on. One with two parents who spent time with him. He'd once mentioned his mother teaching him to cook. The couple of family still frames I remembered seeing in his childhood home had appeared to be happy ones.

In stark contrast, my father was all work and until I was willing or able to contribute, I'd been told to be quiet and out of the way. Working alongside him was the only time we spent together and the only way to gain his attention or approval.

What Isnar and Daniel had together was much better. With Isnar, my son had half a chance of growing up happy.

He caught me gawking. "What?"

I sighed, sorry I'd brought their time together to an end, as well as the tenuous peace between us. Knowing I was going to have to watch every word, my tone, stay calm, attempt to keep any frustration off my face...it all made my neck and shoulders tense.

"I suppose I'm done here, if you're ready?" I said.

He pried himself out of the chair and held our giant of a child as if he weighed nothing at all. I grabbed the sling, pulled my coat on, and turned off the lights. He followed me out the door and as I paused to lock it, I felt him watching me.

"I like the coat," he said.

A compliment? I wasn't sure how to handle that given our current estrangement. "It's as close to a Seeker's robes as I dared get."

He nodded. "It's a nice color. Reminds me of home."

I looked down at my sleeves. The coat did resemble the color of sunset on Artor. His homeworld, that he'd never see again without his link and living in exile with me. "I'm sorry."

Isnar stared at me for a moment and then nodded. He opened the door to the transport and slipped inside, all fluid motions even with the baby. I was very glad his insides had stayed where they were supposed to be so I could enjoy that sight, preferably a few thousand more times. Assuming we could fix this.

We rode home in silence, him making silly faces at Daniel, who squealed with seeming delight, and me smiling. Seeing them together like this, I couldn't help but wonder what his brother would have been like as a father. Would the two of us ever have stopped yelling at one another long enough to find out? Would he have continued to take long assignments away from home or would he have assumed an Artor-based position once the war with Jal was over? And Daniel would be twelve by now. I couldn't imagine what he would be like or how he would sound. What would I be like after being a mother for twelve years? Would I be better at this or still fumbling about, unsure about everything?

My entire body went stiff. Chesser had been adamant about having a family, about carrying on his lineage, his approved genes. How many damn kids would we have running around by now, and would the pregnancies all be as horrible as they'd been with Daniel?

"You all right?" Isnar asked.

"No. Yes," I said quickly, not wanting to explain my sudden brush with anxiety. At least more children was something I'd never have to deal with now. If we could make it through this one without screwing him up, it would be a miracle.

The transport settled into the charging station and the locking clamps clicked into place. I opened the door and got out. Isnar, with Daniel in his arms, followed close behind as we went inside.

"Hungry?" he asked.

If he was asking, he meant to stay, at least long enough to eat. And hopefully, cook. My stomach rumbled.

"Sure. Those spicy noodles you make would be great."

His eyes narrowed. "The ones you refused to eat?"

I searched for something suitably contrite beyond the one apology I'd already offered. Apologies weren't something I had much practice with. I'd had to make too many big decisions with too many lives at stake. Learning how to do that without regret was one of the skills that allowed me to sleep at night. My conscience had learned to deal without apologies for so long that they felt unnatural. Fake. And in this case, with him, inadequate.

And now he was standing there as though he were readying himself for whatever barb I was about to throw at him. I kept my voice calm and even. "Yes, those ones."

He snorted and walked into the kitchen. I stayed right with him and pulled the sling from where I'd wadded it up in my pocket. After taking my coat off, and draping it over one of the kitchen chairs, I put the sling on and held out my hands.

"I'll take him. Show me how to make the noodles. I'm sick of those pastry pockets."

He outright laughed. "Really sick of them, apparently."

"You said you'd show me how to cook." Granted, that was before he'd walked out, but I hoped he still would. I needed all the help I could get. The vids I'd watched obviously weren't enough, given the disaster of the one meal I'd tried.

"You're serious."

I nodded, hoping he wasn't mocking me. If he was, I'd be doomed to grow fat on baked goods and as many pastry pockets as I could handle between sweet fruits or raw or charred attempts at real food.

Isnar glanced down at Daniel. "I suppose you'll need to eat something other than those tubes eventually, won't you?" He sighed theatrically, gaining a toothless grin. "Yes, fine, I'll show your mother how to cook noodles."

He surrendered Daniel to me and started to gather ingredients from the cupboards. I couldn't get Daniel into the sling fast enough to follow everything he was grabbing and from where.

"Stop!"

He spun around, brows lowered and scowl ready.

I held up one empty hand, keeping Daniel's waving arms contained with the other. "Tell me what to get and where and why."

His scowl dissipated. "You really have no idea?"

I shook my head. Though it annoyed me greatly to acknowledge this lack of a basic skill that he seemed to have with so little effort, he was right, Daniel would also need to eat.

"None," I admitted. "Please."

He emitted a slightly positive-sounding grunt and leaned over to set down the bag of noodles he'd had in his hand.

It was then that I realized how short everything was in our kitchen, in the whole house. He had to all but sit on the floor to get the pot out of the cupboard. Filling the pot with water required hunching over the sink.

The prickliness over our bonded connection wavered as he explained about which pot he'd picked and how much water to add. The entire time he sliced the vegetables, his back was set at an awkward angle so his hands could reach the counter. That had to be so uncomfortable for him, but I couldn't recall him complaining about it in the months we'd lived here. The more I thought about it, he had to duck through every doorway. The toilet was low for me, I imagined it was the equivalent of squatting over a bucket for him. The couch in his office was very short, but his feet hung over the end of our bed here too. Nothing here fit him without alteration. It was annoying for me, not quite right for my size, but he was a veritable giant here.

"We could get someone in here to raise this all up, the counters, I mean. Don't you think? It would make it easier for...us?"

He paused his slicing a yellow pepper into thin ribbons but didn't look at me. "Maybe."

At least he hadn't said no or that he didn't plan on being here. I tried to pay attention to what he was doing.

By the time we were working on the sauce, him right over my shoulder while I shook what I hoped were the correct amounts of each spice into a small pan of cream, the hostility I'd sensed through our connection had nearly vanished.

"Yes, like that. Now put it on the burner. Turn it down." He pointed at the knob on the cooktop I'd only used once before.

I put my hand on the knob, attempting to ascertain how much of a twist was turning it down without putting the flame out altogether.

"Here," he said, his hand covering mine as he adjusted the knob. "This line is low. You want it here." With one finger extended, he pointed to the printed black line beside the knob.

If I was wanting his hand somewhere, this wasn't it exactly, but it was another step in the right direction.

Once the sauce was heated and the noodles drained, I tossed them together while he got the plates out. Concerned that I'd splash Daniel with hot sauce, he insisted on distributing the noodles onto the plates and transferring them to the table.

We ate mostly in silence. There were so many things I wanted to say, to ask him about Dugans, about what Weeda had said, if he'd seen anything come of the investigation she'd launched, but all of that could lead to a fight in thirty seconds or less. I wanted to enjoy having him here and eating a real meal. A more neutral topic was in order.

"When do you think Daniel can start eating regular food?"

"You know I've never done this before, right? I know just as much about him as you do."

He knew far more, but I understood what he meant. "I suppose I should ask Weeda. He's just so big already. One of my clients said something about her kid sleeping through the night once they were on solid food."

Isnar shrugged.

"I'll ask." I was hoping he'd start talking, say something, anything that I could run with, but he didn't. Not until we were almost done.

He put his fork down loudly and stared me down. Tingling shocks ran through our connection as his ire again surfaced in full force. "So why wouldn't you eat before? You refused everything, even when I made food I knew you liked."

I physically felt my defenses rise, every muscle tensing. I took a breath and then another and then took one more, letting it out slowly before looking at him. "I'm sorry."

His brows rose, and for a second, I thought I might have evaded the impending argument, but his tone was one I knew well, the implacable interrogating one that he'd honed in my service and perfected in my absence. "Answer the question. Why."

Nerves sang throughout my body, demanding me to get on my feet, to tell him to fuck off. The longer I sat there trying to devise an explanation, any version of one that didn't make me sound like a petty, selfish bitch, I began to conclude that his name-calling, whatever its true meaning, might have been accurate.

Knowing I was about to burst and ruin what little headway I'd made, I got up and took our plates over to the counter. Daniel crouched on the floor, rocking back and forth on his hands and knees like he was warming up to crawl across the room. He didn't need us yelling at one another.

Isnar stayed in his seat, the chair creaking under his shifting weight. His open palm slammed down on the table, making me jump. Daniel went still, eyes wide as he looked up at Isnar.

"Answer the fucking question."

"Language," I pointed at Daniel. "Not in front of him. And keep your damned voice down."

Isnar shot to his feet. "Seriously? Damn is fair game, but fuck is not? Just so we're clear on the rules here."

"I don't know the rules, all right? I don't know how to do any of this." If I could have encompassed the entire planet in my wildly frustrated gesture, it would have been more accurate. "Maybe you had this sort of normal before, or some version of it anyway, because you sure seem comfortable here. I've never had this. I know I'm doing a horrible job of figuring this out, but I'm trying."

"All right then." He stooped down to pick up Daniel.

"What the hell does that mean?" I'd just told him more than I meant to, showed him what I was feeling. I'd answered his damned question. Now he was just going to walk out of the room?

"I don't know yet. The bed I ordered won't be here for a week. I'll take Daniel to my office tonight as per our agreement."

"Take the damned bed. You need to get some real rest so you can fully recover. I'll sleep down here."

"You're not going to like it. The sun will shine right in your face—assuming it stops raining."

"Then maybe we need to do some rearranging."

The bastard just nodded and went upstairs. No thanking me, no offering to help clean up the kitchen. He didn't even offer to help move the couch. I was trying, making personal concessions I'd never stooped to before. I'd told him the truth. Apologized. Twice.

"There's a blanket in the closet by the door," he called down.

I glared at the empty stairway for a moment before sighing and turning back around. Making up for all my nastiness wasn't going to be a quick fix. I'd known that deep inside, but I hoped I had it in me to figure out my Seeker self long-term because he clearly wasn't going to make this easy.

Isnar might have needed to get some sleep, or maybe he wanted to spend time with Daniel. Hell, he probably just wanted to get away from me. But I wasn't tired and there was only so much staring out the window at the rain that I could do. My buzzing nerves demanded that I get up and do something.

The little cleaning bots here didn't have half the functions of the ones I was used to and there was only one for the upstairs and one down here. Most notably, they didn't clean clothes or dishes. It wasn't second nature to do those things myself, but I was getting the hang of it.

I spent the next hour cleaning up the kitchen and the table and then stood in the middle of the common room contemplating the furniture. If he didn't want to help me move anything, I'd do it myself.

On the other hand, maybe the answer was to not move anything at all. What I was supposed to be doing was finding an accord with him so we could perhaps both be in the same bed eventually. Barring that outcome, the bed he'd ordered would be here soon. I'd have my bed back, and I wouldn't need to sleep on the couch.

Would it annoy him more to hear me down here moving things around without him or to not move anything at all?

No, I yelled at myself, I wasn't supposed to be trying to annoy him. Peace, I was supposed to be finding peace.

I screamed into my muffling pillow.

Our fragile truce managed to hold for a couple of weeks. We took turns between the bed and the couch and taking Daniel to work. He cooked, we ate without much small talk. After dinner, he'd take Daniel upstairs, which left me quiet time to work at the terminal, researching treatments for my clients. It wasn't a terrible arrangement in that it served to repair appearances with the local wagging tongues. The less people talked, the more likely we'd evade anyone out for credits or gaining Council favor by killing us.

As glad as I was to have him home and not hovering over me, our arrangement felt strained, like we were trying to fit into roles to which neither of us was suited. The underlying tension made it hard to relax or sleep. After lying on the couch and staring at the ceiling for an hour, I figured I might as well get up and continue with my research for a while.

Distant lightning flashed outside the window. The sound of rain pulled me into a semi-hypnotic focus on healing practices. Isnar came downstairs at one point, breaking my concentration. As tired and edgy as I was, I didn't trust myself to turn around to see what he was doing without throwing a verbal barb his way. Keeping my gaze locked on the words I'd been reading, I listened to shuffling footsteps and cupboards opening and closing. He must have been getting a feeding tube for Daniel. He left without a word, ascending the stairs, and leaving our faux-harmony intact.

Hours slipped by while I read, leaping from one source to another, making notes as I went. Somewhere in the middle of a long-winded article on wound care, I got frustrated when my vision kept blurring and decided that closing my eyes for a few minutes might help.

The familiar weight of Isnar's hand on my shoulder woke me, but I didn't spring awake, alert and ready as usual. At first, I thought it was still raining, but then it registered that the throbbing noise was in my head. I pushed myself upright in the chair. A deep red swath marked the arm that had served as my pillow on the desktop. At least I didn't have terminal indents on my face.

The haloed effect of my vision lent Isnar a glowing aura as sunlight poured through the windows. My stomach rolled. Too much reading and stress and not enough sleep. I knew that's exactly what Weeda would tell me when she stopped by, and she would. Gauging by the concerned look on Isnar's face, he'd be calling her shortly.

My stomach rolled again as the pain in my head spiked. The fish and soft buttery grains that had tasted so good the night before were going to make a reappearance.

Even as I pushed myself to my feet, I knew I'd never make it to the bathroom. I wavered my way to the kitchen sink instead.

He was right beside me as it seemed that everything I'd eaten the day before vacated my body. I wanted nothing more than to curl up on the cool tile floor right there and sleep. The only saving grace of the whole thing was that I didn't have the floating distance that I'd come to associate with an impending seizure. At least not yet.

"Come on," he said. "You're going to bed."

"I have appointments." I considered pushing him away, but I was too lightheaded and he was the only thing holding me up.

"Cancel them." He felt my forehead. "Please tell me you're not getting what I had."

"It's just a headache." I gripped his arm as another wave of nausea hit me.

Once I was done heaving, he handed me a wet cloth. "That's one hell of a headache."

"Remind me to thank the Council for it if we ever see them again."

"Let's hope we don't." He glanced at Daniel who was busy rolling around on the floor. "Don't go anywhere. I'll be back."

"What are you—"

He scooped me up like I weighed next to nothing and headed for the stairs. I might have argued on any other day, infuriated by his assuming I couldn't get myself up to bed on my own, but today I had to admit he might have been right. Closing my eyes helped keep the dizziness under control but the motion wasn't helping my stomach at all.

"Bathroom or bed?" he asked.

"Bed." His chest made a wonderfully firm pillow that put pressure on just the right spot on my temple. I did my best to focus on that rather than each jolting step he took.

He set me on the bed and started to cover me. I waved the blanket away.

"It's too hot in here. Could you please open a window?"

"You're never too hot," he said with a hint of amusement.

He opened the window and stood in front of it as if he were also grateful for the cool air. The rain had left the air clean and fresh. I breathed in slow and deep, talking myself through one of the calming exercises I would have used on anyone else in my situation. While it was good practice, it wasn't as calming as I needed, too much trying to remember the steps and the words, the phrasing, all of it. What did a Seeker do when there was no other Seeker to care for them?

Apparently, they laid in bed, miserable and talking to themselves.

"Better?" he asked.

"A little. It's too bright." It figured I'd get hit with this on a sunny morning rather than one of the long nights that spanned the universal time of several days.

He turned off the lights and pulled the window cover closed except for a sliver at the bottom so the cool air could still come in. Even that seemed too bright but it was an improvement.

"Thanks."

"I better get Daniel. Need anything else before I head out?"

He was leaving. I was supposed to be watching Daniel. "I'm sorry,

I don't think I can take care of him today."

"Of course not."

His dismissive tone hurt. Like he'd expected I would default on our arrangement. Were there enough apologies to make up for our first two months here and could I bear to give voice to all of them?

"I'll take him to work," he said. "Atalina can help with him. I'll send Weeda over."

I didn't have another Seeker, but I did have Isnar. Maybe. "Could you stay? I don't want Weeda. We've used her too much."

"You need her. I can't help you."

I tried to sit up so I could see him better, but my stomach didn't like that at all. Back flat on the pillow with my eyes squeezed shut against the light and the dizziness, I held out my hand to him. "I'll show you how. Just stay. Please."

His fingertips brushed over mine. Then his footsteps thumped out of the bedroom and down the stairs.

FIFTEEN

Jey

It had been over a month since the bombing on Artor and Karin. The investigation by Merkief's people and mine had at least both agreed on the fact it had been bombs, not any sort of accident. But who had planted them and why was still a mystery.

Merkief was sure it wasn't Kess, putting his bet on a Jalvian terrorist cell because the targets were both Artorian worlds. While I wasn't proud that of that my people had formed a terrorist organization, I also couldn't disprove his theory. His logic did make sense. The Hajarta were a militant group, rebelling against all of Kazan's peace deals between Jal and Artor. Even the newsfeeds were full of speculation of their involvement.

The Hajarta had been quiet during Kazan's time in control and even more so during Vayen's. Both of them must have had someone on the inside or measures in place to keep them muzzled. Merkief and I didn't.

My gut told me Kess was involved. Being Jalvian himself, he could be fueling the Hajarta to commit these acts. And if he was, there were sure to be more. The best way to put him on warning was to let him know I was on to him.

Merkief might be willing to hold his half of the Narvan with a grateful smile, but I'd never anticipated holding any of it. Acting as backup for the man who was perfectly suited for the job, sure. Without shame, I'd enjoyed the status and benefits while Vayen held all the shit together. I'd liked that position. Quite a lot, actually, and it seriously pissed me off to have it taken away.

In the interest of freeing up my attention to focus on Kess, I signed off on the long-hammered-out fleet upgrade deal with Merkief and initiated a credit transfer that was much more to my liking than it had been originally. With that task done, I put off my meetings for the day and Jumped to Twelve. Kess had gotten his foothold there first, having taken over the Assassin's guild when Vayen had killed Marin. My couple of contacts in the Nebula had assured me that he still considered it his base of operations, despite having control over Merchess which had a much more upscale ambiance. Kess wasn't an upscale kind of man.

The building that had housed the guild was quiet and dark. But according to what the local network was telling me from energy use and activity, it was fully operational and occupied. A cursory examination of the property made it quite clear that he'd taken lessons from Kazan and put every security measure in place that he could afford. Killing Kess at home wasn't going to be near as easy as offing Marin had been. I'd followed Vayen in the last time we'd been on an assassinate the assassin mission, but Kess knew Marin had died there and who had done the deed. He wouldn't feel comfortable there unless he'd taken preventative measures.

Home base might be out, but thankfully, he'd been busy throughout the Nebula in these past few weeks, making his name known and putting his mark on the local commerce. Specifically, he'd launched a chain of clubs.

Whereas Kazan had preached the benefits of making her mark behind the scenes, of letting the public figureheads take the social accolades and falls, Kess was all about taking credit. If I'd have stopped any of the moderately armored figures scurrying nearby and asked who was in charge of Twelve. They'd all point me to Kess Atta. In a society that prided itself on secrets and keeping to the shadows, he was the one gleaming beacon.

Slavery had skyrocketed throughout the colonies in the Nebula. The Merchessian families had to be loving the change in leadership. Many of those new slaves now worked in Kess's clubs. It seemed like the perfect place to hit him.

I made my way down the street, keeping my face out of the meager light, much like everyone else. Twelve was one of the few places where armed and armored people like me blended in.

"Any sign of him?" I asked my two contacts that prowled this generally inhospitable icy rock.

"Nothing yet," said one.

Another sent the silent sensation of shaking her head. Nexa was always short on words, but the ones she did speak, mattered.

It wouldn't hurt to go look for myself. Of the three clubs he'd taken control of on Twelve, two already had eyes in them. I tried the third. It was farthest from his headquarters so I took a public transport. The fuel fumes inside the maladjusted vehicle gave me a headache, but if it led me to Kess, I'd call it a worthwhile sacrifice.

The line at the door was blessedly short. I stood behind two Jalvian women who were fully clothed in skin-tight black suits with tall spiky heeled boots. It wasn't an unpleasant way to pass the time while the doorman made a show of judging the worth of each prospective customer.

I considered my options. Should I play it safe and go with whichever ID I'd slipped into my pocket that morning or keep any possibly known aliases to myself and offer him a suitable number of credits? The women in front of me were allowed in while I was deciding how many credits this scarred mongrel who was missing two fingers might require. I watched them climb the three steps to the door, light playing off their curves, and then remembered the door mutt. He held out his hand.

I swiped a chip through the reader on his wrist and punched in a number. He raised the one eyebrow that didn't have a wide white scar running through it and consulted the reader. He gave me a quick once over.

"No weapons inside."

"Not carrying any."

He bared the teeth he had left in what might have been a smile. "In case you missed something, there's a weapons check just inside the door."

"Got it."

He nodded and moved on to the next lonely soul behind me.

Up the stairs inside, I found myself confronted with another fringe-job reject. He stood firmly in my path, arms crossed. "The armor stays here."

The rack behind the counter he stood next to was indeed filled with armor of all makes. The shelves opposite the racks held an assortment of weapons that made me feel right at home. Except that I needed mine. Lucky for me, they weren't all inside my coat.

I shrugged out of my armor and handed it to him. The fact that his arm dipped heavily and he had to take a step to catch himself made me smile. He handed me a card written in some Fragian-looking symbols. "You'll get everything back when you leave. House policy."

"Better be everything," I muttered and made my way down the narrow hall. Pounding music seeped through the door in front of me. The women I'd followed in were already on the other side, making their way through the flashing lights and the crowd. The automated weapons scanner wasn't at all hidden, but it didn't pick up anything I had on me. The two guards at the inside door were busy watching the women who'd gone in. The door slid open as I approached. An obnoxiously loud wave of music flooded the hallway. I gritted my teeth and went in.

If Kess was here, he certainly wouldn't be down in the gyrating throng. I peered up at the second level. The strobing lights made following anyone difficult. I needed to get up there.

Making my way through the sea of bodies, any of which could be harboring a weapon just like I was, and without my armor, put me on edge. I almost considered calling Merkief in, but he'd just give me shit for putting myself in this situation to begin with. That was a last resort, and I wasn't there yet.

In the interest of getting above the chaos quickly, I skirted the edge of the dance floor instead of making a clear line right for the stairs. Too many people bumped into me. I kept my hands by my sides rather than patting down my pockets to make sure my weapons hadn't been lifted. I wasn't supposed to have them. No one should be checking my pockets. They were just bumping into me because it was cramped and they were drunk or not paying attention. No one was watching for me. I was safe here. Relatively, anyway. Until I came into proximity with my target.

A woman stood at the foot of the stairs. I thought she was standing on the first one, but she was just that tall. She was also impressively broad. She stared down at me. "You have a pass?"

I leaned in so she could hear me. "I'm meeting someone."

"Name?"

What the hells. I was here. Why not take a chance? Besides, I could Jump if shit went sideways. "Kess Atta."

The stair guard all but rolled her eyes. "Sure, and your name?"

I pulled out my ID and handed it to her. It was easier than trying to remember which name was on the card.

She handed the card back and consulted the datapad she pulled from her pocket. "Sorry, not on the list."

"He's here though? Is he with someone right now? I only need a minute." Or less if I could get a good shot in before he realized who I was.

"Yes, yes, and he has no time for you."

I held up a credit chip.

She knocked it from my hand.

I managed to catch it before it hit the floor and was lost in the crowd of feet. "That was rude."

The woman raised a purple eyebrow. Only on Twelve would a Jalvian discolor themselves in such a way. At least she hadn't marred herself with subdermal facial alterations or any of the host of other modifications the patrons wore here.

"And attempting to bribe me wasn't?" She sneered.

"Paying you for your consideration isn't a bribe."

"The definition of it, actually. Get lost." She shoved me backward.

Before I could catch myself, I knocked into a pair of dancers. The man, heavy on facial piercings steadied his scantily clad female partner and snarled at me, his gaze locked on the towering guard just over my shoulder. If she hadn't been there, he'd likely have taken a swing in my direction and things would have gone poorly for him from there on out. I didn't have time for that.

Kess was close by, in range if only I could get him in sight. If I couldn't do it the easy way, I'd go the more challenging route. Besides, making another pass with the guardian of the stairway was only going to cause a scene—more so than the few people who were currently snickering at me and the pierced asshole still glaring in my direction.

I got lost. Slipping back into the crowd wasn't that hard, there were a fair number of Jalvians here. Anywhere within the Narvan, I would have likely been noticed by now, either by one of Kess's contacts, a vidbot, or any of the general populace who now were learning to know my face. Being a more public figure than Kazan and Vayen had been did have its definite downfalls. Thankfully, Twelve had never been one of my regular haunts.

With the flashing lights and dim club ambiance offering further cover beyond the crush of people, I surveyed the upper level. The railing and milling people above limited my choices of jump points. Establishing one from a skewed angle and not knowing what might be further beyond where I could see wasn't a great call, but I was too close to Kess to just walk away.

By the time I'd finally settled on a point I was confident enough to try, the music had worsened my headache and I was about ready to punch the next asshole to knocked into me regardless of the consequences. How did anyone find this fun?

Oh yes, the women in skin-tight clothing or not much at all, gyrating all around me. All right, so the club did have some benefits. But that wasn't why I was there.

Besides, we had clubs on Jal. But people knew me there. Maybe, if I got rid of Kess or could knowingly avoid him, this wouldn't be a bad spot to meet women when the urge arose.

Quit stalling. I steeled myself to more jostling as I devoted my concentration to forming the new jump point fully in my head and then pulling myself toward it. When I felt the shift of the Jump pass through me, I found myself on the upper level with two women staring in my direction. One shook her head. The other started to say something to a man nearby while still keeping an eye on me.

I couldn't have her alerting anyone to my arrival. Taking a couple of strides over to them, I wrapped my arms around both of their shoulders and hauled them off into a darkened alcove. One of them bumped into the hook that held the curtain door, knocking it free. Both women protested, one squirming in my grasp, the other let out a yelp. I hoped the man she'd been talking to didn't come after them. Knocking their heads together enough to stun them, I dropped them both onto the rounded bench seat. One of their heads fell onto the tall round table in the middle. The other lolled back against the wall. I hit them both with a stunner blast and backed out, closing the curtain behind me.

The man had resumed talking to a group of people, many of which sported distinctive piercings and facial implants that further set them apart from the standards of their races. They didn't understand that fitting in also allowed one to melt into the crowd easier. Then again, maybe they didn't have the sort of occupation where that was necessary.

I made sure my surveillance of the upper level looked as casual as possible by stopping to gawk at a woman or two along the way. I even considered ordering a drink at the bar as there were no lines up here. Having something legitimate in my hand might have helped mask me further.

But then I spotted Kess.

He sat behind a clearplaz wall on a couch with three women. One sat on him, the other two sat on either side. My heart raced to find him distracted and out in the open.

Except, upon a second's more inspection, he wasn't near as open as I would have liked. The clearplaz appeared to be as thick as my fist and the only opening in it was filled with two fringe-jobs that made the door guy out front look like a child. They filled the gap quite thoroughly, shoulders rubbing together and all. One of them spotted me.

He leaned in to the other, saying something that I couldn't make out. The music was slightly less annoying up here in terms of volume, but it was still too loud to hear anyone more than a step away. His body language conveyed what he was saying just fine. Either Kess had put his close staff on alert for my likeness or I just looked like trouble. The second lug turned just enough to start to say something over his shoulder that he created a nice gap for me to sight Kess between his female ornamentation.

In the interest of clearing our reputations with the Council, I wanted the conniving bastard's head intact. I whipped out the gun I'd brought for the job, aimed for his chest, and fired.

Beyond the clearplaz, women scattered. The one that had been on his lap found herself on the floor as Kess sprang to his feet. Her open clothes and his open pants clearly illustrated what I'd interrupted.

I might not have been wearing armor, but he was. It wasn't his regular work armor, but a fashionable fitted coat that went to his waist. No wonder it hadn't looked like armor at first glance.

The two fringe-jobs popped into action, both firing at me despite everyone around. Even over the music, I could hear Kess screaming for them to stop shooting.

Two people near me went down. Fuck. I hadn't intended for anyone but Kess to get hurt. I shot one of the hulking gun-happy lugs in the head. He went down with a thud I felt through the floor. Screams rose above the music. No one bumped into me as they vacated my vicinity with all possible haste.

One of the people on the floor curled into a ball, moaning. The other was still. I swore and went for the remaining guard. He fired again, this time hitting me in the shoulder. Then once again in the stomach before I took him out.

Kess stood on the other side of the clearplaz, one hand pressed against it as he glanced between me and his fallen guards.

It wasn't until Kess's gaze locked onto my wounds and the calculation lit in his eyes, that the effects of those shots hit me. Though I did my best to block out the pain, I knew my focus was slipping fast, my injuries beginning to demand my full attention. If I didn't leave now, I'd be on my ass in a minute or two. That is, if Kess didn't put me there any second with one more shot.

I started to Jump to the tank, but then I realized that my coat and the rest of my weapons were downstairs in the Geva-forsaken weapon's check. Fucking hells. I bolted for the stairs while I still had the benefit of adrenaline on my side. If I didn't get there fast and rescue my shit, Kess could use it against me with the Council. Geva damn the whole fucking shit storm situation.

People dodged out of my way when I hurled myself down the stairs. All the gunfire had cleared out a good deal of the main floor too. The pulsing music sounded hollow without all the conversation to bolster it.

With no small amount of satisfaction, I knocked into the stair guard on the way down. She stood firm, my momentum then sending me off balance and onto the floor. The blood that splattered into the sticky surface with me wasn't something I wanted to see. Nor did I want to consider everything else I was laying in and how very far from sanitary it was for my open wounds. Thank Geva the tank would kill anything I picked up.

Scrambling to my feet, I made it two steps toward the hallway where my coat was waiting before Kess's people surrounded me. Before I could cut my losses and Jump, hands clamped down on my shoulders. A booted foot kicked the backs of my knees, knocking me down on mine.

"Hold him there," Kess called out as he rushed down the stairs.

Hard metal met my scalp as someone pressed a gun to my head. "You want him dealt with?" asked a male voice.

"I'll take care of it," said the female guard from the stairs. She stalked closer, drawing a gun of her own.

Kess made a mad leap down the rest of the stairs. He shoved her aside.

She took two staggering steps before catching her balance and glared at him. "He took out Tag and Mosh."

"I'm well aware of the body count." Kess came closer. "His hands."

My arms were wrenched from my sides by a couple of Kess's thugs. He wasn't taking chances now. Not that I blamed him one bit.

The hole in my stomach started to seriously throb. It grew harder to keep my grimace to myself.

"Now then, I understand you have a grudge."

"You think?"

Kess shrugged. "I believe you were told to let that go."

"I don't always do what I'm told."

"Anastassia never did like subservient men. I suppose we have that in common, you and I." He addressed one of the thugs behind me. "Get his belongings from the armor check. Guessing you didn't arrive like this?" He aimed the last bit at me.

What the hells was he doing? I was kneeling there, bleeding all over his floor, waiting for him to wrap up his little speech and give the command to shunt a bullet into my brain. Instead, he was sending a lug for my stuff?

Logic spoke loud enough to overcome the racing pulse beating in my ears. Of course, he'd get my shit. He wasn't going to leave any sign of my being here that might get back to the Council or Merkief. He'd put the armor back on my body and drop me somewhere that I'd be found. Eventually. He'd set up something accidental or maybe make it look like a local hit, frame someone he was tired of, two birds with one stone and all that.

Someone slapped my face. I realized it was Kess and he'd been talking. "You listening?"

Damn, my stomach hurt. My shoulder too. The fucking thing was screaming with my arm all wrenched up in the lug's meaty hand. Someone behind me had a boot pressed heavily across the backs of my legs. The gun was still at my head too. I wasn't going anywhere. A little voice in my head said that I should have listened to Merkief.

A hefty punch to my jaw brought everything back into immediate focus.

I spit a bloody glob onto the floor. "Your men were sloppy."

Kess nodded. "True. That won't be a problem anymore, though, will it?"

Was he enjoying screwing with me? In the years he'd been itching to kill all of us, he'd never been chatty about it before. I highly doubted he'd had a lengthy conversation with Vayen when that fucking deadly mess had gone down.

"Now then, how about you hold still while Haxel gets the card out of your pocket." He studied me for a second. "Right pants pocket."

A hand reached into the pocket and came out with the claim card. "On it, boss."

"While we wait, we're going to have a little conversation, and you're going to listen to every word, got it?" Kess said.

Did it matter if I agreed? He was going to kill me anyway. "Sure,"

I said through clenched teeth.

"I'm good with our situation. Do you understand me? You have yours. I have mine. We have our instructions."

I was not at all good with the situation. "Fuck you."

He punched me again. Much harder this time. It took a moment for the room to stop shaking. The strobing lights didn't help at all.

"I have a deal to honor. You're pissed. I get it. In light of our last meeting, I'm surprised it took you this long to show up. So I'll give you this one. One. This counts for both you and your partner." He waved to someone behind me.

They came forward with my coat. "Haxel is going to help you get your armor on. Then you're going to Jump. I'm assuming you're in suitable shape to do that yet?"

I didn't buy his dangled hope for a second. Yet, self-preservation made me nod.

He leaned down to get right in my face. "If I see either of you here or anywhere in my territory, the deal is off. I will hunt you both down and no one will know it was me. I will take everything you have. Am I clear?"

"Yeah." Like he meant a word of his deal. I sure didn't.

"Good. Don't waste this." He gestured to the lugs holding me.

"Boss?" said the one he called Haxel. "You're letting him go?"

"Get him on his feet."

"What about Tag and Mosh?" asked Haxel.

"He was right. They were sloppy. Paytel, get someone on the bodies upstairs."

The woman snarled at me before ascending the stairs. Hands hoisted me upward. My stomach violently protested stretching back out as I got to my feet. There were still too many hands on me to Jump, and I had little doubt the gun was still aimed at my head, though I didn't aggravate my shoulder further by turning to look.

Kess clapped his hands. "Let's go, people. I want this place cleaned and re-opened in an hour."

Haxel, an ugly mutt of a man, came forward like he'd been ordered to dress a poisonous viper. He eyed my hands and scowled.

I held out my good arm, my trembling hand reaching for the safety of my armor, but the asshole stood three steps away.

Haxel looked to Kess, who nodded. The mutt shook his head. "Maybe you didn't feel this thing, boss. He's got an arsenal in here."

"I don't doubt it. Be foolish to come after me without one. But really, Haxel, he's plenty armed right now if he's desperate enough to try to off me despite all of you." He took my armor from Haxel and leaned in close again. "Are you feeling desperate? I mean, if you do want to make that move, my honor would be intact. Self-defense, you know."

What was all the prattling about honor? If anyone had less, I'd never met them. "So shoot me already."

"Believe me, it's tempting." His fingers twitched by his side.

I took three quick, deep breaths, desperately trying to maintain a semblance of focus, to find some way to pull out of this fucking mess I'd made.

If I could take the shot, use the one opportunity in front of me… Could I beat the reaction time of the guard holding the gun to my head?

Merkief wasn't involved. A Council probe would find him innocent of this attack. He'd have the Narvan free and clear. The Nebula would be free of Kess and so would Merkief. I could avenge Kazan and Vayen and rid the universe of this perpetual thorn in our side. Hells, I couldn't think of a better way to go out.

Kess's lips were moving but his words didn't matter. My mind was already picturing what I needed to do, my muscles rehearsing for the second of action I'd have. He wanted me dead. I could see it in his eyes.

Pain pierced my thoughts. I gulped three more breaths.

I'd have to go for his head. No use in saving his link. I wouldn't be alive to make use of any of that anyway. It was simply a matter of taking him out with a single shot. After years of single shots and countless opportunities had failed. But I was so close.

Just draw the gun, aim, and pull the trigger. Simple. No way I could miss at this range.

A breath in. A breath out. I released my hold and let my body slip into autopilot.

I drew. Finger on the trigger.

Kess smiled as he drew too, my armor still on his other arm.

A hand registered in my peripheral vision. I aimed.

The hand slammed into my head as I fired. The room went black for a second. When my wavering wits came back online, the club wall made a disorienting arc in front of my face. I hit the floor with a loud crack that reverberated in my head. The lights above me flickered and spun.

A rush of feet surrounded me.

"Stay back. Give me some room to work." Kess came into view. He dropped my armor onto my stomach. The heavy weight on the open wound took my breath away. He stood over me, gun still drawn.

No one was touching me. I could Jump. I had to get to the tank. The thought kept circling in my head but I couldn't quite pin it down enough to put it into action. Kess faded in and out of focus.

"You missed, by the way," he said. Kess switched out his gun for a different one. "You can leave any time you're ready."

Merkief couldn't come in to get me. Not with Kess armed and waiting.

He fired at my shoulder again. Whatever he was using now wasn't at all deterred by bone. Everything was a swirling mass of agony. He went for my hip next, then a knee.

"That should suitably slow you down for a while. If you live." Kess said, his voice distant. "Remember that I could have taken your head. The fucking deal is off."

My vision cleared enough to see him wiping blood from a line across his temple. I hadn't missed by much.

"Hey, boss?" Paytel had returned to his side. "How's he supposed to leave in that shape?"

"He can manage. Kazan's men are hard to kill." He looked down at me. "I'm one of them too, remember?"

That he was, but I'd find a way. I just had to live long enough to do it. Next time I'd bring back up. Even if it wasn't Merkief. I had people, dammit. It was high time I started using my position in the Narvan for my benefit rather than for everyone else's.

I tried for three quick breaths again but couldn't manage more than a slow draw that left my lungs pleading for more.

I'd formed a Jump to the ship in this condition once before, but I wouldn't be able to get the tank going. Vayen wouldn't be there to help me this time.

"Need help," I said to Merkief. *"Tank. Now."*

I closed my eyes to help block out the pain. It honestly didn't do much.

"Where are you?" Merkief asked.

Thank Geva he was waiting. With agonizing slowness, I pulled myself toward his voice, toward the bright lights of the tank room and the blessed clearplaz tube filled with the miracle gel that would hopefully erase what Kess had done to me.

SIXTEEN

Rhaine

My throat threatened to close in upon itself. Tears slipped onto the pillow. I thought we'd been making progress, slow, but some at least. That he was, on some level, glad to be around me to keep his stupid bond under control. That he maybe craved that wonderful tranquility that he'd given me a glimpse of when he'd explained what the bond offered him.

I was wrong.

I'd really broken this. This thing between us that I hadn't wanted, but had come to rely on.

Was *rely* even the right word? Expect, maybe, though that made me feel even worse. I expected him to put up with whatever I threw at him and to be there when I wanted him to be. Which, granted, hadn't been often since our arrival here. But right now was one of those times.

I listened for the door, for the transport to take him and Daniel away. I told myself I should sleep, gather my wits for when Weeda arrived, but between the pounding in my head and the spinning thoughts, that was a futile effort.

The door downstairs remained sealed.

My heart leapt when the first two heavy footsteps sounded on the stairs. The next few were slower. Then they halted altogether.

Daniel cooed. Isnar spoke softly to him in Artorian. Was he talking about me or did he often speak to Daniel that way? I hadn't paid attention to what language he'd used before. Did he plan on teaching Daniel his native language?

To distract myself from the whispers on the stairway and the turmoil in my head, I tried to imagine what Daniel would look like when he grew up. Probably identical to a young version of the man on the stairs that I'd seen in a still frame in their family home when he was all of sixteen. He'd been much younger in the still frame, standing beside his mother with his father and brother looming behind them. An innocent and happy version of the face I now knew so well. Hopefully, Daniel could remain that way far longer than Isnar had. I imagined him working at Dugans, alongside the man who was now his father, learning a business that would keep him out of trouble and earn him a good living.

Would he meet a girl here? Start a family of his own someday? What would Artorian genes do when mixed with Verian? Probably entirely dominate them in every way like they'd done with mine.

My thoughts scattered as the doorframe creaked under the weight of a large man settling against it. Isnar had managed to make those big feet of his silent as a matter of necessity in our previous life, but I didn't mind the surprise here at all.

"Daniel says he wants to stay here today. Since you're in no condition to watch him, I suppose that means I have to stay too."

I held out my hand again. This time he took it.

Though I didn't want to let go, I needed both of his hands free in order to help me. "I'll take him. Sit behind me."

As if he could read my mind, he settled into the same position that I'd taken when I'd done a session for him. With Daniel sprawled across my chest, gnawing on his fingers with great determination and a puddle of drool already penetrating my shirt, I sat up enough to lean back against Isnar's chest.

"I'd coach you through it, but honestly, that's going to distract me from the whole purpose, so I'm going to show you. Hopefully. If we can still make that work."

He didn't say anything one way or the other, but our bonded connection opened as far as I was able to sense it. I went into my memories of the lessons I wanted to show him, trying to pull him along with me, but I didn't need words to know it wasn't working. We'd shared memories before. I knew what it should feel like to have him riding along with me in my head. But my transport had left and he was still standing in the yard.

I wanted to swear, but Daniel was right there. That also ruled out hitting or throwing anything. Muttering threats to the Council probably wasn't the best tone to set either.

Isnar's hands settled onto my shoulders, squeezing lightly. "Probe? You've already got a headache. I doubt it would make it any worse at this point."

He'd have free reign in my head. His highly-honed telepathic touch was deft enough I'd have no idea what he was looking at. Did I have anything left to hide from him?

"Do it."

His muscles jumped beneath me, a twitch as though I'd surprised him. "You're sure?"

I nodded.

One warm hand slipped to the side of my neck, his fingers pressed against my pulse so he'd know if something was wrong while he was busy inside my head. Because I knew he was doing it, I felt him, slithering inside, like an injected drug, the distant sensation of something foreign in my body. Then my mind's natural defenses failed, his presence subtle enough once he was in, that it was as if he wasn't there at all.

As much as I tried not to think about him being in there, to focus on the lessons I wanted him to see, the pain in my head was a distraction I couldn't ignore or block. It tugged me away from the lessons, from even worrying about what all he might be pouring over while he had free access.

The pain suddenly became a spike that took my breath away.

His arms went tight around me. "Oh Fuck. I'm sorry. I'm out. I'm out."

"What did you do?" I asked once I could unclench my jaws.

"Nevermind," he said. "Where should I start? You might still have to talk me through this."

"Tell me what you did."

He sighed. "I thought if I could stimulate the spot where our natural connection is maybe I could kickstart something. Kind of like initiating a bond."

"Not a bad idea, but bad idea."

"Got it. We won't try that again. So, what exactly do you want me to do? Everything was a bit scattered in there."

That wasn't a surprise. I spent the next twenty minutes getting his fingers in the right beginning position before coming to the conclusion that this wasn't going to work like I wanted it to. Couldn't he just magically know what I needed him to do?

"You sure you don't want me to call Weeda? I can try to see where she is on her investigation if we're just talking."

"No, but I wouldn't be opposed to you knocking me out if you still have the urge."

He chuckled, his chest bouncing up and down as he did so. "I might have seriously taken you up on that a week ago. Can I keep that offer for another time?"

"No."

"Worth a try. How about I go feed the slobber monster and then I'll come back and we can try again?"

I nodded.

He handed me the datapad. "Make your cancelations. I'll use the terminal downstairs to call in."

With one eye squeezed closed, I was able to see straight enough to send out short messages to my three scheduled clients. That task done, I tried to block out the world and will myself to sleep.

One of my ears began to ring and my nose stuffed up. With Daniel gone, I swore under my breath, cursing the Council and their last agent who had failed to kill me. Having been sedated, I wouldn't have felt it, and considering what I felt like at the moment, they would have been doing me a favor. Hell, Isnar would still be Vayen, the bond would be dissolved, and he would still have the Narvan in his hands.

But I would've never have the chance to get to know him as Isnar or see him with Daniel, and he certainly wouldn't have had time for either of those things. The Narvan was a demanding and all-consuming mistress.

I'd dragged him away from his quiet life, sure he would thrive in mine and he had. But maybe this, being here on Minor, was me paying some kind of restitution, not what I wanted, but what he deserved. The Council and the demands of the Narvan had been hard on him. He'd earned some quiet, some of that tranquility his bond offered, at least, for as long as he remained here.

No matter how hard I tried to embrace being Rhaine, I knew I would crack and fuck this up again. I'd been Anastassia for too long. There were parts of my mind I couldn't turn off, not like I had when I'd tried to become a Seeker, or even when I'd lost Chesser and found Kryon and the Council. That was all growing forward, experiences building upon one another. Now it was like I was trying to crawl backward, to undo the past twenty years, to figure out who I would have been had I stayed on Prime with Res and not joined the Verian army. The best I could hope for was to try and enjoy whatever normal was supposed to be while it lasted.

Sleep was the only thing that would offer a reprieve from the headache from hell. I clutched a pillow and twisted around toward the foot of the bed to maximize the fresh cool air on my face. As comfortable as I was going to get, I told my mind to shut up and let me rest.

That must have worked because I woke up to a large solid body against my back and the dead weight of a thick arm on my side. I had no idea what time it was and I didn't care. Daniel was quiet, wherever he was. I hoped it was in his own room. Isnar was sound asleep. It was still sunny out and my eyes still weren't having it. I closed them and savored the warmth from behind while the cool air swirled around the front. Other than the intense headache and everything else that was wrong, it felt like we were finally making positive progress.

It was two days later and in utter misery that I caved and allowed a very harried Isnar to call Weeda in. Their voices rose over one another downstairs. I began to wonder if Isnar was losing his temper. We were all in for trouble if that happened.

Daniel let out a wail down the hall that spurred me to get out of bed. With one eye open just far enough to see, I made my way into his room. Isnar had bought him a larger bed, one with slatted walls to contain him. It looked like a cage to me, but I wasn't up for pointing that out. Daniel quieted at the sight of me, holding up his arms. I hefted him out of his cage and settled him on my hip.

From the volume downstairs I wondered if I should venture down there to calm Isnar as well. The thought of attempting the stairs made the dizziness worse. I hadn't been down there in two days. I'd barely been able to keep anything down and my muscles were shaking just standing there holding Daniel.

Isnar's voice rose. "You will get up there and treat my Ishla or you'll find yourself out of a supplier. Is that clear enough for you?"

Weeda said something I couldn't make out.

"No Verian, dammit."

"I said, there are other suppliers."

"Good luck getting them to work with you."

This was going to venture into socially unrecoverable territory very soon. I held onto Daniel with both arms and headed for the stairs.

"You seem fond of threats, Isnar Ka'turoc. Tell me, did Jurson

Dugan retire? I've been hearing a good number of rumors that say otherwise."

What rumors were these? I hadn't heard them. Then again, I only spoke with a fraction of the people Weeda did.

"You're wasting the time you said you didn't have to begin with. Just give her something to fix this and you can go."

"Perhaps I'll just go now," Weeda said.

I'd made it halfway down the stairs before black spots filled my one-eyed vision. With a heavy thud, I sat on the step before I took Daniel head over heel with me. Isnar and Weeda stood near the door.

My voice was loud and grating to every raw nerve in my body, but I wanted to make sure she heard me. "Refusing to treat a patient would violate your colony contract."

"What are you doing out of bed?" Isnar dashed toward me.

I considered waving him off, but I grabbed his hand instead. It was solid and warm and familiar and I needed something to ground me as the lightheadedness took hold even seated. A weight was lifted as he took Daniel from me with his other hand. Freed of my squirming burden, I rested my forehead on my knees. That felt much better.

"I'm fine. I just need a minute," I managed to say.

"If you're fine, why am I here?" asked Weeda, one hand on her hip, the other clutching her bag.

"She's not fine."

"I can see that," Weeda grumbled something in Verian as she started up the stairs. "Get her back to bed. I'll take the baby."

Once he'd handed Daniel off, I let Isnar lift me mostly one-handed to my feet. His shoulder felt just as good as my knees had on my aching head.

"Will you go nuts if I pick you up in front of Weeda?" he whispered.

Grateful that he'd asked first, I couldn't find a reason to argue. Weeda had already seen me at my worst. "Not today."

Within a breath, I was up in the air and on the way back to bed. "Did you off Jersen Dugan?" I asked while I was next to his ear.

"Later."

By his tight and terse tone, I took that as a yes. What the hell had he been up to those first few weeks while I'd been out of it in bed? Maybe Isnar was a little more Vayen than I'd realized.

After I'd been gently deposited on the bed, Weeda handed Daniel back to Isnar. She set her bag on the end of the bed and stood there. She didn't even start sanitizing her hands.

"You need to tell me what exactly happened to you or we're never going to be able to fully treat the mess in your brain."

Isnar's head snapped to her, a scowl on his face. The tension in the room skyrocketed. I grabbed his hand before he could take a step toward her. We didn't need more Vayen on Minor.

"I was tortured over an extended period and it caused significant brain damage," I said. "There was a surgery to fix some of it, but that wasn't as successful as we'd hoped."

"Tortured? Why? Who would do such a thing to a Seeker?"

I ran with her line of thinking. "They wanted to see what made my mind different."

"And they broke it," Isnar added, his voice uncharacteristically thick as he settled down on the edge of the bed next to me. The mattress sagged under his weight. He sat there, stroking my hair with his free hand for a moment.

Either he was pouring it on pretty heavily or he did have feelings for me beyond his self-imposed obligation to keep me safe.

Back in the Narvan, when he'd sprung the bond revelation on me, there had been so much going on. His timing was awful. Then again, I supposed he'd waited two years to be able to announce his bond so I couldn't blame him for that. Still, we'd both had so many issues pulling us in different directions, him running the Narvan with Jey, me dealing with what had been done to me and trying to catch up on everything I'd missed, that we hadn't much of a chance to dwell on feelings.

I wasn't a big fan of those. Every time I'd tried them, life blew up in my face.

Whatever his reasons, it worked in bringing Weeda's aggression down a notch. She opened her bag and brought out her sanitizer.

"You escaped?" she asked, stepping closer.

"I couldn't. When they were done, they let me go."

One of her eyebrows rose as she regarded Isnar. "No heroic rescue?"

His whole body went tight. Heat flared in his hand that I held. I imagined that if we hadn't needed her, Weeda would have been up against the wall with his arm wedged against her throat while he considered where to start cutting until she adequately apologized.

Then I realized it wasn't my imagination. That was what he was envisioning and it was shining through our bonded connection. That image was the clearest thing we'd shared since my surgery. Whether it was possible because he was so focused, it was a strong emotion, or we were touching, I didn't know but I planned on experimenting until we figured it out.

Once I could see and think straight again.

"Rescue wasn't an option. Leave him be. He did what he could."

There was altogether too much talking, too much noise, too many people in the room. I wanted dark, quiet and the cool breeze in my face, nothing else. Well, maybe a few more comforting touches from the man beside me.

All at once, a flood of beautiful tranquility hit me. It swept the edge away from the ache in my head and the irritation everywhere else. I closed my eyes and breathed deep, relaxing more than I had in days.

"You can feel that. I can feel you, almost like before," Isnar said with a clear hitch in his voice. "How? How is that possible?"

I could sense Weeda hovering over me, the sharp smell of the sanitizer she used giving her away. Isnar was getting all bristly again, his space being intruded upon. Our space. Damn, this clarity was amazing. I'd never had such an open window into what he was feeling. This would make getting along with him so much easier. We had to figure out how this was happening and how to make it stay. Maybe my mind was starting to heal.

"You're fine right there," I said. "Let her scan me."

Weeda spent a long time, longer than she ever had before, that I remembered anyway, running her instruments over my head and my neck at different angles over and over. Then she stepped back.

"I need to compare these to what I have on file from your last exam. Give me a few minutes." Her footsteps retreated to the hallway.

Isnar's hand wandered over my face and my shoulders as though he couldn't figure out what he wanted to do. "How are you feeling? How is this working? Are you doing something different?"

"No talking. Just do your zen thing."

"My what?"

Daniel started to squirm and whine.

"I'm going to feed him. I'll be right back." He was up and out the door before I could tell him to stay.

The quiet peace diminished when he left the room, but a whisper of it remained. He was still close by. It was so strange and yet longingly familiar to know that with utter certainty. The knowing was different, not like I'd brushed over his mind with my link, but deeper.

If all Artorian couples had this type of connection, I couldn't fathom how they might ever grow apart or even consider infidelity.

We might not be able to speak mind to mind…yet. Could I recover that too? My heart raced. But this sharing of vivid images and emotions was a giant improvement over the distant and muted feelings I'd been relegated to since our arrival here. If our bonded connection was stronger, that might mean my brain was healing in other areas as well. I might be able to recover more of my telepathy to help with being a Seeker, to one day be able to talk to my son when his natural mind speech kicked in.

When Weeda wandered back into the room, I reached out to her with my mind, to try to brush over it, to get a sense of what was causing the deep furrows on her pale forehead. All I got for my effort was a wave of nausea. I curled onto my side, hoping to keep the dry heaving to a minimum.

"Could you open the window farther? I need more air."

"You need more than air," Weeda said with more compassion than I anticipated coming from her given our previous exchanges. She stood near the foot of the bed, her scanner and datapad clutched to her chest.

I wished the rest of my mental senses would spur into action like the bonded connection had. Her obvious apprehension made my already queasy stomach twist into knots.

As if summoned, Isnar darted in to take his post beside me. "What's wrong?" He looked from me to Weeda. "Someone talk. Now."

Weeda cleared her throat and slid the scanner into her bag. She held out the datapad. "This is the scan from the last time I examined you." She showed us an image of colored blotches, most of which were red or shades of it. "This area," she pointed to a dark region with a few specs of red, "is where the majority of the damage is. When you first came here, this was blue where there were abnormalities and black where there was no function." She turned the datapad back around and swiped her finger across it a couple of times. "This is the scan I just took."

The area she'd zoomed in on was again blue with a burst of purple off to one side and a solid dot of red next to it.

"What does that mean?" Isnar asked.

"New damage. Damage that is cascading into something I can't treat. You're going to need surgery again before this gets further out of hand."

"It's just a bad headache." My words sounded weak as I stared at the blatant evidence to the contrary.

"What might have caused the new damage?" Isnar asked.

"You said this area was involved with your abilities as a Seeker, yes?"

I nodded.

"Did you try something ambitious in the last day or two? Something that may have strained this area? From the size of the damaged area, you had to have felt some indication."

Isnar all but collapsed in upon himself. A wave of utter devastation rushed into my mind. "Oh Geva, no." He shook his head. "I didn't mean to."

Weeda's eyes went wide. "You did this?"

He gazed down on me with a look I'd only seen once before, so full of regret and fear. The last time he'd worn that face, I was getting sentenced by the High Council, when I'd accused him of working with them to get rid of me, when he was facing two years away from me with an unannounced bond and the impending chaos of my safety net and a war.

Seeing him from the inside now, I felt awful for accusing him of trying to get rid of me. He'd proven beyond a doubt that killing me was not an option he was willing to see through.

"You didn't know. Neither of us did. We'll figure it out."

One of his large hands enveloped my shoulder, squeezing with an intensity that verged on pain. He tore his gaze from me to face Weeda. "If you do the surgery, what will that mean for her as a Seeker?"

What his racing thoughts showed me was a wave of panic at losing this newfound bonded connection he wanted so badly that it hurt. I wanted to reassure him that we'd gotten by without it before, but in truth, we hadn't. And to be honest, I didn't want to lose this openness either. When I'd finally acknowledged and accepted his bond to me, I'd gotten glimpses of this, but it had never been this clear, this open. At the time, the thought of him seeing into what was going on in my head, what I was truly feeling, had driven me to keep our connection muted and him at a distance. But Rhaine and Isnar didn't have deadly secrets to hide from one another. They were far simpler people just trying to remain on speaking terms throughout the day and raise a child together.

When I did try to show him that I didn't blame him, that we'd get through this, the pain in my head intensified. No showing then. He was on full blast, but I was a barely dripping faucet.

Weeda turned the datapad off and tucked it into her bag. "I'm going to refer you to a colleague that serves the founding colony. He has a staff of skilled surgeons that can remove the damaged tissue."

"Remove?" I managed to ask through my own panic that I could barely comprehend over Isnar's.

"Seekers do more than just treat the mind, Rhaine. You'll still have all your knowledge and your hands. You can still serve the colony."

I didn't give a fuck about the colony. I needed as much of that part of my mind as I could keep. All of it, in fact. What little that did work at least allowed us a connection, and that was all I had left of the flurry of activity I'd been used to in my head. I couldn't imagine having all of it shut off forever.

Grabbing onto the quivering mountain of muscle and nerves beside me, I hauled myself to a seated position. "So here's what's going to happen. Weeda, you're going to repeat the treatment you used when we first arrived here. I don't care how long it takes. Wake me up when things look better in there."

I shook Isnar's shoulder. "You're going to have to handle this on your own for a while. I haven't been much help so far, so I'm sure you can swing it."

He nodded, but I wasn't sure he'd even understood what I'd said.

"To be safe, let's do this at your colleague's clinic. Send him your notes or whatever you need to do, but no one is touching my brain unless there is absolutely no other recourse. Is that clear?"

Weeda's mouth dropped open. "Rhaine, this is reckless. You need treatment immediately."

"Reckless." Isnar snorted. "You have no idea." He turned to me. "Are you sure about this?"

Though he was asking a legitimate question and trying like all of his hells to sound sincere about it, his hope that I would say yes was overwhelming through our connection.

"You had to decide last time. This one is my call. I'm sure."

He slid off the bed. "Then let's pack. Where is this clinic exactly?" He aimed his question at Weeda.

"You're staying here," I said.

"What? I'm most certainly not. You'll be—"

"Unconscious. This isn't like before." I tried to drill that into his eyeballs rather than his head to avoid further pain. "Daniel needs you, and while I'm sure your staff has business under control, you've already been out for a few days. This could take weeks."

Weeda's brows lowered.

"Or longer," I amended. "I'm sure someone will contact you if there are any changes or decisions to be made."

"I will," said Weeda.

I held out my arm for whatever Weeda was inclined to shove into my veins. "Good, then put me out of my misery, and let's get on with it."

"Could we have a minute first?" Isnar asked in a tone that indicated it wasn't up for negotiation.

"Every minute might matter, but why not at this point." She waved her hand in the air and stepped into the hallway, closing the door behind her.

"If you think I'm going to allow you to…" He grimaced and shook his head. "You're not going alone to this clinic, to another colony, to be surrounded by people we don't know. Not when you're defenseless."

"I am going. They don't know me either. I'll be fine," I assured him. "But before I do, can you do me a favor?"

"No." His aggravation seemed to fill the room. "Fuck no." He stalked around the bed, glancing from the clutter-free floor to the unadorned walls and seeming to find everything but my face as he went.

"*Vearta,* is that raving or selfish? I figured the bitch part out for myself."

His steps paused. "Overheard that, did you?"

"Not the first time I've heard the phrase. Your brother may have used those words a few times to my face. I didn't care to ask for a translation at the time."

He didn't offer to enlighten me.

"Whatever it is, you were both probably right. Well, you were, anyway. He usually deserved whatever I was yelling at him about."

The corners of his lips raised a fraction as he came to a stop at the foot of the bed.

"You don't deserve this, dealing with me, the abundance of Verians, being away from your homeworld and the Narvan." A deep sigh escaped, offering a faint feeling of relief in its wake. No matter how many apologies I made, they wouldn't be enough. "Let me go. Stay and enjoy the bed, the house, the kitchen. Your work. Just don't kill anyone else, all right?"

"You're coming back," he said flatly, also not up for debate.

"I don't have anywhere else to go, so yes. Assuming I don't end up a drooling idiot who can't remember where she lives."

He came closer. "I'd find you and take you home."

If that didn't answer the feelings part of my debate, I didn't know what did. It gave me the nerve to voice what I really wanted.

"That favor?"

He sighed and came to sit next to me again. "Fine. What is it?"

"If I haven't totally burned the bridge and dispersed the ashes to the far reaches of the known universe, can we maybe attempt the us thing again when I get back?"

Silence stretched out to the point I wished Weeda would barge in and save me the indignity of his non-answer.

"Impossible," he said.

Talk about a sucker punch. So not feelings, just obligation. If I could have rolled off the bed and stormed out the door to slam it behind me, I would have, but I was too deflated and dizzy to do more than turn my head away.

Warm fingers pulled my chin back toward him. "The closest translation of *vearta* I can think of is impossible. You are impossible to please."

Oh. I let out a relieved chuckle.

"Not true, but fair, I suppose. I didn't want to be pleased. Not by anything or anyone. But that wasn't your fault. I'm trying."

He nodded as he stroked my cheek. "I don't think we've reached ashes quite yet.

"Is that a yes then?"

"Yes."

Weeda did barge in then just as I was enjoying the first real kiss we'd shared since arriving on Veria Minor.

"Glad to see you're saying your goodbyes. We need to get you sedated and on your way. You'll carry her out to my transport?" she asked Isnar.

"Of course."

"Very good." She grabbed her injector.

I supposed that since I'd offered my arm previously, she took it that I was ready because she didn't ask for further permission. The injection hit me with a burst of heavy warmth that sped through the rest of my body.

"You'll let me know what they say? Where she is? When I can visit? When she'll be coming home?" Isnar's questions all ran together in my hazy mind.

"Ishlan Ka'turoc, I will be quite honest with you. I would be very surprised *if* she comes home. Not in this capacity for sure, likely not at all. We will do what we can, but what I showed you here is dire. She may not be in a condition to take it seriously, but you need to, for the sake of your son."

I tried to protest, to shout at her, to tell her to shut the hell up and quit scaring him, but my mouth was no longer under my control. His fear and anger overwhelmed our bonded connection until that too leveled and then faded, everything turning into a murky blackness. Muffled sounds meandered through the shadows. Something warm registered on my distant skin. Isnar had picked me up.

My last conscious thought was that I was going to prove Weeda wrong.

SEVENTEEN

Merkief

Jey arrived on the ship by some miracle of Geva. For as pale as a Jalvian was on a normal day, his skin was almost blue in comparison. Blood everywhere, exposed bone, and massive wounds. His armor sat in a wad on his stomach. Whoever had done this had tortured him intentionally.

There was only one bastard I knew of who would do that much damage but not finish off a man. Kess. Jey had been talking about going after him. Apparently, he had.

And this is where it had gotten him.

As much as I might want the Narvan for myself, staring that possibility in the bloody face was terrifying. Losing Jey for good was even more so. I stood there for a second, overwhelmed by the ghastly sight, by the thought of Jey being stolen from me like... I shook my head, forcing the thought away.

Pulling off his clothes was a lost cause. I cut off what was left of them. Geva, I hoped the tank could fix this. We'd all suffered extensive damage over the years and come out all right, but this was deliberate. Like Kess knew what the tank could do and had set out a challenge.

Blood and the many causes of it leaving a body were nothing new to me. I'd grown desensitized to it in Kazan's service, but this was Jey. My hands shook, and tears I was glad he wasn't awake to see, rolled down my face.

I shoved the armor aside, along with the remnants of his clothes. His boots were the only thing intact. I pulled them off.

Lifting him onto the platform made my skin crawl. His bruised and swollen face revealed no sign of life. There was no sense in arranging him comfortably. There could be no comfort in his condition. Other than a faint indication that he was breathing, he was entirely unresponsive. I hurried to the terminal to pull up his profile.

Geva, if Kess had done this to Jey, it may have been a blessing that we hadn't recovered Vayen's body. To see him mutilated like this might have made me lose my nerve and run for safety rather than attempt to hold the Narvan.

Within a minute, the platform brought Jey into the healing grip of the gel. I sat there, dumbfounded by his stats, barely alive, the blood loss alone almost terminal. What the hells had the two of them been doing that had taken Jey so long to Jump? And why the fuck hadn't he contacted me before the situation had gotten so dire?

Things between us might be far more strained than they used to be, but we were partners. We'd known each other, sweated and bled beside one another, drank and cursed Kazan's relentless work schedule, and then Vayen's even worse one together.

I'd almost lost him just like... The thought reared up again and this time, I couldn't suppress it.

Wiping my wet face with my hands smeared with Jey's drying blood, I took a deep shuddering breath and then another. The grief I'd neatly contained over the loss of Kazan and Vayen broke free.

As if Jey could see me, I shot up from the chair and blindly made my way to the bathroom where I closed myself in. I stood there, gripping the edge of the sink, eyes closed to the wretched image in the mirror until the worst of it had passed.

Still avoiding my reflection, I washed my hands and my face and then wiped down my armor. Once I was confident that my emotions were back in check, I returned to the tank room to clean up.

Jey's stats steadily rose. He would fully recover. Relief washed away the hollow morbidity and cleared the way for the drive of purpose to resume control.

While I waited for him to wake up and provide answers to what had happened, I had work to do.

I used the office for hours of vid calls. Now that the Jalvian fleet upgrades were off my list of oppressive tasks, there were other issues. One of which was financing for the Artorian University. How the hells had Vayen kept them in business? I tried to prioritize the requests, aligning them with what I wanted and the desires of the Council.

There were many promising projects that might benefit the less than hospitable habitat of Syless. If I could get them self-sustaining with their food supply, the cost of shipping food from Artorian worlds or Frique would drop considerably.

A lot of costs needed to drop considerably. Jey and I hadn't been able to accomplish much in the way of Kryon contracts. More credits would be flowing from Jal to Artorian accounts soon, but the bulk of that would be after the work had been completed. And that was going to take months. The first group of Artorian techs had been dispatched with supplies. What I needed was a team on the Jalvian end to join them, to learn the process so we could ship the parts and bill them right away. That required a lengthy meeting with a department head at the University.

Once that was over, I delved into dealing with Frique. Syless might not need their food soon, but Artor and Moriek would. Though both of them could produce a plentiful supply of their own, the public liked the variety that Frique offered, especially their prantha. The ones raised on Artor didn't taste the same.

By the time my eyes had started to droop, I'd concluded an amicable food deal, but Frique still had no interest in joining my half of the Narvan. The only consolation was that they had no interest in joining with Jey or Kess either.

I crawled into my bed on the ship and allowed myself five hours of sleep. Upon waking only slightly refreshed, which was my new normal, I popped a stim. I'd never been a big user of stims before, but I'd come to see why Vayen had lived on a steady diet of them. Kazan had used them too, though not as heavily. I firmly shoved the thoughts of both of them back down, smothering the raw internal wound with reminders of resentment and what I'd gained from their demise.

Not a tragedy. A blessing.

I drew in a deep breath and let it out. Right then. Back to business.

Jey had cycled out of the tank shortly before I'd awoken. He'd been in for eleven hours. His personal record for sure. And we didn't need a repeat of it. I moved him to his bed to finish out his long recovery sleep.

A thought kept pulsing through my brain, the only reminder of the past day that I allowed myself: I wasn't going to lose Jey to Kess. If Kess could do that to Jey despite his word to the Council, he could do it to me. To either of us, at any time.

If Jey looked that bad, Kess had to be recovering too and he didn't have a tank. I couldn't think of a better opportunity to take him out.

Honor and integrity were not at all on my radar when it came to him. If I'd have had access to his bedroom with his kid and wife in his arms, I still would have planted a bullet in his head. But he didn't have a wife or kids. Not that we knew of. Not that I could even imagine. And if I ever wanted one, I wanted Kess out of the picture, because he undoubtedly had the same lack of conscience.

Coat packed and weapons loaded, I Jumped to Twelve. That was the most logical place for Jey to hit him. I went by his headquarters, which were dark and deserted looking. A deep scan of the local network gave me plenty of confirmation that business was running as usual there. I also found some interesting holes in his security. Places that might have been traps, or simply overlooked. Given the alternative of traipsing around the city to find where Kess might be, I decided to take my chances.

If Kess was recovering from even half the damage Jey had suffered, he'd be in a bed somewhere. Without a tank at his disposal, he'd have doctors on call. He probably had a generous stock of healing gel too, but the commercially distributed stuff wasn't near as potent as what the tank produced.

Using my link, I wormed my way into the building's network. Though there was some troublesome coding, his systems were somewhat similar to the ones Kazan had set up. That wasn't too surprising given that Kess had lived with her for a couple of years before we'd come along.

It was a good thing that I'd worked closely with Jey for a while now and had picked up a good deal of Jalvian security protocols. We'd worked around them on other contracts. I could do it again.

It took me almost two hours of hiding in a dark crevice behind a bush to evade the drones and cameras to verify that the field and grid coverage on the air vent on the roof above me was disabled. I spent another half hour hacking into one of the drones to fly down that same vent to make sure it wasn't a trap. Finding nothing concerning, I let the drone go back on its way and used the image I'd gathered from its feed to Jump directly inside the vent. I slipped for a moment as I exited the void, but caught myself before falling too close to the fans below. It took a few more minutes to access the controls to those through the building network and disable them so that I could drop through the two levels of blades and inch my way down to the channel lined with vent covers. Using the layout I'd found on the network and accessing the internal vid feeds, I found a room that was unoccupied and dropped down into it. With the lights on standby, I could make out a set of chairs and a table of sorts. There were straps on it. So a work room, then. Kazan hadn't employed furniture like this, but from the training I'd had before coming into her service, I acknowledged that it had its benefits. At least, with the lights low, I couldn't see any bloodstains.

I cracked the lock on the door and halted any notice of the breech on the network. Then, making my cautious way out into the hallway, I again consulted the map. Kess lived here. That was a confirmed fact. Jey had told me Marin had been killed in his own quarters. Would Kess have taken those same rooms for himself? Marin had considered them safe, but Kess would have improved security. Kess occupying the main suite was a bet I was willing to take.

Making my way there proved to be a challenge. Kess's people lived and worked at all hours just like we did. While I did fit in here at a glance, I had little doubt that Kess had circulated still frames of Jey and I to his staff.

I used the vid feed to work my way through all the living obstacles as unobtrusively as possible. A trail of bodies would be hard to cover up and if found, would set off alarms on a scale I couldn't control.

It was all going well until I misjudged the distance and travel speed of an alert and undistracted employee. As it turned out, he was the deadly sort. He almost had time to fire before I sent a tight pulse his way. The pulse was quieter than my other choices. I wasn't close enough for a knife and my throwing skills were nothing to brag about.

I found a dark and empty room nearby to drag his lifeless body into. The wall damage was minimal but might attract notice if anyone was looking for it. I'd have to move faster.

One turn later, I found myself face to face with two women. Neither were openly armed. From their minimal clothing, I assumed they'd either come from someone's bed or were heading there. I stunned the two of them. Being that they were wearing next to nothing and likely hadn't ever been stunned before, they went down cold.

If I was near sleeping quarters, I didn't want to chance stashing bodies in dark rooms that might be occupied. The women were going to have to sit this out in the hallway until they recovered. Which meant I needed to move even faster.

I saw the pattern that Jey had mentioned, the rooms and doorways becoming larger and farther apart. Then I came to a locked door, one that wasn't on the map and Jey hadn't mentioned it. Dammit. I didn't have time for this.

The lock wasn't one I recognized and my hurried efforts to work around it weren't successful. Time to resort to Jey's methods. Those tended to be loud and more heavy-handed than I preferred, but they worked.

I fished around in one of my seldom used pockets for a small charge and detonator. With the charge placed, I backed away, activated the connection, and then pushed the button. The explosion was loud. Holding my breath, I ran to the door and tried the access panel. Nothing worked. Cursing the charge and the door, I took a chance and tried to pry it open. That worked. Thank Geva.

A shot hit the back of my coat, just below the collar. Those always made my nerves sing. After taking a second to make sure I wasn't walking into a gun in the face on the other side of the door, I pulsed whoever was firing at me without bothering to see who it was. They were armed. That negated any guilt on my end.

A second shot hit my hand, making me lose my grip on the pulse pistol. It fell to the floor. My hand was bleeding profusely. Fucking hells. I pulled something else with my other hand, knowing by the weight that it wasn't a stunner, and fired. Another bullet hit my coat. I tried slamming my bloody hand on the door controls now that I was on the other side, but I'd damaged them too badly. The only thing the door was good for was cover while I swooped down to grab the pulse pistol. I upped the charge and pulsed the door and everything in the path beyond the opening. A groan beyond the slagged metal told me I'd stopped the bullets from that direction.

I glimpsed enough of my hand in my peripheral vision to know my fingers were all still attached. The tank would fix the rest whenever I got there. I just had to make sure that I was in better shape than Jey had been. He would still be sleeping and unable to help me.

My odds with my off hand weren't preferable, but Kess had to be at a disadvantage too. My one wounded hand was likely nothing compared to what Jey had done to him.

A man came running toward me, firing straight into my coat. That wouldn't have been a problem, but he was using high-powered rounds and they knocked me back with each shot. They also made it hard to breathe. Just as he paused long enough to take aim at my head, I pulsed him. And the wall behind him. And the wall behind that. Dammit, I'd not adjusted the wave and now the thing was empty until it recharged. But I didn't plan to be there that long. I was just putting the pistol away and pulling something else when Kess showed up.

He didn't appear wounded at all. Fuck.

Geva save us all if he'd found a tank of his own. He had to have.

"I take it my work on your pal didn't sink some sense into you?" He drew a gun and aimed it at my head.

"Apparently not." I was seriously starting to wish I'd waited for Jey to wake up.

"Duly noted." He pulled the trigger.

I went with my first reaction, which was to Jump. I spilled onto the floor in the tank room, smashing my face on the tank platform on my way down. Blood gushed from my nose. All in all though, it was preferable to a bullet in the head.

I cursed my lost progress with entering Kess's fortress. He'd surely take more precautions now that he knew we were both after him.

After cleaning myself up, I settled into the chair beside Jey's bed, feeling safer there even though he was asleep. I tried to get some work done on my link, but instead of numbers and words on my eyelids, all I kept seeing was Kess's bullet racing toward my head.

EIGHTEEN

Rhaine

Time passed in a succession of drugged oblivion and occasional hours of consciousness while Doctor Strovel ran his weekly tests. Where Weeda was blunt in her manner, Strovel kept everything tightly under wraps behind his flat face and yellow eyes. Every word was economically wielded. Emotions might have been something he didn't possess. I liked him.

His hair had thinned to the point that his head was mostly bare beneath short, swirled wisps. As he studied his datapad, one hand reached up to smooth them down, one of the few tells he had.

"Still no good?" I asked in Verian, an effort I was willing to make in light of how he was helping me.

Doctor Strovel might have had a halfway decent facility, likely the best on Veria Minor, but that didn't mean he was happy to have me taking up one of his beds indefinitely. Not that he said so, but that was the general feeling I got from his staff. I'd been trying to refresh myself with the language to keep me occupied during my scant waking hours. Listening to the staff talking to other patients in beds nearby was helpful. Not that my bed was exactly near any of them. I'd been positioned off to one end of the long room, a curtain hanging between me and the rest of the patients. Maybe they all had curtains too. I couldn't tell for sure, but their shadows seemed too dark for that to be the case.

"Not good enough. Another week." He measured out a dose from a bottle and injected it into the tube that ran into my arm. Sounds grew muffled and my eyelids heavy. "Good night, Rhaine."

Each time I woke, I wondered how long I'd been there and whether Isnar had come to see me. But I never asked. The answer to either question wouldn't have made me feel better regardless of what it was.

"Good morning, Rhaine." Doctor Strovel swooshed around the side of the curtain as though he had some indication of my waking state. Maybe he did. I wasn't familiar with most of the equipment here. Artorian machines were more familiar than anything else since I'd spent time in their care now and then. The healing tank I'd kept hidden below the surface on Frique had saved me from having to become too familiar with medical facilities on any world.

"Is it?" I asked, not sure it was morning or good or of much of anything else due to an unfamiliar level of groggy thought. "Why do I feel different this time?"

"Different sedation in light of events. Good news or bad news?" He held his arms across his chest with no datapad or scanner in sight.

"Neither is anything I want to hear, I'm guessing, so get on with it." I tried for bravado, but it probably fell as flat as I felt. I wished Isnar was there. The heavy haze was making it hard to comprehend what was going on.

Strovel nodded, his wisps bobbing back and forth on his head. "Your injuries were not healing correctly. However, the surgery was a success."

Surgery. I wanted to scream, to rip Strovel to bits with my fingernails, but my body was too heavy to move. "Does he know?"

"Your Ishlan? Yes. He was not...pleased with the necessity of the procedure."

"I bet not."

Strovel shrugged his thin shoulders, jostling his sky blue tunic. "The procedure was two weeks ago. We can both hope he has found peace with what must be by now."

"We can hope." I threw the canned response back at him. The only bright side I could find was that I wasn't drooling. Though, maybe I was and was just too numb to realize it yet.

"You'll be under observation for a few more days while awake. Your Ishlan has been notified of your impending release."

"Thank you, Doctor Strovel."

He nodded and let the curtain fall as he left.

As my mind slowly cleared from the lengthy sedation, paranoia crept in. Putting my trust in strangers was not something I did. Yet, I had. I'd been here for however long, completely at their mercy, unknowing and unresponsive. They could have done anything to me.

Maybe they had. I wasn't one of them.

The curtain offered a sense of privacy for any curious staff member. Isnar wasn't here to keep them in line and I certainly wasn't up for it. Even as my head cleared, the state of my body informed me I'd been in this bed for a good long while.

That gave Isnar plenty of time to rethink his pledge to take me home no matter what condition I was in. If he was openly displeased by the surgery, I had a sinking feeling I was alone in my head for good. Without even a hint of the bond reciprocated, would it fade away? Did Artorians bond to people with no telepathic gifts? More importantly, did they stay with them? If I'd have had a datapad, I would have been madly researching, but all my fingers had was a thin blanket to worry between them.

I kept thinking of how amazing it had been to know him so clearly, to feel what he felt, even if only for a short while. He'd been so excited to have even that little bit of what he should have had effortlessly with someone of his own kind. I never should have taken him away from that woman he now refused to talk about, Sonia. But he'd been so eager to take the job I'd offered, and he'd been qualified for it, even though he had no idea what he was in for. I'd not exactly been honest with him. Ever, really.

If we'd had that level of bonded connection from the start, or could build from it now, I'd have no choice but to be honest with him and him with me, both of us in a state of utter empathy. But with that option taken away for good, what did we have left? Not much of anything substantial. Familiarity, a common situation, his sense of obligation. Was that enough?

One of the staff came in, interrupting my dismal thoughts, to begin disconnecting me from some of the equipment. "I hear you'll be leaving us soon," she said in a manner that required no response.

I settled back on my pillow, staring at the ceiling while she went about her work. When she left, I didn't feel any more myself, no more in control of the situation at hand.

Hands. I held them up. According to Weeda, as long as I had those, I could still work as a Seeker. But seeking peace of mind and body for myself felt impossible. Both were broken, useless in terms of everything important to me.

What was the point of it all now? Our sham of a joined couple was empty without the bond, relegating Isnar to performing a thankless duty. Daniel had a chance at a peaceful future and an Artorian parent who could teach him about who he was. I had a small shop where desperate clients hesitantly came to the odd off-worlder for what comfort I could offer. I had even less to offer now. They'd gotten by without me. They didn't need me. No one did. I closed my eyes and wished the world away.

As it turned out, my Seeker training did provide something useful. The deep state of meditation that I'd used to sink into my link also worked without it. I could close myself off from the voices, the prodding hands. From the growling in my empty stomach and the nagging of my dry throat. Alone with my thoughts, I began to contemplate how to set Isnar free.

NINETEEN

Jey

I didn't know whether to berate Merkief for his foolish assumption of damage I'd possibly done or be overjoyed that he'd joined me in my quest to kill Kess. The choice was made for me when I got a notification that the shipment of supplies I'd purchased from a source I'd worked with many times before in the Rakon Nebula would no longer be doing business with me. That was quickly followed by an attempt on the life of Karin's faux Premier, eerily similar to the one Kazan had launched when she'd taken control of the moon early in my career, though thankfully, not as successful. Barely five minutes later, I was also hit with a request for backup from Gemmen. Three Cragtek ships docked at the port over Rok had all been hit, their crews assassinated simultaneously.

Maybe Kess had been telling the truth about following the Council's orders unless we struck again. And Merkief had.

If I'd thought advising half the damned Narvan was a lot of work before, this was going to be a drain on every level. Was Merkief up for this new depth of challenge? From his scattered performance lately, I was beginning to question his abilities on multiple levels.

The whole business with Merkief and Marit ran through my mind again. He certainly had no qualms about challenging me. Albeit on his level, not outright. He was a more subtle man than I'd given him credit for and now I couldn't help but second-guess his motives for nearly everything.

I wondered if he'd done anything like this with Vayen, if it had contributed to Vayen's hesitancy to put his full trust in Merkief. Maybe he'd only sensed it. I hadn't. My anger flared again at both Merkief and Marit.

Fucking irresponsible on her part. I'd been doing all I could to be fair to the Artorian world, to not hold any bias against Karin, but now when I read her reports, I had to question if she was still working with Merkief. Were they plotting behind my back? Playing some sort of long game?

My fists clenched. I'd done my best to let it go, to not let his indiscretions come between us for the sake of the Narvan, but damn, it was hard. Vayen had kept him at a distance and it had nearly pushed Merkief away. I couldn't afford that. Not now. Not until we'd dealt with Kess. That was going to take both of us.

I dispatched a team from Jal to do a full sweep of the port over Rok, sent my condolences to Gemmen, and dispatched an additional security detail to Karin until Marit got things back in order there. I'd have to deal with finding a new source for the supplies later.

Fresh from a shower, Merkief popped his head into my room on the ship. "Is he hitting you too?"

"Yes."

"Guess we stirred that up, huh? Think the Council will do anything about him? They said he wasn't supposed to take any action against us."

"And he's not. Directly."

Merkief paused as that seemed to sink in. "You think he'll tell them what we did?"

"I would. Why not use every advantage?"

The Council summons I'd been dreading drove into my head. I envied Merkief for his control over the volume and intensity of everything in his mind, including the link. Even with years of practice now, I'd yet to be able to do buffer or shield my mind like both he and Vayen had implied was possible. Maybe that was a skill Jalvians could never attain.

"You too?" Merkief asked.

I nodded. "Might as well get this over with."

A rare flash of panic took hold on his face. "What happens to the Narvan without us? I mean, if they decide to demote us or worse."

"I'm hoping this is a warning. Advisors don't get demoted. They get killed."

I waited for him to get his shit together. I didn't want to face the Council with Merkief quaking beside me. Why couldn't he keep all this tucked in tight like Vayen had? The only time I'd seen that man outwardly concerned about anything, it had been about Kazan.

"You ready?"

Merkief nodded but seemed to be waiting for me to go first. This one time, I indulged him.

We arrived on Sere to find ourselves surrounded by an escort of grey-suits, the Council's drones. Their empty eyes always made me uneasy. Sometimes they acted as guards, like in our meeting with Kess and the Council. Other times, they were merely present, lingering, watching, acting as guides. They were the Council's eyes and mouthpieces when the cloaked bastards didn't feel like making a personal appearance.

They guided us to a meeting room where three cloaked Council members waited. The door closed behind us. The familiar sound of weapons being drawn behind us did nothing to soothe my nerves. I began to regret not popping a stim before our arrival. If I'd had a tighter focus, I would have felt better about my odds of getting out of the room alive.

"You have violated the peace agreement with Kess Atta," stated a male voice that harbored an Artorian lilt.

Vayen may have had enough of a stone face to shrug the accusation off, but I wasn't feeling that confident. Honesty seemed the safer course of action.

I glanced at Merkief. He'd buttoned himself up properly but he sure wasn't angling for lead on the system now. He returned my glance in full submission mode. Geva, I'd never wanted this shit.

"We did," I said.

"You admit your violation of our direct order?" asked a female voice with a thick accent I couldn't place.

"I do."

She turned to Merkief. "And you?"

"I do," he said more firmly than I expected.

"These actions cannot be overlooked. You will be punished. Kess Atta demands recompense for your actions against him," said the third figure, gliding forward.

Fuck. If we were going down, I was taking Kess with us. "Kess Atta has already collected his due. I don't suppose that was authorized either?"

The cloaked figures went still in what I hoped was a silent conference. Were they all telepathic? Maybe linked? Did they have their own technology? I had no idea.

"Can you provide details?" asked the woman.

I did. Merkief provided a few of his own. Kess had been very busy. How much had launching all those simultaneous attacks cost him? Holding Merchess meant credits probably weren't as much of an issue for him as they were for us. And with only two other small holdings, plenty of slave deals of his own, and Geva knew what else he was into, he had to be doing just fine. He didn't operate with other planetary heads. Kess ran his worlds. If he had demands to meet, it was his choice to play nice or not.

"We find no direct evidence of your claims," stated the woman.

Of course, they didn't. He'd been careful.

"You will be penalized for your actions against Kess Atta. As this is your first and hopefully only infraction of this agreement, you will complete two contracts of our choosing. There will be no compensation for this work. Is this understood?"

Merkief might be openly hurting for funds, but mine weren't endless. Not to mention the time involved in whatever they chose, and I had no doubt they'd make it hurt in every way possible.

We both agreed.

"So we play his game next time?" Merkief asked.

"Yes. Until the game is over."

Set on our plan, we headed to the contract office to take on whatever hell the disgruntled Council doled out for us.

We didn't do a lot of work outside of the Narvan on our own, but from the frequency that the Council had been sending us out lately, I began to wonder if they had other Kryon cleaning up messes in our home territory. Our punishment contracts had involved convincing a mining cooperative that their business needed to move to a Council-designated location and supply Council-designated processing facilities. They took a good deal of convincing. Merkief had done a surprisingly good job on the diplomacy side while I played bad guy, pulling in some of Cragtek's ships to steal shipments, run a couple of attacks in the middle of the night, and be a general pain in the ass.

Once that job was done, we found ourselves on Armin. We hadn't had cause to visit since we'd done a job with Kazan there early on in our time with her. Much like the job then, we'd been tasked with ending a feud between two competing business entities by whatever means necessary.

In an unexpected display of nostalgia, Merkief asked, "Do you want to stay on the station, like last time?"

"Let's drop by and then play it by ear. Who knows if we'll be welcome."

"Good point."

After scoping out the situation on Armin, we tried the jump point Kazan had long ago provided on the station orbiting Veria Prime. Vayen had mentioned on the one time we'd stayed her without her, that Kazan considered the station her home.

I was more than a little surprised when we stepped out of the void into Kazan's suite, both in that I'd remembered the point well enough and that it worked. Nothing had changed in the suite.

"How long did she have a hold on this place?" Merkief mused as he looked around.

"Maybe she set up automatic payments from one of her accounts. They probably don't know she's dead."

Merkief nodded. "I didn't think of that. We should probably notify someone and clear this place out. Not like we're going to need it beyond a day or two."

"Sure. Yeah." This one time, he was right. I didn't want Kazan's stuff lingering out here forgotten. I hadn't left any personal belongings here, but Vayen may have. Probably a stash of weapons or alcohol. I laughed to myself.

Seeing that Merkief wasn't making his way to either of their rooms, I did.

Vayen's was clean compared to the others he'd inhabited. For as meticulous as he had been in business deals, he let it all go when it came to his private spaces. I gathered up the few scattered clothing items. The two empty bottles, I put in the reclamation tube. The stash of weapons was in the closet right where I expected it to be. I put the clothes on top of the locked chest and carried it into the common room. Merkief gave the load an eye roll as I set it on the table.

I went to Kazan's door next and pressed my palm on the pad. The door opened to a room much like all her others, except this one had more personal belongings in it. The closet held clothing I couldn't imagine Kazan ever having worn, plain Verian clothes. There were a few things here in her usual grey and black, but everything else was in colors I'd never seen her wear. A pair of plas clogs like the Verians I'd seen on the station sporting, sat on the closet floor. A couple of books, the ancient fiber kind, sat on the table by the bed along with seven good-sized firestones arranged in a circle around a candle. I checked the drawers and everywhere else I could think of where she might have hidden anything important but came up empty.

Kazan's stash took two loads to move onto the table.

"Anything you want?" I asked.

Merkief barely gave it a cursory glance. "No. I'm going to catch a few hours of sleep and then work by link for a bit before we have to head out."

I nodded. That seemed like a logical course of action. Rather than follow suit, I Jumped the reclaimed belongings to my house on Jal and left them in the appropriate rooms to sort out later.

When I returned to the station, the common room was empty and Merkief's door was closed. I took a deep breath and opened the suite door to have a look at the rest of the station.

It wasn't even five minutes into my wandering that I gained a security tail. I figured I might as well make the nuisance useful.

Turning around to confront her, I asked, "Who would I see about canceling a hold on a suite?"

The Verian security agent's surprise was plain. She took in my armor, which I belatedly recalled Kazan going without during her visit here, though I was pretty sure Vayen had worn his.

"Do you have rules against wearing armor?" I asked.

Her lack of response to either question made me pause. "Do you not speak Trade?"

She nodded. "Mostly, yes. Sorry, it's been a long time since I've seen..."

"You don't get many Jalvian travelers out this way?"

"Not since the occupation."

"Oh, right. That." I hadn't considered that I might be seen as an enemy here. I should have sent Merkief. But after seeing hints at Kazan having a life here, I was curious.

"Maybe you can help me?" I tried again to sound non-threatening. "I worked for Anastassia Kazan. She has a suite here and we need to cancel it."

The little agent pulled a datapad out of her pocket and tapped in a command. She studied the screen.

"It looks like her name is flagged. If you'll come with me to the security office, maybe we can get answers together?"

"Sure." Verians were a frail and petite people. If she or six to eight others decided I was a direct threat, I felt pretty confident about taking them out with minimal effort.

I followed the agent to a lift and then up two levels. All the while, she glanced over her shoulder at me every couple of minutes. When we reached the security office, three other officers were waiting. One was a big mutt from the fringe by the look of his scars and artificial arm that was so mismatched that he didn't bother covering it with a sleeve. It didn't even have skin, instead appearing to be covered in some sort of flexible metal. I tried not to stare at it but I could see how he would be a valuable member of the team of otherwise small people.

"Do you recognize him, Barnes?" asked my escort.

The mutt shook his head. "Not on the wanted list."

"Not yet, anyway," muttered one of the Verian officers beside Barnes.

"He's here to do business for Anastassia Kazan. Do you know why that's a flagged name?" she asked the others.

One of Barnes's eyes lit up with a soft blue glow. It had looked normal until then but was clearly an interface of some kind. Most fringe jobs couldn't afford enhanced replacement parts. Either this one was well off or he'd gotten lucky.

"The commander has been notified of the situation. He'll be here shortly. You will wait," Barnes stated.

I took the offered chair in the main room of the security office. The Verian man took a spot at the desk. The other two stood between me and the door exchanging idle banter, likely in an effort to mask that they were preventing me from leaving.

When a bald dark-skinned human showed up, the others appeared relieved. Now, maybe, I could get some answers.

I stood and introduced myself. He returned the favor, not appearing as apprehensive as the security detail.

"You have the look of one of Anastassia's men," he said.

"I was, yes." Did her people have a polite term for death? She'd never mentioned it and I'd only ever heard her speak Trade in that regard so I stuck with that. "I'm sorry to let you know that she's dead. I've come for her things and to release the hold on her suite."

His face fell and he reached for the seat I'd vacated. I let him have it, remembering how much I'd needed one upon hearing that same news.

After a moment he composed himself. "Was it that other one? That guard of hers with the permanent glower?"

His description of Vayen made me chuckle. "He died with her.

They were together. I don't know how often she talked to you, or anyone here, but I walked in on enough arguments to attest to the fact that they were definitely in a relationship."

He cracked a smile. "That's good. I'm glad she found someone, at least for a little while. Do you know who killed her?"

He knew her well enough to leap to that conclusion so I figured I owed him the truth. "We do. We're working on taking care of him."

The commander nodded. "I'll pass the word along. Thank you for letting us know." He stood.

"If you don't mind, my partner and I would like to use her suite for a couple of days and then the hold can be canceled."

"All right," he said after giving me a stern look. "While you're with us, there are rules."

"We can behave. I promise."

"I would expect nothing less from Anastassia's men, but you won't mind if Mae sticks with you while you're out and about?"

Mae, the poor Verian woman who had brought me here looked less than thrilled with the assignment.

The commander raised his hand. "Not that I don't trust you, but Mae's presence by your side will put the other occupants at ease."

I shrugged. "As long as Mae can show me where to get a drink, I don't mind."

The commander gave Mae a pointed look and waved her to the exit. I followed her. The fringe-job leaned close as I passed by.

"Don't lay a hand on her."

I winked. "Not without an invitation first."

His scowl darkened. I left him to his glaring and caught up with Mae in two strides. Her short legs meant I had to walk slowly from there on out.

While I probably should have bailed on the drink plan and followed Merkief's example, I felt like I owed Kazan a drink in what had been her home for a portion of her life.

At the pace we were moving, this excursion was going to take awhile. I tried to think of something to talk about that would help pass the time.

"What do Verians do for fun?"

"Back home, I'd say pack a picnic or go for a walk in the woods. Here?" she shrugged. "There's a temple, a bar, and a few shops."

"I'd hope there's more to life than that."

"Sometimes I get together with friends to watch a vid. Most nights

I'm happy to sit back in my comfortable chair and read."

"Sounds relaxing." I couldn't remember the last time I'd read something other than a report or funding request.

"And you?"

"Fun?"

She nodded. Good Geva, talking seemed to make her walk even slower. I was going to grow old and die before I got that drink.

"I'm pretty sure I've forgotten what that is."

"Doesn't sound like much of a life then."

"You got me there."

She regarded me with a tentative smile.

"How long are you on watchdog duty?"

Mae consulted a projected display that popped up from a band she wore around her wrist. "Probably until you leave, but officially for two hours."

"All right then, how about a deal. You have two hours to remind me how to have fun. If you're successful, I'll return to my room and you'll never have to see me again. If not, I've got about nine hours to kill before I have to be elsewhere."

She paused for a moment before resuming at an even more hesitant pace. "I'm not sure what Jalvians do for entertainment. I was a kid when your people were here. I've only heard stories."

From the looks I was getting from the few Verians we passed in the corridor, I gathered they weren't complimentary stories.

"I couldn't tell you either," I admitted. "There was a war raging most of my childhood too.

She nodded thoughtfully. "Have you ever considered visiting a Seeker?"

"What's that?"

Mae pursed her lips. "A priest? But also much more. A healer? More like that. Sorry, the words don't translate neatly. They can go into your thoughts and bring peace to a troubled mind."

With the level of confidential information in my head, sharing my mind with anyone was a suicidal idea. Not to mention, I didn't like doing that. Verians and Artorians might be comfortable with sharing thoughts and memories, but that stuff set my teeth on edge. Using my link was as far as I was willing to venture into that territory.

"No thanks."

"Then let's start with a drink." She came to a stop and gestured toward an open doorway.

Familiar sounds beckoned me inside: glasses clanking, people talking, background music at a suitable level to cover conversations from anyone not in the immediate vicinity. Mae led the way to a tall table at the back of the room. She climbed up into the seat that was at a height suitable for me. Her feet dangled far from the ground.

"We could sit somewhere you'd be more comfortable," I said.

"You wouldn't fit at a table made for me."

"I suppose you're right." I waved a server over. "What are you having, Mae?"

She looked at me blankly. "I'm on duty."

"Your duty is to show me two hours of fun. So what are you drinking?"

With our drink orders placed, Mae looked me over with a more calculating eye than before, her gaze lingering on my armor. "I never understood Jalvians."

"Your peace-seeking ways have always been a conundrum for us too. They made you an easy target when we needed an alternate supply chain."

"Do you enjoy fighting?"

Her question caught me off guard. "Had you asked me that when I was a simple soldier, I would have said yes, but now, seeing the whole picture," I shook my head. "No, it's necessary sometimes, but not enjoyable."

That answer seemed to please her. "Do you have an Ishla? Wife? Or whatever you call it in your language?" she asked.

"In my position, there's not much time to develop anything long-term and it would be a weakness for others to exploit."

The server returned with our drinks. I took a quick sip of mine, finding it as weak as I anticipated it would be. "Might as well bring two more for me. Mae's going to nurse that one for at least an hour."

Mae chuckled. "You're right."

It was a long shot, but I figured I might as well ask. "Did you know her? Anastassia?" It felt wrong using her name, but everyone else here did.

"No. Sorry about your..."

"Boss." And much more, but giving voice to any of that would ruin my mood for the night.

"So we're supposed to be having fun. Do you play?" Mae pointed to a gameboard on the wall, far from any of the tables.

"Not unless you teach me."

Her smile turned genuine. "Come on then, bring your drink."

We spent the next hour throwing pointed metal projectiles at a board for points. She won the first two rounds. I won the last. Finished with my third drink, I signaled for another as we made our way back to the table.

"Tell me about your homeworld," I said.

If Kazan had lived here earlier in her life, she'd never talked about it, at least not with me. I recalled her hauling Vayen around with her the one time we were all here, maybe he'd known more. I wanted to know more too but now that seemed impossible.

"I'm actually from Veria Minor. We moved to Prime when I was in my late teens, but they're similar for the most part." She raised the glass she'd finally emptied to the server. "I'll tell you what, we'll trade. Something about my homeworld for yours."

"Sounds fair."

For all of Vayen's bashing of Verians over the years, I didn't see what he was complaining about. Mae seemed perfectly nice, especially now that she'd gotten over her initial unease. They were small but otherwise, just another race from another world. We spent the next hour trading stories of our homes. We weren't that much different really, not in the ways that mattered.

Mae stopped mid-sentence in her explanation of the Verian climate to hold out her wrist and launch the time display. She gave me a challenging stare. "Well? Did you have fun?"

"I haven't quite decided. Answer one more question."

She raised a single eyebrow, waiting.

"If Verians are so peace-loving, how do you explain your security position?"

Mae toyed with her empty glass, running her finger around the rim. "My parents weren't happy with my choice of occupation. They wanted me to stay home, to marry, to find a neat little job somewhere close by, have a few kids. But I wanted to see what was up here. I haven't quite made the leap to going beyond this station, but maybe someday I will. I think it's important to know more about other races, other worlds, so we can be more prepared, not so naive when the next bully comes along looking for an alternate supply source."

"Ouch, but yes. A wise call."

"Thank you." She hopped off her seat, landing squarely on both feet. "So?"

"Yes, I think I had fun."

She flashed a victorious smile while I paid our tab.

"I believe you still need to escort me back to my room."

"You are correct."

We walked slowly, but this time I didn't mind the pace. She talked about her childhood pet, a camping trip, and a prank she'd pulled on her little brother. I let her talk, enjoying the sound of her voice and the images of a much more carefree childhood than I'd ever had. Maybe Verians were on to something we were missing.

"This is you," she said, coming to a stop before a door that looked like all the others, distinguished only by a set of symbols on the wall above the palm-sized panel.

"Mae, you're off duty now, right?"

She nodded.

"So if you wanted to come in and maybe have one more drink you'd be free to do that of your own accord, right?"

She pondered the closed door. "You said your partner was here too."

"He's in his room. He won't bother us, besides he's not near as scary as I am."

Mae laughed. "All right. Just one. I have a shift in the morning."

"Me too." I opened the door and we went inside.

I headed for the little kitchen space to find a bottle of whatever Kazan had stashed there, likely some very aged bottles of red wine. I'd just reached into the cabinet when Mae's hand touched down on mine.

"You know what else might be enjoyable?" she asked.

"I have some ideas."

A blush crept up her neck and over her cheeks. "I bet you do."

I grabbed a bottle, closed the cabinet, and led Mae to my bedroom where I made sure to lock the door so we wouldn't be interrupted. Work would be there in the morning. I deserved a few more hours of fun.

TWENTY

Rhaine

A familiar voice cut through my sluggsh thoughts and the thick dark wall I'd erected to block out the world. Maybe it wasn't so much that his voice cut through, as hearing it made my heart race to a degree that I couldn't ignore the sensation. Despite my conviction to shut my body down until it stopped and several days of effort to see it through, those few jumbled words broke the concentration no one else had been able to touch. Damned feelings.

A heavy weight settled onto my bed. "Rhaine, what are you doing?"

Without opening my eyes, I knew he was shaking his head and sighing. It was in his soft voice. The one thing soft about him, and only on rare occasion.

"Are we back to the hunger strike? They're not going to let you go home until you eat."

Just leave me here, I thought at him, knowing he'd never hear me and unable to give voice to those same words. Whatever else was between us, he was on duty and there was no way he was going to let me wallow here until my body gave out.

I allowed my eyes to open. Once they'd cleared, I took in the man beside me. Concern was etched deeply onto his face. His hair had taken on a wild tousled appearance, too long to stand on end now but too short to pull back as he used to.

What I did not expect to see was Daniel on his lap, holding his hands out to me. He was so much bigger than I remembered. He let out a string of babble, and I caught a glimpse of white in his mouth.

"Teeth?" I heard myself whisper.

Isnar grinned as he looked from me to Daniel. "Six of them. Go gnaw on your mother for a few minutes while I find someone." He set Daniel free on the bed and ducked outside of the curtain.

A rush of conversation erupted on the other side of the cloth, most of it in Verian. I tried to follow along but Daniel grabbed my attention when he appeared to be attempting to stand with one foot on me and the other on the bed. I reached up to grab him and realized that I'd been reattached to most of the monitoring equipment. The tubes were still in my arms, making my grab for him awkward as I also tried to avoid ripping anything out. With him safely settled back on the bed, he played with the fingers on my unhindered arm.

"Om omomomy," he said, looking at me.

"If you say so."

He showed off his new teeth with a wide smile. The curls had vanished from his hair now that it had grown longer. The one thing that might have been from me, gone.

The woman who had been taking care of me more than the others rushed in and grabbed Daniel from me without a word. She ducked out. I heard her scolding Isnar in Verian, not that I picked up all the words, but I knew the tone well enough.

The ruckus faded and then the room resumed its normal sounds of activity, patients talking, someone snoring softly, one of the male attendants relaying instructions.

Staring at the spot where my son had been for a fleeting moment, I wondered where they all had gone and what was happening. It occurred to me that I was no longer sedated and the tubes in my arm were only there because of my self-inflicted shutdown. If I was awake and as healed as I was going to be, I wouldn't need them. With a shaky hand, I yanked the tubes from my arm and sat up.

A wave of dizziness hit me, but not like before, just weak, my body doing some scolding of its own for my lengthy stay in the bed. It took awhile to get my bearings and work up the nerve to get my feet on the floor. The cold tile was a shock to my bare feet, but it was good to feel something solid, something other than a blanket and a mattress. Using the bed, I slowly made my way to the curtain. With one hand on the footboard, I reached out and yanked the cloth aside.

The view was much as I'd pieced together from the glimpses and drugged recollections when they'd been pulled aside altogether to allow more of the staff at my bedside. One big difference, however, was the Artorian in the doorway who looked like he'd just won a large bet. He towered over Doctor Strovel and the female attendant beside him who was holding Daniel. Strovel's eyes seemed ready to pop out of his flat face.

"Not a step farther." The doctor held up a hand and shook his head.

The three of them rushed over. Isnar lifted me up and set me on the side of the bed before I could ask what was going on. My face must have done that for me.

Isnar shrugged. "*Vearta,*. I just happen to have more experience with your obstinate streak than they do."

"You knew I'd get up?" I couldn't believe I'd been played like that, but he did in fact have years of experience.

He leaned against the bed and wrapped one arm around me. "I hoped you would."

I rested my head against his shoulder. It felt good, solid, safe. "Can we go home?"

"We're leaving," Isnar announced.

Strovel's eyes bulged again. "She needs recovery, therapy, to be under observation now that she's fully awake."

"Doctor Weeda will have to assume those duties."

Isnar held out his other arm for Daniel. The attendant handed over the heavy load with a grateful smile.

"Does she require any medication?"

Doctor Strovel seemed to recover his composure. "I'll pass that information on to Doctor Weeda along with your Ishla's file."

"Thank you. I'll see that your efforts are properly compensated."

Compensation was always a priority with him, even though that wasn't how things were done here on Minor. It was his way, and as it had in the Narvan and from the smile on Strovel's face, it gained him favor here too.

Strovel spoke a few terse words to the attendant who then darted off and returned quickly with a wheeled chair. Isnar all but shouldered her aside to be the one to help me into it. He managed the assistance quite gracefully even single-handed. The question of how he planned to guide the chair was answered when he placed Daniel on my lap.

Daniel twisted around on his knees and wrapped his arms around my neck. "Om omomomy."

"What is he trying to say, and why is he saying anything already? The information—" I caught myself before I said too much about our past. "—we were given said he wouldn't start talking until he was a year old. I haven't been out that long, have I?"

"He seems to be taking after my genes. From the information I've found, he's normal."

"This is normal?" I pointed to the child now pulling himself up using my shoulders so he could stand on my lap and bend his knees like he was now contemplating how to jump. Hadn't he just been rolling around on the floor not long ago? Maybe months ago. I sighed, wondering how much I had missed while I was here.

"Yes. Your people just develop more slowly." He chuckled. "Mom or mommy, I think. That is the right word, isn't it?"

I nodded, wondering how many languages Daniel would be speaking by the time he grew up.

"But how does he know to call me that? I've been gone and he's so young."

"Because he's seen you every day."

I thought Isnar had lost his mind when he leapt up on the bed and reached up into the light fixture. With a quick flick of his wrist, he was back down on the floor with something small in his palm that he dropped into a pocket. He glanced at me with a mischievous smirk.

"What? You think I'd leave you here without knowing what was going on? I've been watching. Everything." He drilled that into the doctor.

With that, he grabbed the back of my chair and pushed me out of the long room. Once we were out in the hall, I cranked my head around. "What was that all about? Did he do something I need to know about?"

"No." His eyes were still glittering with no good. "Habit. Keeping the skills sharp. For dealing with suppliers at work," he added.

I nodded and turned back around. Holding my son, I reminded myself to enjoy this, whatever *this* was, while I had it. Habit, my ass. It was a way of life. No matter how much he put into Dugans, it wasn't Cragtek or the Narvan. Isnar wasn't going to be satisfied here for long.

The hum of the transport and Isnar's voice lulled me to sleep for most of the long ride home. Daniel babbled now and then, but it offered more of a comforting background noise than the piercing wail I'd come to expect from him.

Isnar shook my shoulder. "You good to walk inside?"

A quick evaluation of my lazy muscles prompted a hesitant, "Maybe."

"I'll be right back then. Stay there." He ducked out of the transport and was up into the house in no time.

I wondered if Daniel was still able to be contained in his cage of a bed or if Isnar had devised a new method of corralling him. There was so much I'd missed. Daniel was growing more quickly than I'd anticipated. I didn't know as I needed the additional challenge. Or maybe I should appreciate that he would be self-sufficient faster. With a strange pang, I came to the conclusion I'd been gone too long and missed too much. By the time Isnar returned, my emotions were running rampant and there was nothing I could say or do beyond wrapping my arms around his shoulders as he carried me inside. Clinging to him, we made our way up the stairs and into the bedroom. He paused in the doorway and turned me to face the room.

"You cleaned."

"You would have had a fit if you'd have seen it two days ago."

"Thank you."

"That bed I'd ordered finally came in. I swapped it for this one. It's longer."

I nodded, glad he'd made an effort to make himself more comfortable here.

Resting my forehead against his pleasantly warm neck I imagined that glorious tranquility he'd shared before I'd left. I'd never feel that again, not with him, not with anyone.

He sat on the edge of the bed but didn't let go. "You still up for that favor?"

While we lasted. "Yes."

"Good. I've put the mess Weeda launched into our residency paperwork to rest, but we will need to wait until the investigation into Jersen Dugan's disappearance has been resolved. I wouldn't want your reputation further tarnished by joining with me until I'm free and clear."

I sat up and pushed myself away. "Joining? Like legally, for real?"

He paused. "I thought that's what you..."

That's just what I wanted, to be legally tied to someone that I knew was going to leave. He could profess all he wanted, but our bond was no longer strong enough to provide an equitable trade-off for his ambition.

"Not joining." I grabbed his arm before he could slide out from under me. "Let's just go day by day, all right? We both know I suck at this." I forced a smile.

Isnar nodded, but there was a distance there that hadn't been a moment ago. "I'll let you be then. I need to contact Weeda anyway."

As he left, I sensed a wave of disappointment fading with his exit. It came from him. In my head. "Come back!"

He peered around the doorway.

"What did they do? If they removed the damaged section, how can I still feel you, even if it's only faintly?"

"Can you?" From the way his fingers grappled with the door-frame, I was surprised he didn't rip it off.

"Yes."

"I can feel you too. A little. I told them to take only what they had to and not a micron more."

"Why didn't they tell me?"

A wild lock of hair fell onto his forehead. He shoved it back. "You didn't give them a chance."

"I thought it was all gone." And did it matter? Was this little we had left enough? "I'm glad it's not."

"Me too," he said softly just before he turned around and went down the stairs.

I'd hurt his feelings and I could feel it. But that didn't change my mind about joining with him. Did that make me a horrible person? It probably did.

This wasn't the openness he wanted. He deserved someone better. Someone Artorian, who probably would have swooned if he mentioned joining with them. Me, the word made my skin crawl and my mind cramp up. Pretending for our cover was one thing, but to make that commitment honestly, for real, to mean it, brought a cold sweat to my flesh. Joining wasn't for me.

When I woke next, the space next to me was empty and untouched. I got up, used the bathroom, and went downstairs to find all the lights out. The clock confirmed it was one of the rare coincidings of darkness with the universal time. Moonlight lit a large form on the couch. He was sound asleep.

A large chair sat across from the couch, one far more Isnar's size than the one that had resided there previously. I crept into the kitchen, only to find he'd been busy there as well. The counters were all at a more comfortable height and the chairs at the table had thick wooden frames suitable to Isnar's weight and size.

After quietly grabbing a sleeve of crackers and protein spread from the kitchen, I made my way back up the stairs. Daniel was asleep in his cage bed, the walls standing taller than they had previously. Pushing the door open to the extra bedroom, I was surprised to find that the bed we'd had in our room wasn't there. I'd assumed he would have moved it there for future nights when we inevitably would be not speaking to one another. He was far more optimistic than me. No, I chided myself, he'd thought we would be joined, perhaps even happily so. His version of giving us another chance and mine were vastly different. I sighed. How were we going to make this work?

Weeda came by midday. Isnar brought her up and then hung back in the doorway. She went through her sanitizing routine, scowling at me, and an initial pass of her scanner before she spoke.

"You're incredibly fortunate."

I caught Isnar's gaze in the hopes of repairing some of the damage from the night before. "I am."

My effort gained a slight bob of his head.

"For now, everything is as good as it can be. You'll need to avoid straining yourself. While the area appears scarred over, as it were, you have to understand that you've been wounded. Come to terms with what you have and accept it." She turned to Isnar. "And whatever you did to cause that new damage, don't do it again."

He paled and dropped his gaze to the floor. His nod was barely perceptible, but the regret emanating from him was loud and clear.

TWENTY-ONE

Merkief

I loaded Jey's unconscious body into the tank and sank into the chair at the terminal. Kess had been busy, striking at us on all fronts for months. This time the Jalvian giant had taken the brunt of a pulse blast meant for me.

Even working together, we'd yet to take Kess out, but thank Geva, neither of us had ended up in as bad of a condition as Jey had been after his first attempt. It seemed like nowhere was safe anymore. I cursed Jey's submerged body for bringing Kess down on us, for breaking the Council's decree and whatever negligibly honorable deal Kess had prattled on about to Jey that first time.

One of my contacts on Syless sent an urgent message about damage to the aquifer that supplied most of the irrigation water to the test crops I had recently set up. Two months ago the water had been tainted with a compound that rotted all the vegetation. We'd just got the fields replanted and plants growing again, and now this.

I ran my hands over my face and formed a reply. Amid that task, The Artorian Premier demanded a personal meeting to explain my delay in funding his programs.

Jey wouldn't be awake for another couple of hours, but I had established a small force of my own guards. I Jumped to my office on Artor.

One of the three guards I'd personally chosen stood in my office. They were on an eight-hour rotation, similar to what Kazan used to use for us. The big difference was that I only expected eight hours out of each of them and then they switched out. No day-long shifts, no out of whack rotations that took a week to correct, and they all got regular sleep. Most of all, they seemed happy with the arrangement since they were only responsible for me when I was on Artor. I had a set on each of my worlds. This allowed them to have families, to live in their own homes, to have a life, for Geva's sake.

"Advisor." Narantha, the newest hire who had been given the position in place of a perpetually late predecessor, nodded my way.

"How's Artor looking today?" I asked as I walked to the door.

She dropped into step beside me. "Newsbots captured feed of two riots today. We suppressed the feed as per your instructions. The Premier is in a mood. Oh, and it's sunny, so that's nice."

I chuckled. "At least the weather is cooperating."

She flashed me a smile.

Narantha had a good record, nothing outstanding, nothing concerning. Not overly ambitious.

Kazan had hand-picked us based on our performance. Maybe that had worked out how she'd wanted it to, but I had no desire for over-achieving, attention-seekers vying for my favor or making a play for my position once they had enough experience. I planned to retire them out after two years. They were paid well, and at that point, they could live comfortably and I could rest easy. I silently thanked Kazan for showing me what not to do.

Narantha's long legs easily kept up with my pace, armor flowing out behind her as we walked. The sound of her footsteps disappeared under mine. When we reached the Premier's door, she paused with her hand on the pad.

"Not that I don't appreciate the easy job, but is there anything I can do for you during the times when I'm not directly on duty? It feels like I spend a lot of my shifts just waiting to see if you arrive."

At least I thought she hadn't seemed overly ambitious. Maybe I'd read her wrong in the interview. "No, you're doing fine as is."

"All right then." She opened the door and stepped inside first.

The Premier sat at his desk. He didn't stand and he didn't smile. "Advisor. Narantha." He nodded to each of us in turn.

I took the seat across from him. Narantha stood just over my left shoulder.

"I'm sure you've heard about the riots?" he asked.

"Briefly. The cause?"

"Unsafe working conditions. We promised to provide new safety equipment weeks ago. Somehow, one of them uncovered that the order was never even placed."

"Because we don't have funds to provide all new gear to every factory on the planet. I told you to pick the most in-need cities and we'd evaluate from there."

He shuffled through the four datapads on his desktop and pushed one at me.

I picked it up and glanced at the list. It went on for pages. "What is this? Every city on Artor?"

"You choose. You want to be a public figure? Here's how it works: you pick what you think is the most deserving, the most needed, the best option for your people. Ten percent will praise you and be grateful. The other ninety will drag your name through the mud because you didn't pick them."

Under Vayen and Kazan's reign, the Premier wouldn't have dared to be so disrespectful, but they weren't public knowledge. Jey and I had made the call to be just as public as Kess was. However, our holdings weren't unruly territories out in the Nebula. We weren't chosen by the people of the Narvan, not even in a mostly rigged election like majority of the higher public offices. We'd inserted ourselves into their lives with the good intention of transparency and accountability, but no one was thanking us for it. Though my conscience said it had been the right move, there were more and more days lately that I regretted that decision.

From how things had been going so far, the ten percent he'd mentioned seemed more like three in my case. I'd seen my face on the newsfeeds far too often and the number of times it had been accompanied by anything positive could be counted on one hand.

"The only way we're going to be able to finance this is by raising taxes," I said.

The Premier's lip curled. "I'd rather not."

"Neither would I, but if new equipment is what the people demand, we've got to give it to them."

"It's your funeral."

I shot to my feet, slamming my hands down on his desk. "It will be yours first. Would you like me to find a new Premier?"

He went still, keeping his gaze on the pile of datapads before him. "Apologies. I meant to say, would you like to make the announcement, or shall I?"

"You. Your approval rating is high enough to withstand the hit."

Everything I did to attempt to please my people only put me further in a negative light. Too much more of this and there would be an outright revolt, likely not only against me, but also anyone they saw as a supporter of my supposed tyranny. The whole damned government could crumble. That was not the legacy I'd been striving for.

"Understood," said the Premier, cautiously gesturing to the seat I'd abruptly vacated.

I sat back down. While he droned on with other matters that joined a few hundred others on the list I could do little about, my mind wandered to things I'd already set in motion. Things I could do, like making Kess's life miserable. Jey and I had been poking at his operations since he'd turned us in to the Council. If I didn't have Kess and the expensive chaos he caused to deal with, I could have outfitted half the factories on Artor with their new safety gear.

Using the resources of six full planets, Jey and I hoped we could keep hammering at Kess for another couple of months until his own resources started to run dry. Twelve and Thirteen weren't big and the settlements on both were few and far between. Merchess was his prize, but it was only one world and the ruling families would pitch an even bigger fit about any increase in tithes than Artor's citizens would. We just had to ride this out a little while longer. Once we took him down, we'd have Merchess and its credit flow back in our hands and then all would be well in the Narvan.

Our meeting wrapped up. Narantha opened the door and went into the hallway. She gave me the all-clear.

"Any other business?"

"I need to stop at the University to check on a few studies."

"The central jump point?"

Narantha was still getting used to the set of points I shared with my guards, but she'd only been on duty for a couple of weeks. I nodded.

She went first, notifying me through her link that it was safe to join her. It always annoyed me when Jey expected me to Jump first, like he didn't think I caught on that it was for the exact same reason I used Narantha. I wondered if Vayen had made Jey do that for him. I snorted. From the frequent Vayen references Jey made, I was beginning to wonder if our stone-faced counterpart had replaced Kazan as Jey's focus. If that was the case, he'd no doubt taken the fodder role without question.

I stepped out of the void into the center of the University. Narantha waited patiently. We took the stairs up one level to the soil sciences lab where I'd initiated several studies for supplements and improvements for Syless. While I waited for one of the lab assistants to bring me the latest results, Narantha stepped closer.

"I can't believe the Premier had the nerve to speak to you that way. It was very gracious of you to entertain his requests after that remark."

It had nothing to do with being gracious. The problem with the population would be there whether the Premier liked how I dealt with it or not. It was easier having him there, to deal with shit like this for me. Not gracious, necessary. Harming him or anything beyond giving him a little scare wouldn't get me anywhere. Even Vayen and Kazan had known that killing Primes and Premiers was a bad idea.

But I didn't at all mind hearing her thoughts on the matter given the nature of them. I needed a little positivity in my day.

"Thank you."

Narantha smiled. Again. I hadn't made anyone smile in so long that I found I'd been keeping count of hers.

She had a pointed chin and a high brow highlighted by her short, loosely curled hair. The Artorian military uniform fit her well, a fact I had noted during our interview. All my guards wore their home-world uniforms. I wanted them to fit in, to remember where they came from, and if they wanted, when they were done in my service, they could return to what they'd done before a rank or two higher, depending on how pleased I was with their performance. I had no intention of ruining their military or civilian careers like Kazan had done to us. They were guards, perhaps aides in some cases, but they didn't do contract work. They didn't know about Kryon or the High Council. They were just guards and they were safe.

The assistant returned with the samples I'd requested. He launched into an in-depth accounting of the study so far. Then he pointed the way to another lab tech who was overseeing an exper-iment I'd ordered on integrating a batch of rudimentary healing nanites into some of Moriek's livestock to combat two of the illnesses that were decimating their herds.

Once we'd finished there, my stomach was rumbling.

"Are you hungry?" I asked Narantha.

"Quite, actually. You wouldn't think seeing images of animal car-casses would inspire an appetite."

I laughed. "True, but one does need to eat."

"Shall we return to your office on Artor? I'll pick up something for us once I know you're safe there."

I had a sudden flashback to too many meals eaten in an office with Marit before Jey had ended that pleasant distraction. "No, not this time." I flashed her a jump point, wondering how she'd do with a brand new point with no warning.

If I'd caught her off guard, she did a good job of hiding it. "One moment then." It took her a few extra seconds but then she was gone.

After she'd cleared the location, I Jumped. "I'm impressed. You picked that up quickly."

She bobbed her head but kept her eyes on the passing foot traffic outside the empty storefront where we'd arrived. "Thank you, Advisor."

I unlocked the front door and let us out onto the sidewalk. After relocking the door, I headed down the walk, attempting to keep a little distance between me and the public. I didn't have to be in Narantha's head to feel the tension flowing off of her. She wasn't liking this public excursion one bit.

"On occasion, it's beneficial to be seen by the public, doing regular things, like eating," I explained.

"I'd prefer you did this on someone else's watch," she said tightly.

"Are you not feeling up to the job?"

It wasn't like I hadn't been out in public on my own before. Despite being in public figure advisor mode with my lighter-weight armor that closely mimicked the business overcoats worn by government officials, I was adequately armed. I also had eyeballs of my own to watch the rooftops, storefronts, traffic on the street and overhead, and was busy watching the local networks and evaluating the threat level of everyone passing nearby.

It was nice having someone other than Jey beside me at tense times like this. The company was more enjoyable, and the smile on my face for the sake of my public image wasn't quite as forced as usual.

Narantha's brows lowered. "I don't want to be the one that loses you."

She looked so sincere. I slid her into the three percent that I felt confident about genuinely liking me.

"Let's try here." Taking pity on her, I headed into the nearest restaurant instead of the one two blocks over that I knew served the fire-seared prantha that my taste buds craved.

Narantha ran in front of me, dashing inside a step before I could. Being outside of the routine locations that I used her services for, I'd forgotten to follow the instructions I'd set out for all of my guards. I stood outside the dark-tinted door, feeling her absence and too many eyes on me from both inside and out. My confidence vanished.

If Kess was monitoring public feeds, he could send one of his assassins after me. He had a whole fucking guild of them at his disposal.

Without waiting for Narantha's all clear, I hurried inside, cutting the number of observers in half. Breathing a little easier, I found myself under the disapproving gaze of my guard and the frantic one of the young man beside her.

"Advisor Ma'tep. We're honored to have you with us. We'll get a table for you right away. Please excuse me a moment while I prepare that for you."

From the speed at which he launched himself from his post, I wondered if he was about to piss himself. Not that I enjoyed making people uncomfortable, but this new level of deference was a pleasant benefit of my public image. It sure beat skulking around nameless in Kazan's service.

The quaking young man came back covered in a fine sheen of sweat. "Right this way."

Narantha motioned for me to go first so I followed our near-panicked guide into a quiet section of vacant tables toward the rear of the restaurant.

"I hope this will be suitable. Please choose any table you'd like."

I turned to my guard, indicating she should pick.

Narantha chose a table within view of the large tinted window, but not next to it, not at the center of the room, and within a few strides of an emergency exit. A solid choice given our options. I sat, forcing her to take the chair with the view of the rest of the occupants. If there was a threat from that direction, I would have to trust her to spot it. It was a test for both of us.

Once she was settled in her chair and the young man had scurried away, Narantha grimaced at her menu. "Please tell me you don't do this public eating thing often."

"A couple of times a month maybe. Rarely at the same place and never on a schedule, why?"

"That's reassuring, but look at these prices." She grimaced again. "I'm sorry. I don't mean to imply...it's just..." She seemed to shrink in on herself. "Soup. I can do the soup," she said under her breath.

"You don't like the food here? We can go elsewhere."

"And forever tarnish the reputation of this place? They wouldn't appreciate that at all," she laughed nervously. "This is fine. I'm not that hungry."

I set the menu down, giving her my full attention. "Narantha, I might not be able to finance new safety gear for all of Artor, but I can afford a meal for two. Get whatever you want and get dessert. I don't mind."

"You're sure?" she said after a moment.

I nodded, gesturing to her menu.

A slow smile lit on her face, spreading all the way to her eyes. She licked her lips and spent the next few minutes pouring over the options.

After our orders were taken by an only moderately stammering member of the waitstaff, I attempted to relax a little. However, Narantha's earlier comment kept nagging me.

"I like to think I pay you well enough to afford more than soup if it came down to buying your own meal."

Narantha went still. "You do." She squirmed in her seat. "It's just that I have a lot of loans to pay off. School and training aren't cheap. My parents were right in that awkward middle ground between too well off to allow me access to public funding and not well-off enough to help pay my way toward the career I wanted."

"You wanted to be a bodyguard?"

That at least gained me a snicker that seemed to put her a more at ease.

"No, but your pay is much better than the public service field I'd wanted to go into. I ended up defaulting to the military after my second year in training because I needed the credits to keep the bank off my back and the military provided housing. I couldn't take living with my parents another moment. Love them, but, you know?"

I didn't. I hadn't spoken to my family since taking the job with Kazan. They'd made their thoughts on my career choice quite clear. I wondered what they thought of me now as Advisor to our entire damned homeworld. Would that be impressive enough to get back into their good graces? It might, but all the angry words, the disappointment in my mother's eyes, and the bald disapproval on my father's face didn't encourage me to pursue the matter. Thinking of my parents stirred up the ugly severing of my relationship with Jarna, the woman I'd been going to propose a bond with until I'd had my unexpected interview with Kazan. I'd got caught up in the dream of credits beyond counting and the excitement of a top-secret position. My life as I'd known it had come to a crashing halt.

"I'm sorry, did I say something to make you angry?" she asked cautiously.

"No." I forced a smile and shoved the past back down into the shadows where it belonged. "I understand. I'll see what I can do about your outstanding balance."

"You don't have to do that," she said quickly. "Just don't get killed on my watch, all right? It would be hard to get another assignment if that were to happen. Then I'd have to slink back to live with my parents." Her eyes twinkled.

My sour mood vanished. "Right. I'll do my best to stay among the living. On your watch, anyway."

"I'd prefer you did that on everyone's watch, but I appreciate your effort all the same."

Just as I was truly beginning to enjoy myself and her company, a Council summons hit my link. Being on thin ice with them as we were, putting them off wasn't wise.

"I'm afraid I have to leave on urgent business."

She glanced around the empty room. "Right now?"

"I'm afraid so. Tell them to bill me and then take my dinner home and eat it later. It reheats well. I've done it enough times to know."

I stood and ran my hands over my coat, assuring myself that everything was in order out of habit. It wasn't like I was going to use any of it on Sere. That would surely be a mistake I'd not walk away from.

She started to get up but I motioned for her to sit. "Thank you for the meal then, I guess. It will be better than what I would have eaten on my own for sure."

I stood there with the summons pinging impatiently in my head, growing more annoyed by the second that the Council had interrupted this. Whatever this was, I wasn't sure, but I was enjoying it.

"Would you maybe want to try this again sometime? Maybe when you're not on duty?" I suggested.

She outright grinned. "I would, yes."

"I'll be in touch soon then." At least I hoped I would, assuming the Council didn't tie me up with some long, involved contract.

After making sure no one was looking my way, I Jumped to Sere.

A grey-suit escort was waiting for me. They brought me to the room where we'd been busted for going after Kess. Three cloaks were waiting again. Maybe the same three. But this time, Jey wasn't here with me.

Thank Geva I hadn't eaten. My stomach twisted into a knot.

"Advisor Ma'tep," said a female from under her cloak. "It would appear you have too much time on your hands."

"Hardly."

"Then how do you explain the agents you sent to disrupt operations in Ka'opul City on Merchess?"

Fuck. If they'd called me in, they knew I was guilty. The only way they'd know that is if Kess captured one of the team I'd sent and coerced the information out of them.

My nerves went on high alert. This meeting couldn't end well. Thank Geva Jey was safe on the ship and would eventually wake up there to find my hopefully still living body somewhere near the tank.

"Nothing to say on the matter?" asked one of the men.

Shaking my head, I braced myself for whatever punishment they were about to dole out.

One of the cloaks raised a hand. The door behind me opened. Six pairs of footsteps entered. Four Artorian men and two women, all bruised and battered, lined up between me and the Council members.

"Advisor Atta would like to return your people with his regards."

I waited for the catch. Regards, my ass.

"That seems overly kind of him."

"Quite gracious, indeed," said the female cloak. "I assure you that we didn't lay a hand on them."

My people would have been kept in quarantine here to minimize their exposure to the Council, to Sere, to how the known universe was truly run. And if Kess hadn't already gotten the truth out of them, the trepidation and contrition they exhibited upon seeing me confirmed our connection.

"You will need to transport them."

"I will. Thank you."

I waited for the threats, the punishment, some unpleasant decree that would make my life hell, but the cloaked Council members stood silently. Their utter lack of response made my trepidation skyrocket. Had the Council already exacted their punishment in some unknown way? Or had they, perhaps, by some slim Geva-blessed chance, accepted the hostile actions we'd taken against Kess as necessary for maintaining the Narvan?

Near hovering off the floor with nerves, I gave the Council a few more seconds to say something. But they didn't. Counting myself lucky as all nine hells, I grabbed the closest of the two beaten people in front of me and Jumped them to Artor where I'd hired them. When I returned moments later for the next two, the cloaks had left. After all six were safely back on Artor and fervent apologies for getting caught had been rendered, I Jumped to my home and went to bed with a massive headache from the three double jumps in quick succession.

When I woke, I wasn't any better. In fact, I felt far worse. Chilled to the bone, I huddled under my blankets and checked my link for updates.

A virus had hit several cities while I'd slept, and it was spreading fast. People were flocking to hospitals and clinics. Initial reports pinpointed the epicenter. Six bodies had been found there. As their identities flashed on my eyelids, the chills became unbearable. My teeth clacked together as I stared at the faces of the people Kess had returned to me. The people I'd brought back to my homeworld.

The people I'd touched.

TWENTY-TWO

Rhaine

It took a week and a day before Isnar returned to our bed and for the awkward and uncomfortable air between us to clear. He didn't speak of joining again, but his resentment over my rejection didn't need words.

I did my best to smooth things over, prodding him for a couple of cooking lessons, and spending time with him and Daniel after dinner instead of doing the research I wanted to be working on. Had we been back in the Narvan, I would have let him stew until he got over it, but here, we were stuck together in close confines and I didn't want to lose him.

Back in the Narvan, he never would have proposed a joining.

Glad to finally have his comforting weight and warmth in our bed, I didn't rush off in the mornings to my shop that held the quiet I craved. Instead, I lingered at home and cooked the scrambled eggs with hot spicy peppers that he'd shown me how to make. It was one of the few meals I had a fairly solid success rate with.

I took Daniel with me more often than not, offering Isnar more time to sink into his work. Work made him happy and distracted him from his innate urges at home. I asked him about work a lot, letting him talk as much as a man unused to spilling details about what he was doing, did. He was getting better at it, holding a conversation, sharing details, seeming to realize when he was unnecessarily censoring himself.

"I have to go," he said after he'd helped clean up the kitchen.

"I should too. I'll see you tonight."

"Do you want a ride?"

"I'll walk. It tires Daniel out a little."

We parted ways for the day, and I breathed a sigh of relief. I'd made it through another morning without screwing things up. Eventually, I hoped that this outside observation mode, the conscious effort of it all, would become normal. That I could become normal, that I could relax and enjoy this. But that hadn't happened yet.

My day started like most of the others since I'd returned to my regular shop schedule, rearranging things on the shelves, watering my plants, attempting to keep Daniel out of trouble, and the occasional client. Some booked ahead. Some just walked in.

The bells jangled. I looked up from the candles I'd been sorting after Daniel had unhelpfully rearranged them all during my last massage appointment. The person standing there took me aback.

"Roshonomen? What brings you here?" Sure, he was Verian and he had the right to a Seeker just like everyone else, but he was also Isnar's right-hand man. "Is everything all right?"

He swallowed audibly and glanced around the shop. "Your Ishlan is fine, if that's what you're asking."

"That's good to hear, but what about you?"

"I was wondering if we might talk? Me with you as a Seeker, if that would be acceptable?"

Curious, I nodded and waved him to the two chairs I used for that purpose. Daniel headed straight for the candles again. I sighed and let him have at it.

The single lit candle on the table between the two chairs offered a calming scent that helped soothe my aggravation over the loss of order in my shop.

Not knowing where this was going, I sat in relative patience and waited for him to start. He cleared his throat loudly and shifted around in his seat.

"I've heard you had questions as to when your Ishlan came to be involved with Dugans."

"I'll drag that out of him eventually. No need to make it easy for him."

Roshonomen chuckled. "You are a fitting pair."

He had no idea, but I laughed all the same.

"It was my fault and it's been weighing on me. I've come to make my confession."

A confession from this odd Verian piqued my interest. I settled in, tossing out the ritual words to get him started.

Seemingly more at ease now that we were in official Seeker session territory, his tongue loosened further. "You've no doubt gathered that I know what kind of man Isnar is."

I nodded.

"I'd been looking for someone to *take care* of Jersen."

It amused me to hear a Verian talk of such things. For a moment, nostalgia distracted me, thinking of low-level assassination contracts I'd taken in the past, especially at the start of my underworld career.

"Not a lot of that ilk here on Minor," I said.

"Not a one, actually. Or Prime, by the way. If there are, they're too well hidden to get business."

That was good to know, should either of us need an alternate source of income. Not that I guessed there was a lot of business to be had in any case.

"I couldn't take watching the staff suffer any longer. Jersen was getting so used to throwing his weight around that he was becoming impossible to work for. I did what I could to help the others, to talk him down, but he started gunning for me too."

I knew the type. Some people didn't understand that there were limits to how far one can threaten people before they turned on you. Part of me recoiled from Roshonomen turning on his boss, setting up the hit. It reminded me far too much of my first partner, Zsmed, and other betrayals over the years. But I liked this stocky little Verian. He was our kind, in as much as there could be in this sort of society.

"I was about to sink to putting word out with a few of the trade connections, but I didn't know who I could trust, which ones Jersen had in his pocket, you know?"

I nodded.

"Then this giant walks into Dugans with all the right energy rolling off him in waves."

"The wrong energy, you mean."

Roshonomen shrugged. "Right for what I needed."

And here I'd thought Isnar was doing a fine job of keeping Vayen under wraps. Maybe even the toned-down Isnar was dark to the average Verian.

"The two of them met in the office. Jersen always had me in on those sorts of meetings in case he needed anything or anyone taken care of. So I stood there by the door, watching Isnar sizing Jersen up in less than a minute while Jersen bragged about his status and wealth, his pull on the colony, and his network of other traders on Minor."

"That was foolish," I muttered.

Roshonomen gave me a calculating look. "You weren't always a Seeker, were you?"

I gave him my best mysterious Seeker smile, the one we were taught to use when a client tried to deflect a conversation onto us.

He shook his head and continued. "It was like I could see Isnar running the numbers, noting names, counting contacts. Jersen was too busy inflating himself to notice. I doubt he'd considered anyone a threat in years."

Getting comfortable was always a mistake in a position like that.

"Isnar asked to buy in. Jersen turned him down. He didn't want to share. But he offered Isnar a position, one like mine." He held up a hand. "Business was good, expanding. I guess Jersen got enough of the vibe to pick up on how Isnar could be utilized."

Isnar probably would have been fine with that, at least for a little while. It would have allowed him to use his skill-set and completely feel out the operation before making his move.

"Jersen asked me to give Isnar a tour."

"And you gave him your proposal instead." I'd never been good at waiting for confessions to wrap up. I usually had the situation pegged in a couple of minutes. Clients took so long to get to the end. Res had said this was one of the reasons I failed as an acolyte Seeker. There were many reasons.

Roshonomen nodded, not seeming to mind my slip in proper procedure.

"I'd talked to the staff about it, gotten their agreement that something had to be done to stop him from blackmailing most of us, keep his new influx of drugs off the streets, and the sketchy black market deals that were going to get us all busted. Something permanent. We all had to work together to make a story stick, to cover ourselves if we had any hope of undoing some of what Jersen had brought upon us."

"Working together is good." Tossing in a few platitudes now and then had always seemed like a good practice.

"We offered to work for no pay for a full season if he could..." Roshonomen's head dropped as though the weight of his guilt in Jersen's death sat directly on his shoulders.

"Eliminate Jersen," I supplied.

"Yes," he whispered.

"The entire staff of Dugans working for free for a season?" I began to run the numbers myself. Dugans employed a considerable sized staff, in the warehouse itself, delivery drivers, the port transport operators, and the office. A full quarter of no employee expenses would be an enticing sum.

"And he'd still have to buy in?"

He gave me that look again, the one that said Anastassia was slipping out.

"To make the deal official in the documentation, yes."

I nodded, reminding myself to shut up and let him talk.

"He had wanted to wait for a few weeks. He said he was only there to feel out a lead, not to make a move yet. But Jersen had to go. Too many family members of the staff had gone missing or been jailed." He grimaced. "And it was one thing when we held illegal substances over between traders, he made good profits off that, but when he wanted me to short the transfers and sell the offset locally, I'd had enough. I don't want my kids on any of that stuff. The illegal goods stay inside Dugans," he said adamantly.

His eyes went wide and he gave me a nervous once over. "You did say this was confidential, right?"

"Yes," I assured him. "I suppose Isnar should thank you for this confession. Now he doesn't have to make one."

"I'm sure he has plenty of other dealings that are in need of confessing if you're really in the mood to drag one out of him," he said with a good-natured smile.

I laughed. "I hope he's paying you well."

"Very." He sobered. "He didn't take the payment, Ishla. He doubled everyone's pay instead."

That sounded about right. An excuse to take out a man like Jersen was likely an enjoyable bonus for my dear Ishlan.

"But now investigators are asking questions. I thought I had our tracks covered, that Jersen's retirement and the legal buyout would protect us all, especially your Ishlan. I didn't mean to cause either of you harm."

"We'll figure it out. Isnar is good at that sort of thing."

His gaze dropped to the rug. "I pray this investigation is not why you refused his proposal."

"No," I assured him, "the investigation has nothing to do with our personal matter." While I was relieved that Isnar had someone to talk to here, someone he felt comfortable confiding in like he'd done with Jey and Merkief, I didn't welcome our personal issues coming back around to me.

"You need to work together, protect one another and keep your story straight," I said.

"Working together is good," he repeated my offhanded clichéd comment as though it were actual wisdom.

"Just so." I held up my hands in the proscribed pose, recited the blanket text of absolution, and stood. "I'm glad you came to see me, Roshonomen."

He got to his feet with a peaceful smile on his face. "I'm glad Isnar has you. Your balance keeps him from becoming like Jersen, I think."

That balance was called an Artorian bond. Vayen without a bond or ignoring it, could be far more callous and ambitious than local terror Jersen Dugan, but I wasn't about to ruin Roshonomen's delusion.

No matter what evil my Ishlan might enjoy, he did not harm his employees. He was no Jersen Dugan. I smiled, watching Roshonomen leave, wondering at the realization that Isnar and I had both found ways to turn our past lives into a positive here.

I had a sinking feeling that those investigating Jersen's death wouldn't see it that way.

TWENTY-THREE

Jey

Merkief floated in the tank for the second time in a day. When he'd contacted me for a Jump to the tank, it was only an image and three words. *Kess did this.*

He'd been unconscious by the time I got there. Artor was a mess, sick people everywhere. The virus had spread to Karin before someone had figured out what was going on and closed the ports. Thank Geva whatever Kess had cooked up only seemed to affect Artorians. Must be he didn't want his own people to hate him if he managed to take the Narvan.

Putting the Artorians in a desperate place was a wise move on his part. He knew as well as I did that their forces might not be on par with ours but they had the technology to make up for it. They'd kept the Jalvian forces at bay for half my life. A little part of me didn't mind seeing them suffer.

The ghost of the foul-tempered lug that used to stand beside me gave me a glare that made that thought flee my mind. The Narvan was united now. At least, it was supposed to be.

I looked at the smaller man who now occupied that place. He'd been cured after his first round in the tank, but then came in contact with the virus again. Recovery didn't offer immunity and all of Artor was in need of a major decontamination. The high fever this recipe of Kess's brought on, wreaked havoc on their internal organs. Whoever he'd had designed this had keyed it very specifically to their altered genetic makeup. What concerned me was that ours wasn't all that different. We shared the same base, were identical in all the broad strokes. I prayed it didn't mutate and become my direct problem too.

Did Kess have a cure? And if he did, would he bargain for it? I'd sent a report to the High Council, implicating Kess, but all I had was

Merkief's statement. The reply had been slow in coming and when it did arrive, contained only two words. Provide proof.

With people dying and Merkief down, I could either devote my energy and resources to saving the population or investigating Kess's involvement. Both wasn't an option.

I closed my eyes and sunk into my link, pouring over the news-feeds. The death toll had crossed the thousand mark on Artor and was over two hundred on Karin. It had only been two days and over a hundred thousand more were recorded sick. The number multiplied every hour.

Artor might be Merkief's problem, but the pleas of Karin's Premier were mine. I couldn't very well help one without the other, they were too closely intertwined. If I got Karin cleaned up, it would only take one wrong visitor, a freight worker, or a contaminated crate of supplies to set it all off again.

With a heavy sigh, I contacted the Jalvian Prime to begin mobilizing aid to both Artorian worlds.

❧

I'd just sunk into my bed, far from the virus mess, in the safety of the Jalvian house that had been Kazan's, when a Council summons hit me. My first reaction was to reach for my stim tin, but I stilled my hand before I opened it. I really did need to sleep in the very near future. Vayen might have existed on a steady diet of stims during his time as advisor, but Kazan's more cautious intake was my goal.

The one bright side of arriving on Sere was that my escort consisted of only one unarmed grey-suited drone. The room to which he delivered me was also not the same as before. Two cloaks stood waiting, one short, the other taller and broader than me.

"Advisor Te," said the short one with a strange trilling voice that I couldn't clearly distinguish as male or female. It spoke in broken Trade. "We are driven to ask for explore mission you make now."

The broad cloak stepped ahead of the other one. "There are two systems just beyond your jump gate range that require your forces to bring into our fold."

"How far is *just* beyond?" A good number of my forces were tied up with aid efforts on Artor and Karin. The Council had to know that. They seemed to know most everything else.

"The coordinates will be made available at the contract office.

Can we count on your full cooperation?"

"This isn't the best time."

"Explore now," said the short one.

Possibly unwise, but I stared down the fluent cloak. "This doesn't sound like exploring."

"That is the classification given to the task you have been given to fulfill. Do we have your full cooperation?" he asked more forcefully this time.

"Yes." But only because no would have gotten me into a shit pile of trouble. But then inspiration hit. "But due to the health crisis in the Narvan, that you sanctioned, if you will recall, I will require some assurances."

I stood there for three very long minutes, heart pounding, wondering if I was going to get what I asked for or my ass handed to me.

"Speak," said the short one.

I wished it moved under its cloak to give me some indication of what it was or how it might react, but whatever it was remained still. The sleeves hung long and limp. Were there arms involved? Did it have feet? Most of the common races had the same general body form, likely seeded from the same stock and mutating from there, but whatever this was was new to me. Just how varied was the Council? I supposed if they were comprised of members from throughout the known universe, the odds that we all came from a remotely similar mold were quite slim. And in the grand scope of things, I hadn't traveled much.

I drew myself up and did my best Vayen impression. I'd been compliant up until now, but I was sure he'd been far less so than I was. They'd let him live. It was worth a try.

"You know damned well that Advisor Atta hasn't honored your deal any more than we have. This fight has gone far beyond simple jabs. The Narvan's people are dying in droves thanks to your little virus stunt, and don't try to tell me you had no part in it." Damn, that felt good to get off my chest.

The broad one reached out so fast I barely saw his arm move before I felt the impact on the side of my head. And it was the entire side, like a giant open palm of rock had just hit me.

"That doesn't sound like asking for assurances," he said.

"Blame!" shouted the short one.

"You don't like the playing field? Get off it," growled the broad man.

I wished my ear would stop ringing. How in the hells had Vayen and Kazan dealt with their madness? "Is this all game to you? People are dying."

"Pawn. Do job."

"You should listen to it," said the broad one. "People are dying because your partner got sloppy. Rather than blaming us, perhaps you should do something about that?"

"I can't very well do much about anything here if you're demanding I go *explore* two new territories for you."

The giant gloved hand raised again. This time I'd been watching and had time to move enough to avoid the worst of it and brace for the rest. Fighting back seemed like a bad idea, but if he tried for a third hit, I would.

"If I do this for you, you're going to get me the cure for Kess's virus." It might have been their virus for all I knew, but I thought it wise not to push my luck. "And you'll keep him out of the Narvan while I'm occupied." Keeping him out for good would have been optimal, but again, pushing my luck.

"You'll get your cure when the job is done."

"Thousands more will die before that happens. Hundreds of thousands, depending on how far away these territories are."

"Blame that on your partner. His actions against Advisor Atta were exposed. He had to be punished. If he was wise, he would have killed those that not only got caught but also gave him up. Instead, he brought them home and let them go."

Instead, he'd been merciful. I sighed. Would I have made the wiser choice? I wanted to say yes, but my gut said no. What would Vayen have done? I'd stood beside him enough times to know the answer to that in mere seconds. He would have killed them. He'd had no patience for failure. If we were going to keep the Narvan, if we didn't want to hand it to Kess, we were both going to have to let mercy go. That was not a conversation I looked forward to having with Merkief—assuming he didn't keep falling victim to Kess's damned virus.

I tried to see their logic but failed. "You're not punishing Merkief, you're killing the people of the Narvan, the ones who provide the resources and technology you require from us."

"Big mouth pawn!"

The broad cloak stepped closer. "The Narvan is but one of many systems. You are one of many advisors. Earn your cure or let the Narvan be cleansed. Retain your position or hand it to another who is more more agreeable to our goals. The choice is yours, Advisor Te.

"It would seem I have a contract to fulfill then."

He nodded. The other one didn't move. It didn't speak either.

I left the room and went to the contract office to collect the details.

❧

I left two-thirds of my portion of the Jalvian fleet in the Narvan. They ran the usual patrols around the Narvan perimeter, with a high concentration focused on our border with the nebula. The rest were tasked with aid to Artor and Karin in whatever means either Premiere or Merkief requested.

I checked in with Merkief one last time before joining the fleet already en route. He sat on his bed on Kazan's ship. Now it was ours, I supposed, though it felt wrong to think of it that way.

Merkief looked up upon seeing me in the doorway. "I was thinking. How do you feel about cleaning out one of their rooms to turn into a workspace? One of us could use the existing office. That way we could both work from here more often."

It would be safer. But the thought of disturbing either of their rooms made me uneasy, like doing so would unleash some sort of curse or godly vengeance. We had enough bad luck already.

I knew Merkief had cleaned out Vayen's things from his places. He'd probably cleaned out Kazan's too. I hadn't checked. I realized I hadn't been to his houses since we'd split them. We'd always met here, or our Kryon quarters, or on site-neutral territory. He'd mock me if I tried to explain my reasons against his suggestion. Instead, I skirted the issue.

"You can take the office if you want. I don't mind working from my room." Or any of the other rooms. I'd ended up in both of theirs on occasion, hoping for inspiration, looking for hints of where either of them had banked their credits, contact lists, or anything else that might be helpful. Nothing much was. Maybe it was just comforting. I supposed that helped too on some level.

He gave me a hard once over. "They're gone. You've got to let them go."

"Are you talking about their stuff or their vendetta with Kess?"

He scowled, and for a second I thought he was going to go off on me, but he kept whatever it was to himself.

"I like their stuff where it is," I said. "But as to Kess, you need to back off."

He did explode then. "Back off? You were the one pushing to take him out! You started this. Play the game until it's over? Remember that?"

"And look where that's got us. The hospitals on Artor and Karin are overflowing. I've got your people filling my med bays on the aid ships, for Geva's sake. I think you've done enough, don't you?"

Merkief was off the bed and in my face with impressive speed. He gave me a hard shove. "You don't think I regret this whole nightmare enough already? What the hells would you have done?"

"Sent people I trusted could keep their mouths shut." I shoved him back. How dare he attack me when he was the reason for this mess?

"You getting caught handed Kess a free pass with the Council, got him in closer, and pushed us out of favor. Your people are dying because you were sloppy and the Council doesn't give a shit about the death toll. They sanctioned all of this. Now I have to go make up for your mistake by taking on a couple of new territories to buy us the cure from the Council."

His nostrils flared, cluing me in to the punch about to fly. I caught his fist before it connected and drove him back two steps. My patience snapped.

"If you haven't got it through your head yet, this is all on you. I'm trying to fix it, so if you come at me one more time, I will put you in the tank while I reconsider our partnership. Got it?"

"On me?" His face darkened and his eyes narrowed. "Going after Kess was all you."

"And I should have kept it that way." I gave him a sharp jab in the chest.

Fire leapt in his dark eyes. His fists clenched and his jaw went tight. I needed to back off before my anger got the best of me and ended our partnership right there and then.

"If you have anything personal you'd like to attend to before I leave and dump most of my tedious duties in your lap, you've got about five hours."

He faltered. "You're leaving?"

"I'll be working from the fleet for the most part. Though I'll likely Jump back to take care of a few things that need to be done in person."

"And you're handing the majority of the Narvan duties to me."

"Not by choice, but yes."

Merkief nodded, appearing very composed all of a sudden. He

actually almost smiled.

The way he was acting now made me reconsider my plan. By handing him this opportunity, was I playing into whatever long game he had going to take the Narvan solo? Could I trust him to hand over my half when I got back? My gut convinced me to reconsider how much of a workload I could juggle while personally supervising the Council's explorations.

"All right then," he said. "I'll be back here in five hours. You can compose your list of tasks while you wait."

"Oh can I now?" I drew up my own height, which had a couple of inches on him when I wanted it to. "How about you go do whoever put that flicker of a smile on your face and get your ass back here so I can go clean up your mess?"

He Jumped without another word. That was just as well given my inclination to pound on him until he needed the tank again. I hoped he was wise enough to take precautions against catching the virus a third time. If it came down to advising the full Narvan on top of appeasing the Council, I might as well take the headshot myself so Kess couldn't take credit. For now, I needed to keep Merkief beside me.

TWENTY-FOUR

Rhaine

The way Isnar lazily stroked my hair as I lay across his chest would have told me he was relaxed, but his elevated heartbeat gave him away. I enjoyed his warmth and fingers and waited for him to come out with it. He wasn't one for endearing conversation or much conversation at all for that matter, but it seemed he had something on his mind.

"Sta—" he caught himself and cleared his throat.

Oh hell, he was nervous. Was on another join-with-me-bent? While it amused me that I could so unnerve this man who could easily run an entire star system with an iron fist, the topic that brought him to that point did not.

"Are you all right here? With what we're doing, I mean?" he asked.

Well, this was a new lead-in. I figured I might as well see what he was about. "What exactly are we doing?"

"Living here together." His hand stilled and came to a rest on the back of my neck, atop the band I wore that signified our faux joining as per Artorian custom.

"Neither of us planned on being here, but it's not so awful. Is it?" he asked.

I laughed to myself. *Not so awful?* How had he managed to work out delicate negotiations back in the Narvan with tactics like this? But he had. Lots of them, without me around. I was the reason he stumbled over words and occasionally lost his shit.

The large body beside me stiffened as if waiting for a blow. I picked up my head and met his gaze in the morning light. "No, not so awful."

Lately, anyway. It seemed that we'd finally moved past the worst of it all. At least, I hoped so. We were both in relatively good health.

Daniel was on our sleep schedule now and getting to a more tolerable stage, and we both had jobs we enjoyed, given what was available to us here on Minor. This wasn't the life I'd wanted, but I did enjoy the company both in and out of bed. Most of the time.

He relaxed a degree or two, enough so that he sunk back onto his pillow and stared at the ceiling. I sighed inwardly. He wasn't done.

"I never thought I'd have this. A family. The little house. The job," he said.

He had though. I knew that because I'd been to his little house, and I'd met the woman he'd considered starting a family with. But he'd given that all up to come work for me.

If I'd learned anything in my time as a Seeker here, it was giving people the space they needed to talk. Half the time they solved their own problems without anything insightful from me. And if I knew Isnar at all, the last thing he was looking for from me was insight.

I nodded, not willing to commit myself to anything positive or negative on that particular matter. He'd mentioned family first. Was he getting at something with Daniel?

"You never considered having kids?" I left off the 'with Sonia' part that was on the sharp tip of my tongue. Embracing my training wasn't easy, especially with him. We had too much past between us.

He went silent, but the elevated pulse under my hand told me I'd picked the correct path.

"I never thought I'd like it. It was always in the back of my head, an obligation to carry on the family line. Chesser had made it clear that that particular duty would fall to me."

He didn't often speak of his brother. The two of them had been close in their own twisted way. Had it not been for Chesser, I would have never met his brother, or had a kid, or ever stepped foot on Artor. Had it not been for Chesser, I would have never done a lot of things. My life might have been very different. As usual, I both blessed and cursed his memory.

"Well, lucky for you, he took care of the family line end of things," I said.

I rested my chin in my hand, watching his jawline for any clues as to what he was thinking. Our minimal bonded connection was less than helpful at the moment. He'd probably muffled it so it wouldn't give him away.

"I know Daniel wasn't planned and that you weren't at a place in life to be ready to raise him. But what about here? Now?"

"Here and now, you're doing most of the work with Daniel. So, no, it's *not so awful*...as you put it."

His fingers traced the etched pattern on the band around my neck—the replacement for the joining gift Chesser had given me. That Isnar had given me when he'd been Vayen. That he'd made clear wasn't a gift of his own. But even with our connection muffled, I sensed that the metal band was heavy on his mind. Yet, he'd wisely not brought up the word *join* in any manner. Yet.

"And while I'm doing that, while we're prepared, and living in a safe place, would you consider doing it again? With me?"

I lost contact with my mouth and my hands. The room shrunk inward as his words repeated in my head, booming louder and louder. Have another kid? Was he fucking nuts?

The damned Artorians had one thing going for their genetics, they knew how to breed urges into their people. Undying, unswerving damned urges. Join with someone for life, and if you had the approval on your line, get busy pumping out kids.

Grasping for logic, I found a straw to work with. "Isn't one half-breed Artorian enough? Daniel will never be a full Artorian citizen. You wouldn't want to do that to another kid, would you?"

"We're not on Artor." He picked up his head to look at me. Really look at me, with one of his rare sincere, heartfelt gazes that made me melt inside. "None of us will likely ever set foot on Artor again, so what does any of that matter?"

Dammit, I didn't want to crush him, to shut him down like the first time when he'd brought up joining, but he had to understand.

"Your people might be all about carrying on their lines, but let me tell you, mine isn't that great. It could end and the known universe wouldn't care. In fact, it would probably celebrate. You've got Daniel. Isn't that enough?"

While he was formulating an answer, a calm one, by the time it was taking him because his usual terse replies took no time at all, I pulled away. With my feet on the floor, I reached for my clothes.

"I'm asking for one thing. One concession." He kept me locked in that dark gaze as he unfurled his large form from the bed.

Old me would have told him to find someone else to crawl into bed with. But the thought of him in anyone else's bed pissed me off. The fact that he was attempting to guilt me into this pissed me off even more. And to think I'd been annoyed about his attempts to get me to officially join with him. Now he wanted me to pop out a kid for him instead? No doubt he'd insist on the whole joining thing once the pregnancy took. In no way was I on board with any of that. But I needed room to come up with a valid argument, something that would override his Artorian urges. I needed time.

"I'll think about it." That was all the concession I was willing to give.

He nodded as his work face slipped into place, masking all hint of the vulnerability he'd shared with me. Our connection flipped from hope to barbed edges every few seconds, as though he were fighting for patience. That had never been a word I'd associated with Vayen. Isnar, a bit more so.

"I have to get to work," he said. "You good with Daniel today?"

It was my turn. I nodded.

By the time we both finished dressing, it was as though a wall had been erected again, like the last time I'd denied him what he'd asked for. I hoped we didn't have another long, silent agitation settling in between us. But he left without eating, without a goodbye, just walked out the door, got in the transport, and left, taking my sense of ease with him.

&

He hadn't slept in our bed in four days. As much as his nightly absence earlier in our time here had pleased me, now the bed felt empty. The mattress was too soft without his heavy body to take up every ounce of slack. The blankets were warm enough, but they didn't generate heat like he did. Being honest with myself, I missed him there for a lot of reasons that had nothing to do with the comfort of the mattress or the temperature of the room.

I hadn't said anything to indicate he wasn't welcome in our bedroom. I hadn't yelled, or even given him a half-assed dirty look. He simply came home from work, played with Daniel on my days, or handed him off to me on his days. He made dinner. We ate and traded small talk. Then he went up to play with Daniel for a bit before putting him to bed. That done, he went to his post on the couch and closed his eyes. I'd tried hanging out there with him the night before, watching the local vids for an hour, but my attempts to draw out further inane conversation were met with disinterested replies. He was here and yet not here at the same time.

If this was an effort at giving me space to give in to his request, it wasn't necessary. I had no intention of giving in. I had, however, come up with what I hoped were logical reasons to avoid more children.

When he put Daniel to bed and started for the stairs, I blocked his way. "Our bedroom is over there."

He came up short, which was a bit comical given his size and the amount of space he had to stop before plowing into me where I stood at the top of the landing. "You're done thinking already? I figured you'd need a few more days."

"Avoiding me isn't helping."

"I wasn't avoiding you."

I muzzled my urge to give him a dry stare before it caused trouble. "Can we at least go talk about this somewhere else so we don't wake Daniel?"

He nodded and went into our bedroom. I closed the door behind me. It was a step in the right direction. Now I just had to restrain myself to an even tone and keep my face on neutral. Thank goodness for those years of Seeker training.

Instead of sitting on the bed or the chair next to the wall, he stood there, studying me. "Your answer is no."

Hell yes, it was, but it seemed rather harsh to throw that at him. After all, he hadn't asked for anything from me in a very long time. Not a personal request like this, not since he'd pried Cragtek from me.

"I said I was thinking about it and I am." I sat on the end of the bed, hoping he'd follow my lead.

"So you need more time." He started for the door.

"So I'd like to talk to you. Sit."

He did, though he kept glancing at the closed door. I put my hand on his. That seemed to get his attention.

"You said we were prepared. What did you mean by that?"

"We have all the supplies. We're used to the sleepless nights, the feedings, changes, wailing."

I couldn't help but snicker. "Supplies, I'll give you, but the rest? Hardly a selling point. We're just finding our new normal, getting solid nights of sleep. I don't know about you, but I like feeling rested in the morning. I much prefer the babbling over constant crying. And I'm very much looking forward to an end to the changing."

"But we know how to do all that. We know we *can* do it."

"Knowing we can doesn't mean it's a good idea. Think about having to start over, but this time, also dealing with another kid who is getting more mobile by the day. Daniel gets into everything. Can we keep an eye on an infant and on Daniel? What about work for either of us? And right now Daniel has all of your attention. Do you think he'll like having to share?"

He stared at my hand on his before returning his gaze to me. "Wouldn't you like to do it right this time around? Have the kid and raise it from the start? No stasis, no worry about a child being used against you or holding you back?"

"*Do it right this time?* I hadn't planned on doing it at all the last time." My attempt at calm and neutral shattered. "We wouldn't have the option of stasis here. And yes, a second child would definitely hold me back. You too. Like I said, what about either of us working? Taking one kid with us is one thing, but Daniel is distracting enough. I wouldn't be able to hold my sessions if I had to care for a second child at the same time. You think Daniel makes it hard to focus at Dugans? Add a crying infant to that."

"So I'll take some time off."

Dammit, he wasn't listening. "You'd be miserable in a matter of days if you didn't have your time at Dugans. Do you really want to be cooped up here with one kid running around and another one demanding your attention at all hours?"

"So we'll hire someone."

"I don't want a stranger in our house."

He shrugged. "I'm sure I could convince Atalina to take on that duty. You know her and she takes care of Daniel half the time he's with me anyway."

"That woman keeps your entire office in line. You need her there."

He shrugged again. "I could promote someone to take her place. There are several options."

Did he think he had this all figured out without an ounce of input from me? He'd done more than enough of that already, and like hell if I was going to let him do it again. "Here's an option, you carry the baby if you want one so badly."

I hadn't realized how hopeful he'd been of a positive outcome until all hope vanished from his face. I'd crushed plenty of people in my time in Kryon and running the Narvan, but doing it now, to him, made me feel sick.

I wanted to tell him there was no chance I was ever going to be on board with his request, to never bring it up again if he knew what was good for him. But Rhaine wasn't that heartless.

The urge to tell him I needed more time to think about it, to smooth this over somehow, hit me hard. But that was lying to him, giving him false hope. That wouldn't be any more kind in the long run.

I let my barb hang in the air as I got undressed and crawled into bed. He sat there for a while, his back to me, not moving even after I turned out the lights. I tried to will myself to sleep, but the urge to apologize kept me awake. Just when I was about to give in no matter how much of a lie it might have been, he got up and left the bedroom.

My intention was to go to sleep and talk to him in the morning, but guilt kept me awake. After tossing and turning in our big empty bed for several hours, I got up and crept down the stairs. I'd expected to find him on the couch, either sleeping or glaring at the view outside, maybe getting some work done on a datapad if he was in a mindset for it. But the couch was empty. The blanket and pillow he used when sleeping there were still in the closet.

He wasn't in the kitchen. I quietly darted back up the stairs and cracked Daniel's door open. He wasn't in there either. The bathroom was empty as was the extra bedroom. Our house wasn't big enough to hide a giant Artorian anywhere else.

Though I hadn't heard the transport, I ran back down the stairs to check it anyway. It was still there. Where the hell had he gone?

He'd never mentioned having any places to go here, no private haunts like the list Merkief had divulged to me in the past. Other than Roshonomen and Atalina, he didn't seem to be close to anyone at work, and he didn't socialize with them after hours. I checked the terminal, but there weren't any outgoing calls. He was just gone.

At a loss, I sunk onto the couch and clutched my favorite pillow. My heart seemed firmly lodged in my throat, blocking any urge to scream, but the familiar shape brought me a small measure of comfort.

He might have been upset enough to leave me, but he wouldn't desert Daniel. When he'd left last time, Isnar had taken Daniel with him. He hadn't packed anything. He was coming back.

Before he did, I needed to figure out how to fix this, without giving in, because dammit, the last couple of months hadn't been awful at all, and if we were stuck here together, I wanted more of them.

TWENTY-FIVE

Merkief

My first official date with Narantha had gone well, even having been on a moment's notice thanks to Jey running off to do the Council's bidding. She didn't ask anything of me, no favors, no attempts to sway my opinions. We'd just talked. Having someone I could be comfortable around, relax with, was a huge relief. It reminded me of how things had been with Jarna before Kazan happened. It reminded me of normal, of the goals I'd once had.

With Jey off garnering the Council's favor, I was busier than ever, but I'd managed to carve out a few hours for Narantha and enough nerve to let her into my new house, a place I hadn't even allowed Jey to visit.

"This is nice," she said, running her hand over the back of the couch that sat in front of us. "A bit empty, maybe."

"I'm not here much and I like it this way. Less opportunity for jump points."

She held a long sweater in one hand and wore a pair of tan casual pants and a short-sleeved shirt that matched her unadorned pink lips. It was nice seeing her out of armor and a uniform. Ordinary.

"I can see the wisdom in that," she said, "but a home should be an extension of you, show off your personality."

"Maybe you'll have to give me some pointers on decorating."

Narantha laughed. "I'd love to, but I'm guessing you had something more interesting planned?"

"Not really." I pointed to the couch. "All of my days are so intensely planned already that I'd much rather spend a few hours here doing a lot of nothing. With you. If you don't mind?"

She gave me a smile that made my insides turn to liquid.

"I don't mind at all. Shall we sit?" Narantha sat in the middle of the couch, allowing me to pick a side.

I'd left my armor and weapons in the bedroom. It felt very good to sit next to someone without all that, someone I trusted. Narantha made me want to put work aside for a few hours without feeling guilty about it. Hells, she made me feel things I'd forgotten how to feel.

We talked for a couple of hours, not about the Narvan, threats, the virus, or the news, but about her parents, the job she'd wanted but never made it to, and what she'd envisioned for her future. Finally, she raised a hand and quirked an eyebrow.

"Enough about me already. I'm pretty sure you knew most of that already from my file, but I appreciate you letting me ramble anyway."

I shrugged. "Your file doesn't have your voice."

She grinned. "A woman might think you're just pouring on the charm to get into her head."

"Maybe." I reached out and took her hand. "Did you mean what you said about wanting a family? And about living somewhere small and safe where you could do the job you wanted from the comfort of home?"

She stared at my hand on hers, her gaze slowly rising to meet mine. "Well, yes. But...I mean..."

"I'd like that too," I blurted.

"With me?" she squeaked.

"I think so?" I let go of her and put my head in my hands. "Sorry, I'm not very good at this."

She touched my arm. "It's just too fast. You understand."

"Of course. I didn't mean right now, today." Good Geva, I was totally botching this.

Amusement danced in Narantha's eyes and tugged at her lips. "I think it might be best, if you would like to pursue this possibility, that you should hire a new guard."

"Maybe that would be wise. I wouldn't want to give the impression that my other guards might also be in the running."

"That wasn't quite what I was thinking, but yes, I believe I shall have to resign."

"That is unfortunate." But given that she was agreeable despite my utter awkwardness, I didn't at all mind having to hire someone new.

Her presence slipped into my mind along the natural path we'd established during her employment. Each mental caress brought a sense of rightness and ease I'd never had with Jarna.

We spent the next half an hour wrapped up in one another until we'd both worked up a suitable grin on our swollen lips.

I sat back on the couch, pulling her against me. "Before I officially accept that resignation, I have a few things I need to disclose and terms that must be agreed to."

Narantha stiffened. "What kind of terms?"

"The non-negotiable kind."

"You make this sound like a business relationship. That's not what I'm interested in," she said firmly.

"Me either." Far from business. Being with her, even near her made me feel recharged, hells, relaxed even. "But I need to know you're safe."

"Oh. Right, your position would easily lend itself to many courses of manipulation."

"Very much so. Showing any sort of attachment is a weakness I can't afford."

She pulled away to look at me. "So what are you saying?"

While I didn't want to scare her, I took safety very seriously and I wasn't willing to downplay or hide it. "Anything between us must be private. Don't talk to anyone about it. That means no mentioning it in passing, not on any form of social media, and especially not if anyone asks.

"It's not like I want attention over whatever this is or might become, but surely I can at least talk to my parents? And if I give up my position with you, I'd have to return to active duty. They're going to ask why I left."

"Then you come up with something. But don't use names and don't implicate me in any way."

Her jaw tightened and that made me edgy. She was pulling further away, I could feel it both in my head and physically. I reached out, but her unreciprocating posture stopped me short of making physical contact.

"Is all of that necessary? I mean, I get that you have enemies. You wouldn't need me otherwise, but surely it can't be all that bad."

"The threats on Artor aren't the whole of my concerns. Not on any of the worlds I advise, actually. I have bigger enemies than that. The kind that would bring down a virus on all Artorians."

Her eyes widened. "Do you mean what's out there now?"

"Exactly that."

"This is your fault?"

"No." I tried to keep the sharpness out of my voice but failed. "It's my enemy's fault." Layers of them actually, but that was more than she needed to know, at least for now.

Her grimace said that she didn't fully believe me. "Over two hundred thousand have died. Here. I don't even know the number on Karin."

"One hundred sixty thousand and three as of an hour ago. And thirty-six thousand on Moriek. Somehow, someone broke the quarantine protocols and got through."

Narantha slid off the couch. "I...need to go."

The accusation in her eyes burned far more than the conscience-eating guilt that had already been gnawing at me for my part in bringing the virus to Artor. "I'll plan on you keeping your position until you tell me otherwise," I managed to say calmly from the couch when what I wanted to do was jump up and block her exit and make her believe me.

She nodded, grabbed her sweater, and hurried out the door.

After the enjoyment of the previous hours, her absence left me feeling more hollow than ever. I started to understand the extreme focus Vayen had given the Narvan during Kazan's imprisonment. And I hadn't even bonded to Narantha. Not for real, but it sure felt like all my peace of mind had walked out the door with her.

TWENTY-SIX

Rhaine

A buzzing noise from the terminal grabbed my attention. The clock on the wall informed me it was early morning. I'd dozed off a couple of times on the couch, but every creak of the house had woken me with the hope that Isnar had reappeared.

He hadn't.

Hours on the couch and my worry over his absence had left me stiff, making getting to my feet an ungraceful lurch. I made it to the terminal just as the incoming call ended. Pushing my hair from my face and rubbing my hands over my eyes, I attempted to pull myself together.

My Seeker sessions were all booked online. We didn't get many calls, and certainly not this early. What if something had happened to Isnar? I sat down and pulled up the call log. A private call from Dugans. How the hell had he gotten there? It would have been a long-ass walk.

Now that I had a solid lead on him, my worry converted to anger. How dare he just walk out on me like that? What if something had come up with Daniel and I needed him? And what the hell had he been doing all night that he couldn't have come home or called me?

With a deep breath and the best semblance of my Seeker persona on my sleep-deprived face, I returned the call.

The man that answered was not the one I'd expected.

"Ishla Ka'turoc," said a relieved-looking Roshonomen. "Would it be possible that you might, perhaps, come here to...uhh...retrieve your Ishlan?"

Retrieve him? "Could you please clarify the situation?" I asked in my most calm Seeker voice, masking the sudden flare of anxiety surging through me.

"He's—"

A loud banging noise pulled his attention away. Roshonomen winced as one of the glass panels behind him shattered. I realized he was calling me from Atalina's desk right in front of Isnar's office.

"Dammit, Rosh. Where's that bottle?" yelled a slurred voice from inside.

So that's what he'd been doing all night.

"I'll be right there," I said.

My finger was on the button to end the call when Isnar's office door opened. The man who loomed in the doorway with narrowed eyes and a snarl on his lips wasn't Isnar. It was all Vayen.

In public. Here on Minor.

"You better not be calling her."

Oh shit, was that a knife in his hand?

"Get out of there. Now," I heard myself tell Roshonomen while the rest of my brain was scrambling for a way to cover up this situation without having to terminate the valuable man.

A blur in front of the vid told me he'd listened. If only I could have Jumped there and...done something to calm him down. I had no idea what. Likely seeing me would make him worse, but it wasn't as though I could send Merkief after his drunk ass this time.

"You're fired!" He bellowed after Roshonomen's fleeing form.

I glanced at the clock. Only half an hour before Atalina and the rest of the morning staff showed up. A fifteen-minute ride there didn't leave me much time to work. And dammit, I couldn't leave Daniel home alone. I slammed my hand down on the terminal, ending the call.

How could he be so fucking irresponsible? One minute he wanted to start a real family here and the next he was going to entirely blow our cover?

I took the stairs two at a time and burst into Daniel's room with no time for a peaceful awakening. He woke as I hefted him out of his cage of a bed. His piercing cry let me know how grateful he was for the abrupt wake-up call. A better mother might have had calming words or an inclination to offer some reassuring touches, but I wasn't that mother. And his father was armed, drunk, pissed off, and in dire need of corralling before our lives were over here.

Desperation drove me to run out the front door with my coat and child in hand. We went straight to the neighbor's house, where

I pounded on the door. A disheveled and half-asleep woman I'd met once answered. I held out my still-sniffling son to her.

"I have an emergency and I have to go right now. Can you watch him for me? Please?"

"Yes, of course."

Her utter acquiescence may have been due to her sleepy state, but I didn't have time to worry about the intricacies of social niceties.

"I'll be back for him as soon as I can. Thank you." I gave her one of the little half bows I'd seen full Seeker's use when they were being formal with a client and then flat-out ran to our transport.

Inside and breathless, I input the address for the port and sat back to try and form a plan.

By the time I'd arrived at the lot nearest Dugans, I had my coat on and a craving for a stiff drink of my own. It was bad enough that Isnar still garnered suspicious looks over his possible involvement in Jersen Dugan's death, even though no evidence had ever come to light. No one needed to see him in this state, which would certainly confirm any doubts.

Two of the seven minutes remaining on my clock were spent sprinting to the door while trying not to trip over my flowing Seeker-like coat. Roshonomen was waiting there. He kept his hand on the door, preventing me from going inside without causing him physical harm. While I had little doubt I could accomplish that, he was a solid little Verian that might fight back, taking more valuable time. And Seekers didn't use violence. One of us needed to keep our fucking cover intact.

"What happened?" I hoped he'd give me the quick version.

"I came in a few hours ago to accept a late-night shipment. I expected to be alone, but he was here, wandering around the warehouse. Ishla, he had blood on his hands."

Well, wasn't that just great? Now I probably had a body, either dead or injured to hunt down too. "Was he drunk then or after?"

"Then and still." He glanced over his shoulder at the solid door as if he were worried Isnar would come barging through it. "He has knives. He was throwing them into the walls."

This was just getting better and better. I nodded, hoping we'd come to the end of the unfortunate revelations.

"He's quite good with them," Roshonomen remarked offhandedly. "Even as drunk as he is."

While I did appreciate my dear Ishlan's innate skills with a variety of weaponry, I kept that to myself and managed a non-committal mumble. "Is there anyone else here?"

"Not yet, but the first shift will be here any minute."

"And they come in here, at this door?"

He nodded.

In that case, I was going to need some help. "Can I trust you?"

He glanced over his shoulder again. "He's a much better boss than Jersen ever was, even after seeing him like this. It's not a huge surprise. He would have never had a chance of taking care of Jersen for us if he didn't have the darkness in him. So if you're asking if I can be quiet about this, then yes."

"Good. We're going to get him out the back. Preferably, before anyone else sees him."

"How?"

"I'll figure that out. You just show me to an isolated exit and keep anyone else away until I can take care of him."

Roshonomen punched a code into the panel beside the door. "I can see now why he joined with a Seeker. He clearly needs you for balance."

"Indeed." Wise little man, that one. Isnar owed him a raise.

With two minutes to go, Roshonomen led me on a high-speed course through the warehouse. "I'll do my best to keep the staff occupied near the entryway, but I can only give you a few minutes without raising suspicion. I'll unlock the furthermost loading door. The lights are on standby back there unless turned on manually. We don't use that bay much."

"Thank you."

I left Roshonomen to his part of the plan and steeled myself for totally winging mine.

It was quiet inside the office area, but the lights shown down brightly, indicating there had been someone active there recently. Something slammed into what sounded like the wall in Isnar's office. At least whatever damage was happening wasn't out here. Though, there were drops of blood on the floor leading from the warehouse to his office. My heart leapt to see they were red. So not Verian. Not that we were the only outsiders here, but it was still good news.

His door was open. I went in, stepping on something that crunched beneath my feet.

A blade whizzed past my shoulder and into the wall beside the door.

"Fucking hells. Watch it." Isnar shoved me aside two seconds later as if the knife was still in the air.

It had sunk deep into the wall next to a matching blade. Both were surrounded by holes where they had been thrown many times before. How many hours had he been at this? At least he was aiming for a wall and not a body, I supposed.

"Happy or sorry that you missed me?"

"You're not supposed to be here. Get out." He shoved me toward the door.

I got as far as raising my hand to slap some sense into his drunken ass before he grabbed my wrist in a vice-like grip. He might have been that angry or he was just too drunk to realize that he was actually hurting me. I didn't hide my grimace. When that didn't snap him back into bonded male mode, I punched him in the stomach.

The only indication that he noticed the impact was that he gripped my wrist even tighter and wrenched my arm, spinning me around so my back was to him. His alcohol-soaked breath wafted alongside my face.

He held me there, silent and still even as I struggled to get free. I wanted to think he wasn't doing anything more because he didn't want to hurt me, but he already was.

This was the Vayen lurking inside the calm and caring Isnar I'd come to enjoy spending time with. A very distilled Vayen, one that had been bottled up for almost a year now. Back in the Narvan, he would have had plenty of opportunities to exercise these urges so he could be his semi-charming self when we had the chance to be together outside of work. I didn't mind this side of him, I quite liked it actually—when it was called for, but he didn't belong on Minor. Here, other than his body count of one, he'd been doing a masterful job of being Isnar and keeping Vayen sealed away. Until I'd broken the dam.

I might not belong in his office, but neither of us belonged here on Minor. He needed an outlet, a constructive one, and for that matter, so did I.

"Roshonomen mentioned you have a mostly unused bay in the back?" I managed to say somewhat calmly through my clenched teeth.

The pressure on my wrist eased. "What?"

"Would you show it to me? I have an idea."

He stood, breathing beside my face until I wondered if I could get drunk off the fumes. He took too damn long. Female voices were coming toward us. Roshonomen's few extra minutes had expired.

I leaned back to rub my cheek against his. "Please. We need to lock up your office and go."

A pleasant warmth lit in my mind, indicating his drunken state had taken on a more workable direction.

"We could stay here." The slur was much more pronounced now that he was distracted from his anger.

I glanced around the mess that was his office. He'd thrown everything but the terminal off his desk. It all lay against one of the cracked windows. He'd overturned one of the chairs and knocked over the table between it and the couch. Shattered glass glittered on the floor under my feet, likely the remains of the first bottle of whatever he'd downed. His knives were still embedded in the wall.

"We can't. You broke one of the windows." With my free hand, I pointed to the tattered window covering beside the jagged remains of the broken panel.

"Oh."

"And your staff will walk in any second. Grab your knives and let's go."

"Say that again when we get home." He pulled me back against him but let go of my arm as he did so.

I wasn't the only one missing the old me.

He left my orbit long enough to wrench his blades from the ruined wall and tuck them away on his person. I was too busy figuring out what to tell Atalina and her gaggle of office workers to notice where he kept them.

"Come on." I wrapped my arm around his and tugged him toward the door.

He glanced around as if searching for something.

"If you're looking for whatever you were drinking, it's gone. But I'm sure there's more at home."

He nodded, wavering only slightly on his feet.

I let go of him so he could lock the door from the outside. Atalina was right there, her face full of questions.

"We're considering how to redecorate his office," I said. "I'm afraid we got a little careless while rearranging some furniture and cracked a couple of windows." I peered over the heads of the milling office workers who were all watching Isnar with great interest.

"He cut his hand on the glass. Sorry about the mess on the floor. I'm going to take him home to bandage that up and then we're going to spend the day shopping. I trust you can handle things here without him?"

Atalina looked to Isnar who was doing a lot more leaning on me than he had been only moments ago. His hands began to wander. We needed to keep moving before he got any more touchy-feely in front of everyone.

Roshonomen appeared just outside the office. I pulled Isnar along with me as I made my way through the milling workers toward the warehouse and my co-conspirator.

"Make sure that door stays locked and get some new windows on order," I said quietly.

He glanced to Isnar as though not sure he should take orders from me. His boss was busy staring off into the warehouse while doing very distracting things in my head.

I snapped my fingers, gaining Roshonomen's full attention. I also suddenly had Isnar's. His hands began to roam more aggressively. I grabbed them and attempted to curtail his amorous advances.

"Release a cleaning bot in there if you have one around. Otherwise, he can clean up his own damned mess when he sobers up."

Roshonomen gaped. "You speak like no Seeker I have known."

"My Ishlan may have rubbed off on me."

He nodded. "Balance is a precarious thing."

It was, and I was going to lose mine if we stood here much longer. "I'll take him out the back now. Thank you for your help, and I'm sure he didn't mean what he said to you."

"Enough talking." Isnar started for the front entrance with me firmly in his grasp.

I planted my feet. "We're going out the back. You were going to show me that unused bay."

"Later," he said.

"Now."

He muttered something in Artorian but reversed our direction. We headed into the shadows, leaving the chattering in the office far behind.

It was quiet in the back of the warehouse, no movers, no workers. We passed the last towering rack filled with several large boxes bearing writing I didn't recognize. The dim lighting allowed shadows to rule the large open space. A tall bay door filled one wall. The others were made of unadorned brown block. The floor was clean and other than a few cleaning supplies and what appeared to be a broken mover unit along the nearest wall, the space was empty.

"You could turn this bay into a gym. It would give us a place to work out, but you could tell your employees you put it in for them."

"Sure. How far away are you parked?"

His one-track mind had taken over. I'd have to revisit the suggestion once he sobered up.

He let us out the bay door and then locked it behind us. As he punched in the locking sequence I took a good look at his hand.

"Who or what did you punch?"

"It was a long walk here. The bark on those damned little trees is really rough, by the way."

"I'll keep that in mind." I took his arm again to keep him on task with walking to the transport. "I'm sorry I snapped at you earlier."

His steps halted and his body went rigid. Maybe I should have kept my apology for another day. He seemed to suddenly remember why he was here and how pissed he was.

"Go home." He dropped my arm and refused to take another step forward.

"Will you come with me if I promise to give your proposal more thought?"

"You're still going to say no."

He was right. I hated lying about something so important to him, but I couldn't have him roaming the port in this state.

"I can't promise I'll say yes, but I *will* think about it. Right now, you being out in the open like this, trashing your office, that's putting us all in danger. Let's go home. We can fight later, all right?"

His belligerent gaze dropped to his bloody knuckles and then he nodded. He maintained a distance between us as we walked to the transport and even once we got inside, which wasn't a simple thing in such a cramped space.

As though he'd suddenly sobered up enough for logical thought to resume, his gaze locked on to me. "Where's Daniel? Please tell me you didn't leave him home alone."

Did he really think I was that bad of a parent? It was his damned fault I'd had to leave Daniel anywhere at all. "He's with the neighbors. You were on the verge of exposing us, and I didn't have many child-care options."

He at least had the grace to drop the hostility and instead peer out the window in sullen silence the rest of the ride home. Once we arrived, Isnar went into the house.

"I'm going to bed," he announced in the doorway in a tone that made it clear I wasn't invited despite his pawing at me only twenty minutes before.

"I'll get Daniel," I said as the door closed behind him.

It was going to be a long day on no sleep with a hungover Isnar and a kid who was fueled up from a full night's rest. Thankfully, I had a couple of appointments to give me an excuse to leave for a while or the neighbors might have had front-row seats to a screaming match that would blow our cover for good.

TWENTY-SEVEN

Jey

I was tired. Exhausted didn't begin to cover it. Three months of dividing my time between overseeing the fleet while doing the Council's dirty work and attempting to keep my half the Narvan in my hands was nearly impossible. Merkief had hit the ground running with a focus near rivaling Vayen's in my absence. Not that he had the finesse or success that the irritable lug had been gifted with, but Merkief had done all right for himself. Even before I'd handed the Council-provided cure over, he'd had his half the Narvan in fairly good working order despite the health crisis. He'd done an adequate job with the tasks I'd hesitantly given him as well.

Though I'd not handed him near the workload I'd originally intended, I couldn't shake the feeling that he'd sunk his claws deeper into my worlds in my absence. I'd handed one vial to Marit on Karin, to begin manufacturing and distribution and a second one to Merkief for Artor and Moriek.

He'd nodded and half-smiled, taken the vial, welcomed me back with minimal words in a semi-friendly tone, and left. Now that I thought more about it, the smile might have been imagined. Whatever I'd missed had changed him, but not necessarily for the worse as far as advising went. Our partnership, however, remained strained.

While Merkief was suitably occupied and the Council was off our asses, I thought it an opportune time to pay Kess back for all the needless death he'd caused. Quietly and by myself. There would not be another plague in the Narvan on my account.

With my tasks as caught up for the day as they were going to get on a list that never ended, I took advantage of the late evening hour on Twelve and Jumped.

Kess's club hadn't changed since my last visit, except this time I knew what I was walking into. I didn't wear armor and had plenty of untraceable and unscannable weapons on me. If things when sideways again, I could jump without regrets.

The door warden was a different mutt than last time. The line was also shorter. He seemed bored, taking the standard entry fee credits on my disposable chip and waving me through with barely a glance at the throwaway ID I'd flashed. No one was tracing a credit bribe to me on this little excursion.

I walked in, bypassing the weapons claim, and blew past the automated scanners and the two guards at the inside door without any trouble. The club was full at this hour, music thumping, the conversation at a high and steady drone pierced by the occasional high-pitched laughter from a table near the bar occupied by three women wearing garishly bright clothing. I also bypassed the bar, surveying the staff as I wove my way through the gyrating crowd on the dance floor.

The smell of the place, the sounds, filled me with a sudden rush of dread. I'd almost died here thanks to Kess. Thanks to my lack of planning. That wasn't going to happen again.

A flood of rage washed away the dread. Anger wasn't in my favor. I needed a level head, to get my shit under control, keep my mind on the mission. A stim, that's what I needed. That would keep me tight and focused. I worked my way out of the jostling elbows to pull my tin from my pants pocket and toss one of the tiny pills into my mouth. Everyone was popping something here, hells, it probably helped me fit in.

Haxel and the ugly lug who had been at the door last time were on bouncer duty, eyes scanning the crowd for trouble. The sight of Paytel on the stairs made me smile. Her hair was bright pink tonight, spiked up in a row down the middle. I'd save her for last.

As I made my way to the nearest bored bouncer manning the entrance to the bathroom hallway, I contemplated how Kess would go about this. He'd had no qualms about releasing a fucking virus on an entire population. If this were my club, he likely would have walked in and started shooting everyone or maybe released something deadly into the air filtration unit. Thankfully, for the innocent patrons, I wasn't Kess. His staff, on the other hand, were fair game.

The music was loud enough that I didn't worry about anyone picking up the low and tight pulse blast to the bouncer's chest. Normally, I preferred bullets for this sort of work, but I didn't want to take a chance on Kess having a way to trace those to me. A pulse left nothing behind but devastation. I slid the man with the hollowed-out chest down to the floor and left him there. Now I was on the clock.

I hadn't had cause to do much work like this since the early days with Kazan. For some reason, she favored Vayen for this kind of thing. Or maybe he asked for it. But when he wasn't available or the need arose, I'd gotten my hands dirty too.

I hadn't exactly missed it. The one upside this time was that I knew Kess would be livid. The only thing that would really make this good in my gut would be to take out Kess, but after last time, I knew that was unlikely. At least not here. I'd have to settle for pretending each body was his.

The door lug was next, a quick knife to the throat from behind. He was a big man and not wanting to get tagged with his blood, I had to let him fall to his knees and keel over from there. That thud didn't need to be heard, it was felt. Heads swiveled in his direction. I'd already headed for Haxel.

"Hey," said a thick man who slid into my path. "I know you. You're that sorry ass who got the shit blown out of him."

Like I needed to be reminded of that utter failure?

I rammed a knife between his ribs and shouldered him up against the wall. Vividly remembering Kess, flanked by his staff while he blew out my shoulder, hip, and knee, I jabbed the man a few more times before letting him slide down into a limp bloody pile.

With the body count rising on the floor, it was just a matter of time before someone tripped over one of them.

Haxel, the oh so helpful soul, seemed to notice his pal was missing and started making his way over. I sunk back into the crowd and let him come, considering how to best take him out in a manner that would convey my wrath to Kess. But then Paytel seemed to notice something was wrong too. She signaled to someone on the second level. A second later, a bright beam of light joined the flashing of the colored beams cutting through the smoky haze. It swiveled overhead, panning over where I'd just been. A heartbeat later, it stopped on the last body I'd dropped on the floor.

I needed to move faster.

With the light slicing through the crowd, some of the patrons were starting to realize something was happening. Half of them stood in Haxel's way, looking around for the cause of the bright light. The other half skittered away from the beam. I moved with them.

Another of Kess's fringe rejects crawled out of the woodwork. By the way his eyes widened as he came rushing in my general direction, I gathered that he also recognized me. Kess's show had left a lasting impression.

Subtlety was a luxury I no longer had. The man got a pulse to the chest the moment I had a clear shot. I ran for Haxel now that the crowd was thinning. My cover would be gone in moments.

"You," was as far as Haxel got before my knife slashed across his throat. He stood there, holding the gaping wound as blood gushed between his fingers. I would have liked to slash him a few more times, but Paytel spotted me.

She let out a shrill whistle that carried over the thumping music. The bright white light circled the dance floor, searching.

Paytel needed silencing. I shoved my way through the clump of bodies lurking in the same shadow. They scattered, which left me plenty of room to move but also left me exposed to the light. I dodged into the shadow of the stairs beside her. If they got me on surveillance footage, I'd be screwed.

With my options limited, I let the rest of my pulse charge go on the underside of the stairway. The structure gave a great metal-wrenching scream before collapsing in a plume of plascrete and twisted metal framing. Paytel, bleeding from two cuts on her face, leapt out of the pile and over the railing. She let loose a flurry of bullets. One hit my shoulder, another hit my arm. Thankfully, the stim had kicked my adrenaline on high. The vibrating energy pulsing through my body distracted me from the pain.

Paytel ejected the clip and reached for another. I tackled her. She went down thrashing and clawing at my face.

"What's going on down there?" Kess yelled from above.

The music abruptly stopped, leaving a thumping echo in my ears. The beam of light danced through the heavy cloud of plascrete dust.

"Turn up the filters," Kess said. "Paytel, are you all right?"

I clamped a hand over her mouth. Her wide eyes regarded me with pure hate. It was mutual. I parted her armor and slid my knife between her ribs. She bucked and kicked but couldn't get out from under me. I jabbed the knife in four more times just to make sure she wouldn't be recovering. Then I decided not to take my chances. Kess had come back from worse. I couldn't chance any witnesses. Better to be sure than let her bleed out like I wanted to. Ramming the knife into the artery on her neck wasn't exactly satisfying but it did the job.

Her eyes took on an unfocused glaze. I let her go and slipped further into the rubble to Jump.

Kess had killed hundreds of thousands of people. I hoped the loss of a few of his key members would convey my feelings on the matter. If not, he had plenty more clubs I could hit.

TWENTY-EIGHT

Rhaine

The bruise around my wrist kept getting darker. I kept my sleeve pulled down during both therapy sessions and was grateful I didn't have any massages or adjustments lined up for the day. Using my hand for even typing my notes at the end of those sessions hurt to the point that I began to wonder if he'd broken something.

It wasn't often that I was grateful Daniel was walking on his own, because he managed to get into everything now, but at least I didn't have to carry him—as long as I wanted to walk slowly and stop to look at every rock and bug along the way. Today I wasn't in a hurry to face what waited for me. I locked the shop door and we headed for home.

The normally short walk took us an hour and a half. Daniel babbled in a mash-up of Verian from Atalina, Trade from me, and Artorian from Isnar. At least I followed two-thirds of his commentary. I smiled and nodded and held his hand when he wasn't busy filling his pockets with rocks. The bugs, I convinced him to leave behind.

No lights shone in the windows when we approached the house. The neighbors were out planting flowers in front of their home. I waved to them because that's what Isnar told me normal people did. They smiled and waved back. Social niceties accomplished, I made Daniel empty his pockets into the rock pile we'd started near the doorway.

"You can show your father later. He's not feeling well today."

That sounded like something a mother should say instead of the truth. Maybe I was finally getting the hang of this parenting thing.

We went inside. Isnar wasn't in sight. Thankful, I set Daniel on the couch with the vid on and with a bowl full of crackers and dried fruit, and then I went to the kitchen to down a few painkillers. They weren't something I'd had much need for when I'd had the tank at my disposal, but now I was grateful for their ready availability at the market. I hoped they and the icepack I put on my wrist would do the trick. This wasn't an injury I wanted to explain to Weeda.

I settled in next to Daniel, arm propped on my favorite pillow with the icepack and decided to allow my eyes to close for just a few minutes.

A hand on my shoulder jolted me back to wakefulness.

"Look, Daddy, Mommy hurt," Daniel said, brushing his chubby little fingers over my hand with the lightest touch.

I blinked the sleep from my bleary eyes and took in the kid surrounded by the half-eaten remains of the contents of the bowl I'd given him. He was looking over my shoulder. The one with a large hand on it.

Yawning, I prepared myself for the fight we were about to have. "Why don't you go upstairs and play until dinnertime?"

"He shouldn't be on the stairs by himself. I've told you that." Isnar scooped Daniel up and, with him perched on his shoulders, to Daniel's squealing delight, carried him up to his room.

He probably had told me that, but I was too tired to think clearly. My hand still hurt like hell. I pulled my sleeve back to examine the large, hand-sized bruise around my wrist. It was a lovely shade of violet. At least it wasn't overly swollen.

By the fact the ice pack was at room temperature, I gathered my nap had lasted a couple of hours. I turned the vid off and sunk back onto the couch. My eyes wanted to close again. Isnar's heavy footsteps descending the stairs convinced me to remain awake.

He settled into the newer chair that fit him and stared hard at my arm. "Where were you earlier?"

"I went to work. Why?"

"Did you sleep last night?"

"Not really, no." I rubbed one hand over my face and pushed the stray hairs out of my eyes. "I was worried about you. I didn't know where you were."

His face took on a pinched look. "Have you eaten anything?"

"I don't remember. Can we drop the fifty questions thing and just get to it? I'm tired and, if you're done up there, I want to go to bed."

He nodded and drew a deep breath, finally looking me in the eye. "Your wrist?"

"What about it?

"Are you all right?"

I held up the bruised and throbbing object of conversation. "Does it look all right to you?"

Damn, it felt good to let my passive Seeker persona slip for a few minutes. His hungover ass deserved a full-on tirade of my old self proportions.

When his gaze didn't waver, I gave my tongue free rein. "So which is it? Do you want a family here or do you want to slink back to the Narvan? Maybe you'd like to expose us all and save yourself from making the choice. We're all going to be dead if you don't keep your fucking head down."

He nodded.

"That's all you have to say? A fucking nod? Seriously?"

"I…" He stood and walked into the kitchen.

I wanted to scream at him, to throw something, maybe give him a few bruises of his own to mull over, but Daniel was upstairs playing quietly and I wanted to keep it that way. My blood raced as badly as if I'd taken a stim.

He returned just as I'd decided to get up and corner him in the kitchen, quietly if I could manage it. The plate and second ice pack in his hands threw me off. He put the plate bearing two slices of thick toasted bread topped with still warm and melting cheese on the table by my knees and then gingerly replaced the warm ice pack with the fresh one. He stood there staring at the large angry bruise like he could erase it if he concentrated hard enough.

The regret rolling off him was palpable. While I appreciated that, the sheer weight of it in such close proximity reminded me far too much of his constant hovering during our first months here.

Torn between shoving him away and consoling him with the reminder that I'd been going to slap him when he had grabbed my wrist, I stayed put and eyed the food he'd brought. My empty stomach prompted me to swallow what I'd been going to say and take a bite instead.

Rather than looming there, attempting to touch me, or even offering to get me anything else, all of which I fully expected him to do given his past behavior, he retreated to his chair. He sat there quietly while I ate, alternately gazing at his shoes and the stairway.

The clank when I set the empty plate down on the table seemed to echo through the house.

"I just…"

Two whole words this time around. I shook my head. "How much of last night do you remember?"

"Most of it. I think."

"Then I'm not going to tell you how to run your business, but you better apologize to your buddy Rosh and keep him damned close because he could sink us both. Got it?"

"Yes," he all but whispered.

"You're also redecorating your office so I suggest you spend the evening doing some shopping and keep Atalina out of there until you've fixed or covered up that wall. And for the love of all that's fucking holy, keep your damned knives put away in public places."

The lip curl could have been a snarl or a smirk, but the tone said restrained annoyance. "Anything else?"

"Watch your son. I'm going to bed. I have several day's worth of adjustments and massages to reschedule in the morning."

"I didn't mean to hurt—"

I held up my good hand and got up from the couch. "I know. Drunk and pissed off has never been a good combination for you. Goodnight."

He watched me head for the stairs and then got up. Instead of following me, he picked up the plate and the ice and walked into the kitchen. By the time I'd finished in the bathroom and crawled into bed, he'd crept up the stairs. Though his footsteps lingered outside our doorway for a moment, he retreated to Daniel's room.

Maybe we were both finally learning how to live with one another.

When I came downstairs in the morning, Daniel's hand in mine as per his father's instructions, Isnar sat at the terminal. He must have slept on the couch because he didn't appear tired.

"I took care of things," he announced as Daniel climbed into his lap.

"Good." I picked a couple of eggs out of the basket on the counter and washed them.

He cleared his throat. "I also ordered equipment to set up that workout area in the back bay."

His drunk memory was better than I anticipated. "How soon will it be ready?"

"A week or two. I'm putting a partial wall in to further separate the space from the rest of the warehouse, adding lighting and updating the climate system."

He might be a violent ass on occasion, but he did not go halfway on anything. "Perfect. Let me know when it's done. You're not the only one with energy and aggressions to burn." I cracked the eggs into a bowl. "Do you think Atalina would be up for some after-hours babysitting while we vent together?"

He shot to his feet so quickly that his chair tipped over backward. Daniel watched with wide eyes as Isnar put him down only to dart over and pick me up. Air vacated my lungs as he squeezed me so hard I couldn't speak.

"I'll make sure she's up for it."

I nodded, my cheek rubbing against his. Before he managed to suffocate me, I pushed against his shoulder enough to loosen his hold. If he was this happy about working out together, maybe he'd drop the request that brought us to this point in the first place. I dearly hoped so.

TWENTY-NINE

Merkief

When I arrived on Artor and saw that it was Narantha on duty, I swore under my breath. I'd been timing my visits there to when she was off.

"I switched shifts," she said in answer to my muttering.

"Why?" I started out the door.

She dodged in front of me. "Because I wanted to talk to you in person." She opened the door and nodded to me once she'd ascertained the negative threat level.

"The cure you distributed has eradicated the virus."

"I wish we'd gotten it sooner."

So many had died needlessly because Kess was an evil asshole. Because the Council wanted to punish me. And then Jey had the idiotic nerve to go hit Kess's staff at one of his clubs. Surely retaliation was coming. Would this ever be over? Would I have to go through every day of my life waiting to see what awful thing Kess came up with next? And if we didn't retaliate, would he let this feud go or would he take that as a sign of weakness and hit us harder?

"I'm impressed you found one that quickly."

"Don't be," I snapped.

Narantha stepped aside, putting space between us as we approached the Premiere's door. She went through the motions, opening the door, verifying the room was safe, waving me in, with tension in every movement.

"Sorry, I'm in a terrible mood today."

She nodded, shoulders easing a fraction as she stepped back to take up her post behind me.

The Premiere wasn't happy with the public's response to our tax hike. Now that my unadoring public was healthy again, they were back to protesting. Using the influx of tax profits, I'd been making progress with outfitting the manufacturers with the safety equipment they'd demanded. Still, no one was happy.

Our meeting dragged on until I felt like I was doing nothing more than beating my head against a wall. There were no agreeable answers. And I'd thought my mood was terrible before.

Narantha quietly accompanied me to the University and then to a public appearance that probably should have been put off to another day considering my mood, but I plowed forward anyway, knowing that postponing my speech would only draw more criticism.

I checked the time and noted that Narantha's shift was nearly finished. "We can talk after this is over. If you're still inclined?"

She nodded, most of her attention on the surrounding buildings and the restless crowd that had gathered to hear my public response to the accusations that I'd had the cure all along and had made the planetary leaders pay for it to save their people.

My opening went smoothly enough and I'd just gotten into the real reason for the tax increase when Narantha's shoulder hit me hard. A sharp pain erupted in my head. Screams filled the air.

My instant reaction was to call out to Jey. I realized I was sprawled out on the stone steps I'd been standing on a second ago. Narantha gripped my shoulders tightly, yelling at me. I couldn't make out what she was saying. And then Jey was there, shoving her aside. The last thing I saw was the tank and Jey's frantic face.

I came to in my bed on the ship. Jey sat beside me.

"Thanks."

He nodded. "That was too close. No more public speaking until we get whoever did this."

I sunk into my link, skimming over the reports and updates that had come in while I'd been out. News of my assassination filled the vid feeds. I watched a clip and went cold seeing the bullet hit my head. Narantha's panicked face made my throat clench.

I had to let her know I was all right. "I have to go."

Jey scowled. "I don't think that's wise."

"I'm just going to my house. Nothing public, I promise. I have to talk to someone."

"You can do that from here."

I could, but I very much wanted to see her.

"In person." But in person meant I'd need to take shower and get dressed.

As I started to compose a message for her, an update for my news story pinged for my attention. My assassin had been caught. Vid feed of Narantha hauling a squirming Artorian man toward a herd of enforcers brought me a little joy. If she'd caught the man, he couldn't have been sent by Kess. This was someone who wasn't linked.

"He's been apprehended. It wasn't Kess," I announced.

"I just saw that. Nice work by your guard. You owe her a raise."

"I'll let her know you offered."

He shook his head. "If this wasn't Kess, I feel better about the odds of it not happening again. Go on then, but for Geva's sake, be careful."

"I will."

I sent a message to Narantha, asking her to meet at my house on Artor then got cleaned up and went there to wait. She must have had a jump point nearby because a transport pulled up to the house barely ten minutes later.

She got out and ran to the door, pounding on it. The second I hit the open command, she burst through the scant opening. Upon spotting me, she rushed over and wrapped her arms around me. Despite all that had just happened, everything instantly seemed all right. I relaxed in her embrace, pulling her closer, basking in the smell and feel of her.

"I don't know how, but thank Geva your alive," she said next to my ear.

My throat thick, all I could do was nod. The next thing I knew, she was sobbing.

I held her until we'd both regained our composure and then steered her to the couch so we could sit. I prayed this talk went better than the last one.

"I thought—" she shook her head, sniffing.

"It was very close, but thankfully no. Thanks to you. Nice job catching the assassin."

She wiped her face on her sleeve and nodded. "I had help. The local security team shit themselves when they realized you'd been shot on their watch. They may have let the guy slip through the cracks initially, but they made quick work of closing in on him after the fact."

"I imagine it's all fine and good to want me dead, but no one wants Advisor Te to take Artor."

Her gaze met mine. "There was talk of that, yes. I didn't want you dead."

"Bad for your job prospects if I were," I said, hoping to steer her toward the heart of the conversation we needed to have.

Narantha grabbed my hand, clutching it to her chest. "That's not the reason."

Warmth rushed through me. "I'm glad to hear that."

Pulling her closer, I noted how she molded to me perfectly. While things were going well, I decided to get to the heart of it before I lost my nerve. "So what did you want to talk about this morning?"

"This," she said nuzzling against my neck.

"I like this very much."

"Me too." She sat back just enough to be able to look at me. "I had a long talk with my parents about my future." She squeezed my shoulder. "And no, I didn't imply that you were involved in any way. They want me to be happy and have a family. Most of all, they want me to quit my job, especially after today. My father has already called me twice to tell me so."

"I'd prefer you weren't hurt either."

"Well, there's one thing you all agree on."

Her nervous smile made my stomach twist into a tight knot.

"What is it?" I asked, steeling myself for her answer.

"If we do this, will it be like waiting in that office, never knowing when you'll show up?"

"No. Maybe a little, but you'll know where I am, at least generally. We have the links, and if we have a bond in place, you'll always know if I'm safe or not."

She turned away. "I won't be able to do anything about it."

"Actually, you will."

Her eyes lit up.

"If you feel anything off through our bond, you'll be able to contact Advisor Te using your link. He can help me like he did today. Think of the bond as an extra layer of security I don't currently have, something only you can do."

"Is that all I am for you? An added layer of security?"

"Certainly not." I opened my mind to her along the natural pathway we'd forged together, giving her access to the overwhelming flood of emotion she elicited that I tried very hard to control on the outside. Letting myself go wasn't something I was comfortable with.

Narantha smiled softly. Her warmth in my mind made me tingle all over, making me crave far more.

"You'll lock me away in this house," she said after a moment.

"You can pick whatever house you want, it doesn't have to be this one." I gestured at the general blandness of it all. "As you can see, I'm not all that attached. To the house, I mean. Not like I am to you."

She chuckled. "But I'd still be stuck there."

"Not exactly. It just needs to appear that you've dropped off the radar. Staying out of the public eye means no assassins are looking for you. No one is trying to use you for blackmail. No one is torturing you to punish me for whatever I've done to piss them off."

"Do people really do that?"

I considered again pointing out the virus Kess had recently unleashed, but since that had been the cause of her last exodus, I thought better of it. "Yes."

She was silent for a few minutes. With our connection still open, she had full access to how badly I wanted her safe and how much I wanted her to stay with me. But this was her choice to make.

"Would I meet him? Advisor Te? Actually meet him, I mean, beyond the knocking me out of the way to grab you sort of meeting."

"Yes. I would want him to be able to help you if anything should happen to me. Like today. Or if you needed help and I couldn't get to you."

She nodded. "Is he like they say he is on the vids?"

"Sometimes, but for the most part, no. Am I like the vids portray me?"

Narantha snickered. "No."

"There you go then."

"Are you sure you want to do this? I mean, you barely know me."

"I'm sure." I knew plenty, probably a lot more than she realized. Our conversations, the very sound of her voice, every expression, the slightest touch, they told me everything I needed to know. She filled a part of me that had been empty. Having her back now, feeling complete with her beside me, I wasn't sure I had the strength to be apart from her again if she turned me down. "The more important question is, are *you* sure?"

"I'd like a day to think about it first. If you don't mind?"

A day was more than reasonable, and yet far too long. I swallowed hard and threw a smile on my face. "Good Geva, no. Take whatever time you need."

"A day will do," she said confidently.

We spent a couple of hours that I really didn't have, sitting there together and talking. When she left this time, it was on much better terms. Even so, being away from her and uncertain of her answer, made me itch all over. This was sure to be the longest day ever.

Needing a distraction, I went to go have a talk with my assassin.

They'd placed him in a cell, under guard. There was plenty of deference upon my arrival, along with shocked faces upon seeing I had no visible injury.

I approached the desk of a uniformed enforcer who openly gaped at me. "Turn off any surveillance on that cell. I will talk to him alone."

"Yes, sir." The guard's fingers tapped on his terminal. "You can go on back. I'll recall the guards in that zone now."

He handed me a paper with the cell number and returned to tapping on his terminal.

I used my link to access the network and find a map so I didn't need to ask for a guide. I didn't particularly want any witnesses. My public image was bad enough already.

When a couple of enforcers passed me going the opposite direction, I gathered I was in the right area. Seconds later, shouts came from near my destination. I sprinted for the cell.

My assassin lay sprawled out on the floor, eyes reddened and bulging, and white foam dripping from his mouth. Even with the containment field active, I was close enough to do a probe. His chest fell and didn't rise again. Too late. I was too fucking late. I spun around, confronting the prisoners across the row and next to him.

"Who assisted him? What did you see?"

"Nothing. No one," said the man from the next cell.

"He pulled out a tooth. Looked like some kind of capsule inside," said the man across the hall.

Furious, I stormed back to the main office. "I want to know who searched him. Names. Now."

Not only had the enforcers allowed this assassin to get through security at the press conference, but they'd also done a shoddy job of processing the prisoner. Now I'd never know who sent him. His lack of a link said it wasn't Kess, but his level of commitment made me wonder. The local enforcers hadn't prevented him from taking a shot at me, they'd only caught the man with Narantha's help, and now they'd let him through processing with a means of suicide.

My gut told me that the ninety-seven percent of my own people against me had taken a step up from protests and riots. If that was true, I wasn't safe anywhere and everything was on the verge of falling apart. The urge to Jump to the ship, to hide there until the situation improved hit me hard. Teetering on the edge of the Jump, I thought of Narantha and her impending answer. A whisper of calm flowed through me, pushing the paranoia back enough for me to think. The situation would never improve if I hid myself away.

Those against me considered me a dictator and nothing I'd done to appease them had changed their minds. Perhaps it was time I took hold of the role they'd cast for me and attempted to steer my half of the Narvan from there.

I returned to my unadorned house where I strategically set about ending the careers of various levels of politicians and public servants. If they didn't want me alive to keep their world in order, I'd replace them with people who had a more vested interest in me.

It wasn't until I finally pulled out of my link and hauled my lonely ass to bed that I considered what Narantha might think of my actions. How would my new appointees manage the news feeds? What public speculation would fly? Would she know what I'd done and hate me for it? By the time I'd chewed down a second fingernail I realized what I was doing.

It was too late to turn back now. I shoved my hands firmly under the pillow and closed my eyes. I'd have her answer tomorrow.

THIRTY

Rhaine

Our twice a week private workout sessions were going splendidly. I met Isnar after work and Atalina took Daniel home with her and fed him dinner. We got to work out our frustrations on one another in a constructive manner, take a quick shower that often devolved into quick sex in the new bathroom he'd had put in at Dugans, and then pick up Daniel on our way home after locking up. We both seemed to be more relaxed. Our life here felt more natural, balanced as much as it could be. I didn't even make a single comment when he started openly drinking at home. He kept it to one or two and it wasn't an every night thing. Sometimes I joined him.

However, splendid ended the afternoon I showed up at Dugans for workout night when Atalina met me at the front door like usual, but then she shook her head. I'd been looking forward to a good sweat both on the mat and in the shower afterward, but this change to our several months of routine brought my mood to a crashing halt.

So much so that my Seeker demeanor slipped. "What do you mean no?"

"Sorry, he's in a meeting. He said he'd see you at home later."

"Go with Lina?" Daniel asked, holding his free hand out to her.

"What kind of meeting?" It had better be a damned important one. And the more I thought about it, I couldn't think of anything important enough at Dugans that would warrant blowing me off without any notice. He was definitely going to hear about this when he came home.

Atalina patted Daniel's head. "Not tonight, sweetling." She straightened her coat on her shoulders and took a step out into the lot before turning back to me. "Oh, I almost forgot. Could you please tell him that I was unable to find a lead on the gestation unit he asked for? Artorians and their odd technologies. Unnatural for a baby to be in one of those things." She shook her head. "Sweet of him to consider though, given your age and health."

"My age?" And just what had he told her about my health?

"Don't worry, dear." She smiled. "Nothing wrong with being a mature woman."

Just how old did she think I was? For that matter, how old did Isnar think I was? He might be eight years younger, but I wasn't even forty yet for fuck's sake. Atalina had to be in her mid to late fifties. Did I honestly look that old too?

For Daniel's benefit and our cover, I restrained my explosive response to a nod, hefted my son onto my hip, and marched back to our transport. Like hell was I sending it back for him. My sweet Ishlan could find his own fucking way home.

"Rhaine?" he called out with clear apprehension upon opening the door to the dark house.

I'd long since fed Daniel and put him to bed. Whatever important meeting Isnar had been in had gone quite late. I'd been waiting.

From where I stood only a few feet away in the darkness, I could smell alcohol on him. It was the certain scent of it that paused my plan for a second. I knew that smell. My faithful bodyguards had called it Hewr's piss. It was made on Artor and it wasn't available here. I tabled that question for later and let my attack fly. Literally.

He got a couple of hard hits in, but he'd been caught entirely off guard, had been drinking, and I was determined. It also helped that I knew his moves by heart after having been practicing together for a few months. I had him down on the floor in half a minute.

Rather than bask in my accomplishment, I spoke before he went for one of his knives. "Not bad for an old lady, wouldn't you say?"

"Rhaine?" he asked with more trepidation than before. "What are you doing?"

Shifting around on top of him, I located one of his knives and pressed it to his throat with zero remorse. "Answer the question."

"Who said you were old?"

"Apparently, you did." I sat back on his chest. "Atalina asked me to pass along that she was unable to find a supplier for the Artorian gestation unit you were looking for. Such a considerate request given my age and health."

I found his sharp intake of breath quite satisfying.

His response was a moment in coming. I waited, knife in hand, making sure it glinted in what little light the moon had to offer.

"That was her supposition to my request. I didn't say anything of the sort."

"You didn't deny it either." I gave him a heavy thwack in the chest before getting up. "Do you even know how old I am?"

He got to his feet just as quickly as he did when we sparred at the gym and backed away. "Can't say as it ever really mattered, so no."

"Care to guess?"

"Not while you're still armed." A soft thump indicated he'd reached a wall. The lights came on a second later. "You made it clear you didn't want to carry a baby, so I was seeking out other options. That's all."

So he hadn't given up. He'd merely been mulling over solutions to the problem. I shook my head and held the knife out to him. He made no move to take it so I set it on the table beside the couch. "When I said you could carry it yourself, a gestation unit was not what I meant."

"Why not? It's the perfect answer."

I had to agree with Atalina on this one. "It's unnatural."

He stood there blinking, looking at me like I must be blind to his perfect answer.

"No child of mine will ever come into being in such a cold and impersonal environment. There's no bonding, no attachment, no getting to know one another. Why do you think your mother didn't use a lab?"

"It's not a lab." He shook his head. "The units provide a whole environment, enrichment, learning, the whole works. We could set it up here, in the house, so we could all get attached."

That didn't sound so awful and he had that pathetically hopeful look about him again. I groaned inwardly. "Be that as it may, it doesn't provide a solution to my reservations beyond birth."

"I'm still working on that."

Great. It still wasn't going to happen. Rather than drive him out of the house like the last time a baby had come up, I went for a distraction. "Tell me about this meeting and why you smell like Artorian liquor."

His answer was too quick in coming and he did that momentary glance at the floor thing that always gave him away when he was lying to me. "I was exploring my own lead on a unit."

My old self would have stared him down and demanded the full answer but my knocking his ass on the floor had left me satisfied enough on that aggressive front for now. Instead, I took a my sized chair, settled into it, and delved into my Seeker self. "And how did that go?"

"He didn't have any and didn't think he could get one. The government keeps a strict inventory on them."

"And this person you were meeting with, he was also Artorian?"

"Yes, but I didn't know that before he hit the surface."

Again with the visual dip. I found it endearing that he could pull off a steely-eyed lie with anyone else, but with me, he had a tell.

Isnar strode over and took his seat across from me.

"Was that wise?" I asked.

"He didn't recognize me, if that's what you mean."

"You're sure?" For all I knew he could have been posing as a trader to feel out a lead on a contract. One that could take Isnar from me.

"I'm sure. And yes, that was before we shared a couple of drinks."

At least he was being careful. Mostly. I couldn't exactly blame him either. I was used to being on my own, different among the many, but he'd left his people behind for me and there wasn't another face similar to his for several colonies around us. It had to be comforting to talk to someone in his own language for a change. And to get word from home.

"I imagine you asked him about the Narvan?" My own heart raced with anticipation of any news.

"I did. He had nothing detailed to offer. Business as usual from what I could get out of him without seeming too focused on worlds that shouldn't matter to me."

The ache in his voice was clear enough. They mattered quite a lot. Guilt hit me harder than any of his punches had.

"Any luck getting meat imported from the Narvan?"

He shook his head and sighed. "Minor is too...minor. The big trade ships don't stop here. We get the ones who can't afford the jump gate fees. The route is too long between the stops to make proper containment profitable."

"That's too bad."

He'd stopped complaining about the meat here months after we'd arrived, but he had to be damned sick of fish by now. I had a feeling his lack of complaint was more because of the futility of it than any level of acceptance.

Isnar eyed the couch. "The ache in my back and shoulder inform me that you're pissed, but do you mind if we save the rest of this for tomorrow? It's been a long day."

It had, and the lack of news regarding the Narvan left me filled with disappointment. "Sure."

He went to the closet and pulled out the blanket and pillow. His fingers made quick work of the clasps on the overcoat he wore and his shoes. A minute later, he was under the blanket with his eyes closed.

From what I remembered, that particular potent drink had always mellowed him out pretty heavily. I'd limited myself to a couple of sips when he, Merkief, and Jey had often shared a bottle after long or messy contracts. I watched him for a moment, considering telling him to get up to our bedroom, but from the slow rise and fall of the blanket, I gathered he was well on his way to sleep already.

I turned off the light and felt my way up the stairs, nursing a couple of well-earned bruises of my own.

THIRTY-ONE

Merkief

Narantha's day had turned into two. The newsfeeds were buzzing, but it seemed my new appointees were doing a much more favorable job of managing the media in my favor than their predecessors. However, Narantha was a smart woman, and I didn't put it past her to read between the lines.

I'd barely eaten since we'd last talked and the jittery feeling and whispers in the back of my head that she was going to turn me down refused to abate. Jey, sitting across from me in the small office on the ship, slammed his hand down on the desk.

"What is up with you today?"

"I'm waiting for an answer on a bond proposal."

He gave me a blank look.

"Not the financing kind, dammit. I sort of proposed a joining with Narantha."

The blank look continued, but with a more baffled edge.

"The guard who was with me when I got shot. We've sort of been seeing each other for a few months."

"That's a lot of *sort of* for something as momentous as you lot make your bonds out to be."

"I know." I sat back and sighed. "She's probably trying to think of a safe way to turn me down."

He leaned back in the chair that had once held Kazan and then Vayen. He looked at home there. "So, the guard huh? Taking a page out of Kazan's book?"

"Not exactly. She has no knowledge of anything I'm involved in off of Artor. Beyond the advisor title, I mean."

"Are you going to tell her? Assuming she's agreeable to the

joining."

"I don't think so. I don't want her involved in any of this. The farther off the Council's radar I can keep her, the better."

"They'll know. Maybe not right away, but they will. Especially if you file the proper paperwork."

I hadn't thought that far ahead. He was right. Would Narantha agree to join if we couldn't go through the proper channels? Or if we did, what would the Council do about it? It wasn't like she was a security threat.

"We'll figure that out when I get her answer."

"I'll want to meet her."

I nodded. "I already warned her about that."

"Warned her?" He laughed. "I'll have you know, I do not make a habit of scaring women away."

"No, that's hardly your problem. Even the timid little Verian ones can't stay away."

Jey grinned. "I'll behave with yours though."

"You better."

With the proposal out in the open, my mind settled on the tasks ahead of us. We'd just about wrapped up the last of the day's issues when Jey stopped midsentence.

"Karin is under attack," he said.

"By who?" And then I got a ping too. "So is Moriek."

"Why hit two Artorian worlds?" Jey asked.

"Let's go find out who we're dealing with."

❧

The ships were unmarked and unknown.

"Retaliation for the territories you took for the Council?" I asked Jey from my bunker on Moriek.

"Or Kess found some allies. Notice how they know where to strike? Their attacks aren't random. They know the cities and where prime targets are."

"Good point. Either way, we can't let them send in ground troops."

"They won't get that far," Jey said with certainty. *"The Jalvian fleet is flanking them as we speak."*

If this was Kess, he'd know we'd pull in the big guns. I had a hard time believing he'd throw away all these ships. Unless they weren't his and he was maybe getting rid of a troublesome ally in a two-for-one type of deal.

While the Artorian forces that had launched from both Karin and Moriek did a fine job of making a sizable hole in the attacker's fleet, there were still too many missiles making it to Moriek's surface. Karin wasn't faring much better. We were going to have our hands full with clean up and recovery once this was over.

It was another hour of chaos before the Jalvian fleet vented the atmosphere of the last ship. With the worst part of it over, we sent salvage crews out to grab the wreckage so we could identify our attackers.

"Did you get your answer from Narantha yet?" Jey asked.

"No idea. That hasn't been a priority."

"I've got this. Go get your woman situation figured out so you can get your head back in the game tomorrow."

What I wanted to do was take a shower and sleep, but he was right. As much as I was dreading her answer at this point, I needed to know.

I Jumped back to my house on Artor and stood there in the middle of the common room debating whether hearing her refusal in person or at a distance would be less painful. A hollowness settled into my stomach.

Taking a chance that I might be catching her at a bad time, I reached out over our natural connection. *"I've been told I'm quite distracted while I await your answer."*

Narantha didn't respond.

She was likely in the middle of pretty much anything, it was the middle of the day on Artor, after all. I distracted myself from a hundred imagined ways she'd turn me down by taking a shower to pass the minutes.

I'd made it into bed and was staring at the ceiling, caught in a loop of knowing I should sleep but also waiting anxiously for the sound of her voice, when Narantha finally answered.

"Can I come see you?"

"Sure. I'm home."

"I'll be there in ten," she said quickly and then was gone.

I hauled myself out of bed, suddenly exhausted. At least she was going to let me have it in person. Did rejection require getting dressed? I didn't figure it did.

Wearing only the loose pants I'd planned to sleep in, I went to the couch to wait. True to her word, she was at my door in ten minutes. I didn't feel like getting up, so I accessed the controls through my link.

"Merkief?" she called out.

"I'm in here." I realized I hadn't turned the lights on either. The window coverings were all closed like I usually kept them for security reasons. Maybe I was legitimately more exhausted than I'd realized.

She approached cautiously and sat next to me, but on the edge of the cushion. "Sorry I didn't get back to you sooner," she said in an exhale of words.

I shrugged. "I did tell you to take however much time you needed."

Narantha started, seeming to take in my lack of actual clothing. "Oh, I'm so sorry, you're tired. You were probably dealing with that tragedy over Moriek and Karin."

"I was. Jey kicked me off the clean up so I could talk to you. Then I sat down. And now it's all catching up to me."

She reached out to fix my hair. I'd been running my fingers through it while I'd been waiting in an effort to stay awake.

"If you could put me out of my misery quickly, I'd appreciate it. I have a lot to do."

"Misery." She snorted, settling back onto the couch and resting her head on my shoulder. "You have no idea. My parents have been grilling me for two days straight."

"Can't say as I blame them."

"Good. Then maybe you'll agree to their terms so we can both get past the *misery* portion of this and move on to enjoying ourselves."

My heart leapt at the mention of enjoyment. "Terms? Moving on how exactly?"

She took my hand, threading her fingers through mine. "I told them I had a bond proposal. They were ecstatic. Then I explained that I was going to have to move away, that I likely wouldn't see them again, and that I couldn't tell them who it was. They were decidedly not on board."

"I see." I started to pull my hand away, but she held on tightly.

"But I was. So we hashed out some terms. If you'll agree to them, we have their approval."

Approval would be nice, but pleasing parents wasn't something I excelled at. "What do they want?"

"To meet you."

Would they be in my three percent? The odds weren't likely, especially in light of me whisking their daughter away. The contents of my stomach churned at the thought of having to meet her parents.

"I suppose."

She nodded. "To have a secure line of communication so I can talk to them even if I can't visit in person."

That made me grimace. "Any leak of an association with me could put them in danger."

"They wouldn't put me in danger. Surely you can arrange a secure line for vid calls?"

"I don't like it, but all right."

"And they want to meet your parents," she said quickly.

My stomach revolted further at that thought. "That one I can't do."

She hit me with a hard stare. "Don't you try to pull the 'they're dead' thing on me. They're not. I found them. And if they can live happily and safely out in the open while their son is the Geva-blessed Advisor of all of Artor, then I think you're being overly paranoid about all of this."

I wrenched my hand from hers and slid off the couch. I needed to walk, to move, to subdue the nerves singing throughout every inch of my body. "They're only living safely because I have security on them. I haven't talked to them in seven years. We didn't part on good terms."

"Did you force a bad situation to put them at a distance for their safety?" she asked.

"No, our falling out was quite unplanned."

"Is your relationship with them something that can be fixed?"

It was more a matter of deciding if I wanted to fix it. They hadn't made any effort. Neither had I. I studied Narantha's face, her hopefulness that I'd agree to her parents' terms written clearly in her pleading eyes.

"Maybe."

Relief shown in her smile. "I could go with you if you want. To talk to them. If that would help?"

Showing up with a proposed bond mate would give me a reason to stop by and a neutral topic to start with. Probably to end with too. But for her, I'd try.

"That would be nice."

Narantha nodded. "That's settled then."

"Is it? Just three demands?"

"Yes, and you can thank me for that later." She winked. "Get some sleep and then let me know when you're ready to visit your parents."

"Never?" I said, only half-joking.

She gave me a stern look. Damn, what was I getting myself into? Hells, if Vayen had dealt with Kazan... I chuckled. Narantha was nothing compared to that level of power struggle.

❧

What did one wear to confront estranged, bitterly disapproving parents?

Picking up on my hesitation, Narantha pointed to the dress uniform I wore for public appearances. I'd been wearing one like it when I'd taken a bullet to the head. Would she attempt to save me today too?

Dressed and filled with trepidation, I got into Narantha's transport. I didn't have any jump points near enough to be of use.

Knowing the address, she took care of entering our destination. I don't think I could have brought myself to type it in.

"I'm going to get some work done," I announced.

She didn't protest, even though we had an hour and a half ride there. I supposed she had her own link to keep herself busy.

I dove into anything that was outside of Artor to keep my mind off the impending disaster. When Narantha nudged my shoulder, I managed to stay busy for a few more minutes before she resorted to a shove I couldn't feign not noticing.

"We're here," she said.

Knowing there was no evading this, I got out of the transport and took a few seconds to take in the home where I'd grown up.

The modest two-story single-family home stood wedged in a row of twenty-six others, sharing exterior walls along either side. A box of orange flowers on trailing vines hung from the large first floor front window. Three smaller windows marked the second floor bedrooms.

They'd changed the exterior color from rusty orange to pale yellow, but the door was the same imposing deep brown. When it opened, I involuntarily took a step back.

Narantha caught my arm, gently pulling me forward. "Don't worry, I'm not off guard duty just yet."

If she hadn't been there, I would have gotten back in the transport and left before we reenacted the ugly memory of my leaving home for what I'd thought had been for good.

"I've seen you deal with the Premier like he's no big deal. I'm sure you can handle your parents," she whispered.

I didn't care about the Premier or what he thought of me. I just needed him to do his job. A job he was very comfortable and familiar with thanks to the advisors who had come before me. My parents were a very different story.

As we approached the two older versions of the people from my past on the doorstep, I could no longer avoid looking at them. My father's hair contained more silver and the lines along either side of his mouth were deeper. They'd always lent him a stern look, even back in the days when I'd done my best to please him. Then, when I'd attained a job due to all the achievements he'd driven me toward, he'd been livid, adamant that I was throwing my life away on a crazy pipe dream.

Having enjoyed long careers of their own, my parents had waited until later in their lives to have me. They'd been involved in every aspect of my childhood, always there, always pushing me to do better, and then they were suddenly against me.

Upon seeing my mother's face, the pain of that severing crept up from the depths of my gut where I kept it buried.

Her shoulders were hunched a bit more, arms, bare from the shoulders down, thicker, as was her waist. She stood beside my father, hands clasped in front of her, watching me with eyes I'd always considered kind until the day I'd left.

When I dreamed of seeing my parents again, it usually turned into a nightmare, either they spurned me worse than before or someone showed up to take me out and killed them in the process. On rare occasion, they would smile and my mother would hold out her arms like she'd done when I was little, welcoming me home from school each day. In reality, none of that happened.

They both stood there, faces carefully composed, giving nothing away. Neither did they say a word.

Never had I been more grateful for easy-going Narantha who marched right up to them.

"We spoke yesterday, I'm Narantha. It's so nice to meet you."

"Yes," said my mother.

One word and I was nearly undone. It had been so long since I'd heard her real voice. The version of it in my head was as furious and spiteful as it had been the last time.

"Come in," said my father, opening the door while he blatantly analyzed Narantha.

Neither of them acknowledged me, but neither did they bar my entry. Smiling politely, Narantha pulled me along to follow my father inside. My mother closed the door behind us.

The inside of the house hadn't changed much since I'd left, every surface clean and colored by souvenirs of my parents' lives—their travels around Artor, their jobs, my childhood. My father led the way to the common room right off the entry hallway. We sat together, Narantha still holding onto my arm, which was good because I might have drowned in memories if left unanchored.

My mother appeared from the kitchen, carrying a tray laden with filled glasses and a plate of baked treats. My childhood had been full of the smells of her baking. I couldn't remember the last time I'd had a homemade sweet.

"So." My father finally acknowledged me with a stern and disapproving gaze. "This fine young woman tells us you've proposed a bonding?"

My tongue seemed to be glued to the roof of my mouth. Narantha nudged me with her knee.

"Yes," I said, not missing the implied censure that I should have been the one to tell them about the proposal. I wasn't going to apologize. It wasn't like I'd been hiding since I'd taken over the advisory position. They could have reached out at any time.

The knots in my stomach tightened. I pressed my lips together to keep what I wanted to say locked safely away.

Narantha smiled brightly and reached for the tray. She held a frosted handcake out to me and took one for herself.

"These look wonderful. Did you make them?" she asked.

My mother nodded. She'd yet to look me in the eye.

Narantha took a bite and gave me another knee knock.

My mind spun, trying to think of some trivial, non-combative string of words I could utter that might break the near critical level of tension in the room.

"I like the new color outside."

"We did that three years ago," my father said woodenly.

I shoved half the handcake into my mouth and took my time chewing it. Geva, it was so good. I ate the other half in a single bite and reached for a second one.

"Hungry?" asked my mother flatly, her frown illustrating her disapproval of my manners.

"I forgot how good these are," I said around the second cake I was shoving into my mouth. It wasn't until after I'd said the words that I realized I'd spoken them out loud.

"I'm sure the Advisor of all of Artor has plenty of cakes any time he wants them," she snipped.

Narantha let out a burst of sputtering laughter. "Are you kidding? He barely eats. He's too busy getting pulled in every direction."

My mother waved Naratha's comment away. "I'm sure you have a staff of the finest bakers and chefs."

"He certainly does not," Narantha said just as dismissively.

While I did greatly appreciate the effort she was making on my behalf, being talked about like I wasn't there annoyed the hells out of me. The sweetness in my mouth vanished. Despite trying to make this reconciliation work for Narantha's sake, being here, with them, under their disapproving gaze despite all I'd achieved, it was all too much. Words I'd tried to keep from saying marched through my lips with no mercy.

"I do not have a staff, a lofty estate, regular fancy meals, or much of anything else. I stay under the radar so I don't get another bullet in my head. And for the record, I'm advising three worlds, not just this one. That job takes every moment of every day, so if you're going to continue pretending I don't exist, that's fine. I have plenty of other matters I need to attend to."

Mortified that I'd ruined the meeting, I got up and walked out of the room. Narantha didn't follow.

"Feel better?" she said flatly.

"No."

"Did you forget we have terms for the joining?"

"No," I said contritely. And now, not only did I make things worse with my parents, if that were possible, I'd pissed Narantha off too. *"I can't go back in there."*

She sighed in my head. *"It would probably be best if you didn't. I'll work damage control here and take the transport when I'm done. I'm assuming the house is safe enough since you have it under guard?"*

Except we'd arrived publicly. I cringed at the thought of letting her stay without me after we'd taken that risk. Narantha's link skills were good enough to Jump me if need be, but I didn't want her slowed down with attempting to double jump complete strangers.

As I quickly scratched a jump point pattern into the trim of the bathroom door, I said, *"Contact me immediately if anything happens and Jump. I can be there in seconds to get my parents if need be."*

"*I will.*" The annoyed tone she'd used earlier was gone, replaced by her usual good-natured one.

"*Narantha?*"

"*Yes?*"

"*Thank you,*" I whispered, meaning so much more than I could adequately say.

THIRTY-TWO

Rhaine

Daniel squirmed on the couch beside me, wanting to go play outside, but I wasn't feeling well. These minor illnesses were an unpleasant reminder of the fortunate life we'd left behind. I'd been off work for two days with an unsettled stomach and runny nose. I had a vague memory of being sick like this as a kid. I hadn't enjoyed it then either.

The local vid channels offered something to do while my body fought whatever this was. It wasn't worth bothering Weeda. We'd finally settled into an amicable working relationship, but I didn't want to push my luck.

"Outside!" Daniel demanded for the third time in five minutes. He got to his feet and jumped up and down on the couch. The motion did nothing good for my stomach.

"Sit. Down," I said with a sharpness that hadn't slipped out in a long time. The face that accompanied those two words must have also conveyed how thin my patience was because he dropped to the cushions and sat stock still, staring at me like he might burst into tears.

"Thank you," I said, managing a more motherly tone before blowing my nose and tossing the tissue into the nearly full bin beside me.

The local news came on, opening with a story about a new colony starting up just beyond ours. They'd started excavations and clear-cutting. And they'd discovered a body. One identified as Jersen Dugan.

I grabbed the controller and turned up the volume, all sense of my ailing body gone as my entire focus locked onto the face of the man who had been causing us issues since shortly after our arrival.

"...a stab wound that pierced his lung. The body was identified through medical records as it had been in the elements for well over a year and suffered additional damage from local wildlife. The initial medical investigation indicates that the injury may have been self-inflicted. However, no immediate apparent form of transportation accounts for how Jersen may have come to be in this undeveloped place on his own. Authorities are searching for the actual location where the death may have occurred as animals have extensively disturbed the area. No weapon has yet been found."

The reporter's face was replaced by a panning shot of the clear-cut area with an array of equipment in the background. It looked suspiciously like a secluded place I might bring someone to die a slow death. Somewhere a body could rot without being discovered—in a manner that wouldn't reveal foul play and could destroy any possible evidence left at the scene. If only someone could account for how he'd gotten there.

The feed returned to the reporter. "Dugan's absence has been under investigation. Now that his body has been found, Isnar Ka'Turoc, who took over Dugan's business, has been formally charged."

The image of my dear Ishlan from our colony identification chips flashed across the screen.

"Daddy?" Daniel asked, pointing at the vid.

My blood ran cold. How could they do this? Put us out in the open like that? Show his face to everyone? I grabbed Daniel and slid him onto my lap, heedless of any germs I might have been spreading.

The reporter went on to talk about projections for the upcoming storm season as though my world hadn't just come to a crashing end.

The terminal in the kitchen buzzed. Fucking hell, we didn't need this attention! Any attention. Ever again. Why couldn't Isnar have just vaporized Jersen's terrorizing ass? But there weren't any readily available locations in our colony to do that. Isnar had used a knife. Something simple and not near a suspicious-looking as a gun or pulse blast, both of such weapons were securely locked in a chest in his closet. With his armor.

The terminal buzzed again.

If they came to search the house, they'd be found. A large stash of weapons wouldn't help Isnar's case at all.

I set Daniel aside and ran to the kitchen to answer the terminal.

Atalina's face came into focus. "Ishla, they took him!"

"I just saw the report. Please tell me he went without resisting?"

She nodded. "He was surprisingly polite."

"Thank his gods for that." I shook my head, feeling only a fraction of relief. He was playing innocent—not something Vayen had ever excelled at. I hoped Isnar was more convincing.

"Do you want me to come over and watch Daniel? If you wanted to go speak with him? I don't know how long he will be detained."

"As long as they can, I would imagine."

Roshonomen appeared next to Atalina. "I'm sending a transport to your home. I was told that you had some items that need to disappear?"

I had to give Isnar credit for thinking fast under unexpected circumstances. All his dropped comments about keeping his skills intact rushed at me. He'd never really relaxed here, never given into this life, always keeping his toes dipped in the old one. Just as I knew he might walk away at any minute, he'd known his cover could be blown, that his past might catch up to him.

"Put Atalina in that transport. It needs a legitimate reason for being here. I'm assuming you have the disappearing under control?"

Roshonomen winked. "Completely."

With the immediate details taken care of, I picked up Daniel and carried him around the house, not sure what I was doing or where I was going. Waiting set my nerves on fire. Having someone solid in my arms helped. Daniel rested his cheek on my shoulder and sat quietly in my arms as if he too could sense something was terribly wrong.

A knock sounded on the door. I hurried over to open it. "Thank goodness, your here."

But it wasn't Atalina. Two uniformed colony officers stood on my step with dour expressions.

After a second to collect my wits, I said, "I was expecting the babysitter. I'm not feeling well. How can I help you?"

"My Daddy was on the vid," Daniel said proudly.

One of the officers raised a brow. The other smirked. "Yes, he was. That's why we're here. If you'll excuse us, Ishla Ka'turoc, we've been ordered to perform a search of your home."

"Of course." I backed away from the door for lack of any immediate line of defense. If Isnar went with the cooperative route, I figured I might as well play along.

"Please excuse the mess. As I said, I've been sick." I set my loudmouth son down and made a show of bustling around the common room to tidy the pillows, dispose of my tissue mountain, and clear away the dishes from our midday meal in front of the vid.

"Do you have any weapons in the house we need to be aware of?"

asked one of the officers who followed me into the kitchen.

Another knock at the door interrupted my attempt at a workable answer. "Excuse me a moment. Watch out for the kitchen knives, I suppose."

This time it was Atalina. "I'm sorry, I came as quickly as I could," she whispered.

I waved her inside. "I appreciate it on such short notice. I was just about to take a nap when these nice officers arrived to search the house."

The officer who had remained in the common room gave Atalina a long look. "You work at Dugans."

"Yes. I often care for Daniel when his father brings him to work."

"Lina!" Daniel ran over and jumped into her arms, nearly knocking the small woman over.

The officer pulled out a datapad and jotted down what I assumed were notes.

"Anything upstairs?" he asked.

"Just bedrooms and a bathroom."

He gave me a pointed look. "Weapons, Ishla Ka'turoc. Are there any weapons upstairs?"

"Yes, my own. I don't like being home alone. I was kidnapped once before. Not here," I said in answer to his unasked question. "Doctor Weeda can confirm this."

"Doctor Weeda is busy examining the body of Jersen Dugan."

Wasn't that just wonderful. Couldn't they have found someone less competent? "I'm sure she'll do a thorough job. We work together quite often so I can attest to her skill."

The officer nodded. "Upstairs then? I'd like to examine these weapons of yours."

"Sure." I led him up the stairs, leaving Daniel in Atalina's care. "You don't think I had anything to do with this Jersen mess do you?"

"As a Seeker, no, but your Ishlan is a suspect. There have been questions about his takeover of Dugans."

"I'm sure all the paperwork is in order." Isnar was usually very thorough with that sort of thing.

The officer offered a non-committal nod.

I brought him to our bedroom where I kept my single knife and gun in the drawer beside the bed. I opened it and stepped back.

"You don't keep them in a secure location? With a child in the house?"

"He isn't able to get into our room on his own. I suppose I will need to do that soon."

"Immediately, yes." He gave me a chastising glare.

The officer pulled a scanner from his overcoat and waved it slowly over my gun and knife. Then he picked them up and examined them carefully. A sudden scowl made my heart skip a beat.

"What is it?"

"This gun is loaded. It is illegal to store loaded firearms in your home."

I let my exasperation slip out. Sure, that seemed like a safe practice for an average person, but I needed to be ready in seconds.

I *used* to need to be ready. No Kryon had shown up at our door. No one had taken any extra notice of us beyond general suspicion of non-Verians. I wasn't supposed to have any reason to think I needed a loaded weapon. I was supposed to rely on the colony officers to spot threats and deal with them. Time to play stupid.

"I... What am I supposed to do if someone breaks in? Ask them to wait a moment while I load my gun?"

"No, Ishla, you notify us and we'll take care of it."

If that wasn't the stupidest thing I'd heard. They were ten minutes away, and the terminal was downstairs in a room with a single path of entry. No way in hell would I put my life in their hands. But I smiled and nodded contritely.

"Yes, of course."

"Are you aware that your Ishlan keeps weapons on his person?"

I nodded. "Traders can be a dangerous lot. He meets with all sorts and some can't be trusted."

"He uses knives."

"Yes? They are easier to conceal than a gun."

"Yet, you have both."

"I'm not the one dealing with jumpy trade partners."

His sigh sounded less than satisfied.

My nose started to run again. I sniffed. "If you don't mind, I'm not feeling well."

"I'll just take a quick look around up here then, if you don't mind?"

I waved him onward and sat on the edge of the bed.

He opened my closet, sweeping his scanner over the contents. He went over to the chair covered with Isnar's dirty clothes, the chest at the end of the bed where I kept the extra blankets, and finally, he opened Isnar's closet.

I reached into the open drawer beside me, deciding whether I could take this officer out quietly if I used a pillow as a somewhat silencer. But what then what would I do with the one downstairs in front of Atalina and Daniel? What would the repercussions be if Isnar was still in custody?

The other officer called out, "I'm all clear down here."

"Just about done," said this one.

The scanner pinged on something on the floor of the closet.

I wrapped my hand around the gun, lifting it out of the drawer.

The officer reached in and pulled out the folded armored coat. "What's this?" he asked, turning toward me.

I didn't have time to get the pillow up and shooting him would only bring down more problems. I made a clumsy show of popping the clip and showing it to him. "There, all better."

He looked nervously at the gun in my hand. I put it back in the drawer. What I hoped he didn't see was me palming the knife just in case I needed a last resort plan.

"Oh that? It was his brother's. Family heirloom. He was in the military. Killed in action."

The officer shook out the armored coat that probably weighed half as much as he did and was just as tall. "Not if he was wearing this."

"Head shot," I said offhandedly while my mind played Chesser's death in vivid detail. My throat went thick and my eyes blurred. I ducked my head, rubbing my temples against the intense headache that was quickly forming. Damned stressful situations always brought them on.

If the scanner had picked up traces of weaponry on the empty armor, it might well pick up the horde of weapons inside the shielded chest right below it. It figured that they would have halfway decent investigative technology, but had never heard of stims. What I would have given for one of those.

A halo shone around the officer. I started to shiver as the distant feeling that accompanied my seizures spread over me.

"Ishla, are you unwell?"

Hadn't I been saying that since their arrival? I needed them to leave right now. For once, I embraced the misery of my condition and didn't mask an ounce of it. "Yes, very much so. Could you send Atalina up on your way out? I'm sorry, but I do need to rest now."

His suspicion turned to outright concern as he looked me over.

"Of course. Sorry to keep you." He bobbed his head in a slight bow, returned the coat to the closet, and backed out of the room.

Nausea swept over me by the time his feet started down the stairs. I dashed to the bathroom where I reaffirmed my friendship with the toilet.

"Ishla?" Atalina called out from the other side of the bathroom door.

"I'll be out in a moment." Pale and shaking, I washed my face and sought out the injector from the cabinet.

When I emerged from the bathroom, Atalina immediately shooed Daniel into his room. "Go play. I'll be there in a moment, sweetling."

She took my arm though I didn't offer it and helped me to the bedroom. "He was worried this would happen." She tsked and made a fuss about me taking off my shoes and then getting into bed. "Comfortable enough?" she asked after arranging the pillows and straightening the blankets.

Unlike Isnar's annoying hovering, Atalina's efforts struck me as sweet. Like something a mother should do. In the back of my mind, I noted her actions and tone of voice in the hopes that someday I might emulate them without conscious effort.

"Yes, thank you. I'm going to take my medicine now. I'll be out for a while. I hope that's all right."

"Don't worry about me or that sweet boy of yours." She patted my arm. "And I have a feeling your Ishlan can take care of himself."

A heavy peace swept through my veins as the injection began to work. "Let's hope so."

<h1>THIRTY-THREE</h1>

Merkief

Jey's interrogation of the few prisoners taken from the ships in the recent attacks had left us feeling mostly secure about the situation. They had been retaliating from Jey's rampage into their system. It just so happened that they came toward the Narvan by way of the jump gate near the Rakon Nebula. Kess, having gotten wind of the ships passing through, had taken the opportunity to provide prime target coordinates.

Knowing Kess would deny any involvement, we opted out of going to the Council with accusations, instead, looking for ways to retaliate on our own.

I left that plan to Jey as my head was mostly wrapped up in other matters, like fulfilling the terms set out by Narantha's parents. She'd set up a another meeting.

The second trip to my parent's house was much different than the first. This time, Narantha's parents accompanied us.

As we pulled up to the house, she turned to me. "Remember, they agreed to be hospitable. That means if you go off on them, it's on you."

I nodded, all the while silently repeating to myself, 'keep your mouth shut'.

Narantha carried a plate up to the door, her other hand in mine. Her parents followed behind us. I wished we could have all Jumped directly inside the house, but I didn't want to explain what links were to either of our parents. We didn't need unholy Artorian tech in our heads to further worsen the situation. Not to mention, Jumping them for the first time would likely make them nauseous.

Her parents were nice people, ordinary and kind. It was easy to see where Narantha got her personality.

This time my parents greeted us all with smiles. Neither of them looked directly at me, but they did seem genuinely happy to see Narantha. I supposed that was progress in the right direction. Since she was on good terms with everyone, I let her take the lead.

Under Narantha's advisement, introductions took place inside. Drinks were passed around, polite conversation was made, and my mother actually complimented Narantha on the handcakes she'd brought. I'd sampled a couple before we'd left.

Having had my fill of Narantha's baking, I left them all to getting to know one another, wandering off into the kitchen for a little quiet in a long-missed place.

"I thought you might have left again," my mother said quietly.

I turned away from the still frames of my childhood on the wall next to the small breakfast table to find her standing in the doorway of the kitchen where I'd watched her happily baking, where nothing but good memories abounded. I couldn't find it in me to break the tenuous truce Narantha had brokered. Instead, I shook my head.

"I'm glad you didn't," she said.

'Are you?' was on the tip of my tongue, but I kept it to myself.

She held out her arms.

I didn't remember moving forward, but I found myself bending down to be encompassed by them. It was awhile before either of us spoke, and even then, she only backed away a few inches.

"You chose a good mate, even if her cakes are a little dry."

I chuckled. "They are, aren't they? I didn't have the heart to tell her."

Her eyes glistened as she patted my hand. "I'll show her how to make them right."

A connection I hadn't felt in years unfurled in my mind as my mother hugged me both inside and out.

My father, probably summoned by the stirring emotions over their bonded connection, hurried into the kitchen. He came to an abrupt stop, clearing his throat loudly.

"Marda, is everything all right in here?"

She stepped back, nodding and wiping her face on her sleeve. "Fine. We're fine. I should see to our guests." She hurried back to the common room.

He stood there awkwardly for a moment, head cranked around, watching my mother leave, but also noting I hadn't moved.

"You haven't had any trouble here, have you?" I asked to break the silence.

He shook his head. "Not that we know of, anyway. Narantha told us about your watchers."

"Good. That's why they're there."

"She tells us you're going to lock her away. That what you big advisor types do? Keep your mates like prisoners?"

"I plan to keep her alive and happy. That's what we *advisor types* try to do for all of you."

For all his avoiding setting eyes on me previously, he scanned every pore and follicle now. "We saw you get shot in the head on the news not too long ago. You look fine now, not even a scar. That some sort of stunt to gain sympathy from the public?"

"As if the public has any sympathy for me. I'm sure more of you were rejoicing than not." The urge to unburden my resentment on him was near overwhelming, but then I remembered Narantha and her parents in the other room, and why we were here.

"The one good thing I do have as Advisor is excellent medical care. If you have any doubt about that bullet in my head being real, you can ask Narantha."

"I saw she was there with you." His ire dropped a few degrees. "Saved you, I suppose."

"That she did. She caught the would-be assassin too," I said proudly.

"Geva be praised for that." He sounded like he meant it.

Surprised, I observed him just as thoroughly as he had me earlier. He bowed his head a couple degrees and nodded. It wasn't the hug I'd shared with my mother, but it was a start.

Feeling a little more at ease, I returned to Narantha's side where her presence could hopefully keep me calm before I screwed anything up again.

With the approval of Narantha's parents gained, I'd initiated the bond and went out the next day to commission her joining gift.

Two weeks later, I'd presented it to her at a fancy dinner eaten in my house. I had no desire for anyone to catch wind that we were together in anything other than the employee/employer relationship that was already very public thanks to the feed from my near assassination. Narantha, now wearing the ring that I'd given her, seemed to be understanding, though I could tell she was disappointed at not being able to share the news with friends or enjoy the spotlight that such a position should have offered her.

While I was fully enjoying the courtship phase of our joining, I had to sever our relationship on the employer end. That meant I had to interview prospects to take her place in the Artorian guard rotation and hire a few to keep an eye on her from a distance. She was quite adamant about not wanting anyone looming over her shoulder all day and night. I was confident about her self-defense capabilities, but I knew firsthand that we all let our guard down sometimes. Having that extra layer of protection made me feel better about letting her maintain her cautious level of freedom. For now.

When she wasn't dropping cryptic hints of gifts she wanted in order for me to fully win her consent to our joining, she spent a lot of time with her parents. My mother seemed to also be making good on her comment about giving Narantha pointers in the kitchen. She'd spent a few afternoons there as well, this day was one of them.

For me, working on Thirteen, it was the middle of the night. Jey and I staked out what was supposed to be a meeting place for Kess according to the information we'd gained from mostly trusted sources.

One could never fully trust anyone in Kess's orbit.

"What did she ask for today?" Jey asked from the top of the building across from me, where he sat with a rifle.

"A firestone. Like I have time to hunt one of those down."

"You're in luck. I happen to have a few. They were Kazan's. I'm sure she wouldn't mind if you used one as a gift."

His suggestion struck a chord in me, like maybe the universe was working in my favor for once and things were falling into place. There was a rightness in involving Kazan in this small way. I couldn't help but think that she'd approve. *"That would be great. Thanks."*

"Someone's coming."

I crouched lower, hoping to all hells that the shadows concealed me as well as I thought they did. The pulse pistol in my hand was charged and ready. Waiting. We'd been waiting for hours.

"It's not him," Jey said, sounding as disappointed as I felt.

The man walked into the lot and stood there, looking around. Then he walked the perimeter, passing within a single stride of me on his route. After ten minutes of this, he whistled softly.

"Here we go," Jey whispered in my head.

He had the night-vision scope so I had to trust him. If we could finally eliminate Kess, I'd breathe much easier and I could grant Narantha more of the freedom she craved.

Kess and a woman, probably someone he'd borrowed from his guild, strode into the lot. Buildings loomed on two sides, and a tall solid plascrete barrier stood on the far end, leaving one end open. Jey had posted himself on the tallest of the two buildings. I hung in the shadows of the shorter one. They joined the man in the middle. All three stood there together looking in three different directions. Within minutes, two more people showed up. In the darkness, it was hard to see who they might be. If Jey had any idea, he didn't say anything. I crouched, waiting for the signal. The two incoming bodies joined the three in the middle. An exchange took place. Whatever it was was too small to make out from my position. They spoke too quietly for me to overhear what they were saying. I'd been in plenty of similar situations where all I did was wait for my part to come into play, but this was Kess. And he was right there and I wanted him dead very badly. So did Jey.

"What are we waiting for?"

"Kess isn't here."

"That's him. I can see him right there."

"Not him. A decoy."

"So he knows we're here."

"Very likely, yes."

I swore silently. *"We should leave before they flush us out."*

"I agree. I'll touch base with you tomorrow before our check in with the Council."

"Can't wait."

I loathed our meetings with the Council. How anyone could relax and remain fully composed while having their every action examined was beyond me. It was like the worst sort of employee evaluation. And they demanded these meetings every eight days. I didn't recall Vayen or Kazan having to meet that often, but maybe they did without us. It wasn't like I took a guard. No one else was allowed in the room. Jey and I were interviewed separately. We tried to meet beforehand to make sure our reasoning aligned on anything we felt they might find questionable. They always had a lot of questions and often not about the things we thought they would, keeping us on our toes. Maybe that was the purpose of it all. It was a technique I used myself on many of my contacts. If they never got comfortable, they didn't get ideas of abusing the system. However, I didn't appreciate it being used on me.

I also didn't appreciate the information leak. I waited until I was pretty sure Jey had left and then set my pulse to a wide heavy beam. Faux Kess and his agents must have decided we weren't going to take the bait. They started to spread out, slowly backing away from one another, watching the rooftops and shadows with particular attention. Weapons openly slid into hands. They continued to talk, though I still couldn't hear what they were saying. The words likely didn't matter anyway. It was all a ruse. The moment they all fit within my estimated swath of destruction, I emptied the pulse charge. Before any survivors figured out the exact trajectory of my shot, I Jumped.

Feeling victorious, I stood in my empty house on Artor in the dark. I wished Narantha was there.

THIRTY-FOUR

Rhaine

When I woke from my drug-induced sleep, I made out the sound of the vid downstairs. In the hopes that I might find Isnar on the couch, I changed my deeply creased clothes, washed my face, and headed for the stairs.

The voices before I got to the bottom crushed my hopes. Atalina was still here. She spun around as I entered the common room.

"Ishla, are you feeling better?"

Isnar's face wasn't on the vid, so maybe a little. But he also wasn't home. "Somewhat. Any news?"

"He called for you. I let him know you were sleeping, that you'd taken your medicine."

Great. Now he would be worried and want to be home, and who the hell knew what he'd do to get here.

"Can I call him back? I'm not sure how the legal system works here in that regard."

"He's been fully processed and was able to make a call himself, so it's worth a try."

"They're really charging him?" Blackness tinged the edge of my vision as my pulse thundered in my ears. I felt my way to my chair and sank into it.

Daniel slid off the couch and climbed up onto me. I held him tightly, grateful for his solid warmth.

Atalina bowed her head and averted her gaze. "Doctor Weeda has ruled that the injury was not self-inflicted. The force was too excessive. Too deep, I think." She gestured vaguely. "I'm sorry, Ishla. I wish there was something I could do."

It wasn't like I could ask all of the Dugans staff to come forward and divulge what sort of business Jersen had been running, what he'd done to deserve his non-self-inflicted end. Doing so would only unleash a massive investigation on the business, and from what Roshonomen had implied, he and Isnar were still utilizing many of Jersen's business practices and partners. None of them would appreciate investigative attention any more than we did.

"We'll figure something out."

I rubbed my temples, wishing I had a clear head. Weeda's medicine had knocked the headache down to a tolerable level, but my sinuses were throbbing, and now that I was up and conscious, my nose had turned into a faucet again. Atalina leaned over to hand me the tissues I'd left on the couch.

"Thanks."

Once I thought I'd expelled all the mucus a body could naturally generate, I made my way to the terminal in the kitchen. After a little searching, I located the non-emergency contact for the colony office and began the convoluted game of getting connected to the right person so I could speak to my Ishlan.

I cursed Weeda and her accurate findings while I waited on hold to be connected to the next person. My heart faltered when a familiar face graced the vid in front of me. For all the excess moisture in my head, my throat went dry.

Isnar offered me a tired smile. "Are you all right? Atalina said—"

"I'll be fine. What about you?"

He smoothed his hair back with both hands, his gaze taking on a more calculating angle. "They found the knife and where they think it happened."

The way he phrased his statement led me to understand our call was being observed. Which made sense, but I was so used to being able to talk openly with him. He was the only one I could do that with. Having that taken away made me angry.

"Why did they charge you with murder? You didn't do this," I said, playing the distraught Ishla role.

"Doctor Weeda thinks I did. Something about the angle of the puncture wound and the force inflicted." There was a momentary flash of Vayen in his gaze, enough to let me know that he'd silence that medical expert in a heartbeat if given the opportunity.

"Does she only think this or does she think she has proof of your involvement?"

"Just her expert opinion."

"Normally, I respect her opinion, but this time, she's wrong," I said forcefully.

He merely nodded.

He looked well enough, other than being tired. They'd left him in his clothes, likely because they didn't have any inmate clothing in his size. Back in the Narvan, it wouldn't have surprised me to see him roughed up a little, or a lot, given who he was and what enforcers might have to prove or do to keep him subdued, but he appeared untouched. Maybe the Verian system was kinder than most.

Isnar held up his hands, showing me that they were locked together in a pair of restraints. They did have those in his size. I supposed they had enough off-world visitors with the port right here to account for being prepared in that regard.

"My hands are tied in this matter," he said.

I shook my head at his terrible attempt at humor. Or was he telling me that I needed to take action for him? When a half-hearted, smart-ass smile didn't make an appearance on his face, I nodded.

"Stay calm. I'll say a prayer for you," I said, milking the Seeker angle. Though he did his fair share, Isnar knew I wasn't the praying type. "I'm sure this will all be cleared up soon."

It would be if I had anything to say about it.

"I would appreciate that. I have no desire to sit in a Verian prison for the next thirty years."

From the underlying growl in that last bit, I took the hint that his extremely limited patience was running out. If we didn't want our cover blown by a rampaging Artorian, I needed to do something fast.

"Take care of yourself, Rhaine."

Was he talking about not pushing my luck with the headaches? Because until he was back beside me, my stress level was going to hover on the headache threshold indefinitely. Or was that code for 'be ready to run with Daniel' if he did let Vayen out? His face and tone gave no clue either way. Damned observed call.

"You too."

The call ended before I could say anything more. I wondered if he terminated it or someone else had. I hadn't seen his arms move.

With the call ended and my thoughts spinning, I ventured back into the common room. "Atalina, do you need to go? I've certainly kept you long enough."

"I made a call to my Ishlan last night. But yes, I should go check up on him, make sure he's taken his medication."

I went to stand in the doorway to the common room. "Has he not been well?"

"He's been ill for some time. Since he worked for Jersen."

Others of the Dugans staff had come to me with similar stories, spouses or children fallen ill with a lingering disease. Most were treated with medicine Jersen supplied in lieu of a portion of their wages. Other spouses and children had gone missing or been arrested. After talking to Roshonomen, I was putting together Jersen's employee motivation plan and why they all were willing to work for free to make him dead.

"Isnar is getting the proper treatment for him, I hope?"

Atalina nodded. "At no cost. Blessed man."

"He has his moments." I herded her toward the door. "Thank you for staying with Daniel."

"No problem at all. You'll let me know if there's anything I can do to help?"

I nodded, holding the door open for her.

She took my not at all subtle hint gracefully, and having gathered up her coat, she got into the company transport she'd arrived in. A moment later she was headed down the street.

After taking a few minutes to make a small batch of Isnar's favorite eggs, because that was something I could do on autopilot, I sat down to eat with Daniel.

"Where's Daddy?" he asked, gazing at his father's vacant chair.

"He's on a business trip. It's just the two of us for a few days."

Daniel sniffed. "He didn't say goodbye."

"He's sorry about that. He didn't mean to leave so fast."

Daniel ate his eggs in sullen silence.

Meanwhile, I took advantage of the quiet moments to contemplate a plan. I needed to get Weeda to change her testimony. Somehow.

I put the empty plates on the counter and then sat down at the terminal. "You can go play for a bit. I have to do a little work and then I'll read you a story, all right?"

Daniel nodded, wandering back into the common room to play with the pile of toys Atalina had brought down for him.

I placed a call to Weeda.

She answered with a scowl. "Is this regarding a patient or your Ishlan?"

"Both. Many patients, actually. Are you available to stop by?"

"I suppose you mean immediately," she grumbled.

I was about to say that it wasn't a life or death matter, but then I remembered the look in Isnar's eyes and realized it could well be. Especially hers, if I couldn't convince her peacefully.

"I would appreciate that, yes."

"I'll be over within the hour."

I ended the call and went upstairs to get the storybook datapad, my gun, and my knife. I hoped I could sway Weeda as a Seeker, but if not, I had other methods. And I had a lot more experience with those.

Daniel and I passed the time with a few stories, wherein I continued to add to my Artorian and Verian vocabulary. Not that there were many advanced words involved, but even rudimentary words were helpful when it came down to it. And if Isnar ever lost his blanket or his toys I would know what he was talking about.

I laughed out loud. Daniel gave me a questioning look. "Nevermind."

Weeda's knock saved me from further explanation. I got up and let her in.

She took in the mess and my no-doubt ruddy nose and glassy eyes. "That's been going around," she said, pointing at me.

"I noticed. I picked it up from one of several clients last week."

"And I'm guessing those aren't the ones you were referring to in your call." She glanced expectantly at the chairs.

"Shall we sit?" I gestured her to the chair I usually used which was far more her size while I sat in Isnar's. Daniel sat on the floor at my feet, chatting in Artorian to himself.

"Is this about the murder charges?" she asked.

"Yes." There was no reason to skirt the issue. We both knew why I'd asked her over. But I did try to keep my tone in the Seeker range rather than indulge my urge to put a knife to her throat and demand she retract her statement.

"And the patients you mentioned?" She eyed me levelly as if she somehow knew I was holding back.

"You mentioned you've treated most of the staff at Dugans at one point or another."

"Yes? Most of them have lived here since I've been practicing medicine in the colony."

"And did you notice more calls for your services in the past few years than usual?"

I shouldn't have been surprised when she pulled a datapad out of her overcoat and consulted it. Of course, she'd come prepared. She probably had her treatment bag out in her transport.

"I suppose that could be said," she stated after a few minutes.

"Do you have any theories as to why this might be?" It aggravated me to have to go the long way around, to play Seeker when I wanted to get right to the point. But I respected Weeda, even if she grated on my nerves most of the time. She deserved a chance to find her own way out of this. A way where she got to live.

"Off-world shipments skipping quarantine? Not following proper handling procedures? Avoiding safety protocols? Jersen tried to run an efficient operation. It wasn't his fault people cut corners."

I wished we'd done this meeting at my shop. The smells were wrong here. I wasn't in the proper element, the one that solidified my Seeker-self. Breathing in and out, I tried to find my balance.

"What leads you to believe it was Jersen's staff that was cutting corners and causing themselves injury?"

She scoffed. "He wasn't the one requiring my services."

My fingers twitched, wishing for the familiarity of a weapon during the interrogation. But it wasn't an interrogation. Not intimidation. Just a conversation, an enlightenment. A revealing of the truth. If I could do this without resorting to threats, I could prove that I didn't need to be Anastassia to get things done. I could do this a more peaceful way as Rhaine. I imagined what Res would say about that, about who I was trying to be now. Would I finally be *good* enough for him?

"What if I told you that Jersen was causing those illnesses and injuries?"

She stared at me blankly. "Why would he do that? Why hamper his staff?"

"Why pay them when he could force them to work for a fraction of their worth in order to get what they needed to live? To keep their family together? To prevent their sons and Ishlan's from ending up in jail or disappearing?"

She blinked. Once, then twice. "Surely the authorities would have caught up with Jersen if that were the case."

"And if Jersen were to compensate the authorities to look the other way?"

"Our colony officers could never be compromised."

"Couldn't they? And if only a small portion of the Dugans staff dared report any wrongdoing due to fear of retribution, would the authorities feel they were being overly compromised or merely looking the other way on occasion?"

"Rhaine, if you have evidence that this is true, you must bring it to light."

"My sessions are confidential. All of them." I gave her a pointed look. "The man who perpetrated these crimes is dead. He cannot be prosecuted. He can't pay for his actions. He can't seek forgiveness. He's no longer a danger to them. My testimony is moot."

She seemed to ponder this for a few moments.

"You're asking me to overlook a murder. An outright murder committed by your Ishlan on a member of my colony."

"Our colony," I stated firmly.

"So you do not deny that your Ishlan is guilty."

The victorious gleam in her eyes made me reach for my knife. I sat there, fingertips on the hilt, listening to my son talking to himself at my feet. Was I prepared to throw it all away? Daniel's peaceful childhood, my mostly happy life here with Isnar, and his chance at being normal like he deserved?

I was finally learning to like this life, to enjoy it. I didn't want it to be over yet. It would surely be over someday, but not now, not if I could help it.

"I don't deny that he took care of a problem that the authorities were willing to overlook."

She surged to her feet. "You confirm his guilt."

The time for Seeker talk was over, but I still left my knife in its hiding spot. "I also confirm that our colony officers were bribed and that you looked the other way despite evidence that an inordinate number of health issues were apparent at Dugans."

Weeda's mouth fell open. "You would accuse me of neglecting my duties?"

"Were you?"

She sat back down. "Can you prove what you say is true? If it came down to that?"

"I could. However, I do not wish to cause Jersen's victims further trauma. I would also prefer not to disrupt their livelihoods or the flow of supplies to the colony by freezing the workflow of Dugans in order for outside officials to conduct an investigation."

"I see."

She watched Daniel play for a few very long, silent minutes. All the while, my nerves sang. It was as if I had Res sitting on one shoulder and my old life on the other. If she darted for the door, I could drop her. In my mind, I rehearsed the motions of grabbing Daniel with one hand, keeping his eyes averted, while shooting Weeda with the other. It would be fast. If I could get her with a neat headshot, clean up would be minimal. I'd have to bury the body, but on my hunts for local plants for my shop, I'd discovered a few places that would work, places that were not ideal for future development. We might be able to maintain our lives here.

"Rhaine."

"Yes?" I shook my head to clear my dark thoughts.

"I said, what do you want me to do about Isnar?" She chewed her lip. "I can't very well say that I randomly changed my mind about the cause of death."

"Perhaps further medical investigation could find that Jersen had been drinking heavily or using drugs, something that would account for his excess strength, the angle, or lack of restraint in his efforts at meeting his own end."

"I don't want to know how you came up with that so quickly."

"Let's just say I've seen and heard a lot of things."

She nodded. "As you say."

If she was going to throw Seeker-speak back at me, I could relax. At least a little.

"If you might find it in your means to conduct those tests and convey your findings this evening, I would deeply appreciate it. My Ishlan's patience is wearing thin. In fact, I've never seen it hold out this long. Your people have been a good influence on him."

She gave me a smile that might have almost been warm. "Our people, Rhaine."

I smiled back. "As you say."

THIRTY-FIVE

Jey

Narantha was about what I expected. She was a good match for Merkief, someone to keep him in touch with reality. That was something easy to lose touch with in the behind-the-scenes lives we inhabited. And after his little stunt with blowing away Kess's decoys that I'd been quietly dealing with the retaliation of for the past few days, I hoped that having a mate would give Merkief a reason to get home instead of causing more trouble we didn't need.

Having been his guard, even if only for a short time, she'd proven herself competent. I wasn't at all opposed to him having someone else to keep an eye out for him while he was at home. And it sounded like he was determined to keep her there so he wouldn't have to worry about her. No additional distractions was also agreeable for me. She knew just enough of what we did to understand the reasons for that level of caution. And she'd managed to reconnect him to his family. That alone seemed to make him a more agreeable person to be around. Yet another positive in her favor.

I'd given him my approval. As if he would have pushed her aside if I hadn't, but it was, all in all, much smoother to have us all in agreement. She was also linked, which gave me another contact in his camp if I needed information.

They'd had a private joining ceremony. While I'd been in attendance, I felt more like I was working security the entire time than a guest. Maybe he was more relaxed because his parents were there and Narantha was by his side. Her parents seemed more friendly with him than his own. In a small way, I was envious.

I had zero contact with my family and didn't feel I was missing anything from them. We'd never been close, they'd shipped me off to school at an early age, and after a couple of years, I'd stopped missing them. They'd sent messages for a few more years after that, but then those had also dried up.

Merkief seemed happy to be tied down to those connections. They were probably comforting after most days or nights or series of days like we had, but I didn't have the same family drive he did. It was probably an Artorian thing.

I held up both halves of the Narvan for a week as my gift to the newly joined couple, giving them time together that they'd likely never get again without a massive bribe to convince me otherwise.

Word of his joining didn't make it to any of the media outlets, which was our goal. Now it was up to him to keep his mouth shut about it out in the open. If he slipped, that was on him. I had no reason to be talking about it.

However, there must have been some evidence of what had transpired on my face, or maybe it was just in the air because in my next meeting with the Jalvian Prime, the subject came to light.

"Did I ever tell you about my daughter, Dayana?" he asked at the tail end of a discussion regarding fleet rotations between Jal and Rok.

"No, your offspring has never been a topic of interest for me."

"Hear me out," he said, "She's a nice girl. You'd like her."

"Not interested." Not without seeing her, and absolutely not for the reason he was bringing her up.

"She lost her husband over a year ago now. Her daughter could use a father in her life."

"I'm sure."

It wasn't going to be me. Merkief might be hardwired to produce offspring now that he'd had the mysterious Artorian correction procedure and joined with a willing mate. I, on the other hand, had made it a practice to prevent offspring at all cost. Well, not *all* cost, abstinence was not in my vocabulary. And taking on someone else's kid? Definitely not.

"She's a charming little girl. Very bright."

"You must be very proud."

He leveled his stare on me. "I get that you're playing the field as it were. I would too in your position. However, think of the benefits a marriage contract such as this would offer. It would solidify your ties to Jal, to your people. To me."

Ah, fuck. He was playing that card? "You're already tied to me. And if you're tired of me, I'll find someone else. You may be firmly entrenched, but have no doubt, I can pry you out if need be."

A scowl took up residence on his lined face. "It was a civil offer. There is no need for threats."

"I didn't think so either," I said, letting him know I'd seen through his thinly veiled *offer*.

Entertaining any marriage contract with a position of power would be seen as playing favorites. Jal was my homeworld and I already spent more than my fair share of time and focus here. Rok was a close second. If anything, if I were to entertain a political marriage, I should turn my eye to Karin. Not that Marit was my type, especially not after she'd entertained Merkief. But any woman from Karin would mean figuring out how to live with an Artorian on a personal level. As much as I had and did respect certain Artorians, I knew our races were different enough that such a thing would never work out. Not with me, anyway.

On the whole, it was just easier to continue onward as I had been, finding entertainment for a night or two when I wanted it. Why screw with a system that worked?

"Is there anything else?" I asked, already getting bombarded with requests for my attention elsewhere.

"No," he said tightly. "We're done here."

"Good." I backed away from his desk and Jumped to Cragtek on Rok.

I used the public jump point, not wanting to disturb the office that had been Vayen's. Gemmen kept it like a shrine. I understood where he was coming from on that.

Each time I visited, Gemmen seemed to have aged a couple more years. He insisted he was in good health, and he seemed sharp enough, but his eldest son Gamnock had stepped in to do some of the heavy lifting lately, and while Gemmen might have resented that, I endorsed the move.

On this visit, much like all the others, he offered me a drink, which I politely declined. And as usual, he seemed disappointed, as though I'd deprived him of an excuse to have one for himself. Like he couldn't bring himself to drink alone. I supposed that would have given Gamnock more ammunition to use against him.

"What brings you by today?" he asked after I'd settled into the chair across from him.

"I'm looking for a quick credit source. I was hoping you might have some leads, maybe something I could assist with for a cut."

"I'd appreciate the help, but honestly, that viscu Kess has our extra ships tied up with escort duty. We can't run even a simple attack and grab anywhere near the Nebula. He's got ships watching for us. We've lost three shipments and four ships to that bastard. He's been bad for business.

A business Kess knew I got a cut of. He knew Cragtek. Hells, he probably had a contact or two still inside.

"We're going to have to clean house."

Gemmen nodded. "I had a feeling you were going to suggest that. You know everyone hates cleaning."

"Not my favorite activity either. I'll have Merkief recommend a few people. All your employees agreed to mandatory probes as needed. I'm afraid this one's needed."

"I don't suppose you could do them? The staff would take more kindly to one of their own in their heads."

"I'd love to boast that I'm just as adept at probes as an Artorian, but I'm afraid links don't function that way."

He nodded reluctantly. "I'll put the order out and watch for any runners. Maybe we'll get lucky and flush them that way."

"Maybe." But we both knew Kess's people were more professional than that. If they were still in place, they were in until we dragged them out. "I'll have Merkief contact you. Let me know how it goes."

"Will do."

With that funding avenue closed, I resorted to a visit to Sere. Our advisory positions offered a steady flow of credits from the Council, but Kess was also drawing that same income. We all had three planets to finance and advise. The playing field should have been even. But his three worlds were credit rich and, with the exception of Merchess, those credits mostly flowed directly to Kess. Even then, the sheer number of credits that Kess extracted from the Merchessian families alone was far more than what we could draw from taxes on any single world in the Narvan, despite our worlds being more vastly developed and populated. Slavery and slave labor provided a lucrative income source.

We were driven to take contracts for the additional income, and those took time away from our efforts to thwart or eliminate our problem. Usually, we took contracts we could do together because the bigger jobs paid more, but this one time, a particular contract caught my eye.

I sat at one of the desks in the contract office, flipping through available jobs. The name Isnar Fa'yet caught my eye. I'd met the man a few times, mostly in the context of working with Vayen, but from what I'd understood, he'd been a longtime friend of Kazan's too. He was Kryon, and now he was missing.

According to the provided details, the date was within days of Vayen and Kazan's deaths. Had Kess been involved with Fa'yet's disappearance too? But if that was the case, why not cash in on three bodies instead of just the two? It wasn't like Kess to pass up an opportunity like that.

Kryon didn't often go missing. On the off chance one did, a body turned up eventually. Fa'yet had been missing for two years. Either someone didn't want him found or he didn't want to be found.

According to the contract, I wasn't the first one to look into his disappearance. Four other Kryon had gone before me. Eluding that many skilled and resourceful sets of eyeballs was impressive. Or, I considered, he'd been vaporized and there wasn't anything to find. Given the previous effort and the time span, my gut was partial to that explanation.

I didn't exactly have the time to waste on what was likely a dead end, but this was something I could work on alone and inbetween other obligations. I supposed he could be in hiding for whatever reason or maybe even being held. Being Kryon, he had to have a wealth of information locked in his head.

If Fa'yet was out there somewhere, given his connections to Vayen and Kazan, he might also want a piece of Kess. My allies and options were running as low as my finances. As Kryon, he'd be useful in both capacities. With nothing to lose, I put my name on the contract and hoped I'd be more successful than the others.

THIRTY-SIX

Rhaine

"Don't touch those!" I yelled at Daniel for the tenth time as he put the candle back into the bin. He'd been intent on rearranging my displays all day. While I relished the fact that my shop was my space and I didn't have to wrangle any staff for once in my life, a small part of me wished I had an Atalina around to foist my rambunctious son on during my appointments. Thankfully, my clients were understanding, or perhaps they were just desperate for my help since there were no other Seekers to choose from.

"Sorry about that." I ducked back behind the curtain to finish the last spinal adjustment of the day.

"He's fine," mumbled the gnarled old Verian man as I got him arranged in the proper position.

After a satisfying crack of his spine and a sigh of relief, I helped him off the table and back out into the main room of the shop to see what my son had managed to get into now.

"You should just let him play. He's not hurting anything." The old man smiled at Daniel, who smiled back.

Sure. That wouldn't create a mess at all, and Daniel would never consider breaking anything. I snorted quietly while packing up his weekly supply of medicinal tea.

He set a few coins on the counter, patted Daniel on the head, and left. I put the coins in the jar I kept in a locked cabinet. While I didn't charge for my services, people often left some form of payment if they could afford it. I only used what I needed to replenish my stock and kept the rest on hand to pass along to others who needed it far more than I ever would. Isnar's income from Dugans and the fortune he'd set me up with had made sure we were financially free to do pretty much whatever we wanted.

"Come on, your father will be here soon to take us home."

"Walk?" he asked.

"It's too cold and windy today." The winters here were blustery and temperatures hovered right around freezing. While the lack of a sunny sky for the past two months made it easy to sleep with the off-kilter universal time days, I looked forward to some natural light again once this season was over.

I scooped Daniel up and attempted to occupy him with a book on my lap while we waited. He squirmed until the lights on the transport shone through the front window. Daniel leapt off my lap and pressed himself against the door. Thankfully it was too heavy for him to open on his own. I wasn't sure how I was going to contain him once he'd gained a few more inches and enough strength to escape.

After wrestling him into his coat and getting into mine, we ventured out and climbed into the transport. Daniel hopped onto Isnar's lap and began a rambling account of his day. I closed my eyes and let the vibrations of the transport move through me in an attempt to relax for a few minutes.

The ride home was short and my respite was over too quickly. Daniel tore through the house, toys scattering in his wake. Isnar settled into his chair. He grabbed Daniel anytime he came within reach, tickling him and then setting him free again. Laughing wildly, our son filled the common room with his chaotic energy. I left them to it and retreated into the kitchen. Not to cook, that was Isnar's task, but to sit at the terminal so I could enjoy a few uninterrupted minutes of research on the conditions that were plaguing my clients.

The knock at the door wasn't expected. My first instinct was to locate a weapon. The note of nervous surprise in Isnar's voice when he answered the door, made me follow my gut. I grabbed a knife from the block on the counter and crept to the open archway that led to the common room to assess the situation.

"You did sign up on the foster rotation," said a Verian woman with an infant in her arms. Another woman stood beside her with a bag on one shoulder and a datapad in her hand.

"I did. I just didn't expect to take anyone so soon." Isnar glanced over his shoulder to where I was standing.

"Could we come in? It's cold out here."

"The wind is quite wicked this evening," said the one with the datapad.

"Of course," he said, stepping aside.

Daniel ran up to the women. "A baby?"

The one with the baby knelt to give him a good look. "Yes, he'll be staying with you for two weeks. Won't that be fun?"

Fun? Our bonded connection might have throttled my input to just above nil, but I made sure even that little trickle conveyed my feelings regarding this surprise. Isnar seemed to wither, assuring me he'd picked up on what I was projecting.

Daniel clapped his hands and jumped around. As much as I wanted to vanish to our bedroom for the next two weeks, or perhaps move into my shop, I didn't want the injury of an infant due to the unsupervised enthusiasm of my son on my conscience. I returned the knife to the block on the counter and hurried into the common room to contain Daniel.

"You must be Ishla Ka'turoc." The woman with the datapad smiled at me. "Thank you for taking your turn with one of our foster children. It's rare that a non-Verian family volunteers. Gerod is very blessed to live in a home with a Seeker."

I managed a semi-polite nod but made no effort to take the child they offered in my direction. Isnar stepped forward and took him instead. Tiny Gerod nearly vanished in Isnar's large hands. It was going to be an interesting two weeks because I had no intention of taking part in this. I certainly hadn't signed up for it.

Seeing that I wasn't reaching for the offered bag of supplies either, Isnar said, "Could you please set that on the table there?"

"We'll be back in two weeks and checking in remotely every few days. Please contact the agency if you have any concerns or issues. Any donations you'd like to offer to Gerod's belongings would be greatly appreciated," she said with a heavy hint.

Everyone in the surrounding colonies seemed to know we were financially well off. I supposed it wasn't a huge surprise with Isnar owning Dugans and our investments in several other companies.

For a moment, I considered this the perfect excuse to clean out Daniel's outgrown clothes. The kid grew at such an accelerated rate—at least it seemed that way to me, Isnar claimed it was normal—that he didn't have a chance to wear anything out. But then it occurred to me, seeing the tiny baby kicking in Isnar's hands, that Daniel had been almost twice Gerod's size the day he'd been born. Gerod was small even to me. We were going to break this kid before our time was up. Who the hell had thought this was a good idea?

I retreated to the couch where I could contain Daniel on my lap. Isnar thanked them and the women left. What he was thanking them for was beyond me.

Before I could launch into my scathing tirade, he sat down beside me. "I only signed up this morning. I intended to talk to you tonight. I certainly did not expect them to throw a baby at us the same day."

"The correct order would have been for you to talk to me, at which time I would have firmly said hell no, and you never sign up for this. What were you thinking?"

Daniel squirmed on my lap. I loosened my hold on him. He reached out to pet the baby who was now blinking up at all of us.

Isnar sighed. His head rested on the back of the couch and he stared at the ceiling. "Rosh suggested that volunteering for foster rotation might help smooth over our social standing in the colony, make us more integrated."

Yeah right. "He randomly suggested this?"

"Not exactly."

At least we were being honest. "And?"

"And I was hoping this would help you see that we could do this again. But if I'm wrong, we're only in this mess for two weeks."

He was definitely wrong, but that he'd left himself an out made me smile. On the inside, anyway.

"And where is Gerod going to sleep?"

"I'll move some of Daniel's old things into the spare room." He gave me a hesitant look. "If you could hold him for a few minutes?"

I held out my hands. "What about dinner? I have research to do."

Isnar's gaze darted from me to Gerod, Daniel, the stairs, and the kitchen. He offered a pained smile. "Guess I'll find that sling. I'll be right back."

And so progressed our quick descent into chaos. For the first six days, I let him suffer. He took both boys to work, he came home looking more exhausted each day, and though he attempted to utilize our bed, he ended up sleeping on the floor of the extra bedroom more hours of the night than with me. He cooked, he took care of all the things he regularly took care of, and he was more dead on his feet than I'd seen him since we'd left the Narvan. Even more exhausted than when he'd been recovering from a drug addiction and took on two full week's worth of solo bodyguard shifts.

It was that realization that made me take pity on him even though I'd taken Daniel that day during my appointments and he'd only had

Gerod to deal with at work. And also, he was right. People did notice we had taken on a foster shift and they appreciated it. Most of my customers mentioned it and I didn't even have the kid with me.

Isnar walked into the house, eyes half-open, gaze unfocused, with Gerod in the sling across his chest. The kid was wailing. On autopilot, Isnar tossed his coat over the chair by the door, uttered some incoherent words in our direction, and headed for the kitchen.

"Hey."

He didn't even pause.

I gave Daniel a look that made him giggle and got up to go after my zombie of an Ishlan.

It took me standing in his way before he seemed to notice I was speaking. "Sit." I pointed to a chair at the table.

"I've got to make…"

I shook my head. "You're going to sit and eat whatever half-assed dinner I make and then you're going to bed. In bed. Got it?"

He cast a pitiful downward glance at the angry baby on his chest. "But what about Gerod?"

"Don't argue with me."

A shrug accompanied his nod.

By the time I'd toasted some bread and sliced cheese to melt on top of it, he was mostly asleep despite the high volume of wailing right below his face.

We didn't exactly enjoy the dinner I'd made given the loud accompaniment, but it was over quickly, and clean up was next to nothing. I stood in front of Isnar and held out my arms.

"Give him to me."

"You didn't… you said…" He shook his head. "I've got this."

"One night. That's all I'm offering. Go on. Sleep."

The gratitude flooding my head, even in our muted state brought a tear to my eyes. He was as exhausted as he looked.

Isnar stood and removed tiny Gerod from the sling to place him in my arms. He pulled the sling off and draped it over the chair, hugged Daniel, and trudged his way up the stairs. Since I didn't hear any thunderous crashes, I gathered that he'd made a controlled fall into the bed before losing consciousness.

Daniel pointed at the baby in my arms. "Mine?"

"Only for another week. I suppose you want one too?"

He didn't answer as he took my offered hand so we could go upstairs safely as per his father's instructions. I was sure he could manage just fine on his own. The kid seemed to be invincible given the number of tumbles and scrapes he'd already encountered. Not much slowed him down. Rather like his father. I chuckled to myself.

After getting Gerod changed, I settled into the big chair Isnar had brought into the bedroom. With one giant kid and one tiny one, I proceeded to read them stories that Isnar had loaded on a durable, near childproof datapad. Gerod didn't care, but he did stay relatively quiet, which with the exception of his exit from our house, was all I could ask for.

The datapad allowed for multiple translations of each story. Isnar, always thinking as he seemed to be, had loaded at least two if not all three languages for most of them.

"Do you know any of these words?" I asked Daniel out of curiosity, pointing at the three lines of text under the picture of the next story I'd started.

Daniel nodded, slowly sounding out a few simple words in both Trade and Artorian. I didn't count myself as any sort of expert on anything child-related, and I knew he was talking and walking early, but I was pretty damn sure he should not have been reading for a couple of years yet. What kind of mutant kid did I create? How was he going to fit into the school here or even with other kids? I compared the two children in my lap and found them vastly different.

Gerod might have fit in my arms more comfortably, tiny as he was, but he felt wrong. Too small, too frail, like I might break him at any moment. How did Isnar, who was larger than me, deal with such a delicate child all day? Very carefully, I supposed. So did I. He wasn't ours to break.

After a few more stories, I put both boys in their beds and went to check on my full-grown one.

He was fully clothed with one leg and a hand hanging off the side of the bed. Though he could have used a shower and something clean to sleep in, I let him be.

I'd slept for all of three hours when Gerod's crying woke me. Isnar didn't even stir. Any other night, I would have shaken him, pointed him to the door, and gone back to sleep, but I silently crept out of our room and into the one where tiny Gerod lay screaming. He quieted in my arms as we went downstairs to heat a feeding tube. We had a long week ahead, but that was Isnar's problem. I hadn't asked for this, but if he wanted a fully immersive illustration as to why we shouldn't have another kid, I couldn't have asked for anything better.

THIRTY-SEVEN

Jey

Merkief wrapped up the final probe of the three men we'd been hunting. He glanced up at me. "I've got everything we need."

"Sorry, we have to wrap this up," I said as I aimed for the head of the first in line.

The restrained men all lay on the plascrete, bleeding and wild-eyed. The crazed look might have been a byproduct of Merkief's probes. After the insults they'd spewed while he did the first mind-jack, I wouldn't have been surprised if he was none too gentle with the rest of them.

"Think of it as me doing you a favor. Your boss wouldn't be so merciful after learning what you've given us." I ended their suffering quickly with neat head shots.

"We should go. Enforcers are likely already on the way," said Merkief.

I consulted my link. "Security is two minutes out. Anything useful on the bodies?"

Merkief did a quick pat-down of our victims while I kept an eye out.

It was sad that we'd come to this, resorting to stealing credits and anything else we could find from our marks. Not up to Kryon standards, that's for sure. But this wasn't a Kryon job.

After Kess had crashed two Kryon contracts with very determined efforts at taking us out, we'd been wary of doing much official work on that front. If he had details on our Kryon contracts, someone on Sere was feeding him information. Unfortunately, we couldn't pull a house cleaning effort on Sere like at Cragtek where Merkief's men had flushed two of Kess's agents.

We'd been trying to cooperate in every possible way with the Council's demands for the Narvan to stay in good favor. It seemed someone still wasn't impressed.

Small local contracts in the neighboring systems were bringing in a trickle of credits. It was better than nothing.

Merkief rifled through the last man's pockets and stood. "Let's go."

We stepped out of the void and onto the ship. I'd been spending a lot of time there. Merkief, understandably, opted to sleep at his new home on Artor—one Narantha had chosen.

"Anything good?" I nodded toward his pockets.

He was silent a moment, and at first, I thought maybe he hadn't heard me, but then he grinned. "A few credit chips. I'll check them out and see if they're worth the risk of converting over."

"All right then, so what are you grinning about?"

"Narantha. She just told me she's pregnant."

"By headchat? Shouldn't that be a face-to-face announcement?"

He gave me the dry stare he always used when I broke out the mind shit slang. I shrugged it off. Sometimes the man had no sense of humor.

"I'm assuming that was your goal, so congratulations?"

Again with the unamused stare.

"Go on then." I shooed him away. "Go celebrate or whatever one does. I'll let the contact know the job is done and we can deliver the information when you're available."

He shook his head. "Little wonder you're single."

"I work hard to stay that way."

My refusal of the Jalvian Prime's offer had caused a good deal of tension I didn't need. It wasn't worth unseating him just yet, but I'd looked into what that would take.

With Merkief occupied with family matters, I used the little office on the ship to do some more digging on the Fa'yet contract. At least that was one Kess couldn't hunt me down on.

All I had was a lot of dead ends. The only semi-promising lead I'd found was at his home, which had taken some digging to locate. Had I not had the influence of Advisor to Karin, I likely would have come up empty-handed. It also helped that I knew Kazan's methods. I figured if they'd been friends, they might have picked up techniques from one another. With Merkief busy, I figured this was as good of a time as any to go check out the house.

On the outside, it was similar to most other single-family homes in the area, detached from one another by a modest distance, a plascrete walk with no landscaping to speak of, neat but nothing out of the ordinary. As I expected, everything was locked and sensors blinked inside. If he was dead, who would get the notification of a breach? If someone showed up, they might have information. I broke out the corner of one of the window panels—not enough to create havoc inside if it wasn't repaired anytime soon, but enough to trigger an alarm.

Though there wasn't an audible sound, I picked up the signal on my link. If I stood out here much longer in the light, the neighbors were going to notice me. When the alarm didn't bring anyone. I broke out a little more of the plaz to be able to reach up and open the window. Thankfully, the windows were generously sized so that I could fit through.

The lights were off and no command of mine turned them on. I checked the public records for the address and found utilities had been turned off within days of Fa'yet's noted absence. The property was paid for and wasn't for sale.

When I'd seen the man, it had been on Sere. Vayen had mentioned meeting often at Fa'yet's house, but I'd not been involved in any of those interactions.

I made my way through the house, grateful for the natural light from the few windows. Like Kazan, he'd favored a home with minimal entry points. Things got interesting when my boot rolled over a bullet casing. Several more were scattered nearby. No blood. No body. No sign of missed shots that might have left a bullet for me to examine.

The irony of the fact that I was doing the investigation that we did our best to prevent was not lost on me. All I did know was that there had been an attacker, they hadn't missed, and whoever had been attacked, presumably Fa'yet, hadn't fired back as there were no other casings. The fact that there were casings at all, which would have normally been considered sloppy by Kryon standards, made me think that someone had wanted it known that shots had been fired.

I pocketed the casings for further examination and was about to head back to the ship when a High Council summons hit me. I Jumped to Sere and was directed to the meeting room we usually used for Narvan business. That boded better than a grey-suit escort squad to one of the seldom-used rooms where only bad things seemed to happen.

The broad-figured cloak and another sat at the table. I took a chair at the other end, my usual location.

The melodic female voice from one of my previous meetings greeted me. The small talk ended there. "How would you feel about holding sole control of the Narvan?"

My breath caught in my throat. "Why? What did Merkief do?" If he'd gotten caught going after Kess on his own again, I was going to strangle him whether he was going to be a father or not.

"Answer the question," said the large male.

"It would be a lot of work. I thought we had an agreement that it would be both Merkief and I?"

"That was your predecessor's wish. Not ours. We prefer one advisor."

"Is this about the cost of having two of us?" I had no idea what they'd paid Vayen or Kazan, but what we were getting was barely enough to scrape by. I supposed, if we hadn't been shunting credits into aggravating Kess, or able to take more Kryon contracts without having to worry about Kess being after us, we'd be better off. Maybe. We'd been hurting since the day we'd taken over. It sure seemed like we were at the bottom of the advisor payscale.

"No. You could be making double what you are now. How do you feel about that?" said the female.

"I feel like my costs would also be double."

"Your predecessor did a better job than both of you. You worked closely with him. This makes you the logical choice for the position."

"If your Rakon Advisor hadn't killed my predecessor, he would still be here doing a better job than I can do. But instead of punishing the man who took out one of, if not the top advisor you had, you rewarded him. And now he's harassing us. And he's getting leads from one of you on our Kryon contracts. So maybe if you want me to do a better job, you should take care of Kess and your leak."

I sat there, heart thudding, both aghast at what I'd allowed to fly out of my mouth and damned proud of standing up to them at the same time. They wanted me to be more like Vayen? Well, he wouldn't have put up with their shit either.

The female turned to the broad cloak. "Perhaps the secondary Advisor will be more willing to take on the solo position?"

"I wouldn't suggest calling him that to his face if you want him to play into whatever you're scheming here," I said.

"Perhaps you should prove to us again why we allow this unusual arrangement to continue before we choose for you," said the broad cloak.

What the fuck was that supposed to mean? Did they get off on convoluted threats? I'd probably pushed my luck far enough for one day so I adopted a more agreeable tone before I smart-assed my way out of a job.

"What will it take to allow us to continue as is?"

"Advisor Atta has been tasked with claiming new territory for the Council. You will do the same," said the female.

"I did that for you already."

A giant fist slammed onto the table, shaking it all the way to my end. "You will do it again. Coordinates will be provided in the contract office."

"Maybe you should task whatever candidate for advisor you have in the chute with taking this territory? I'm not fond of sacrificing my people for a system we'll be ordered to hand over to someone else. Again."

"You were allowed to make trade deals last time," said the female.

"I think you're confusing me with my predecessor," I said, using the term they often used for Vayen that made me grit my teeth. He had a fucking name.

The female waved a gloved hand. "Claim whatever salvage then and make your deals, take whatever spoils necessary to appease your forces, but leave the territory intact. Is that agreeable enough?"

"Fine, I'll do it, but tell me first, am I competing with Merkief or Kess for the Narvan?"

Neither of them answered. They got up and walked out.

I fingered the casings in my pocket. The Fa'yet contract was going to have to go back in the unsolved folder. If our position with the Council was as precarious as these two implied, I didn't have time to waste on a dead man.

I left a summary of my findings in the file in the contract office on the off chance anyone was feeling generous with calling that good and would give me the payout. With the coordinates of my Council redemption in hand, I Jumped to the ship to get my plans in order and some sleep before heading out on another months-long distraction I didn't have the time or funds for.

THIRTY-EIGHT

Rhaine

Gerod had been gone for two weeks. The house seemed too quiet, even with Daniel on full speed. My dear Ishlan had recovered from his sleep deprivation, but I'd caught him standing in the spare room over the empty crib several times. Each time, upon hearing me, he reached down to pick up something to carry back to Daniel's room. He was dismantling our makeshift nursery in slow motion.

Daniel asked after Gerod on an hourly basis. Whether he thought of Gerod as a new toy we'd taken away or had genuinely enjoyed having another small person in the house, I didn't know. My brother and I had never been close. He'd been eight years older. We'd had nothing in common, nothing to talk about until I'd been old enough to assist him and my father with their research. Would it make Daniel happy to have a sibling?

I cringed upon further analyzing that thought. How far was I willing to go to ensure he had a normal childhood? Normal, in as far as a quick-developing hybrid child could have with two highly unsuitable parents. Well, maybe just one. I had to admit, Isnar had this parenting thing down pretty damned well.

Maybe I'd been too young to remember my father playing with me, smiling and laughing with me, reading me stories. Or maybe he never had.

Daniel's father did. And he enjoyed it. Even a blind person could have picked up on that.

Isnar wouldn't be home for another hour yet and he had Daniel with him for the day. I hung my red coat in the closet and found myself going upstairs to wander into the spare room, to stare at the empty crib. Oh hell.

Compensation. That was Isnar's thing. He liked to keep things on the level with his contacts, his suppliers, with anyone he did business with. Did I owe him compensation for all he'd done on my account? My gut screamed yes while my thoughts writhed, squirming away from this suggestion with great haste.

I'd carried Daniel for six months. Six hellish months. Isnar had given up his link, his position, his homeworld, and connections to everyone he knew. He'd almost died from a Verian virus because of his decision to be here with me. He'd left that all behind and he'd only shoved it in my face once, and only when I'd driven him to it. I sighed and sat in the big chair beside the crib.

Six months. That would be his compensation.

I sat there, taking in the quiet of the house, the emptiness of it with Daniel and Isnar gone. At any other point and place in my life, I would have been overjoyed for the lapse in obligations, the moments of peace. But now I was here. I was Rhaine Ka'Turoc, joined with Isnar, mother to Daniel. Here I was a Seeker who sought out peaceful solutions, who offered comfort and understanding. Here, I'd learned to bend.

Caught up in my clarity and resolution, I went downstairs and called Weeda. The connection buzzed through long enough that I almost ended the call but then her harried flat face appeared on the vid in front of me.

"Rhaine? What do you need?"

Always right to the point. That was probably just as well, less time for doubt to talk me out of this.

"I need you to do a quick procedure for me." I took a deep breath and said words that I'd never thought I'd give voice to. "I need my reproductive inhibitor removed."

Weeda's jaw went slack. She sputtered a moment before the same questions in my mind rolled off her tongue. "Are you sure? Is that wise? And at your age?"

"Yes, probably not, and I agree thirty-eight isn't ideal, but it's still well within safe parameters."

Weeda chewed on her lip. I could almost see her running calculations in her head. Eventually, she nodded. "When?"

"Can you come by my office tomorrow? We can do it in the back room. I was told it would only take a few minutes. I can send you the details."

"I'll see you tomorrow after midday."

"Thank you, Weeda."

She chuckled. "Your Ishlan might, but you'll likely be cursing at me for the duration of the pregnancy if what you've told me of your past experience repeats itself."

"I'll try to keep my cursing to a minimum." I reached out to end the call but paused with my finger on the button. "Could we keep this between us? I don't want to get Isnar's hopes up. I've been on the inhibitor for a long time, and the hybrid part could make it harder for a pregnancy to take at my less than ideal age."

Weeda nodded. "That sounds wise. It shall be as you say."

"Thank you." I terminated the call.

❧

My first client the next morning made me wonder if Isnar had our house bugged. I hadn't recognized her name when she'd booked the counseling session, but when a familiar face showed up at my door announcing herself as Marilee, I braced myself for a subtle jab from one of Isnar's office girls.

She took the offered chair and fidgeted with her fingers. If Isnar was going to send someone to fish for details on my talk with Weeda, he'd chosen poorly. I began to wonder if this was a legitimate session and what Marilee might have to say in light of the surprise session I'd had with Roshonomen.

"What brings you here today?" I prodded.

She cleared her throat and straightened herself in the chair. "Roshonomen said you're safe to talk to? That you won't file any reports?"

"Our sessions are confidential, yes." And if this had anything to do with Isnar and Jersen, I hardly would have reported anything anyway.

Marilee let out a relieved sigh. "You never met Jerson, did you?"

I shook my head, attention locked on the petite woman in front of me.

"He could seem charming. At first, you know, like some men can?"

"Yes." I lived with one of those, according to people in our colony. In truth, he was the opposite, the charming side was secondary. The dangerous, imposing part was definitely first.

"Jersen wasn't like us, like the men around here."

"He wasn't Verian?"

"He was." Marilee glanced at the door. "But he didn't act like one of us. He never would have come to see a Seeker."

I'd heard enough from Roshonomen to gather Jersen's brain had been wired differently than the average Verian. "Maybe if he had, I could have helped him."

"Perhaps." Marilee smiled sadly.

"Is there something you need to tell me about Jersen? He's gone now. He can't harm anyone."

"He took our son," she blurted.

I had to catch myself to keep my mouth closed when it wanted to fall open. While others in their sessions had alluded to incidents like this, I'd yet to speak to anyone directly about it. There were so many questions to ask. 'Does Isnar know' was top on my list, but he hardly needed his name inserted into any of this farther than it already was. "Took how? Did you report this?"

"My Ishlan worked here, at Dugans I mean, Jersen befriended him. He came to our home, met our children. Two days later, our son, our oldest, who was nine, was gone. Just gone." Her voice shook.

I couldn't imagine having Daniel suddenly missing from my life, and I'd only been around for half of his short time with us. "That must have been awful."

Marilee nodded.

"What leads you to think that Jersen had something to do with his disappearance?" And why was she so concerned about the authorities hearing any of this?

"My Ishlan was arrested three days later. He's still in prison." Tears welled in her eyes.

I shook my head, trying to piece her scattered story together so I could feasibly offer some sort of resolution or comfort. "Why was he arrested?"

"They claimed he'd been running drugs with one of Jersen's trade partners. They said they had witnesses, that there was plenty of evidence."

I had a hard time picturing any Verian running drugs. Then again, maybe that made them the perfect carrier.

"What did your Ishlan say?"

"That he was guilty. That I needed to protect our children and keep quiet."

"What about your missing son?"

"Jersen's insurance that I'd do what my Ishlan said. If I worked for him, my son would be treated kindly and my Ishlan would live out his sentence and come home."

"Your Ishlan took the fall for Jersen's drug run gone bad," I said, thinking out loud.

Marilee's gaze locked with mine. "You think my Ishlan isn't guilty?"

"I'd have to do some digging, but I'd give that fifty-fifty odds. And even if he was doing the deal, it was only because Jersen forced him too, likely by threatening to harm your family."

"Why would you think such terrible things?" she asked.

Because I'd done deals just like Jersen? "I've seen terrible things," I said instead. "Jersen has been gone for two years. Why are you telling me this now?"

"If my Ishlan is guilty, he should serve his time," she said resolutely. "But others have said that your Ishlan has helped them. With problems Jersen caused, I mean. I don't want to cause any trouble, to bring another investigation down on your Ishlan or the company, but my son is innocent. All the children are."

Merilee's hand flew over her mouth. "I'm sorry, I shouldn't have said that. It's not my place." She sprang up from the chair. "This was a mistake. I'm sorry."

"All the children?" I jumped out of my chair, leapt over it, and blocked her escape. It wasn't a very Seeker-like thing to do, but my mind was distracted with running suppositions and how to go about my investigation without gaining attention.

She halted abruptly, just short of running into me. "How did you move so fast?"

I pointed her back to the chair. "Our session isn't finished. I will help you, but I need more information."

Marilee gulped. She seemed to gauge her chances of getting around me and opted for returning to her seat. "To keep them safe, I was told to do my Ishlan's job for half the wages he made. I could barely pay our bills."

"And you're not the only one in this situation?"

She shook her head.

That explained the high number of women working at Dugans and why they were so fond of my Ishlan who paid them a more than fair rate.

"All right then. We'll sort this out. I'll need Isnar involved. He knows Jersen's connections. Do I have your consent to share what you've told me?"

Her hands twisted on her lap. "He's so busy. I would hate to be a bother."

"You're not. Think of it as giving him a redeeming task to make up for what he did to set you all free," I said, rather proud of my sudden onset of Seeker-sounding wisdom.

Marilee smiled. "As you say, Ishla. I will tell the others."

"Let them know they can talk to either of us. Whichever they find more comfortable."

"Thank you."

"Anytime." I finished our session with a traditional chant and blessing and sent her on her way, all the while counting the minutes until I could talk to Isnar.

THIRTY-NINE

Jey

Taking a break from the neverending job that was the Narvan, seemed frivolous in light of all that I needed to do, but I didn't want to slight Merkief or his mate. He'd been tied up at home for a week after the birth of his daughter, and I'd been doing my best to cover for him. I'd already had one meeting with the Council this week about his lack of focus. That was on top of the two other similarly-themed meetings over the past few months since my return from the latest Council-required territory acquisition.

At this point, I was fairly certain I didn't have to worry about Merkief taking the Narvan from me. While it may have been on his radar when we'd first taken on the position, his attention was now elsewhere. If I didn't want the Council to cull him and have all of the Narvan dropped in my lap permanently, I was going to have to find an amicable way to tell him to get his ass back in the action.

"Isn't she perfect?" Merkief asked, gazing down at the blanket-wrapped bundle in his arms.

I nodded for lack of anything constructive to say. What I should have pointed out is that she was a diversion he couldn't afford. *We* couldn't afford. Having a mate waiting at home was one thing, but this? How long until they popped out a few more, and he needed more time off? Even with this one, he was going to want to Jump home anytime she sneezed, for Geva's sake. One thing I did know for sure about Artorians was that they were very protective of their families. To a fault.

Narantha, looking tired but otherwise healthy, pointed at me. "Let him hold her. That will be worthy of a still frame for sure." She laughed.

Before I could decline, Merkief carefully held out his child to me. Ah fuck.

I did my best to mimic what he'd been doing and not crush or drop their tiny liability. To my great annoyance, Narantha captured a still frame.

"That will go in her memory box," she assured me. "When she gets older, you two will have something to laugh about."

The two of them were doing plenty of laughing already. I didn't need to see the image to know how comical it looked.

"If you're done giggling, take her back." I held the baby out to Merkief.

Narantha took her instead. "Are you afraid she's going to contaminate you with domestic urges?"

I snorted. "Yes, that's definitely a concern."

Narantha snickered her way into the kitchen with the baby tucked under one arm. She looked so comfortable with it, like it was natural and ordinary. I turned to Merkief to find him watching her walk away with a sickeningly blissful smile on his face.

Maybe the Council was right. Maybe I should take the sole advisory position and let him have this. He seemed happy here, at peace.

"We named her Anasta," he said quietly.

The question I'd been about to ask got stuck behind the sudden lump in my throat. "She'd be honored, I'm sure."

He nodded, staring after his family, now out of sight in the kitchen. Plates clanked together. Water ran in the sink.

"Sounds like dinner is almost ready," he said. "How long has it been since you've had a home-cooked meal?"

"No idea. A very long time." And this one would undoubtedly be Artorian in nature, probably shellfish, as that was my least favorite of what he and Vayen would pick up back when we'd all shared meals in Kazan's service.

Before I lost the opportunity, I asked, "Would you want this full-time? I mean, if it were an option?"

"This?" Merkief glanced around the house that was a stark contrast to Kazan's homes that we'd shared.

People lived here. There were flowers on the table, pillows out of place on the couch, baby paraphernalia all over the common room. An unfolded blanket had been tossed over the back of the couch. Still frames hung on the wall, including one of the two of them at their joining ceremony that I'd taken for them. There were little bits of both of them everywhere I looked.

"That would be great, but that's not an option, is it? We have the Narvan to run and Kess to keep in check," he said.

Gathering my nerve, I cleared my throat and prayed for something friendly to come out. "I could, if you wanted, deal with the brunt of it all so you'd have more time here. If you wanted to step down, I mean."

He froze. "Give up my half of the Narvan?"

"It's not like we're having the time of our lives or rolling in the credits and glory of it all. The position is a huge weight to carry. Maybe you'd like this better? You could still help out when you wanted to. I'd need your help for some things for sure, but it would be less stress, less time away."

He watched the doorway for a long moment and then his head snapped toward me. "You think you can take my half of the Narvan? I earned this position every bit as much as you did."

I held up my hands. "I'm not taking anything. It was just an offer."

Narantha popped out of the kitchen. She held Anasta out to Merkief. "Can you take her while I get everything on the table?"

He nodded and took the baby. His movements were stiff as he walked over to the table and sat down. I followed at a cautious distance and sat across from him.

"You can keep your damned offer and forget you ever made it," he said tightly.

"Maybe I should go," I suggested.

He sure as all hells looked like he was going to tell me to get the fuck out, but instead he said, "Narantha worked all day on this. It would be a shame to disappoint her."

Just when I thought the night couldn't get any better, Narantha walked in with a giant platter of steamed shellfish.

She smiled widely. "I hope you're both hungry."

FORTY

Rhaine

Isnar had an incredulous look on his face after I told him about Marilee's situation. "I can't believe she didn't say anything."

I pointed to his plate on the table. "Your dinner is getting cold."

"A woman's mate is in prison and her son is being held somewhere thanks to that viscu Jersen, and you're worried about my dinner?"

"You don't want to go rampaging off on an empty stomach."

He slammed his open palm on the table. "I'm not rampaging anywhere."

I regarded him with a raised eyebrow. "That's good to hear. Now eat. We can talk this through and then tomorrow you can use your sources to get to the bottom of this. Marilee suggested that others of your staff suffered similar circumstances. I'm sure we'll have our hands full with sorting this all out for a while."

Isnar shook his head, pushing food around on his plate with his fork. "I knew he'd blackmailed them, most of them, for various things. That's how he roped them into working for next to nothing, but I didn't know that he'd gone this far. I was far too kind with his end."

"No, you were smart. Flaying him alive would have looked very suspicious. Besides, letting the wild animals eat him was a nice touch."

"I thought so," he said around a mouthful of flaky fish.

We spent the rest of the meal discussing how to proceed with the investigation and leads he would check into in the morning. Daniel ate in relative silence, letting us hold a mostly uninterrupted conversation. And to think I was considering ruining that by granting Isnar's wish. I sighed.

"What's the matter?" he asked.

"Nothing." I gauged the mess he'd made in the kitchen with the energy level of our kid and my intentions for the rest of the evening. "How about you take that dirty little creature upstairs for a bath before bed and I'll clean up here."

"Sure."

He carried a load of plates over to the counter and then swung Daniel up onto his shoulders. Daniel squealed with glee as they bounced up the stairs.

Cleaning up the table and the counter took less time than washing a giggling kid. Listening to the two of them made me smile. This was what he deserved. Both of them.

By the time they were done in the bathroom and several stories had been read, I'd committed to giving him what he wanted. If we were going to do this, I had every intention of at least making this end of the process as enjoyable as possible.

Isnar turned out the lights in the hallway and opened our door to find me stretched out naked on his armor.

"I miss the smell of this, don't you?"

He may have answered with words, but I was too caught up in the searing heat flowing through our bonded connection to pay attention. His lips and hands took over from there.

At some point he'd shed his clothes because he was naked the next morning, sprawled out on three-quarters of the bed. I was too tired and sore for very enjoyable reasons to care about his space-hogging tendencies.

"You're going to be late." I poked him again.

He grunted and finally stirred.

"I'll take Daniel today. I'm guessing you'll have your hands full."

"Sure. Yes. All right." He shoved his hair behind his ears and rubbed his face. Still looking half-asleep, he pulled on a pair of pants and headed for the bathroom.

I got up slowly, stretching as I did so. After that long and gratifying night, I was going to need to do a little muscle untangling on my mat. Smiling to myself, I picked up the apparently aphrodisiac armor and returned it to the safety of the closet.

❧

"I found three of the kids," Isnar informed me over dinner.

"Already? You work fast."

He grinned. "I had a few good leads."

I'd done some digging between clients that morning and sent him what I'd uncovered. "Glad they panned out."

"Jersen had been supplying a workhouse with slave labor for years. I'm guessing we'll find a few more missing people there. Verians tend to stand out on other worlds."

I nodded, enjoying his good mood. "Anyone else come forward?"

"Two more. Once Marilee spread the word and Rosh backed her up, it loosened a few tongues."

"Good. I'm booked up all next week. I'm guessing some of those are your people too. Most are anonymous session requests.

"I'm glad they're able to talk to you. They're grateful, but nervous with me."

I'd noticed that same thing. They knew what they'd dragged into their midst when they'd made their offer. He was an evil they needed and appreciated, but he was still an evil.

"You want me to put Daniel to bed?" he asked when we were done eating.

The mischief glinting in his eyes was not lost on me. "Yes, that would be great."

And so we launched into a new pleasant routine. Gym nights at Dugans, updates on undoing Jersen's deeds, early to bed with Daniel, and more enjoyable evenings than not in the bedroom.

Everything was progressing nicely until one morning, three months later, I woke up in a murky cloud of nausea that was nothing like one of my headaches. The fun had ended. It was time to make good on my compensation for his sacrifices.

I'd given it four more weeks just to make sure. I knew the signs well enough that I didn't need Weeda to confirm them: exhaustion, nausea, headaches, and a bloated feeling that just kept getting worse. My only question at that point was how long was this going to take? I broke down and called Weeda to do an exam at my shop.

She sanitized her hands and took the scanner from her bag. "Are you excited?"

I answered honestly with a pained grimace. "To get this over with? Yes. How long?"

"The pregnancy took quickly," she said as she moved the scanner over my suddenly rounding belly, which was part of the reason I needed information before springing this on Isnar.

"It seems Artorians are good at that." It had only taken a few times with Chesser, and while I'd definitely encouraged the quantity with Isnar, I had a feeling I was well on my way with this one too. Most of our efforts had likely been after the fact.

She nodded. "Strong heartbeat. That's good. You mentioned Daniel was large from the start?"

"That's what my doctor said, yes. Normal gestation for me would be nine months but Artorians run six. He was six. Please tell me that's all this one will take too. I'd love to know I only have to put up with this for four more months."

She pondered her scanner for a few minutes and then consulted her datapad. "You can sit up," she said absently.

"Well?" My patience had left a month ago. I'd struggled to keep my Seeker persona intact every day since.

"Hybrid children are hard to gauge. You understand that, right?"

I nodded, feeling guilty for being short with her. My damned emotions were all over the board. Isnar was already worried that my headaches were worse lately, and I snapped at him far more than I meant to.

Weeda held up her scanner to show me a still frame of a tiny body trapped inside mine. "Rhaine, meet your daughter."

A lump formed in my throat. I wanted to cry but I was petrified at the same time. I had no idea how to parent a daughter. Would Isnar want a girl? He loved roughhousing with Daniel. I supposed he could do that with a girl too if it came to that. My heartbeat evened back out after a moment.

"From her development, I'd guess you're three months in. But she's small for an Artorian. Have you been eating and sleeping?"

"No, on both."

"I'm going to give you something for the nausea, but you will need to sleep. How did you manage the first pregnancy?"

"My doctor helped. He did acupressure." I sighed again. "I tried to show Isnar how to do it once."

She smiled. "Show him again. I'm sure he'll be happy to help you any way he can."

Oh heavens. The hovering. I swore in Trade but Weeda picked up on most of it.

"You may want to keep that to yourself when you make your announcement," she said, chuckling

"I will. Thank you for coming."

"I'll be back next week."

"Weekly? Is that necessary?"

She stared me down.

"Right. I'll see you next week."

Weeda nodded and then packed up her things and left.

Taking a deep breath, I collected my wits and called Isnar.

My anxious Ishlan burst into my shop with a jangle of bells on the door. He set Daniel down and hurried over to where I stood by the counter. It was a good halfway point between the door so I could see when he arrived and the bathroom where my midday meal had just gone.

He took my shoulders in his hands. "Are you all right?"

"As well as can be expected. Sorry, I didn't mean to make you rush over here." I laughed nervously. I was sweating. His concern filled our connection.

"Do you need me to call Weeda?"

"No, she was just here."

"Is it the damage again? I thought we had that under control."

"It is." I grabbed his arms, needing something firm to hold onto. "I'm pregnant."

He stood there staring at me, frozen.

"Did you hear me?"

A grin spread over his face. "Really? You're pregnant?"

I nodded. For a moment, to see the joy on his face, the misery of all of this was worthwhile.

"Is everything all right? From what you said about carrying him," he pointed to Daniel, "this wasn't easy."

"We think so, but she's small so Weeda is going to do weekly check-ups."

"She?" His grin grew impossibly bigger.

Well, that answered that concern. A girl was fine by him.

"Yes."

He kissed me and then crushed me to him before letting go to grab Daniel and swing him around. "You're going to have a sister."

Daniel giggled and squealed until Isnar put him back on the floor.

He was suddenly right back in front of me. "What do you need? What do you need me to do?"

"If we're both going to make it through this pregnancy, you need to back off."

"Right. Backing off." He took a step backward. "What else?"

"Remember when I tried to show you how to do the acupressure like Peter used to do for me, like the lessons I learned as a Seeker?"

He nodded.

"You're going to need to learn how to do that. Fast. And I'll try to be patient, but it's really hard for me right now so please don't be mad when I snap at you." I suddenly wanted to cry for no fucking reason.

He took a step forward and then got a twitchy look and stepped back again. I waved him closer and was engulfed in his arms once again. This was going to be tough to navigate with my emotions all over the board. *Vearta* even.

"Is this why your headaches have been worse again? Why you've been feeling sick?"

"Yeah, and I have at least three more months to go. So I hope you're up for this nasty ride. It's only going to get worse."

"Worse? How much worse?"

He was pouring on the concern again.

I pulled out of his grasp, needing room to breathe. "I'd show you, but I can't. You'll just have to trust me on that."

"Are you done here? Would you like to go home and rest? You look tired."

I'd looked tired for weeks, but at least he'd had the grace not to point it out until now. "Yes, that sounds wonderful."

Seeming grateful for something concrete to do, he did a quick once over of the shop, tidying up the counter and putting the sheets I'd left on the massage table after Weeda's visit into the washing machine. It warmed my heart to see this towering and dangerous man cleaning up after me. Not only because he'd made the effort to know just how I preferred things to be, but because the word tidy did not describe him at all when left to his own devices.

While he finished, I utilized the bathroom yet again and then collected Daniel and my coat. He met us at the door and was doing his best to maintain at least a two-step distance until we got in the transport. During the ride, he stared at my stomach with that silly grin on his face. It made me laugh despite feeling sick.

When we got home, he hung out in the yard with Daniel for a bit, sitting on the front step while Daniel showed off his newest additions to our ever-growing rock pile. I watched them out the bedroom window for a few minutes, imagining another little body running around out there. Imagining Isnar with a daughter, and instantly pitying any boy who might consider looking her way. Chuckling, I crawled into bed.

Isnar woke me a couple of hours later. "Are you hungry?"

I nodded. "Toast maybe."

"That bad? You need to eat better than that."

"It's that bad."

His mouth opened and I had the feeling he was struggling to keep quiet on the topic, but he closed it again, got up, and went down to the kitchen.

I took one of the anti-nausea pills Weeda had given me, wishing it was a stim. What I would have given for a burst of energy just then.

By the time he returned with a glass of juice and a plate of buttered toast, my stomach was feeling more settled. Hopeful of a meal that might stick with me, I dove in.

"Where's Daniel?" I asked between bites.

"Playing in his room. Quietly even."

"Enjoy that while it lasts. Quiet will soon be a far-off dream again."

"That's fine." He settled onto the bed beside me and reached out tentatively to my stomach.

"You can't feel anything yet, but have at it."

He did. I didn't have to have our full connection in working order to pick up on the peace rolling off of him. It was all over his face and the light touch of his hand. I missed having his zen vibrantly in my head, but this wasn't so bad either.

Eventually, his gaze tore away from where his daughter grew to rest on my face. "I'm pretty sure this couldn't have been an accident. What changed your mind?"

"You asked for this one thing." I said, searching for the right words. "After everything you gave up to be here with me, I owed you."

His hand retracted. The peace shut down abruptly. For a moment, I thought *he* might be ill.

So much for him understanding my method of compensation.

He picked up my empty plate and glass and headed for the door, every move wooden. "I'll check on you later," he said quietly before closing the door behind him.

Merkief

Jey insisted that his current exploration missions were at the order of the High Council, but I saw through him. He was trying to impress them so they might grant him lead on the Narvan.

Even more aggravating, Kess seemed to know every time Jey left. He doubled down on his subtle attacks and I was left to face them alone.

Running the Narvan together, my ass. This was the fourth time Jey had slipped off with the Council excuse. I'd had enough. I sent a message to my Council contact, requesting a meeting.

Narantha popped her head into my office at our house. I'd been working from there more often than not, handling as much business as I could through my link or vid calls. That was safest, given Kess's spike in activity. "What's wrong?" she asked.

"Just work," I repeated the same answer I always gave her. It might not have been specific, but it was true.

She came in and sat down. I wanted to tell her to get out, that I had major issues to deal with, that I was in the middle of something, the middle of everything really, but she looked exhausted. I snapped out of my flurry of tasks to realize it was the middle of the night here.

"Go back to bed. I can take care of Anasta if she wakes up."

"It's not just work, is it?" She tapped her temple. "Don't lie to me."

The one downfall to our bonded connection was that she could sense everything I was feeling. Just as I could with her. The connection provided honesty and empathy. We were a couple now, joined of one mind. I hadn't considered that the vows were quite so literal, that the overheard comments and good-natured gibes between bonded men were not exaggerations. Narantha might not be able to read my mind, that would go against everything we believed in, but our ancestors had dialed us in as close to that as possible.

"You're angry all the time, distracted, busy, always busy." She shook her head. "I can't sleep with all this in my head."

Guilt slammed into me, guttering out my accusations against Jey, my retaliation plans against Kess, and my frustration with the incessant mess that was the Narvan and its far too many moving parts. It wasn't the baby wearing my mate down, it was me.

That realization sunk in further. I thought about how many nights I'd sat in here working, maybe grabbing a couple of hours of sleep beside her. Being caught up in near constant meetings and aspects of the Narvan I didn't want to share, I barely spoke to her about day-to-day things beyond the care of our daughter. Once I acknowledged it all, the muffling dam I hadn't realized I'd erected between us broke, flooding me with her frustration, exhaustion, and concern.

Unable to move under the weight of it all, I could only plead for forgiveness. "I'm sorry. I didn't realize—"

Narantha came around my desk to stand behind my chair. She wrapped her arms around me and rested her chin on my shoulder. The peace she offered when we were like this drove away everything that had been on my mind and let me relax.

"You're tired too," she said in my ear. "Come to bed."

I was. I leaned my cheek against hers, enjoying the warmth and comfort of this simple thing.

Reality crept into the cloud of peaceful bliss. This was why I kept my mate at a distance. I couldn't afford to relax. None of what I'd been working on was going to slow down or stop. If I went to bed, there would be twice as much to deal with when I woke up. I cursed Jey for his selfish fucking mission to Geva knew where this time.

"Merkief, you're fighting it. Stop. Just for one night. Please."

I nodded. One night. She deserved a lot more, but I could give her what was left of this one.

We went to the bedroom together. I didn't dare let go. If the peace between us wavered, my resolve would crumble and I'd be back to work in a heartbeat. With Narantha's hand still on mine, we settled onto the bed and closed our eyes. Everything else faded as I gave in to the calm she wrapped around both of us.

❧

It was early morning when the Council summons intruded on my sleep enough to drag me into wakefulness. I hated to wake Narantha but I also couldn't just take off without a word. I opted for making more noise than necessary while changing out of the clothes I'd fallen asleep in.

Narantha wiped at her eyes. "Leaving already?"

"I've got an important meeting."

"They're all important, aren't they?" she muttered as she slid into the middle of the bed and pulled the blankets around her.

"Some more than others. I'll try to be back by midday so I can help you with Anasta."

Damn it, why did the Council have to drag me in now? I needed to spend some time with Narantha beyond falling into an exhausted sleep beside her.

She waved me off. "Do what you need to do so you can maybe come to bed at a reasonable time tonight."

Seeing her there, like that, I regretted turning Jey down on his offer to take lead on the Narvan. Should I step back and enjoy more time with my mate and our daughter? I let Narantha's calm wash over me, imagining what it would be like to have the leisure to enjoy this for full days at a time, to spend more time with Anasta, to not have the weight of the Narvan weighing me down.

I stood there gazing at the warm and cheerful woman I loved. She was everything I'd hoped for, far more than I deserved, and even as annoyed as she got with my position, she still put up with me. Geva, I could cut my losses with it all, grab what credits I had readily available and start over with my family on a little no-name planet somewhere far from the threats and stress of the Narvan and the Council. My heart raced as the idea took hold.

She eyed me curiously. "Merkief?"

I took a step toward her, the words on my tongue.

The Council ping hit me again, shattering my dreams of escape. Maybe once Kess was taken care of, once I knew Jey had the Narvan firmly in hand, knew that my people would get the guidance they needed to flourish, then I could go.

Or if I were able to stomp out the competition and firmly establish myself with the Council, then I wouldn't have to look over my shoulder so much. I'd have more time to spend with my family. The best of both worlds might be on the other side of this meeting. After everything I'd been through, that I'd lost and gained, worked for, bled for, I had to try. If it didn't work out, I'd revisit my escape-it-all plan.

I leaned down to kiss Narantha's forehead. "I'll do my best to be home for dinner for once."

She smiled. I took one last deep breath within the peace she exuded and Jumped to Sere.

❧

A helpful grey-suit directed me to a meeting room.

Two cloaks sat at a long table. I took a seat toward the middle so I wouldn't have to yell and got right to business.

"How would you feel about a single advisor of the Narvan?" I asked.

"We're not opposed," said a male voice from a very large cloak.

"Do you feel you'd be the best option?" asked a female voice.

"I'm the one here running everything while my partner keeps wandering off on adventures in the great unknown."

"We've noticed," said the female. "Your hold on the position is improving."

Improving? Like the past two and a half years had been some sort of training exercise? I gritted my teeth in an attempt to keep my annoyance to myself.

"How is your family?" asked the male.

How the hells would they know I had a family? We'd kept everything quiet. The guards I had watching the house hadn't mentioned anyone paying undue attention to it. Narantha only Jumped directly to her parents' house or mine. We hadn't chanced a transport since we'd gotten joined. For that matter, she'd barely left the house since Anasta had been born, using vid calls for her family visits.

I had to give them something or they'd suspect I was hiding information from them. How much did they know? "My parents are fine, why?"

They were silent longer than I was comfortable with, but I sure as all hells wasn't going to offer anything further without reason.

"And Advisor Atta, has he been cooperative?" asked the female.

"Hardly, as you likely know. Someone here has been feeding him information."

"We'll look into that," said the male in a tone that led me to believe they'd do no such thing.

"And your relationship with your partner?" asked the female like they were working off a damned checklist.

"Tolerable. Better when he's doing his job. He claims you sent him off on this mission. Is that true?"

Again with the silence.

"So what do I need to do to make this a solo position?" I asked on the off chance I'd actually get an answer.

"Prove yourself," said the female.

"I'm already doing everything you ask of me. What more do you want?"

"Your predecessors took care of those things that prevented them from getting or doing what they wanted."

Took care of to what degree? Did they simply mean I should talk Jey into the backseat position so he could go off and explore as much as he and the Jalvian fleet wanted? Were they implying that I should take Kess out? I'd been trying, dammit.

Would asking for clarification make me seem dimwitted? Surely Vayen hadn't ever asked for more details. He'd just done whatever the fuck he'd wanted. With as many contracts as he'd completed while juggling the entire damned Narvan, the Council was unlikely to have censured him about anything. Jey and I weren't that lucky.

"All right then. I'll see what I can do."

"We'll be watching."

If that wasn't ominous, I didn't know what was. I had no doubt they'd been watching before, but now that I'd made my intentions known, I'd invited them to watch my every move.

As I got up and walked out, I wanted to slap myself.

In order to have time to take another stab at Kess, I needed to deal with a few matters first, most of which were his fault. Kess had moved from destroying my crops on Moriek back to sabotaging the ones on Syless. At the same time, a lab on Artor that had been manufacturing a promising vaccine for a new virus, also likely from Kess, had been bombed from the inside, destroying the entire building as well as all the others nearby. And there were plentiful rumors of an upcoming tax increase on Moriek. The public wasn't buying my denial, instead reveling in social unrest.

I spent my day hunting Kess's agents on Syless while delegating the elimination of his riot-causing agents on Moriek to a few of my deadly contacts. The bomber on Artor was likely long gone, but I also sent aid to help the wounded and assist with clean up, issuing a statement that the explosion had been a tragic accident. A lot of tragic accidents had been happening over the past couple of years and the Primes and Premieres were starting to put that together, demanding answers. I doled them out as vaguely as possible through my link.

I managed to catch two of Kess's agents in the midst of destroying one of the seeding machines on Syless. While I dearly wanted to take care of them myself, that wasn't the image I wanted portrayed on the news vids, certainly not anywhere that Narantha or our parents might see. Following proper procedure, I contained them and referred their location to the local enforcers with the orders that a statement would be made divulging they'd been sent by Kess. Then they were to be publicly executed.

If I could give the public someone other than me to blame for all of our troubles, I'd have the Narvan behind me in storming the Nebula. And if Kess's actions went public, the Council wouldn't be able to offer him protection any longer. Taking him out one on one hadn't worked. It was time I try something larger scale, something to make the Council take notice. They'd told me to take care of him, bringing the entire Artorian fleet against him would certainly do just that. I grinned as I Jumped home for dinner.

Jey burst into my head. *"What the hells are you doing?"*

"Taking care of Kess, once and for all."

It had taken a month of going hard after Kess's operatives and multiple public executions on every world in the Narvan with the exception of Frique, but I now had the Artorian fleet in agreement to attack the Nebula. The remainder of the Jalvian fleet that hadn't gone with Jey was on standby in the Narvan in case Kess sent more of his mysterious allies in our direction while we were occupied.

"Where are you?" Jey more demanded than asked.

I sent him my location on the bridge of one of the Artorian ships that was preparing to leave the station where it had been docked.

He stepped out of the void with one arm raised and promptly punched me in the face. Before I could react, he clamped his other hand on me and Jumped us both to the ship.

"Are you fucking insane?" he yelled. "You cannot go after Kess like this. It will void our position with the Council. We had an agreement, remember?"

"We did, until they started working with Kess."

He shook his head. "It could be a single leak within the Council. We don't know how much support Kess has.

"They want me to prove I can take care of him. They said so."

He looked at me like I'd lost my mind. "They said that you should take a whole fleet and hunt down one man? The one man we're not supposed to be in open contention with?"

"Not the fleet, but that I should take care of him." I shoved him back. "What do you care? You're not even in the Narvan anyway."

"Did you think I just walked away? I'm doing what the Council asked me to. I didn't *want* to be gone."

"Really? Because they wouldn't confirm that."

His lips drew into a thin line and the one prominent vein on his forehead bulged more than usual. That was never a good sign. I stepped back.

"Did it ever occur to you that they might be trying to pit us against one another? That if they wanted Kess to swoop in and take the Narvan, it would be much easier with just one of us to deal with?" His brows lowered as a scowl settled over his face. "No wonder they keep sending me out. They're driving you to screw up so they have an excuse to hand the Narvan over."

I thought back to the Council's invisible checklist and them watching my every move. They'd shown no indication of their thoughts on my actions since I'd made my declaration. Did I actually have their backing to make a big stand against Kess or was I handing them an open violation of our initial agreement to get me tossed out of the advisory position for good? Doubt crept in, shadowing every thought.

Was now the time to run? Even as I started to take stock of my available finances, my conscience couldn't accept the idea of cutting my losses, not if it meant the Narvan falling into Kess's hands.

"Are you even listening?" Jey snarled in my face. "You cannot take the fleet into the Nebula, do you understand? Tell them to stand down. Now."

Taking orders from Jey made me grit my teeth, but until I had time to sort through what he'd said, to consult with the Council and get some clear answers, I couldn't take the chance that he was right. I gave the order.

The fleets were none too happy about the de-escalation. There was a lot of grumbling from both Artorians and Jalvians. After all the public attention I'd been giving this matter lately, I didn't even want to consider what the news feeds were going to say about me now.

FORTY-TWO

Merkief

Jey had been impossible to deal with since his return to the Narvan. The partnership we'd once had was now held together by a few fragile strings. If we continued down this path much farther, I'd have another Kess-like rival on my hands.

He wouldn't budge on our trade policy review that I'd been trying to hammer out for almost three months now. We needed to come to an agreement fast or my funds were going to run dry and he damned well knew it. He wanted me desperate so he could get his way. He'd taken to hiding in a house he'd bought somewhere on Karin because he thought I didn't have a jump point there. The last time I'd seen him, I'd taken the opportunity to slip into his very aggravated mind and harvest a point in case I needed to catch him unaware. It was an integral piece of the plan if I decided to take that final step toward claiming the Narvan for my own.

I'd yet to work out how to get that by Narantha. For all her trepidation over meeting Jey initially, she'd grown to like him and had insisted on having him over numerous times for dinner. I think he knew how much it grated on me after his offer that first time, to have him in my home, eating with my family, because no matter what he was in the middle of, he accepted her invitation every damned time. She didn't even bother to ask if I wanted him there, just assumed that because we were partners, whatever was stressing me out certainly couldn't be him. And he, being Jey in the company of a woman, was well-mannered and polite, and not at all the asshole I had to deal with.

If I did take Jey out, Narantha, with our now fine-tuned bonded connection would inevitably pick up my feelings of gratification and start asking questions. The bond made it difficult to lie to her. The best defense from the darker parts of my job was to make sure they never came up. Which meant putting up with Jey. For now.

Which also meant that when the Council called, I answered. I needed to maintain their favor until I'd taken care of the competition.

I Jumped to Sere where I was pointed to the contract office. So it was one of those 'prove yourself' summons. They'd been doing those more often lately. Maybe they were getting closer to making a decision. Like always, I shoved my Narvan duties aside, let Narantha know I'd be busy until further notice, and set off to do the Council's bidding.

The contract was easy, as far as Council jobs went: intercepting a hand-held shipment between exchange points and eliminating both of those points so the interception wasn't immediately realized. It was the kind of job I'd been taking through other channels outside of the Narvan—quick, simple jobs for enough credits to help fulfill some of the smaller requests for my financial assistance.

The job went off easily with two well-placed bullets. I grabbed the sealed black plastube and slipped it into my coat. As I did so, I took someone else's well-placed bullet in the stomach. I groaned as another shot hit my armor at the shoulder. I didn't have time to take in the bodies well enough to Jump them. Leaving them to be found here would void my contract. I wasn't about to have this mess on my Kryon record, dammit. I popped a stim, took another bullet to my coat, and then took off after my attacker.

From the startled look on her face, I gathered that she'd hadn't expected me to be in any condition to give chase. She got as far as spinning around to run before I put a bullet in the back of her head.

Even with the stim, it was a painful half hour of Jumping dead weight and disposing of three bodies. I'd have to use the tank before delivering the shipment to the contract office. The delay would imply that I wasn't as efficient as I wanted to be known for, but showing up wounded from a simple contract also wasn't an option if I wanted to maintain my image.

The ship and tank were empty when I got there, the lights on standby. They flickered to life within seconds of my arrival. I pulled up my profile, undressed, and got onto the platform. As the platform rose, I ran through the blurred seconds between gaining possession of the tube and the bullet hitting my stomach. That woman had been waiting to take the shot, to take advantage of any distraction I might have had. Waiting to take me out. Was it Kess and his Council insider? The Council themselves? Someone else? The only thing I was certain of as the gel crept over me was that if I didn't gain the Council's favor, the next Kryon contract might be my last.

When I woke, I quickly showered, got dressed, and Jumped to Sere. The delivery of the shipment to the contract office went off without comment beyond an acknowledging nod from the woman behind the counter. I took my time wandering back to the designated jump point, waiting for the summons to a private meeting that I'd been hoping for, but my link was only plagued by funding requests and dismal news reports.

A hollowness settled into my stomach. Would the Council ever be satisfied? I'd done everything within my means that they'd asked of me, but my hold on the Narvan felt as tenuous as ever. Maybe now was the time to give up and run.

The sudden urge to go home, to see my family, to take comfort in Narantha's peace hit me hard. I'd give voice to my escape plan this time. She'd become the keeper of my conscience, the scraps of me that were still good. She'd know the right thing to do. I tried to put a positive spin on my thoughts so I wouldn't further burden her and Jumped home.

The house was quiet when I got there. The light was on in the foyer, where I'd set my jump point. Narantha always left it on for me so I wouldn't be in the dark when I got home. The rest of the house was set to night lighting, just enough to get around in without bumping into furniture. The hollow feeling intensified, spreading into my limbs, and making me sweat. The calm that usually washed over me when I was near Narantha didn't come.

My anxiety skyrocketed, sending my heart into an erratic beat that made me light-headed. I reached out to the two guards who were stationed outside within view of the house. The connection to one of them was gone, the other too faint to make full contact.

The urge to call out to Narantha was overwhelming, but my tongue was too thick to make a sound. All I had to do was reach out over our bonded connection and I'd realize everything was fine, that I was overreacting, that this anxiety was just the culmination of weeks full of shitty days. But something my mother used to say about asking questions I didn't want truthful answers to shook loose in my brain.

When my boot knocked into a soft shape, my breath hitched. Forcing myself to look down, I made out one of Anasta's stuffed toys by my foot.

Good Geva, I needed to calm the fuck down. With all the anxiety pouring out of me, I expected Narantha to come running out of the bedroom any second, whether she'd been sleeping or not.

But she didn't.

I turned the corner to the hallway that led to the stairs. A dark smear marked the wall and continued upward. Specks of darkness littered the carpet, and by halfway up, they became blotches. With my heart now lodged in my throat, I activated the rest of the lights throughout the house.

Knowing on some level what I was walking into, I contacted Jey. I didn't know for what exactly, maybe help, maybe accusation. Like Jumping to the tank room, contacting him was a reflex when shit was going to get ugly.

He didn't acknowledge me. I left it at an open ping so I could decide how to proceed when he did respond.

The bloody blotches became bloody footprints. I glanced at the walls, noting several bullet holes. It was easier than acknowledging the bloody, bare foot protruding from Anasta's open doorway. When I couldn't put it off any longer, I forced my feet to take a step closer. Then another. Each seemed to take an eternity.

Narantha was just inside the room, face up, a gun in one hand. Blood covered the clothes she'd worn to bed. Bullet holes riddled her chest like whoever had done this had stood right where I was standing, emptying the entire clip into her once she was down. Once she had no hope of getting back up. No hope of fighting back. The brutality of it was entirely unnecessary.

I tore my gaze from the body on the floor to the wall of the hallway. She'd emptied her gun as well by the looks of it and, judging by the height, she'd tried for headshots. From the lack of a body and the amount of blood on the floor and walls, she'd had to have been weak and in a panic. Even my accurate-shooting mate could have missed under those circumstances. She *had* missed.

Turning back to the body on the floor, I suddenly found myself on my knees next to it. To her. To Narantha, dead on the floor of our daughter's room. Silence threatened to crush me.

Anasta had to be gone. They'd taken her, whoever had done this. I'd get a message any minute, demanding credits or that I do something for them. I'd do whatever it was and then I'd have my daughter back.

I pulled myself over to the crib, begging Geva to show me that it was empty.

But it wasn't.

I could see Anasta there through the slats under the white fluffy blanket I'd bought for her. The soft sound of her breathing I'd grown so used to as I rocked her to sleep was missing.

A hit on my mate was one thing, but no self-respecting assassin would do this. No one would take that contract. No one was that heartless.

I managed to get my feet under me, to get my hands on the side of the crib and hold on as my vision blurred with a flood of tears. A fine spray of red covered the blanket. They'd shot my daughter in the head. My baby daughter, executed in her crib.

I picked her up and held her as I slid back down to the floor. A vacuum filled the room that had only a day ago held a cooing child and lullabies. Now it was only a screaming emptiness. I reached out for the comfort of Narantha's hand only to find it cold.

Time stopped as I sat there, aware only of the empty place inside me where the bond had been. Hot tears streamed down my face.

They were both gone.

In lurching thoughts, my mind slowly regained function.

They'd been taken from me while I'd been sleeping off the gel or in the tank unable to do a damned thing about it.

So that's why my attacker hadn't gone for the headshot while I'd been distracted. Someone wanted me alive. They wanted me to see this. To suffer.

With every ounce of my being, I needed a name. Someone was going to pay.

The guard who might still be alive outside, had he seen anything? Gently, I set my daughter down next to my mate so they could be together here as they were now with Geva.

Forcing myself to leave the room, I ran down the bloody stairs and then outside, heedless of who might see me. It didn't matter anymore. The news bots could report the location of my home and the death of my family all they wanted. Narantha hadn't gotten her fame in life, but everyone was sure as all hells going to know about her now. All of the Narvan would know what had been taken from me, my calm, my center, my beautiful mate. Our daughter. Grief strangled me, making it hard to breathe.

My family was dead. The one thing I could do for them was find their killer.

Following my instincts on the most likely positions for the house guards, I found the dead one first. The semi-live one took me a few minutes longer. He'd been shot numerous times. The puddle of blood surrounding him indicated he didn't have much left to lose.

Under normal circumstances, I wouldn't have chanced a probe on anyone so close to death, but nothing mattered beyond finding who was responsible. I dove in.

"Show me who did this," I demanded.

The image was blurry. A man in armor similar to mine. Jalvian. That was all I got before the image began to waver and fade. I pulled out just as the guard drew a shallow, gurgling breath. Seconds later, he went still.

There were two Jalvians who had connections to the Council, who could have gotten a lead from them, who had agents that could have been planted to take me out on a contract. Both of them had a lot to gain by my death, or if that failed, by murdering my family to weaken me.

But I wasn't weak.

I didn't have to worry about maintaining a good image for Narantha now. Whoever had taken my family from me was going to suffer a fate far worse than mine.

The Council wanted someone ruthless like Vayen? Like Kazan?

I checked the weapons under my armor.

Those two were going to have nothing on me.

FORTY-THREE

Jey

I woke to the screaming of my house alarm system and the distinctly unnerving feeling of a gun to my forehead. Instinct made my hand reach for the gun under the second pillow beside me but the jab of metal against my head halted that motion before I followed through.

My eyes opened to Merkief's rage-twisted face in sharp focus where he loomed over me.

"What's going on?" I asked, as though my mouth hadn't quite caught up to the situation yet. When I'd ignored his earlier message in favor of getting some sleep, I'd hardly expected this extreme of a response.

"Get up," he snarled, backing off a single step.

Comforted by the fact that he hadn't yet fired what I realized to be a fucking pulse pistol, I did as he requested, making sure to keep my empty hands visible. "Mind if I turn the alarms off?"

"Only if you can do it from here."

I would have preferred the two minutes to stroll downstairs to the security station in the kitchen so I would have had time to think clearly, maybe access news feeds, or covertly grab one of the six weapons I had hidden between here and there. But instead, I accessed the interface through my link, returning the house to silence.

"How'd you get in here?" I'd purposely not given him access to this new acquisition to prevent shit like this from happening.

"You've never been very sensitive to probes."

While dealings between us had been tense since my unwise offer to let him step down, I didn't think that warranted bursting into my house and putting a gun to my head. I brushed over my link connection with Narantha, hoping for some insight.

There was no connection on the other end. My blood ran cold.

I stood there, shivering, wearing only the pants I'd slept in while Merkief gave me a full once over with a gaze tinged by more than a sliver of crazy.

"You're not wounded," he stated flatly.

"Should I be?"

A flood of bloody images pummeled my brain, too fast for me to make out clearly, but I couldn't pretend not to understand what it was. There were bodies, a woman and a baby.

He reached out with his empty hand, grabbing my arm. The next thing I knew, we were in the foyer of his home on Artor. He shoved me ahead of him. "Upstairs."

The chill took hold in earnest in his quiet house, making me shiver. When I rounded the corner to the stairway, I didn't have to ask why I was here. Or why he was out of his mind. Or, most tragically, why I'd not been able to reach Narantha. The blood-smeared handprints all the way up the stairway told me everything.

"I didn't do this. You know I would never harm—"

He shoved me so hard I had to catch myself before I landed face-first on the next step. While I could have probably dodged forward far enough to give me the few seconds I needed to Jump away, it would only seal my guilt in his eyes. I was going to have to let this play out and pray for the best.

I walked down the hallway on autopilot. I'd never been up there but the blood on the floor and walls pointed the way to what he was determined to make me see.

Bright and cheerful Narantha lay in a thick puddle of drying blood, her body riddled with bullet holes. The single shot to Anasta's head brought bile to my mouth. I shoved my way back past Merkief and lost my last meal in the hallway.

Once I had my stomach back under control, I pointed to the family I'd half-started to think of as my own for as often as I'd been here and had talked to Narantha by link. "I did not do that. I would never do that."

"I've seen you do plenty of shady shit," he said with the pistol still in his hand. At least it was aimed at the floor now.

"Not to your family, dammit. You know me better than that."

"Do I?"

I didn't like how his trigger finger twitched or the crazed look that had taken hold of him.

"Yes. You do," I said firmly

"Where were you during the past seven hours?"

"Sere, for a private meeting and then a Kryon contract."

My stomach threatened to rebel again. I sat on the floor, back against the wall, staring with blurry eyes at the holes opposite me where Narantha had fought back.

When the Council had called me in for a meeting about Merkief, I'd assumed it was a routine check in, making sure he was doing his job and not fucking around with Kess again. They'd asked about his family, if they were a security risk for Kryon business and if I felt he'd be able to ever fully focus on the Narvan again. They'd asked about his loyalty to the Council. Nothing in their inquiry had set off any alarms for me. They'd known about Narantha and Anasta, they'd known where the house was. Surely that was because Merkief had told them. It wasn't because the Council was asking me questions while some telepathic bastard did one of those subtle-ass probes like Merkief had done to get the location of my house.

If this was my fault... I put my head in my hands.

"What?" He got down in my face, pistol still in one hand. "What did you do?"

"You told the Council about your family, didn't you?" I whispered. "They knew, didn't they?"

The dangerous, steely look Vayen had often worn made a very unwelcome debut on Merkief's face. "They didn't hear a word from me. If they knew, they never made that clear."

He put the pistol to my head again.

Looking at the dead woman and her child only a few feet away, I didn't have the inclination to protest.

"What did you tell them?" he asked.

"Nothing they didn't already seem to know."

"Did they probe you?"

I couldn't say with a clear conscience that they hadn't. I dove into my memory of that meeting, trying to detect if I'd noticed the slight slithery feeling of someone slipping into my head. I didn't think I had. But then, I hadn't noticed when Merkief had stolen the house jump point from me either. My defenses were good, dammit, but so was Merkief. The Council had probed me after Vayen and Kazan had been killed and I hadn't felt that either.

"Did they fucking probe you?" he yelled.

"I don't know."

He hit me with the pistol. The hard thwap reverberated through my head. Seconds later, blood ran down my forehead from a cut I felt there. It trickled down my nose, over my lip, and off my chin onto my chest. I sat there, watching the blood drip.

"Of course you don't fucking know. Your inferior Jalvian defenses got my family killed." He hit me again, with his fist this time.

I didn't stop him, but after the third punch, I stumbled to my feet and lurched down the hallway to put some space between us, between me and the bodies in the bedroom.

"We don't know they probed me," I said.

His snarl said otherwise.

There had to be a way to know. I needed to know. "Can you get in my head and see? Maybe trace whoever it was, if there was a probe?"

The slight shake of his head killed that little hope. "Not unless they did a piss poor job, and anyone associated with the Council or Kryon is above that."

"But there were only two cloaks in the room. The Council wouldn't do this."

"If they're good enough, anyone could probe you from the next room or the hallway, anywhere close by, for Geva's sake. It could have been Kess for all we know."

"Kess is Jalvian."

"He could work with someone who could probe you." His crazy level dialed down to an eerie calm. "Clean this up. I'll deal with a service when I get back." He didn't say *if*, but it was there, silent and ominous.

"Let me get dressed, I'll come with you."

He raised the gun and aimed it at me. "I already gave you something to do. Do it."

"Sure. All right. Just don't get yourself—"

He Jumped.

Caught between concern that he was going to get killed and wondering if he was just crazy enough now to give him a no-holds-barred edge over Kess, I realized that neither of those things immediately mattered. I'd deal with the outcome either way when it came to pass. For now, I had something I could do, something I needed to do to try to make up for what I may have had a hand in.

The heavy weight hanging around my neck told me that I had definitely had a hand in it.

As though all my muscles had stiffened at once, I worked my

way back down to the floor and sat there shaking, staring at the bare, bloody feet of a woman I'd considered a friend. I doubted Merkief had any idea how often we'd talked. She'd needed to vent and I was the only one who knew everything, the one she didn't have to worry about letting anything slip with. And now she was gone.

Using my link, I contacted the local enforcers, apprising them of the situation. Within half an hour, they swarmed the place, finding me there in the hallway, still on the floor, half-dressed with a bloody face.

By that point, I didn't have it in me to do more than explain that this was Merkief's family, their Advisor's family. That they'd been murdered. That, in his grief, he'd left and no, I didn't know where he'd gone, but that their bodies should be held until he resurfaced.

They declared they'd do a thorough investigation, that they'd report all findings to their Advisor. They suggested I leave, get my head looked at, and get cleaned up. They knew where to find me if they had additional questions.

It wasn't until after I'd left that I realized they hadn't asked how I'd come to be wounded or what I was doing there. But they'd also let me go. They wouldn't have done that if I were a suspect.

Using the tank to erase what Merkief had done felt wrong. I dragged out a med kit and sat in front of a mirror, trying not to see my own face, trying to only focus on the gash that I closed up and slathered with healing gel.

Not knowing when or if Merkief would return, I decided to hold an Artorian service of my own. Sitting in the dark house, I thought about Naratha's laughter and her cheery conversation. The woman barely had a drop of darkness in her. She'd been good for Merkief. Hells, good for me, and I wasn't even involved with her.

Hadn't been. Another person I was going to have to get used to referring to in the past tense.

I drank a good half of my bottle before it occurred to me that with Merkief off on a broken-bond-binge somewhere, I should probably remain generally sober. But really, it was bad form to not empty the bottle. Narantha and her daughter deserved a proper send off. The Narvan could limp along on its own for a while. I sat and I drank.

FORTY-FOUR

Jey

Merkief sat behind the desk in the office on the ship. Even though three months had passed since his family had been murdered, that off-kilter gleam in his eye remained. What he'd done when he'd taken off after their deaths, I didn't know. He'd simply reappeared and offered no comment. The public ceremony for his family was poorly attended, mostly representatives from the planetary heads who had all bowed out of attending in person, and those who were looking to earn his favor or funding. His parents and Narantha's had attended, but neither of them spoke to Merkief. While Narantha's parents seemed entirely devastated by the loss of their daughter and grandchild, his own parents glared daggers in his direction. What goodwill he'd regained with them had vanished.

That might have been the fault of the media coverage, which Merkief was also livid about. The news outlets had put their own spin on my presence in his house—saying that unable to reach her mate, Narantha had called on me. I'd been knocked unconscious while attempting to defend his family and they'd been killed. All anyone knew for sure was that the suspect was a Jalvian male and it wasn't me.

But it was. I hadn't pulled the trigger, but I'd very likely provided everything else for the killer.

And so when Merkief had demanded to pull lead from now on, I didn't argue. When he made unpopular decisions, I did my best to smooth them out. Like now, when tensions on the Jalvian worlds were running high. I could see all of the work we'd done to unify the system falling apart before my eyes.

"You'll have to sort it out," Merkief said in the unyielding tone he'd adopted from Vayen's handbook on Narvan domination.

"I'll do what I can."

"We need the Jalvian fleet fully behind us, so you better make sure that you do."

Were I not feeling like a complete piece of shit, I might have pointed out that constantly and vehemently declaring that a Jalvian had killed his family was not working in his favor for holding Jalvian loyalty. A more level-headed Merkief would have spotted the issue himself and maybe attempted to fix it, but this one, he just stormed his way through each day like all the known universe could just fuck off.

The only upside to the tragic situation was that Kess had been leaving us alone and so had the Council—other than their occasional private demands, like the current one for me to do another foray to one of their planetary targets.

"Is there anything else?" I asked. My assigned task list was already quite lengthy and balancing the Council's demands with Merkief's was going to be challenging.

"No." He shut me out like he'd flipped on an ignore switch and focused on the terminal in front of him.

Considering that as polite of a dismissal as I was going to get, I left for Jal to meet with the Prime.

It wasn't as though Merkief had sat down with my half of the Narvan and told them I wasn't running the show anymore, but they all seemed to sense it. Maybe it was the news story about me failing to protect Merkief's family that tarnished my reputation or my general lack of being able to fund much of anything. Whatever it was, they were still mostly respectful, but there was a level of doubt hanging over me, and they were definitely testing my ability to enforce anything.

I'd barely stepped inside the Prime's office when he bypassed all manner of greeting and hit me with, "Let me guess, by the look on your face, you're going to ask for half the fleet again so you can run off and conquer some nameless world."

Maybe my people were less respectful than I'd realized. At least this Prime. Then again, we'd been on uneasy terms for quite awhile.

"You would be correct."

He nodded. "And why should I grant this request?"

"It wasn't a request."

He held his hands clasped together on the top of his desk, body relaxed, looking for all the world like I was just some lowly general with the itch to go conquer something. "Are you financing this proposed *exploration?*"

I sat down, which was probably admitting defeat in his eyes, but I didn't really care anymore. All I needed to do was get him to give me half the fleet, at his cost, to keep Merkief off my back and the Council happy. The Prime getting ticked wasn't near as big of an issue as my rage-filled partner who could go off the rails at any moment and take my access to the tank with him.

"I'm currently between granting funding requests," I said.

"You have been for a while now. I'm starting to think your well has run dry."

It had. "The fleet always returns with a bountiful haul and the crews are happy with the action. Isn't that enough financing for you?"

"That would mean I break even. There's no profit," he said.

I shook my head. "You're starting to sound like an Artorian."

He chuckled. "I'm starting to sound like a leader who has to rely on his own finances because my Advisor has cut me off."

"I didn't cut you off." I sighed. "Look, I need the tax intake from this mission as badly as you do. Can we just agree to do it for both our sakes?"

His lips curled into a predatory smile. "Not without some negotiation."

He *had* turned into a fucking Artorian. I waved a hand in the air and sat back. "Fine. Name your terms."

"We're flipping the percentage on the incoming goods and you'll meet my daughter."

Oh hells, we were back to that again? "Meet not marry?"

He didn't look happy about the differentiation, but he finally said, "I'll work with meet."

It had been months since I'd been inclined to meet a woman for any purpose. While my body might have been on board, my head wasn't in it. Narantha, who hadn't even been my mate, had left a hole in a place I hadn't realized she'd filled until she was gone.

Meeting the Prime's daughter might not only get me through this deal, but could be a test run to see if I might possibly be interested in finding someone to maybe not settle down with exactly, but... Oh hells. I almost burst out laughing. Narantha had quipped about me holding Anasta leading to domesticated urges, but instead, it was her.

"The percentage stays as is if you'd like to keep your position, but

I will meet your daughter."

His scowl grew more pronounced. "We return to threats?"

"It would seem so." Dammit, I really didn't have the time or energy to replace him, but if he kept pushing me it would have to happen.

The Prime's fists clenched and unclenched on his desktop, fingers flexing as his nostrils flared. "Then I leave it all in Dayana's hands. You want your ships? She has the final say."

"That's a very unwise move for a man in your precarious position. Are you sure you want to take it?"

He stared me down. "I do. Dinner tomorrow night at her place. You'll have the address shortly."

With a heavy sigh, I stood, adding finding a new Prime for Jal to my task list. As I walked out the door, I figured why the hells not, and also added dinner with the Prime's daughter.

I rode the lift to the top of the plex. Feeling naked without my armor or any sort of uniform, I took a deep breath and stepped off onto the elite floor. This meeting wasn't near as important as the Prime thought it was, I'd already started looking for his replacement, one that would hand me half the fleet without question. I was only here to test the waters, to see if I was ready to entertain the idea of female companionship on any level. Dinner with Dayana was merely a convenient opportunity.

If I was inclined to find a wife, it would be a marriage with advantages, likely political. Dayana would be good practice.

My prior dealings with women had not been set up by others. They'd always been a matter of yes please or no thanks and happened organically, usually in a bar or somewhere similar, and they lasted a few enjoyable hours. They were never anyone important, at least not that I knew of. I didn't often ask who they were or remember names. They were certainly never a Prime's daughter and they didn't happen in fucking plexes.

The towering structures had always seemed so grand when I was a kid living on the ground, like some magical place I'd never go. But now, having done too many contracts in them, taking out the rich and powerful who lived there, my nerves prickled just being inside one.

Of course, the Prime's daughter lived in a top floor suite. I walked the rounded corridor, searching for her number. Discovering I'd missed it, I doubled back. Finally spotting the right one, I raised my palm to the panel just as the door opened.

"Did you have any trouble finding me?" asked the slight blonde woman inside.

For a Jalvian, Dayana was short, almost petite. Like Kazan had been. But whereas Kazan had plenty of muscle and fire that more than made up for her size, Dayana was all soft curves.

"A little. I always get lost in these things." Always. Or just this once, when I was too out of sorts to read simple damned numbers.

She nodded, stepping aside to let me in. "My father tells me you prefer single-family homes."

"Easier to secure," I said, then regretted it instantly. I was supposed to be an all-powerful Advisor, for Geva's sake, not some paranoid hermit.

Outside of political meetings or intimidation, I'd not had cause to make idle conversation with a woman of her status before. My nerves frayed a little further.

Standing just inside like a looming idiot who didn't belong, I considered fabricating an excuse to be called away before this went any further. Dayana touched the door control panel to shut it and stepped further inside.

Dammit, now I was in. Tossing an excuse at her now would be awkward. I sighed inwardly.

"You do know that plexes have security teams and checkpoints, especially at the entry and ground levels?" she said.

"Of course." And I'd bypassed them every time I'd worked in a plex. But that didn't seem wise to say. I was supposed to be all civilized. Advisor-like. Whatever that was. Alone, consumed with work, and verging on a stim and alcohol problem?

If I could make it through this night without her slamming the door in my face over some social misstep, it would be a miracle.

"Wine?" she asked as she led me into the main open room that was anything but common in the giant suite.

Two staff members were busy in the kitchen. The noise of their efforts reminded me of Narantha's cooking and her smiling face. I swallowed hard.

"Yes, please." The whole bottle would have been even better.

Dayana gestured to one of the women in the kitchen who darted off to a cabinet and pulled out a bottle. She hurriedly opened it and located two glasses.

While I would have preferred a couch or somewhere more relaxed to begin the requisite small talk, she opted for the table. And not just any table, but a long semi-transparent work of art on legs with a chair on either end. Fuck, if I had to figure out what fork to use, I was going to be busy consulting my link throughout dinner instead of paying attention to the conversation.

I habitually avoided fancy dinners and ceremonies that required this level of society manners. Had I never taken the job with Kazan, this sort of thing might have been a goal to aspire to someday, working my way up the ranks and retiring with a few wives and the beginnings of my own dynasty. But that wasn't the avenue I'd gone down. I didn't belong here. Not without armor on my shoulders, a gun in my hand, and a contract for some rich man's life.

Dayana's brows drew together. "Are you all right, Advisor?"

"Yes. I'm fine." I settled into the chair, only to realize it was one of the high-end, conform-to-your body models that some famous designer had come up with ten or so years ago. I couldn't remember the name of the line or the designer. It hadn't been important at the time. I started to access my link to find out but then wondered if that was something she expected me to know or care about. What the hells were we supposed to have in common? And where was the Geva-forsaken wine?

As if summoned by my discomfort, the woman with the wine appeared beside me. I stopped myself from reaching for the glass once she'd poured it. This wasn't a club. I sat back, watching her set it carefully on the table in the precise place it apparently belonged in the intricate place setting. How did one address house staff? Was I supposed to thank her? I decided to play it safe and possibly rude by keeping my mouth shut.

Dayana watched me somewhat covertly, her gaze darting from my face to the glass. Was she attempting to poison me for her father? I watched her right back.

Once I saw that the woman had poured for Dayana from the same bottle, my suspicions were lessened. Was this what my dating life was going to be within this echelon of women, wondering if their primary goal was to kill me? I hadn't realized how carefree my prior relationships had been until now. Then again, they'd never actually been relationships, had they?

I hoped I wasn't being rude by draining half my glass, but it was either take the edge off or run for the door.

Dayana watched me over the rim of her untasted glass, which she was breathing in and rolling around. "Do you like it?"

Right. Not a fucking club. No slamming the drinks. Truthfully, I hadn't even noticed the taste. It was red. It had alcohol in it. "Yes, very good."

She smiled. "My father sent it over. It's from one of his vineyards."

Of course he had his own vineyards.

"Do you own any?" she asked, finally taking a sip.

"No."

In terms of owning anything, my list was very short. Kazan's house on Jal that was now in my name and the now compromised two-story row house on Karin. Every other credit I had to my name was wrapped up in investments to finance my half of the Narvan. And a fine job I was doing of that lately.

I took a restrained sip of wine, copying hers.

One of the kitchen staff returned with a tray of food, which she set at my end of the table. She held a serving utensil in one hand, smiling nervously. What was I supposed to be doing? I didn't remember eating at the same table as my parents when I had lived at home. Meals at the academy had come on pre-portioned plates. During the time I had served, it was a free-for-all in the mess hall. Meals with Kazan often were eaten out of a box or reheated on a plate. It hadn't occurred to me that I might need to study for this damned date.

I forced a smile and improvised. "Ladies first."

Dayana beamed as the woman bustled down to the other end of the table with the tray. She indicated her choices with the point of a finger and sat back to be served. With that mystery solved, I racked my brain for something appropriate to say. My usual lines were far below someone like Dayana.

"This is a nice place you have here," I said, making my meal choices.

"Thank you. I'm sure it pales in comparison to what you're used to."

I choked on my first bite. The serving woman looked petrified. I waved her off. After another sip of wine to clear my throat, I struggled to figure out how to answer that. Avoidance seemed appropriate.

"What exactly has your father told you about me?"

She ate delicately, chewing tiny bites that seemed hardly worth the effort of raising the fork. Seeing that I wasn't eating, she set her fork down, took a drink, and sighed.

"That I can't hope for a more prestigious marriage contract and that I should do everything possible to impress you. Clearly, I'm failing."

I waited a moment to see if she was kidding, but her gaze remained on her plate and her face had taken on a pained look.

"And you also know I'm only here because it is a condition of his granting me half the fleet for a mission," I said, playing along with the Prime's deal to see her reaction. How far had he pushed her to go?

She took a much healthier gulp of her wine and waved for one of the women to refill our glasses. Dayana sat back in her chair, her shoulders sagging. "He told me you stick to business. I thought maybe this would be different, here, not in his overdone toybox of an office."

I laughed, the nerves running out of me like a plug had been pulled. At one point I was pretty sure I snorted. I wiped at the tears running down my face, wheezing the word, "Toybox."

A smile cracked on her lips that grew into a grin and then she started to laugh too.

"I promise I won't tell him you said that," I said, wiping my face with my napkin, "but that's exactly what I'm going to think the next time I'm there."

"I take it your office isn't similar?"

"Not even remotely."

She leaned forward, looking more relaxed too. "What does an Advisor's office look like?"

For a moment I considered lying, spinning some grand tale, but if this was going to be a true test of carrying on an honest audition for a possible wife, they'd need to know at least a degree of the truth. Narantha had had that. She'd been happier, knowing what she was in for, at least on a base level. I owed the same to anyone I might drag into my life.

"I'm more into bare walls and simple spaces. Honestly, none of this." I gestured to the over-the-top luxury of her home.

"And no vineyards," she said with a tentative smile.

"No properties beyond two unremarkable houses. I don't even own a transport."

Her mouth dropped open.

"Look, I don't know what he told you, or why he's so sure I'm the prospect of a lifetime because I can wholeheartedly assure you that's not the case. My life is pretty much me working and sleeping in-between working. I eat takeout from the box. I don't have a staff in either house, and I have no idea what most of this is for." I pointed to everything on the table in front of me.

Dayana was quiet for a moment, emotions playing across her face in ripples. I wasn't sure what it ended on, other than it wasn't obvious disappointment. I considered my gamble of truth a win.

"I don't care what fork you use," she said at last. "Just eat. They've been working hard on this meal for most of the day."

"Gladly." Since we'd dispensed with the pretenses, I dug into one of the best meals of my life. We'd finished a second bottle of her father's wine by the time the meal was over.

"Are you ready to escape or would you like to move to somewhere more comfortable?" Dayana asked.

She'd talked about her daughter and the charity work she did throughout Jal in her family's name. I only divulged watered-down truths when she asked. Mostly I let her talk, gathering information on topics this type of woman might discuss so I'd be better prepared when I wanted to try this for real.

Dayana was far more tolerable to be around than her father. Perhaps she'd gotten her personality from her mother.

"I can put off escaping a little while longer."

She smiled and led me from the table to a large sitting space that featured the clearplaz dome of the plex overhead. Stars twinkled in the sky between clouds. I took one large, very comfortable chair and she took another next to me. A veritable wall of potted plants of all sizes stood between us and the two women clinking dishes together as they cleared the table and put the kitchen in order.

"So other than your father attempting to bind me to Jal, why is he so intent on roping you into another marriage contract? You appear to be doing just fine here on your own."

"Do I?" Her lips quirked. "Johnus was a captain. A good one, if he and my father are to be believed. His family was well off even before our marriage contract. This was his home."

"Seems a waste for a captain to spend all his credits here when he lived on his ship for the most part."

"Are you really that out of touch with the concept of social status?" she asked, then quickly covered her mouth. "I'm sorry, that slipped out. Too much wine."

"Don't worry about it." I waved her apology aside. "Zero concept. Don't care. I'm not part of it."

"You're the Advisor to three worlds. How can you not be a part of it?"

I shrugged. "Never have been. Don't care to start."

Her brow furrowed. "How is that possible?"

"My family comes from a long line of dutiful soldiers, their sole purpose seems to be churning out more bodies to fill the ranks. I lost touch with them after I'd entered the system as a kid and never felt inclined to reestablish any connection. I work. I always have. That's how I got here."

"That sounds very lo—"

"Tough to live with. As I said, not the big catch your father set me up to be. If anything, I live much more like the average low-ranking soldier than any level of the socially elite."

Dayana toyed with the fringe on what was likely some high-end designer pillow, given the rest of the surrounding furnishings.

"You do know that most of our people don't live like this, right?" I indicated her lavish apartment.

"I know," she said quietly.

For being the Prime's daughter, she didn't appear to be as out of touch with reality as I assumed she would be. Pampered, to be sure, but not haughty.

She watched the sky overhead for a few moments. "I don't suppose you have a view like this in your house?"

"Only if you walk outside and look up."

Though my comment made her smile, I kept waiting for her to turn her nose up, for her to declare her father was an idiot for attempting to shunt us into a marriage contract or to cut the night off with a clear indication that we were done here. Instead, her gaze danced over me and then traveled around the room before returning to the pillow on her lap.

"The apartment contract is up in four months. With Johnus gone, I've been living off what remains in our account. I'm sure I could find something more affordable to make the credits last a lot longer. My father insists I renew."

"For the status of living in the plex?"

She nodded and let out a long exhale. "It's where the daughter of a Prime should be," she said in a mockery of her father's voice. "I don't suppose you'd entertain the thought of a marriage contract?"

"Are you mad?"

This was supposed to be a trial run, practice. Obviously I hadn't shared enough of the truth to dissuade her from her father's plan.

"I'm sure your father would be proud that you're willing to sacrifice yourself to a marriage contract for his benefit, but my answer is a definite no."

I started to get up. Trial over. I might even have called the night a success, but it was time to leave before things got ugly.

Dayana leapt from her chair and stood in front of me. "Hear me out." She held up a finger. "In return for granting me the position of Advisor's wife, you'd get my father's loyalty and a big popularity boost with our people in general."

A popularity boost would be handy, but there were so many other factors against this.

"I already have your father's loyalty."

She gave me a dubious look.

Surprised that she had the nerve to hold her position, and curious what else she had to bargain with, I pointed to her finger. "Other than living the glorious life of the rich and influential in my mythical secret estate. What else would you get?"

"My father to quit grilling me about finding a new husband." A quick smile flashed over her face. "We can live separately if you prefer. I'd only need you around when my father comes by so he thinks he got what he wanted. As I said, I have my own credits to live off of. I'd just need to find something suitably fitting while still affordable."

"You're serious."

Dayana nodded. She stepped back and returned to her seat.

The Prime had put his trust, his career and future in Dayana's hands with his gamble. It seemed he was a smart man after all.

I sat back down and weighed my options. Did I find a new Prime, discredit the current one, let a rigged election run its course, take the fleet to do the Council's bidding, and also find time to hunt down a prospective wife? Or take the deal dangling before me on date one, keep the Prime, get the fleet in a matter of days, and keep the Council and Merkief happy? The leadership on Karin and Rok wouldn't be pleased, but on all other fronts, option two seemed to be less painful. I certainly didn't need the Council thinking I wasn't on board with their demands or edgy Merkief doubting my loyalty.

"If I agree to entertain this idea, you'll tell your father to give me the go on the mission?"

She gave me a long look that verged on becoming uncomfortable. "If I said you already had my approval on the mission, would you bolt for the door?"

Could I make this work with her? We barely knew one another. A political union had certainly been on my radar, but to commit to a virtual stranger? I did know her father pretty damn well, but that wasn't a selling point.

She seemed real enough, not a flighty socialite. Could we find some comfortable middle ground and settle into a good-natured friendship like I'd had with Narantha?

But Dayana came from a high-standing family, one in the public spotlight, one that would have expectations of my end of the marriage contract.

I grimaced. If she was serious, she needed to know the truth before any deal was made. "I'm not what you'd consider marriage contract material."

"Oh, I don't know about that."

"I do," I said sternly. "And there are security risks. I'm sure you recall the murder of Advisor Ma'tep's family?"

That made her pause. "I will address that with my father, but I'm quite used to having guards nearby. The security of a Prime's family is not so different than yours in that regard. Other objections?"

A business deal was not how I'd envisioned a marriage contract happening, but at least that was familiar territory. "I recommend a long and private courtship. Feel free to make it on and off again if the urge strikes. And if you change your mind at any time before we eventually have to follow through with the contract, you're free to go."

"And you'll be discreet in the meantime?"

I nodded. "Standard operating procedure for me."

"That explains the lack of swooning prospects in the rumor mill." She tapped her chin, glancing at me out of the corner of her eye. "Between your status and mine, I'd say we could drag out your proposed quiet courtship for a few years before my father and the public gets restless and demands that a contract be fulfilled."

"Good." A few years left me an out. Her too.

She nibbled on her lower lip for a moment. "There is the matter of public appearances? We'll have to work on your table manners."

"Oh, no." I shook my head. "I'm busy for all social occasions. Meetings, travel, skirmish with the Fragians, you pick the excuse. You're welcome to join me for mandatory public speeches and other obligations I can't get out of so you can get your publicity in the news feeds."

"I can work with that."

"As it happens, I'll be out of the system for a couple of months so maybe start slow with the news of our big date tonight?"

Dayana nodded. "Thank you for getting my father off my back."

"And thank you for getting your father to allow my use of the fleet." The man owed her big for saving his position, and possibly his life, depending on how gracefully he might have taken losing his job.

If we were going to make this a business deal, we might as well do this politely. I held out my hand.

She reached out to take it. "I look forward to further refining our arrangement."

I smiled at the woman who might well become my wife someday. "As do I."

FORTY-FIVE

Rhaine

"Remind me to never ask you for anything ever again," Isnar said as he held my hair back while I hovered over the toilet.

"It's not your fault that Weeda's anti-nausea pills stopped working." I took the blessedly cold cloth he offered me and washed my face.

"Don't go anywhere. I have to check on Daniel a minute," he said before dashing out of the bathroom and down the stairs.

It was more likely that he was running downstairs to call Weeda to see if there was something else she could give me. There wasn't. I'd asked at my last weekly checkup. Four months in and I'd lost more weight than I should have gained.

Isnar returned before I had the inclination to attempt the return walk to our bedroom on my own. He stood Daniel on his feet and shooed him toward his room.

"What did you do for the nausea last time? Maybe I can wrangle something from one of the trade ships."

"This pregnancy is different than last time." I took his offered arm, and we made our way to the bedroom. "It was more headache-intensive with Daniel."

"More? I don't think that's possible." He helped me onto the bed and waited until I got situated before placing the one blanket that was just the right weight over me. "You're so skinny."

"I noticed." I tried to smile but I was too tired. "I was thinking about names."

"Oh?"

He settled onto the bed next to me, pushing up the pillows on his side so he could sit up with a datapad on his lap. He'd been working from home for the most part for the past couple of weeks, calling Atalina to the house to keep Daniel occupied when he had to be at Dugans in person.

"You should choose her name. I had my turn with Daniel."

"We could pick one together," he offered.

I patted his hand and closed my eyes, feeling calmer now that I was laying down and knowing he was right there. "I'd like her to have an Artorian name. Surprise me."

"I suppose you'll want me to pick a name you can pronounce too." He squeezed my hand, his warmth penetrating my cold, dry skin.

"I would appreciate that. I'm sure she will too in the long run."

He chuckled. "Sleep, before I knock you out."

While I might have welcomed that respite given my state, I knew he was joking. I drifted off to the sound of him grumbling about gasket pricing and incorrect quantities under his breath.

"For the love of Geva, please wake up."

I came to with the vague impression that Isnar was holding me. Blinking my eyes several times didn't help bring the room into focus. Every muscle in my body ached.

"You have to do something. She can't go on like this much longer," he said.

Realizing I was staring at his shirt, I slowly got my head turned enough to catch a glimpse of Weeda by my knees.

"She's coming around. Keep a hold of her."

Weeda let go of my legs. I only then realized she'd been holding them because of the sudden lack of pressure. She reached into her bag and came out with a scanner.

"How is she?" Isnar asked.

She ran the scanner over me. "Rhaine is stable. The baby...we'll have to deliver her soon."

His arms tightened around me. "How soon?"

Weeda mulled over whatever she saw on her scanner. "As soon as I can find someone to assist me. I think I have everything I need in the transport. Normally, I'd ask Rhaine."

"I'm busy," I whispered.

The relief on Isnar's face filled me with a warmth that chased the chill and distance away. Except that meant I could feel all of my body, and it hurt. Everywhere. I couldn't hold back the moan that slipped out.

"I'll help you," he said.

Weeda's brows rose. "You've assisted with births before? Complicated ones?"

"Do you have another option close by?"

"Sadly, no. The doctor I'd like to have here is two days away." Her face lit up. "Do you have a datapad handy? Could you set up a vid call on that?"

"Be better on the terminal downstairs, but yes, I can make that work. Reception might not be good up here. The datapad doesn't have much range for that kind of signal. You could set up the call downstairs and forward it to the datapad."

"Perfect. I'll go make sure she's available and hopefully get a few things clarified with her first before we begin. Stay here with Rhaine."

Like he was going anywhere. "Getting a front-row seat for the birth of your daughter?" I asked.

"Wouldn't miss it." He brushed a hair off my forehead and smiled.

"If you really want to throw Weeda off, pull everything but the sheet off the bed and lay down a couple layers of clean towels. Move the lamp down to the end of the bed and set the chair beside it."

"You trying to make me look good or are you just that anxious for this pregnancy to be over?"

I managed a weary grin. "Yes."

He set me down gently and hurried around the room, following my directions. "You do realize that this is a couple weeks early, and she may have to surgically remove the baby?" he asked without looking at me. His apprehension wriggled into my mind through our bonded connection.

"However this is going to happen, I don't want it to be down on the kitchen table where we eat. Do you hear me?"

He turned toward me and nodded.

"And if things get dicey, you pick the baby." I pointed at him. "No arguments on that. I've had my turn. She gets hers."

I didn't need a fully operational bond to know that his anxiety had just skyrocketed. He was back by my side instantly, hands on my arms and face, as though he was attempting to absorb me.

"Could that happen? I can't lose you. I thought this was safe, that Weeda knew what she was doing."

"Maybe on Artor they've got this all figured out and death during childbirth is a thing of the distant past, but we're not there. And this isn't a standard birth. And I'm gathering by the fact that I just had the third seizure in a month, that I'm not in great health. So yes, losing me could happen even though Weeda does know what she's doing."

"I never should have asked for this," he said brokenly.

"Don't blame yourself. All you did was ask. I knew the risks and went ahead with it anyway." I grabbed his arm. "Now help me get undressed and onto the bed."

Once I was settled into place, he held out the one blanket I liked. I nodded.

"Why would you agree, if you knew this could happen?" he asked as he covered me up.

Because he deserved a child of his own. Because I *did* owe him. Because, despite who he'd been in the Narvan, he was a good father. Because I loved him.

I smiled at him gazing down at me. "Because maybe life here together isn't so awful."

He choked out a broken bark of laughter and kissed my forehead. "I'm going to go help Weeda carry everything she needs up here. Don't move."

❧

I slipped in and out of consciousness, aware that Weeda had given me something that put me slightly outside my body. I could feel Isnar holding my hand and hear Weeda talking with another woman on the datapad, but it was all a breath or two removed. Each time I woke, the two of them had moved. One sitting in the chair at the end of the bed, the other standing beside me or pacing next to the bed.

"Yes, we're going to try it the natural way first," Weeda was saying this time.

"Are you sure that's safest?" asked Isnar.

A tinny voice on the datapad answered, "Doctor Weeda has everything prepared and waiting if further complications arise."

I realized it was a tightness in my abdomen that had woken me, my muscles in a vice-like grip for several breaths before easing up. They'd induced contractions. I tried to recall how many times I'd woken before this.

"She appears to be fully dilated," announced Weeda. "It won't be long now."

The grip on my stomach came again. An intense pressure built between my legs. I needed to push. Why weren't they telling me to push? They must have had a reason, and I tried not to, but my distant body wasn't listening to me.

Weeda shot to her feet. "Stop. Don't push. Rhaine, you need to stop."

The pressure came again. A shooting pain hit with it. My body didn't listen when I told it not to yell either.

Isnar appeared. He stood facing me, hands firmly on my shoulders, gaze locked on the pillow beside my head. "Do whatever it is you're doing faster," he said over his shoulder.

"The baby is stuck," Weeda said. "I'm trying to guide her into the right position."

The pain came again. Weeda's hands pushed and pressed. I wanted her gone. I wanted her hands off of me. I wanted this baby out of my body.

"Faster," snarled Isnar.

"Yelling isn't helping," growled Weeda.

The pressure hit hard. I couldn't ignore it. I grabbed Isnar's hands on my shoulders and pushed.

And suddenly the pressure eased. I sank back onto the bed.

"We've got her," announced Weeda triumphantly.

Isnar spun around. "Why isn't she moving?"

While all I could see was Isnar's back, in my mind I rehashed the steps for delivering a baby. Weeda was cleaning the mouth and nose, maybe giving the baby a little poke or jiggle. The silence stretched on.

And then the cry came.

I sank into the pillows, dimly aware of the tears dripping down the sides of my face but too far from my body to care. The baby was free of me now. I could finally rest. I closed my eyes, drifting off, thinking of the first meal I wanted when I woke up.

"She'll be all right now," said Weeda. "I've stopped the bleeding."

"Who's bleeding?" I asked, feeling like I'd woken from a three-day-long nap.

Isnar slid onto the bed beside me with a blanket-wrapped bundle in his arms. "You were. Weeda has everything under control."

Being that he looked far more relaxed now, I took his word for it. "And the baby?"

"Small, but healthy," said Weeda, who came over to stand by my other side. "I've given your Ishlan instructions on the special care she'll require for the next few weeks. You need to rest and regain your strength." She turned to Isnar. "Call me if you need anything. I'll see myself out."

Once Weeda's footsteps hit the stairs, Isnar scooted closer. "Do you want to hold her?"

I'd never had the urge with Daniel, downright dreaded the thought of it even, but here, in our bedroom with Isnar beaming proudly down at the bundle in his arms, I wasn't opposed to the idea. "Sure."

We'd just managed a successful infant transfer when Daniel burst into the room and bounded up onto the bed. Isnar corralled him. Daniel peered into the blankets as I moved the wrap aside to take a look at what we'd made.

Only slightly larger than Gerod had been, our daughter slept in my arms. A dusting of blonde hair and pale skin made my heart jump. "She looks like me?"

Isnar nodded.

"Can we tell her the name?" asked Daniel, his excitement ready to burst at the seams.

"Ikeri," said Isnar.

Running through the Artorian words I knew, I tried to find a match. "Star?"

Daniel shook his head.

I dug deeper. A word in one of his stories had been similar. "Light? Something to do with light?"

Daniel let out an exasperated sigh and rolled his eyes. "Mommy needs to work on her words."

Isnar laughed. "To be fair, the direct translation is rough. Morning light. Sunrise?"

A new day. I found myself smiling at my daughter. "It's perfect."

THE NARVAN CONTINUES WITH:

CHAIN OF GREY

BOOK 2

I didn't think my shipping business was overly successful, not to the point where anyone would want me dead because of it. But as I lay there on the floor, observing the fine spray of my blood on my office wall, I had to consider that I might be wrong.

Heavy footsteps drew closer.

Damn. I knew I was rusty, but it was still disappointing to know that I'd not done any serious damage with the two knives I'd managed to throw before toppling from my chair. I tried to peer around my desk, but my body wouldn't cooperate.

Rhaine was going to be pissed when I missed dinner yet again.

The footsteps stopped. Something tingled inside my head. The telepathic barriers I'd erected years ago dissolved as my strength faded. The tingle came again as someone invaded my mind. It was a familiar touch, one that sent my head reeling as much as the blood loss.

I didn't think my shipping business was overly successful, not to the point where anyone would want me dead because of it. But as I lay there on the floor, observing the fine spray of my blood on my office wall, I had to consider that I might be wrong.

Heavy footsteps drew closer.

Damn. I knew I was rusty, but it was still disappointing to know that I'd not done any serious damage with the two knives I'd managed to throw before toppling from my chair. I tried to peer around my desk, but my body wouldn't cooperate.

Rhaine was going to be pissed when I missed dinner yet again.

The footsteps stopped. Something tingled inside my head. The telepathic barriers I'd erected years ago dissolved as my strength faded. The tingle came again as someone invaded my mind. It was a familiar touch, one that sent my head reeling as much as the blood loss.

The blurry form of my killer loomed over me. "Oh Fuck! Vayen? Is that really you? You're alive?"

❧

Whispers told me I was dreaming, but I ignored them in favor of enjoying a quiet meal with my family. We sat around the table in our little house on Veria Minor, Ikeri shoving sweet yellow fruit into her mouth until her cheeks were bulging, Daniel looking guilty, and Rhaine giving me a look that said I should ask why. I didn't. Instead, I slowly ate the meal I'd made after coming home from my day at Dugans, savoring this normal moment I'd never thought to have.

A moment that wouldn't exist if the High Council hadn't drugged me into forming a bond with my partner. If they hadn't demanded that I kill her. If we both hadn't had to give up what we'd worked so damned hard for and ended up here, around this table.

Ikeri giggled. Juice dripped down her chin. I laughed, ignoring the pressure in my head that was likely the warehouse informing me of a late shipment. Rhaine and I had agreed on no work or datapads at the table. I'd deal with it in the morning.

Except, it occurred to me that it wasn't a message on a datapad. I tried to will the pressure away. I'd closed off all my telepathic contacts from my previous life. Other than Daniel, who was sitting right there picking at his dinner, no one else in our colony was telepathic. Beyond that, my link was gone. No one should be in my head in any manner.

My hand itched for a gun, but I hadn't used one of those in five years. They were safely locked away in a chest in a closet under the armored coat I'd folded up upon arriving on Minor. For peace of mind, I allowed myself two small knives when I left the house, but I was home now and they were put away. I didn't need weapons anymore, certainly not in my own home.

We were safe here. I picked up my fork and ate another bite.

Ikeri slid off her chair and grabbed my hand, tugging me toward the common room where we sat most nights to watch the local vids. Rhaine was talking as I stood. I had the sense that she was telling me what trouble Daniel had gotten himself into, but the words I heard were wrong, muffled, confused. It wasn't her voice, but a familiar man's voice. One I didn't want to think about. Ikeri tugged at me again, more insistent and with more strength than I expected. I started to fall.

I woke with a gasp to a view I never thought I'd see again. I prayed to Geva I'd stepped out of one dream and into another, but when I blinked for the tenth time, the cold metal room was still there. The grey metal ceiling, metal walls, crisp white sheets on the narrow bed, my old clothes on the shelf beside me—my room on the buried ship on Frique.

Merkief stood over me with his hands clasped together as if he'd been praying. "I'm so sorry. If I had had any idea you were Isnar K'tu-roc, I would never have taken the job. I swear. It wasn't one of your known aliases, and it was just a quick and easy contract, no setup." He grimaced. "Sorry, not to make you feel insignificant."

"It's all right. That's what I was going for."

Had I ever really been gone? Being on the ship again made my years on Veria Minor seem almost surreal.

He burst into a grin. "We thought you were dead. I mean, Kess killed you. Or he claimed he did. We didn't want to believe it, but he had proof."

"Why the hells were you taking contracts in the Verian Cluster anyway?"

"We need all the credits we can get without Merchess to help finance the system. I spot a good contract, I take it."

At least someone had put enough credits on my head to make me a worthwhile target. Though, was that a bragging point in my new life? I supposed not.

The life I'd left behind hadn't treated Merkief well. He'd acquired deep lines on his forehead and around his eyes, and his hands and face revealed a gauntness hidden elsewhere by his armor. The armored coat was the same, the weapon lumps were in the same places, but his stance had changed, more wary, guarded. The good-natured grin I fondly remembered faded as the silence between us grew.

Not that I wasn't happy to see that he was also alive and well, but we'd received little news of the Narvan System on Veria Minor, and for my own sanity, I'd done my best not to look. I was done with that life. With my link implant removed prior to our going into hiding, I had no way of knowing or even guessing at Merkief's current affiliations.

"So where does this put us?" I asked.

He glanced at the door. "In a Geva-forsaken mess, I suppose. Jey will be here in a minute."

"How long have I been out?"

"Six hours maybe seven? It was a clean shot. Honestly, I was too busy hoping the tank would heal you using your old profile to pay much attention to the time."

Alarm plowed through my momentary nostalgia at seeing Merkief and the ship again. Rhaine would be beyond pissed and into panicked territory by now. Merkief might have been polite enough not to come out and ask about her, but Jey would. Now that they knew my current alias, they could search Veria Minor's network to determine our exact location.

The peace of the past five years began to unravel.

About the Author

Jean Davis writes an array of speculative fiction and plays with chickens. When not ruining fictional lives from the comfort of her writing chair, she can be found devouring books and sushi, weeding her flower garden, or picking up hundreds of sticks while attempting to avoid the abundant snake population that also shares her yard. She lives in West Michigan with her musical husband, an attention-craving terrier, and a small flock of chickens and ducks.

Read her blog, and sign up for her mailing list at www.jeandavisauthor.com. You'll also find her on Facebook and Instagram at JeanDavisAuthor, and on Goodreads and Amazon.

If you enjoyed this book, please consider leaving a review. They are much appreciated. Thank you!

www.ingramcontent.com/pod-product-compliance
Lightning Source LLC
Chambersburg PA
CBHW071346300726
48976CB00006B/1789